FOX *and* WILLOW

VOLUME ONE:
CAME A HARPER

ALLISON PANG · IRMA 'AIMO' AHMED

FOX & WILLOW CREATED BY ALLISON PANG & IRMA 'AIMO' AHMED

WRITTEN BY ALLISON PANG

ILLUSTRATED & LETTERED BY IRMA 'AIMO' AHMED

FOREWORD BY ALANA JOLI ABBOTT

COVER & LOGO DESIGN BY MICHELLE DREHER & ANGIE BAYMAN

GRAPHIC DESIGN BY JEREMY MOHLER

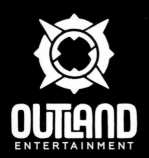

OUTLAND ENTERTAINMENT

Jeremy D. Mohler
Publisher & Creative Director
Alana Joli Abbot
Editor in Chief

3119 Gillham Road
Kansas City MO, 64109
P. 785.640.4324
Email. jeremy@outlandentertainment.com

WWW.OUTLANDENTERTAINMENT.COM

FOX & WILLOW VOLUME ONE: CAME A HARPER
First Printing. Published by Outland Entertainment LLC, 3119 Gillham Road, Kansas City MO, 64109.

For international rights, please contact: jeremy@outlandentertainment.com.

Printed and bound in China.

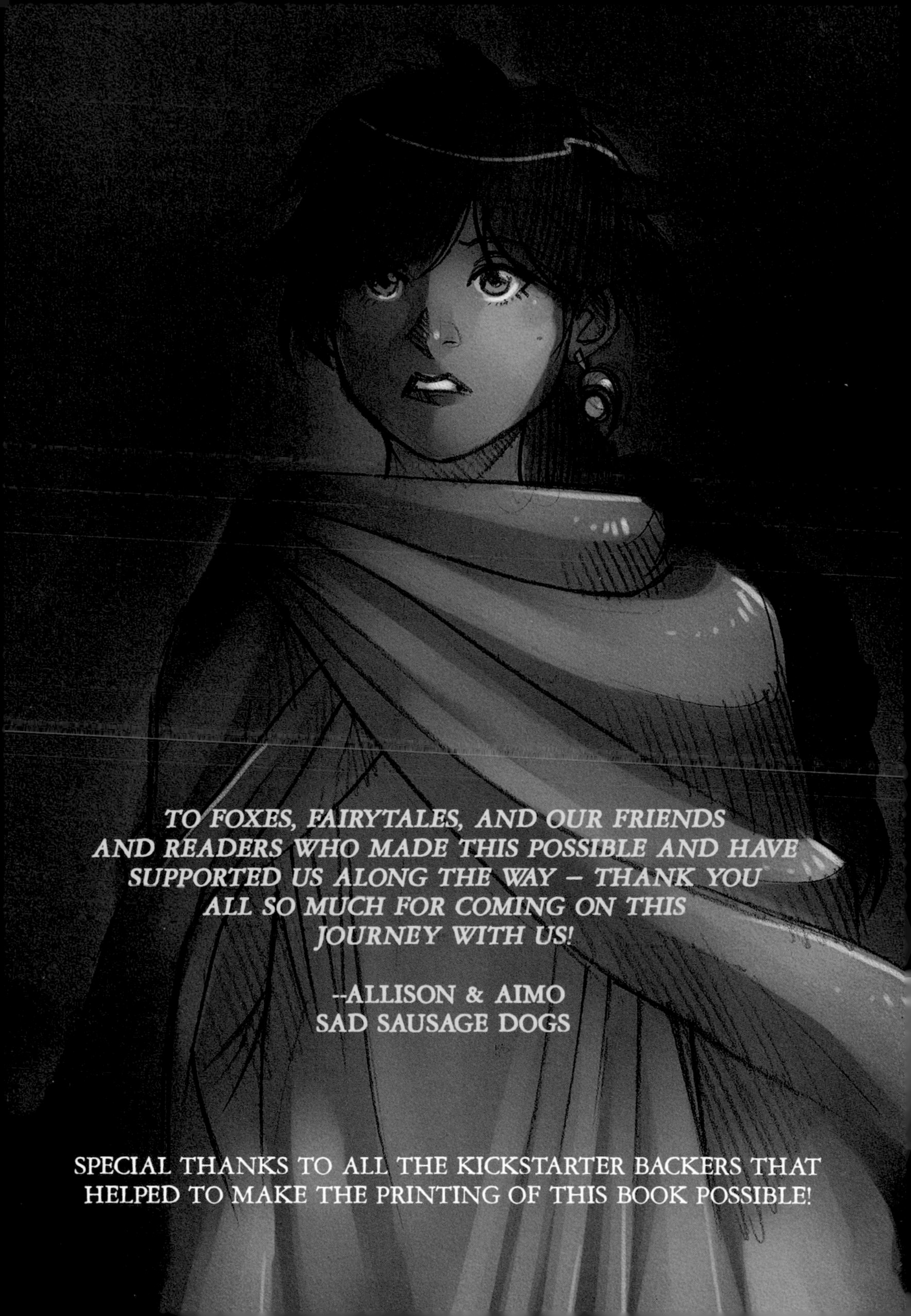

TO FOXES, FAIRYTALES, AND OUR FRIENDS AND READERS WHO MADE THIS POSSIBLE AND HAVE SUPPORTED US ALONG THE WAY – THANK YOU ALL SO MUCH FOR COMING ON THIS JOURNEY WITH US!

--ALLISON & AIMO
SAD SAUSAGE DOGS

SPECIAL THANKS TO ALL THE KICKSTARTER BACKERS THAT HELPED TO MAKE THE PRINTING OF THIS BOOK POSSIBLE!

FOREWORD

I first encountered the work of Allison Pang in her "Abby Sinclair" urban fantasy novels. They feature a tiny unicorn that lives in Abby's underwear drawer. That was all the hook I needed to pick up the books, but it was the storytelling and worldbuilding that kept me there, following her adventures.

And after I finished the third novel, I went searching for more of Allison's work, because I'd had so much fun in her world. Which is how I first discovered *Fox & Willow*, the story of a princess on the run, her supernatural fox companion, and the trouble they get into as they encounter characters from fairy tales. I' d thought I was a fan of Allison's before this, but *Fox & Willow* took me straight from casual-fan to forum-posting, refreshing-the-webpage-on-update-days fan.

The story and character are both so clear on the page, right from the very beginning, that I sank in immediately. Irma 'Aimo' Ahmed's art is gorgeous, and her use of color—sometimes full, sometimes just subtle highlights—makes the illustrated pages a joy to look at. Allison's dialog feels both authentically spoken and also in perfect keeping with the fairy-tale tone of the tale.

In "Came a Harper," the story you're now holding in your hands, Willow and Gideon are in the middle of their own story when they encounter a skeleton. Readers are immediately presented with the sense that they're coming into the story late—that both the skeleton and the protagonists have a story that begins far earlier than these pages. And while those hooks may leave you wondering as you turn the last page of this volume, rest assured, the answers do come. Part of the fun is wondering when and how we'll learn just how Willow and Gideon got into this mess.

A while ago, Outland was considering reaching out to some comics to see if they wanted to find a print home. Of course *Fox & Willow* was at the top of my list! Just as I got approval from the team to reach out to Allison and Aimo, I saw in the comic's Patreon that they'd signed a deal with another publisher. I was happy for them to have found a home, but sad it wouldn't be with Outland. As the fates had it, however, the situation with their other publisher changed, and this time, I didn't hesitate—

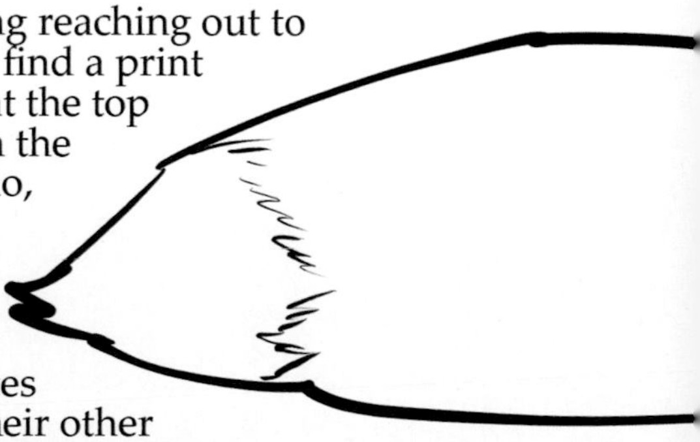

and I was thrilled when Allison and Aimo agreed to bring *Fox & Willow* over to Outland, so we could bring you this beautiful print edition.

I'm grateful to all the Kickstarter backers who helped bring this book to the world— and I'm so excited to help *Fox & Willow* reach a new audience in print.

I hope you love it as much as I do.

Alana Joli Abbott
Outland Entertainment
August, 2020

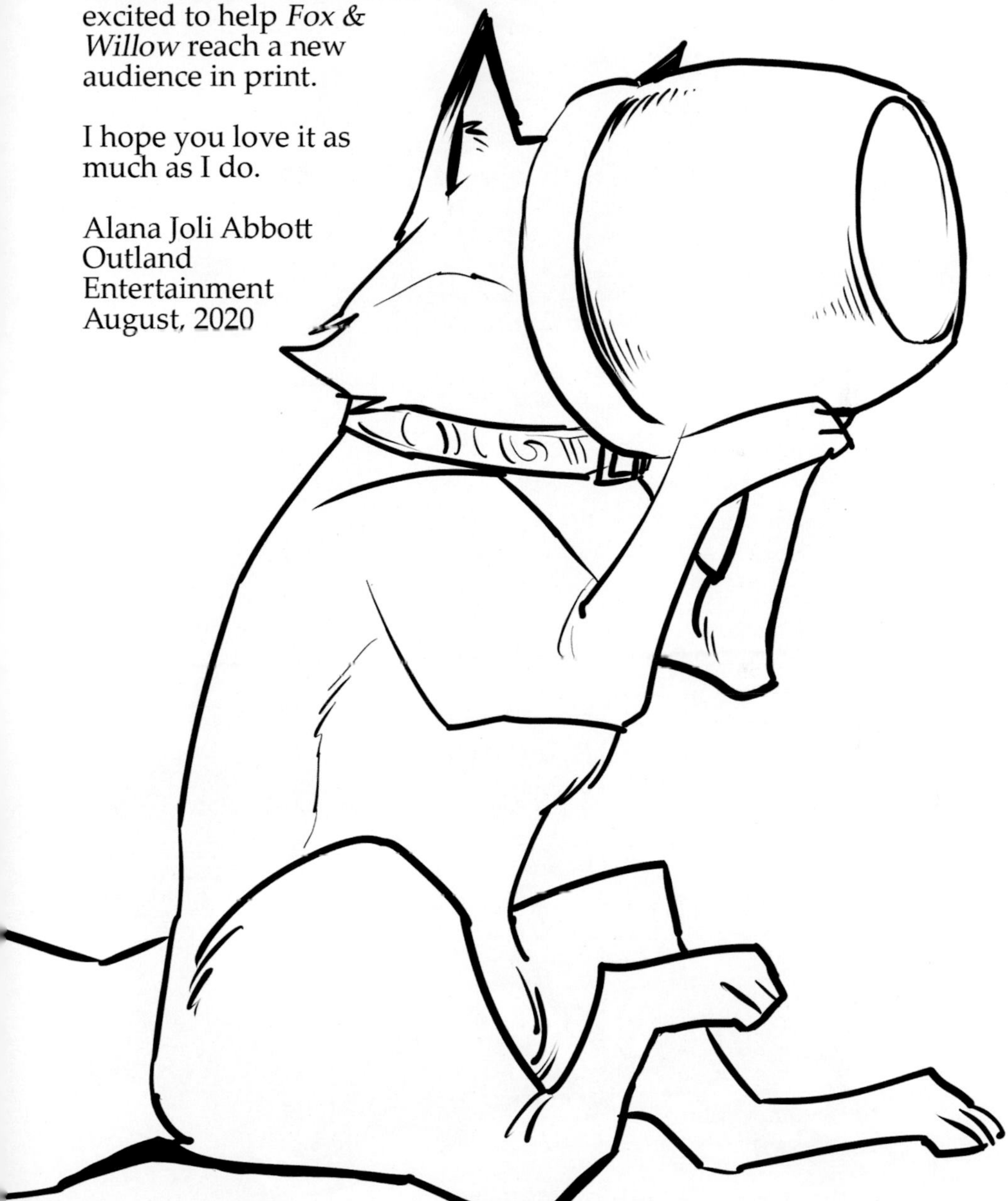

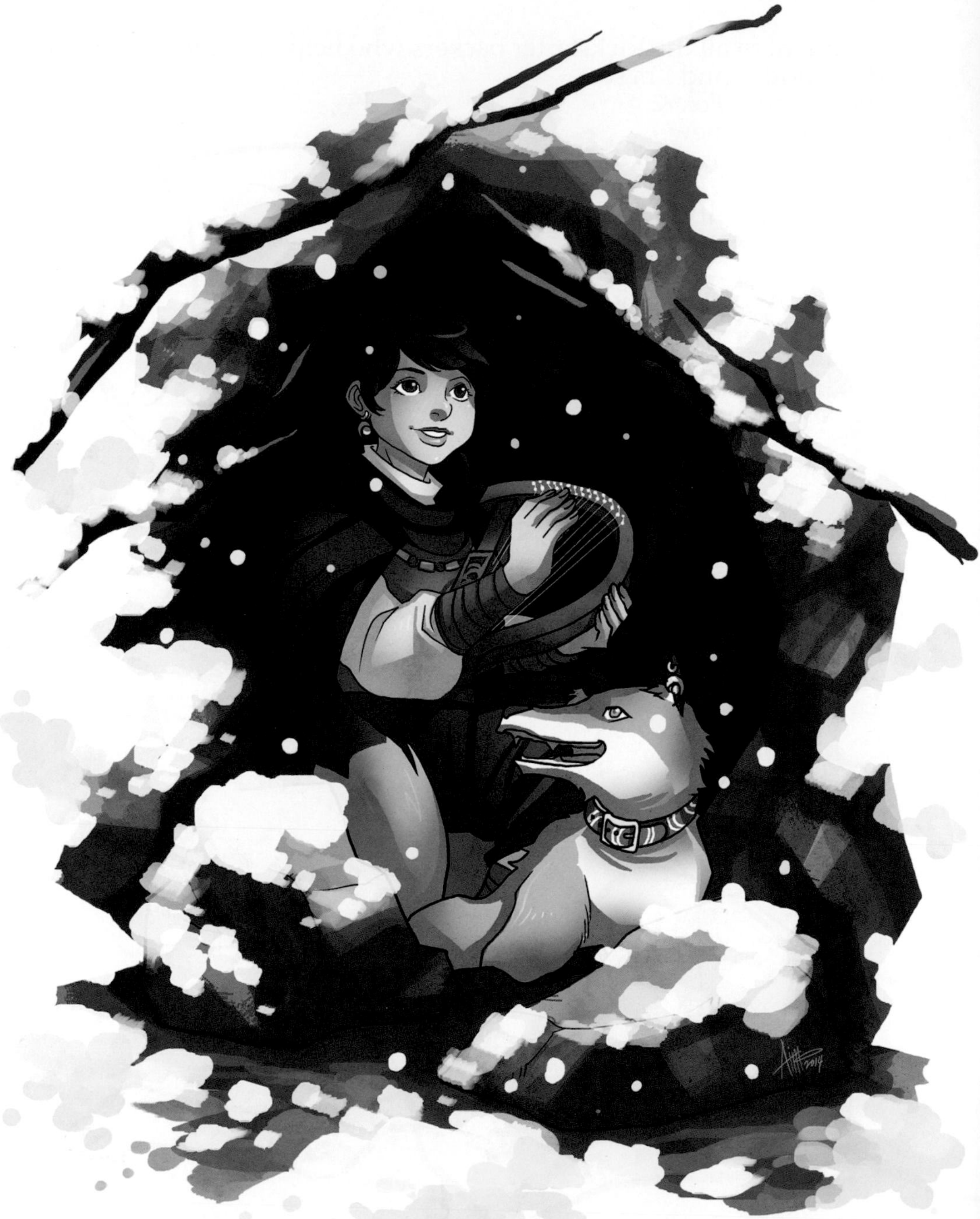

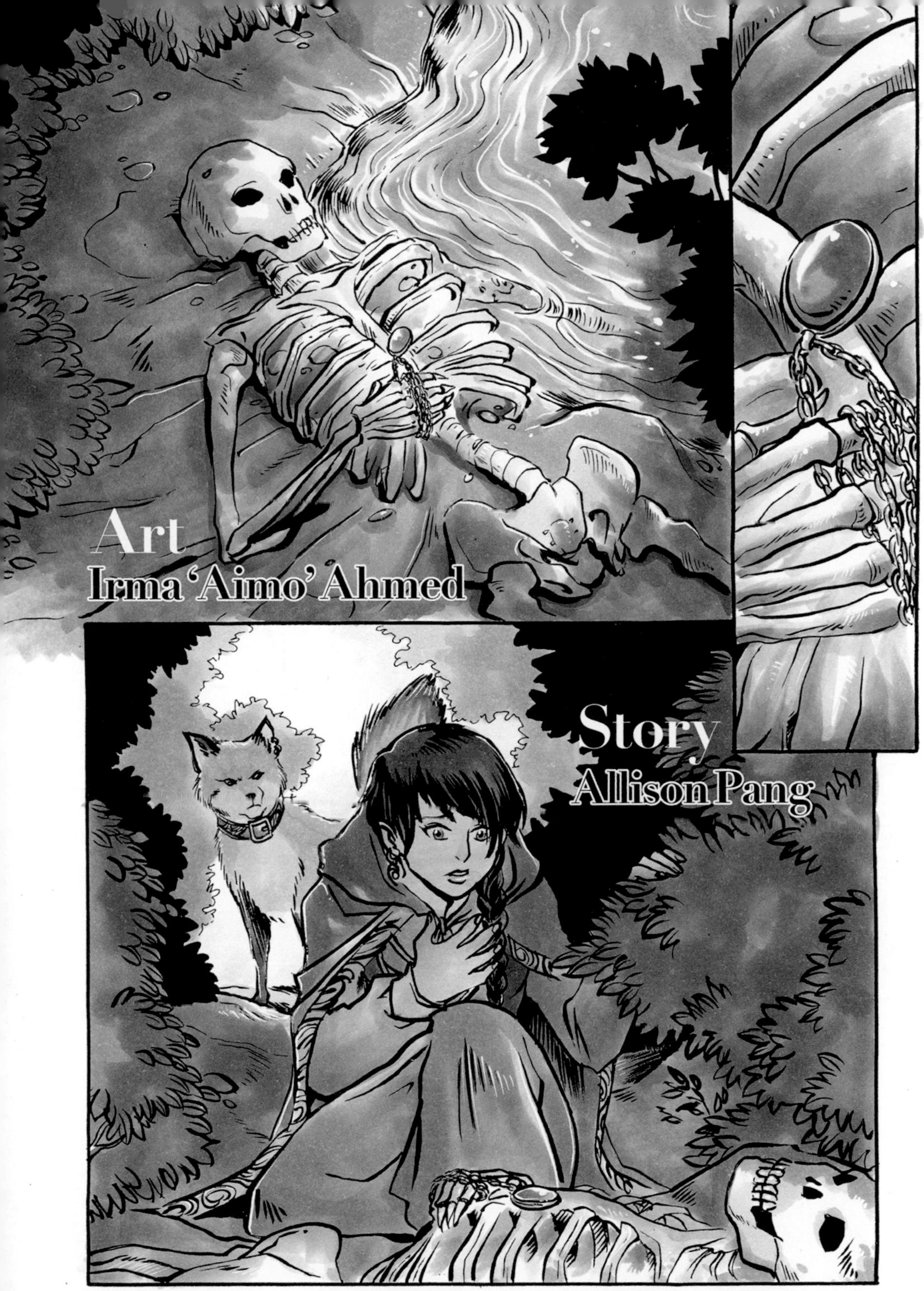
Art
Irma 'Aimo' Ahmed
Story
Allison Pang

Chapter 1: Came a Harper

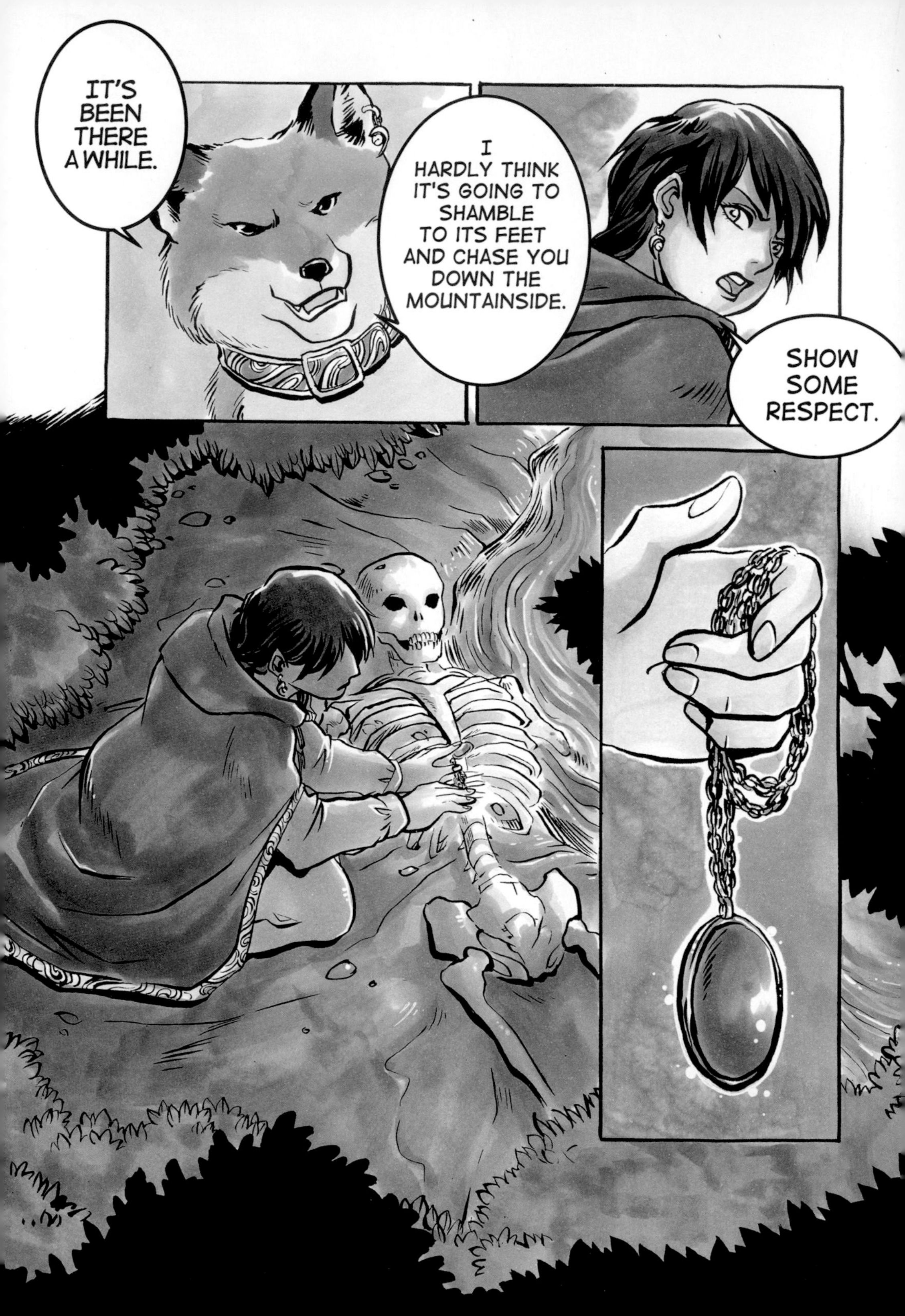
IT'S BEEN THERE A WHILE.
I HARDLY THINK IT'S GOING TO SHAMBLE TO ITS FEET AND CHASE YOU DOWN THE MOUNTAINSIDE.
SHOW SOME RESPECT.

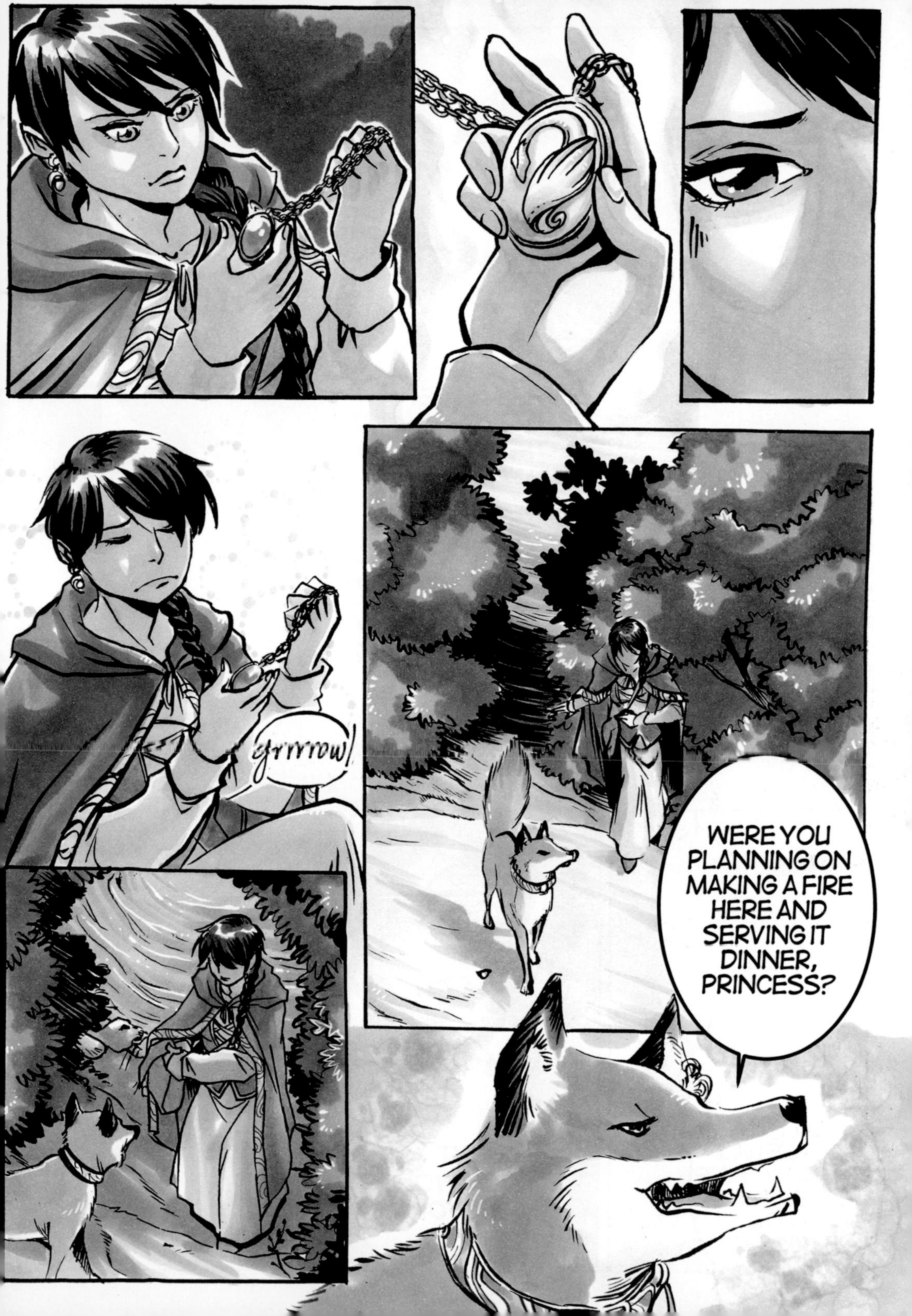
grrrrow!
WERE YOU PLANNING ON MAKING A FIRE HERE AND SERVING IT DINNER, PRINCESS?

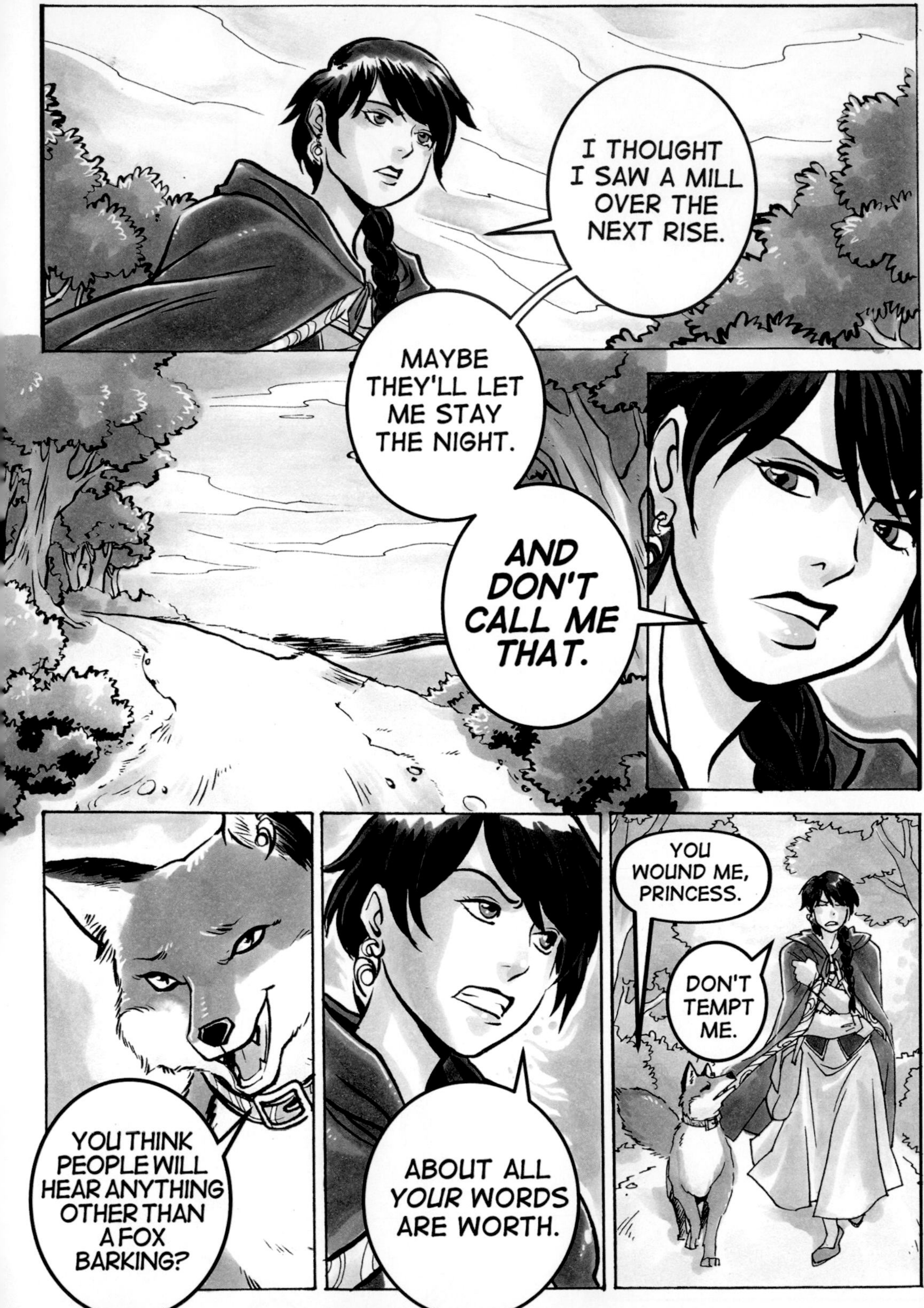
I THOUGHT I SAW A MILL OVER THE NEXT RISE.
MAYBE THEY'LL LET ME STAY THE NIGHT.
AND DON'T CALL ME THAT.
YOU THINK PEOPLE WILL HEAR ANYTHING OTHER THAN A FOX BARKING?
ABOUT ALL YOUR WORDS ARE WORTH.
YOU WOUND ME, PRINCESS.
DON'T TEMPT ME.

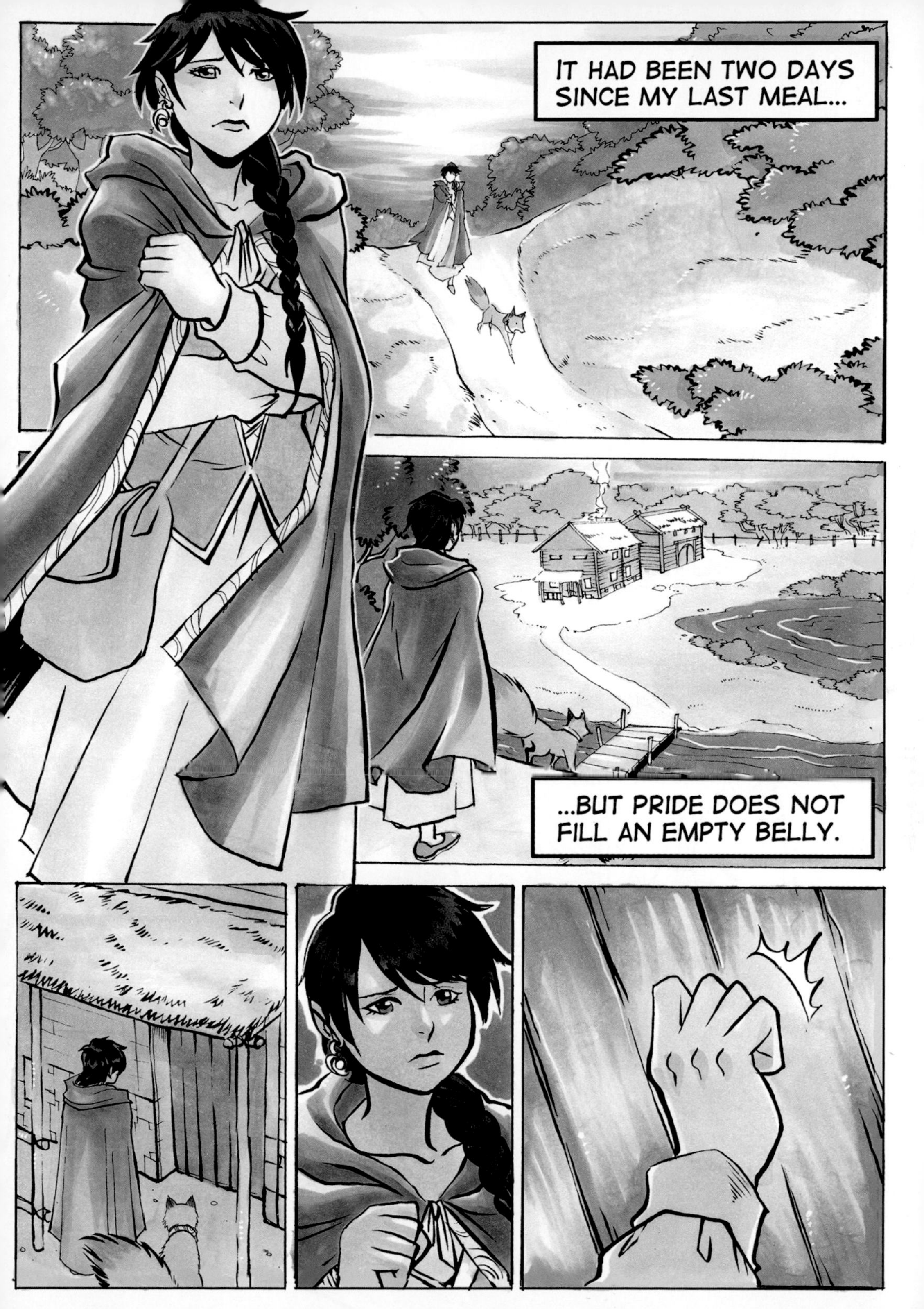
IT HAD BEEN TWO DAYS SINCE MY LAST MEAL...
...BUT PRIDE DOES NOT FILL AN EMPTY BELLY.

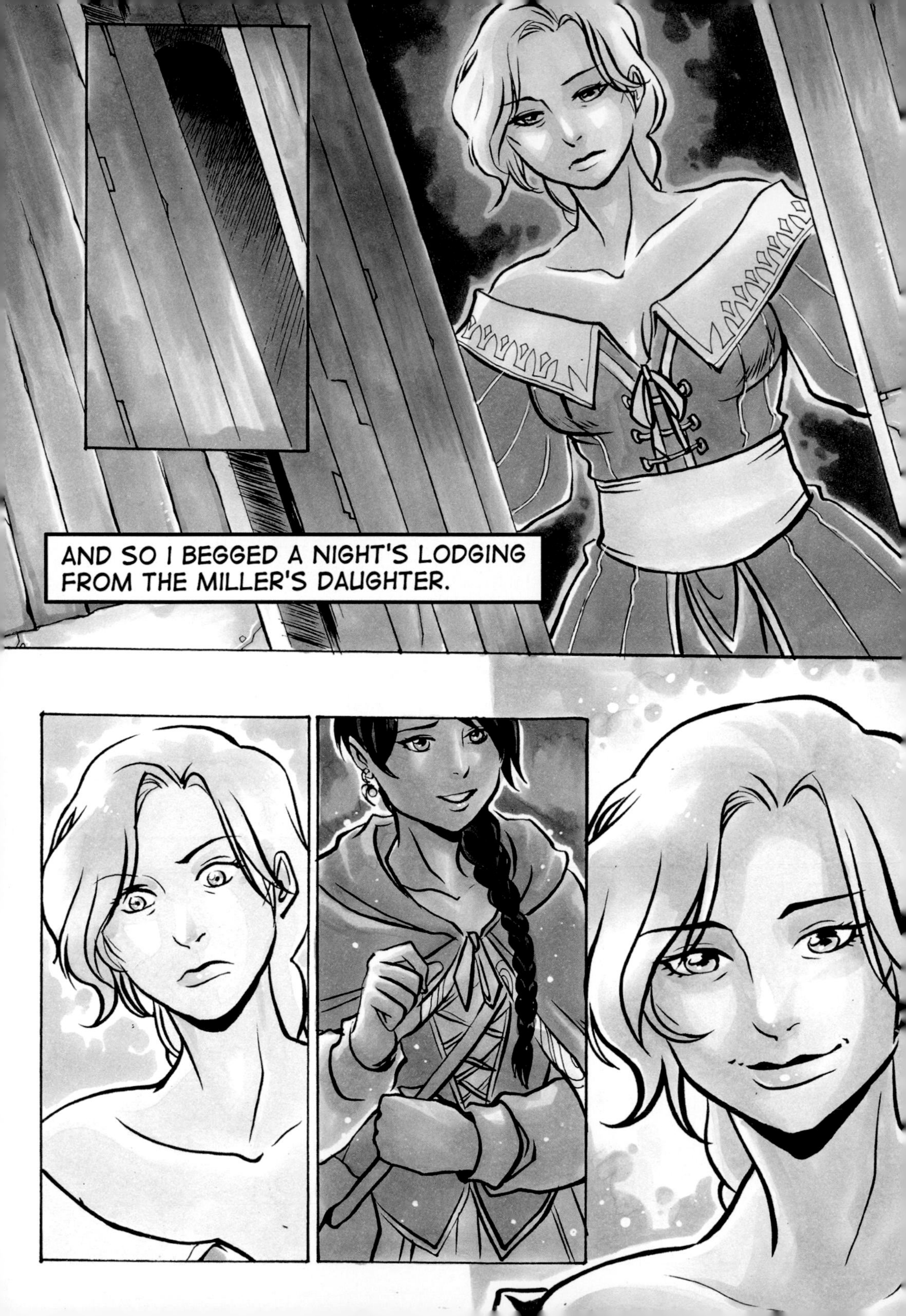
AND SO I BEGGED A NIGHT'S LODGING FROM THE MILLER'S DAUGHTER.

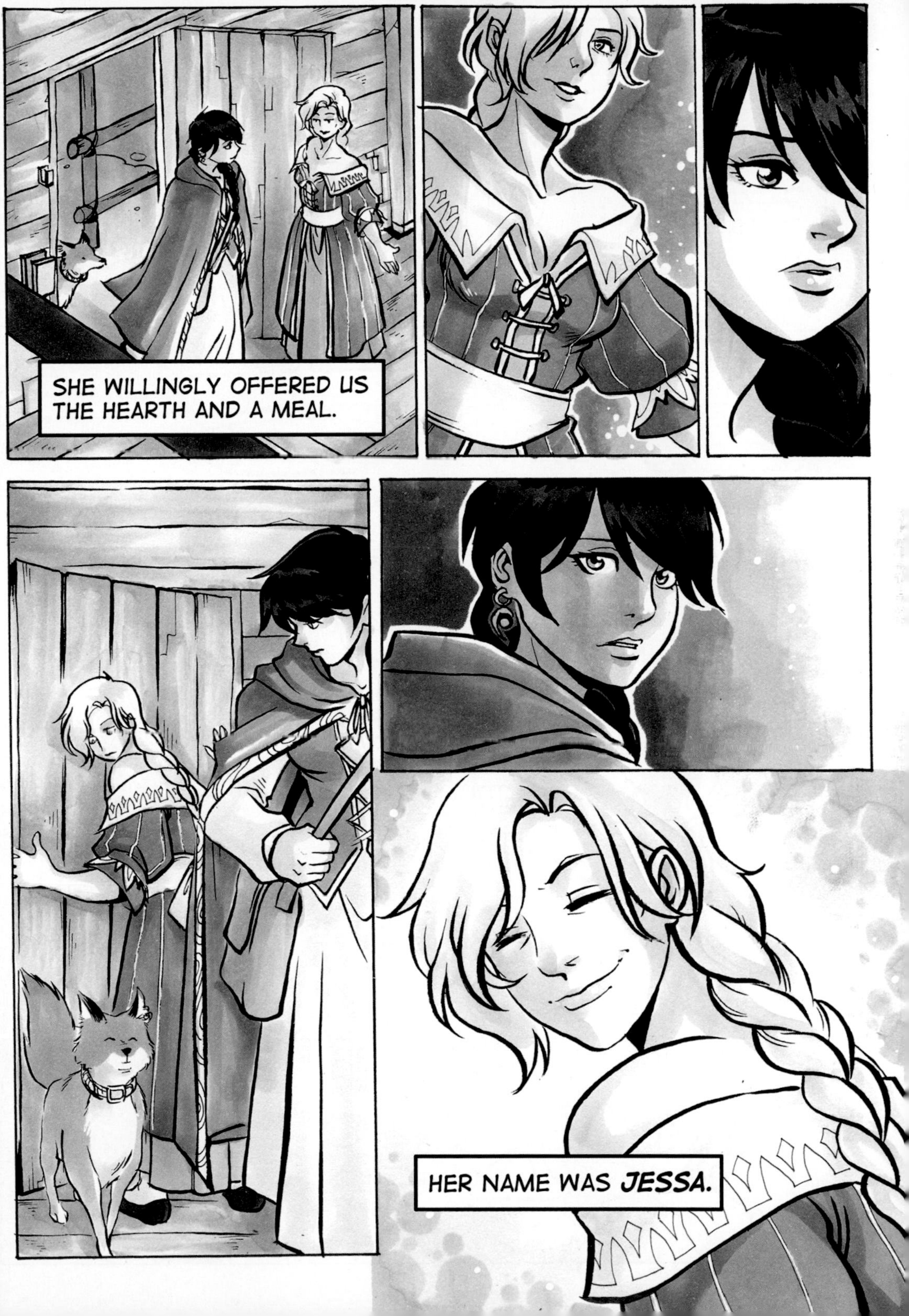
SHE WILLINGLY OFFERED US THE HEARTH AND A MEAL.
HER NAME WAS *JESSA.*

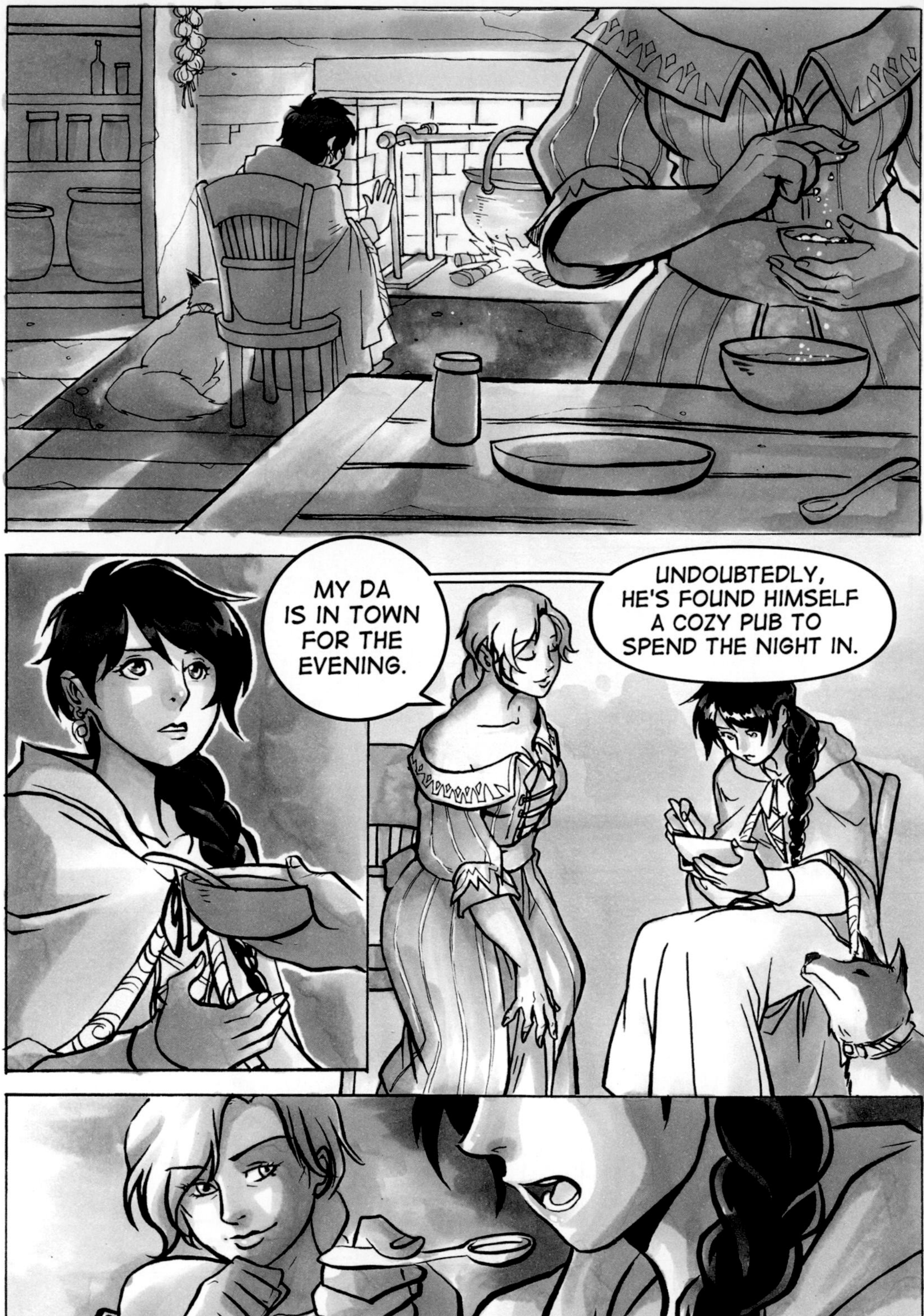
MY DA IS IN TOWN FOR THE EVENING.
UNDOUBTEDLY, HE'S FOUND HIMSELF A COZY PUB TO SPEND THE NIGHT IN.

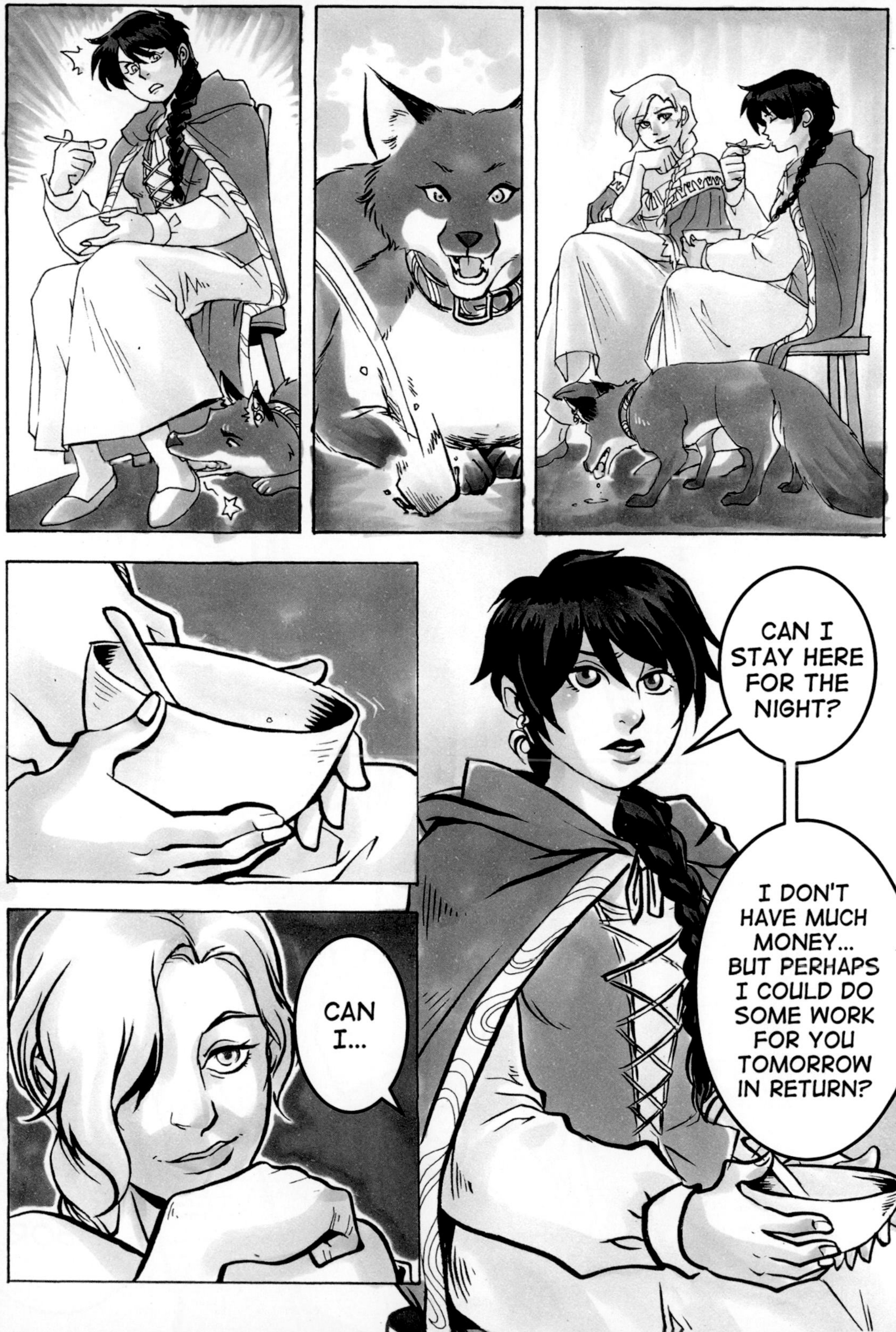
CAN I...
CAN I STAY HERE FOR THE NIGHT?
I DON'T HAVE MUCH MONEY... BUT PERHAPS I COULD DO SOME WORK FOR YOU TOMORROW IN RETURN?

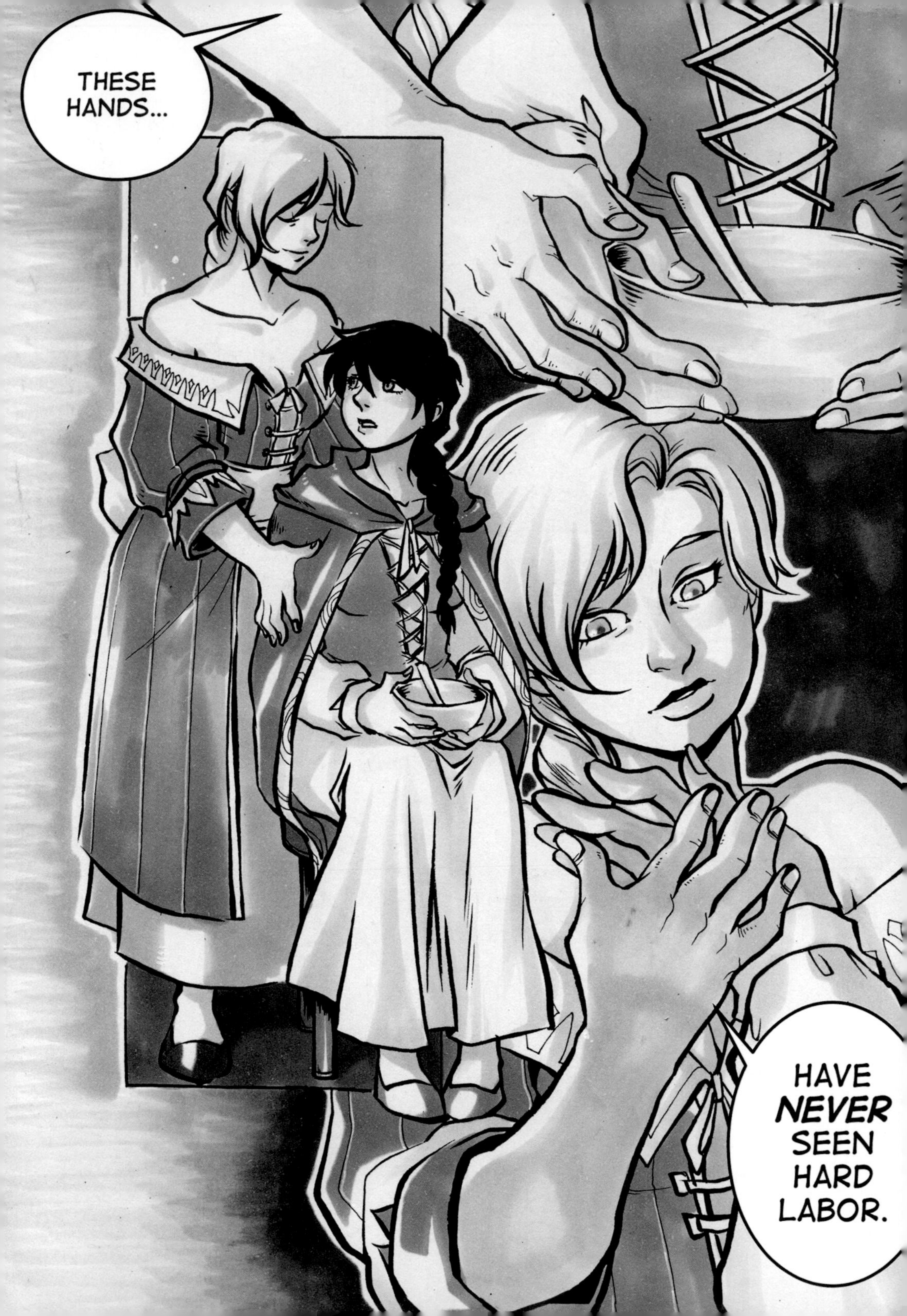
THESE HANDS...
HAVE **NEVER** SEEN HARD LABOR.

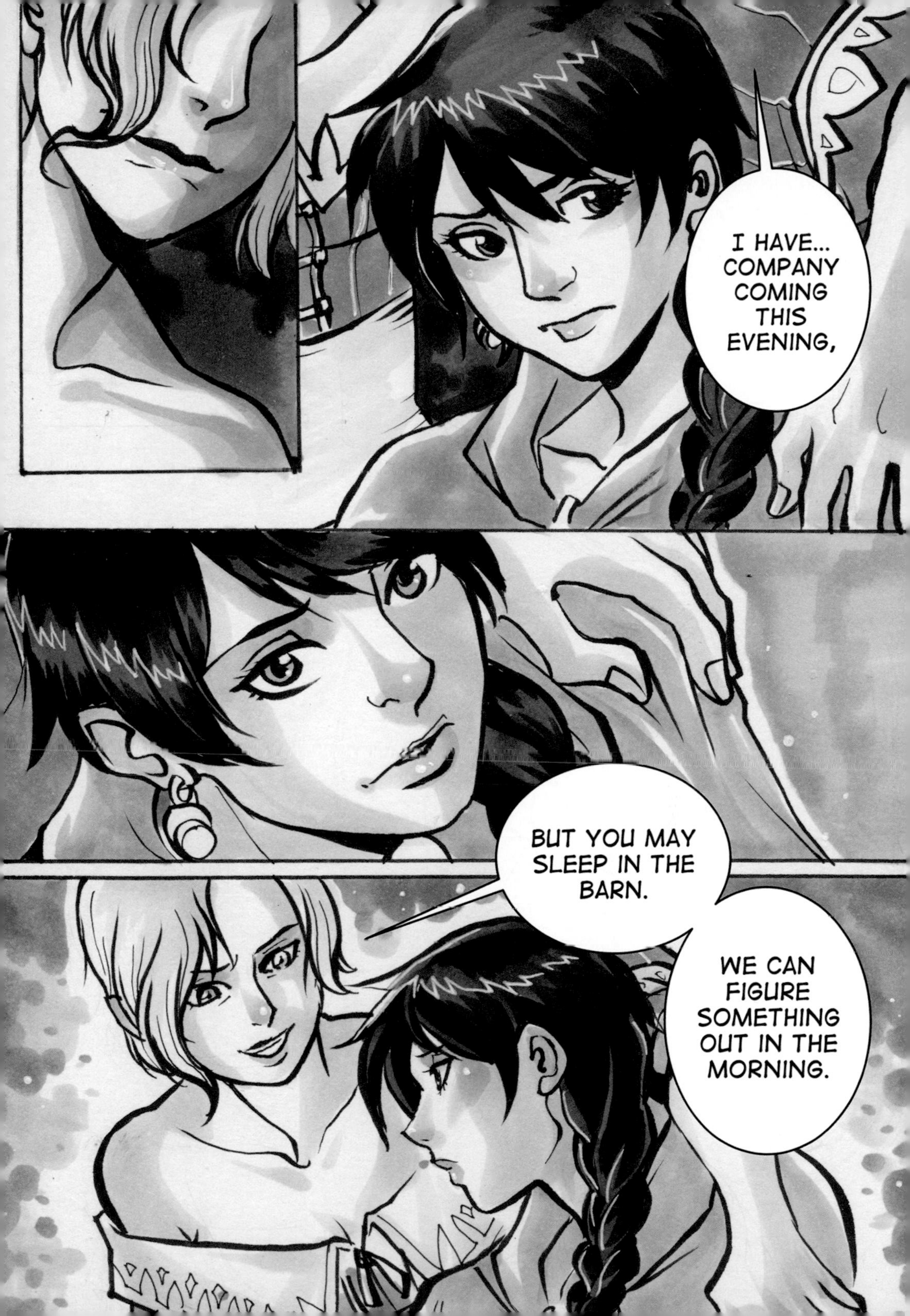
I HAVE... COMPANY COMING THIS EVENING,
BUT YOU MAY SLEEP IN THE BARN.
WE CAN FIGURE SOMETHING OUT IN THE MORNING.

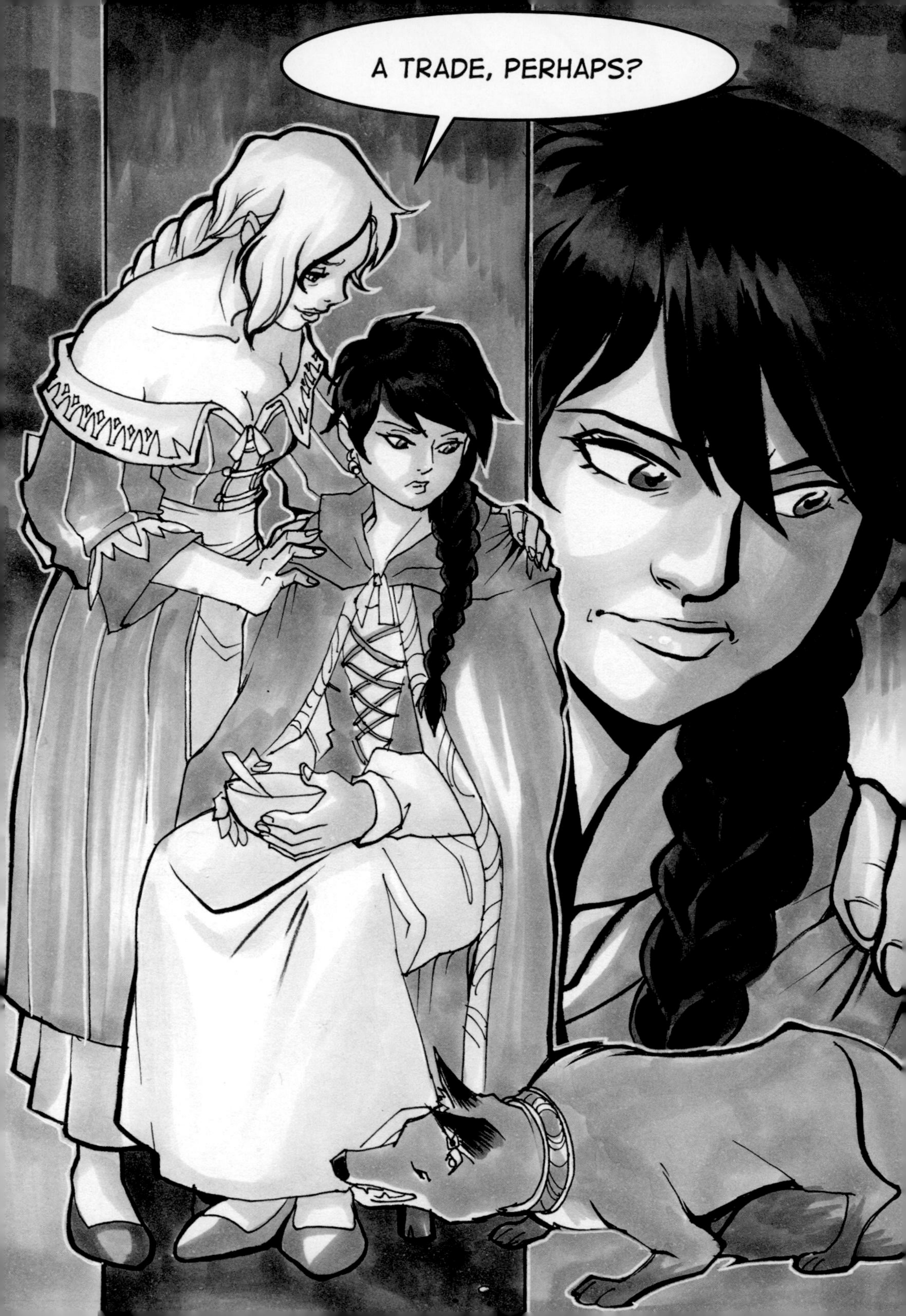
A TRADE, PERHAPS?

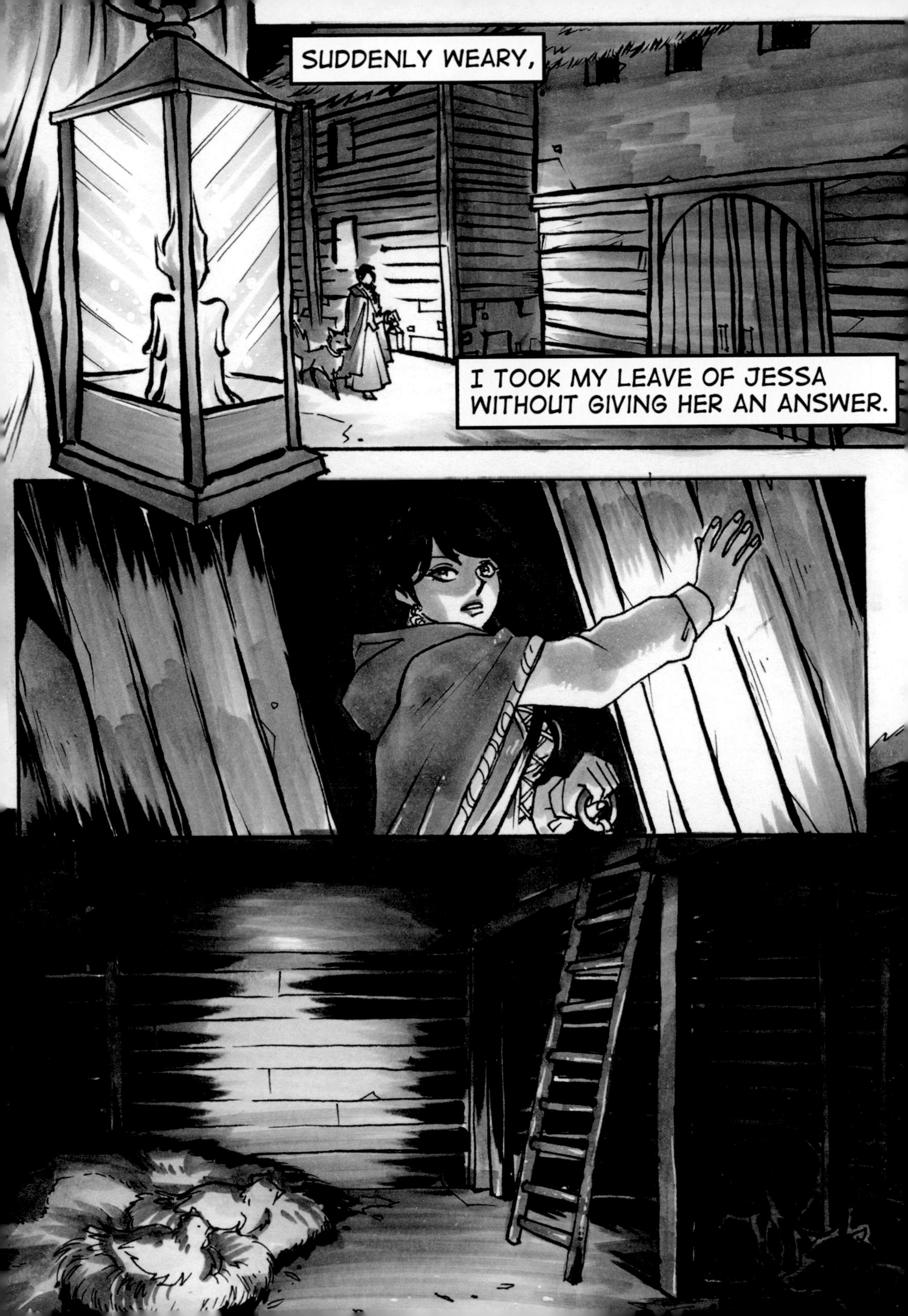
SUDDENLY WEARY,
I TOOK MY LEAVE OF JESSA WITHOUT GIVING HER AN ANSWER.

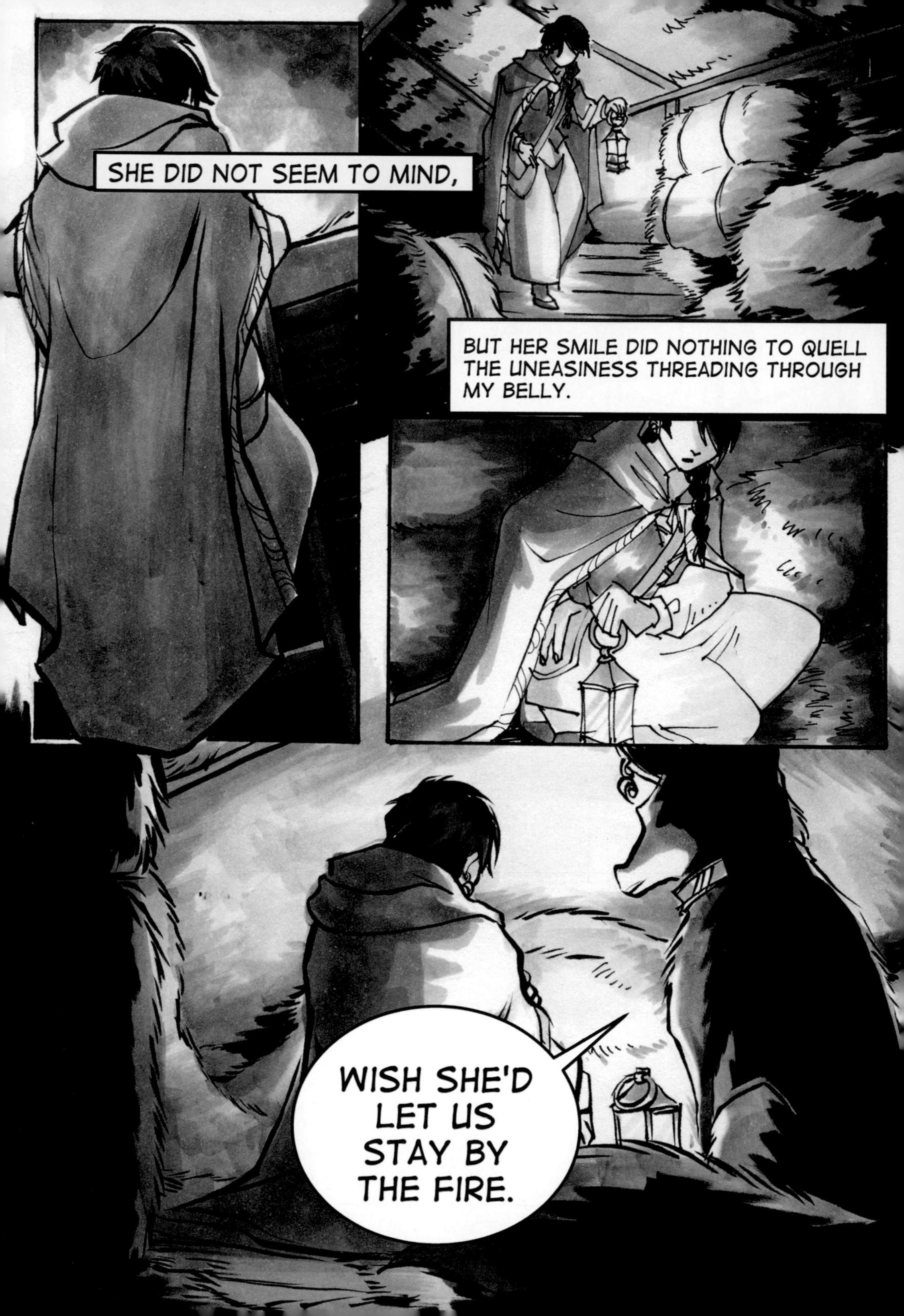
SHE DID NOT SEEM TO MIND,
BUT HER SMILE DID NOTHING TO QUELL THE UNEASINESS THREADING THROUGH MY BELLY.
WISH SHE'D LET US STAY BY THE FIRE.

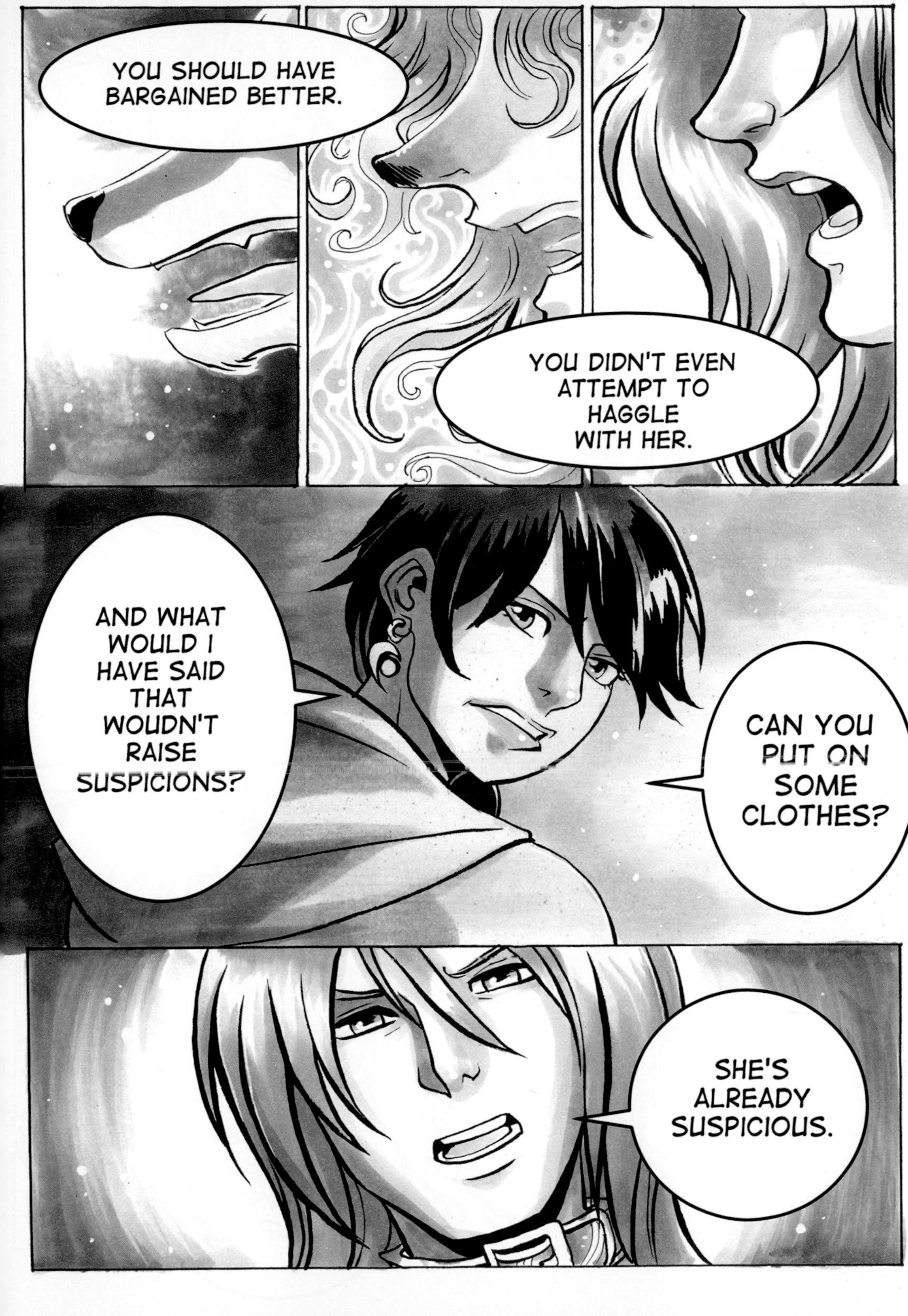
YOU SHOULD HAVE BARGAINED BETTER.
YOU DIDN'T EVEN ATTEMPT TO HAGGLE WITH HER.
AND WHAT WOULD I HAVE SAID THAT WOUDN'T RAISE SUSPICIONS?
CAN YOU PUT ON SOME CLOTHES?
SHE'S ALREADY SUSPICIOUS.

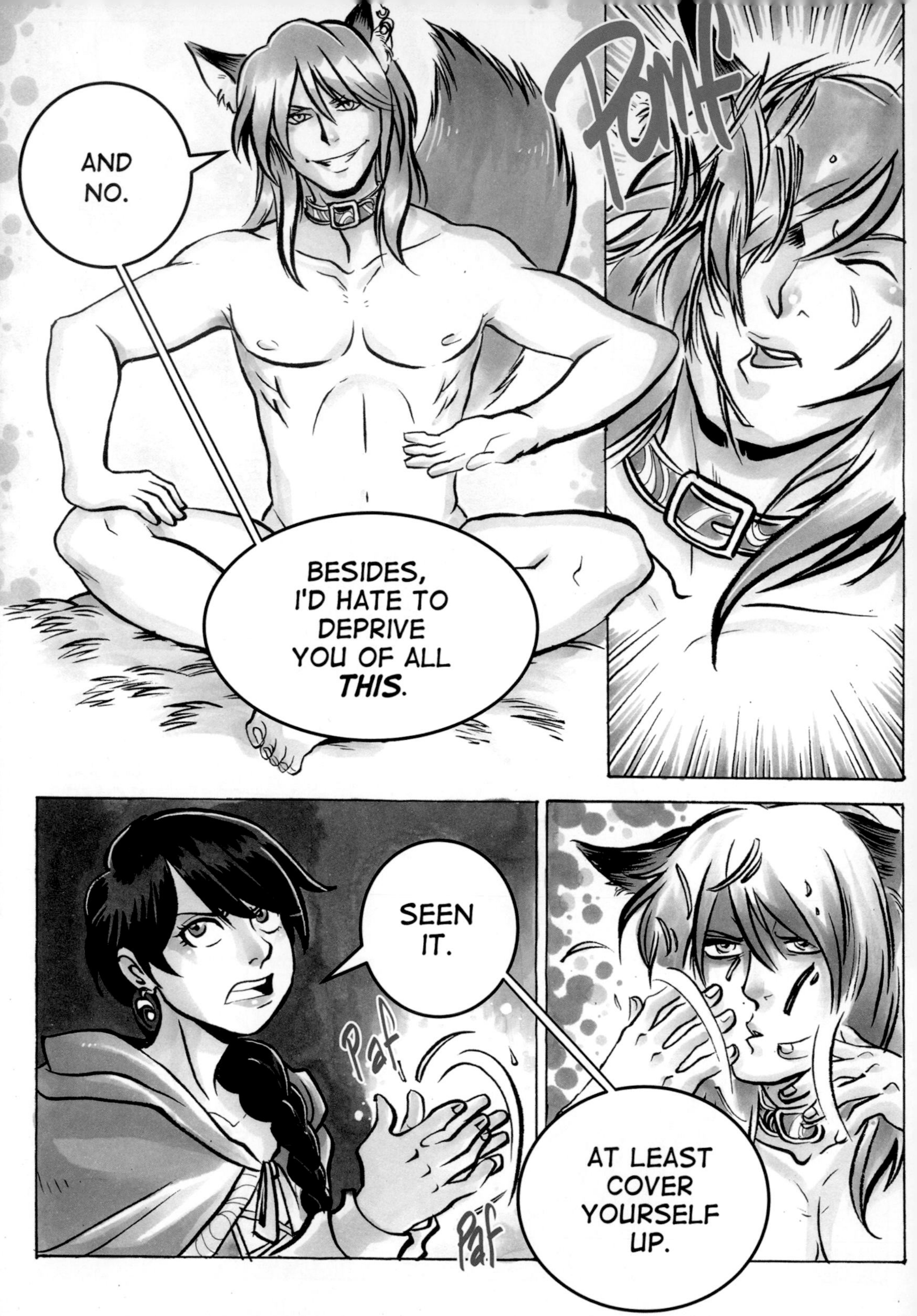
AND NO.
BESIDES, I'D HATE TO DEPRIVE YOU OF ALL **THIS**.
Pomf
SEEN IT.
Paf
Paf
AT LEAST COVER YOURSELF UP.

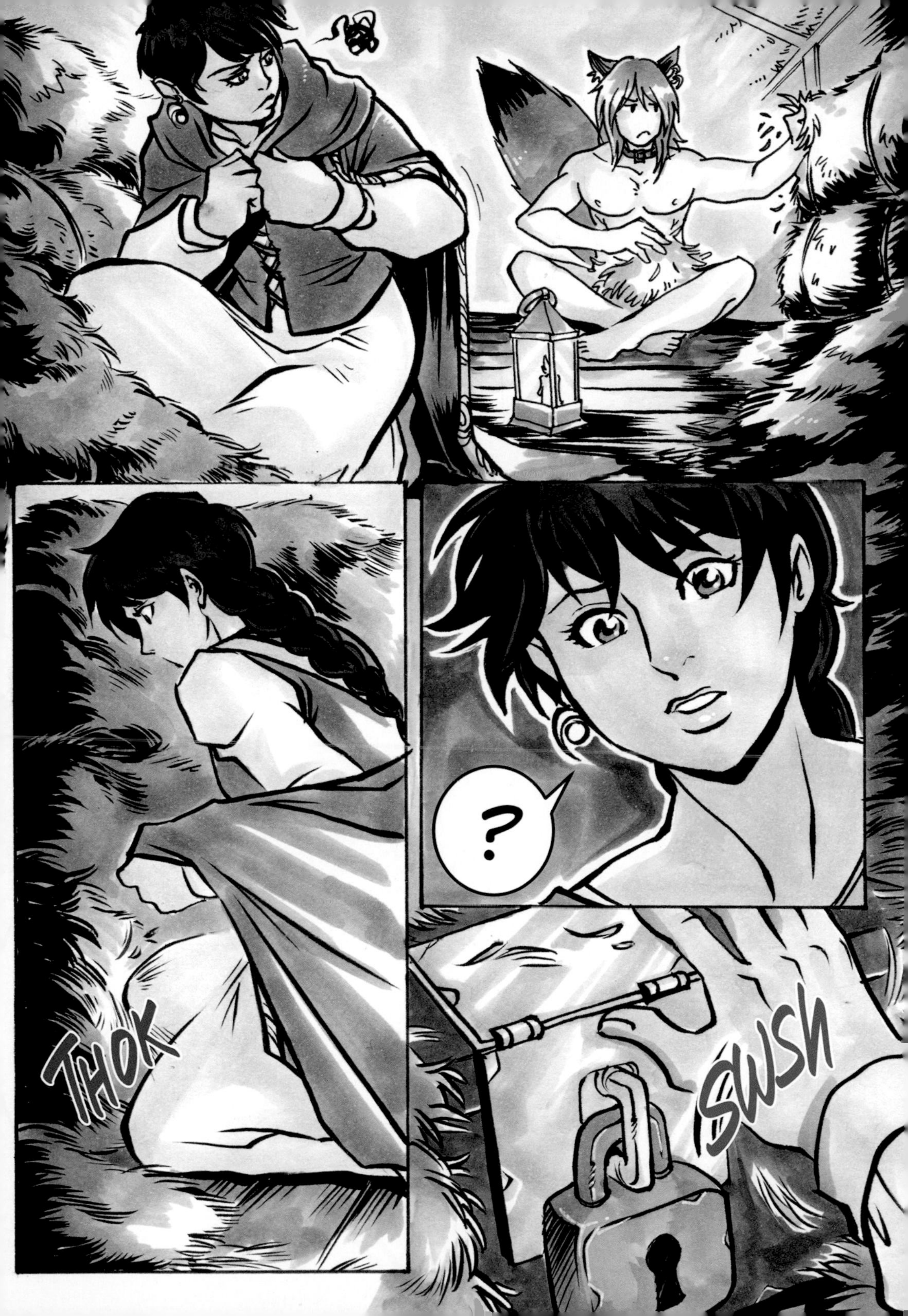
?
THOK
SWSH

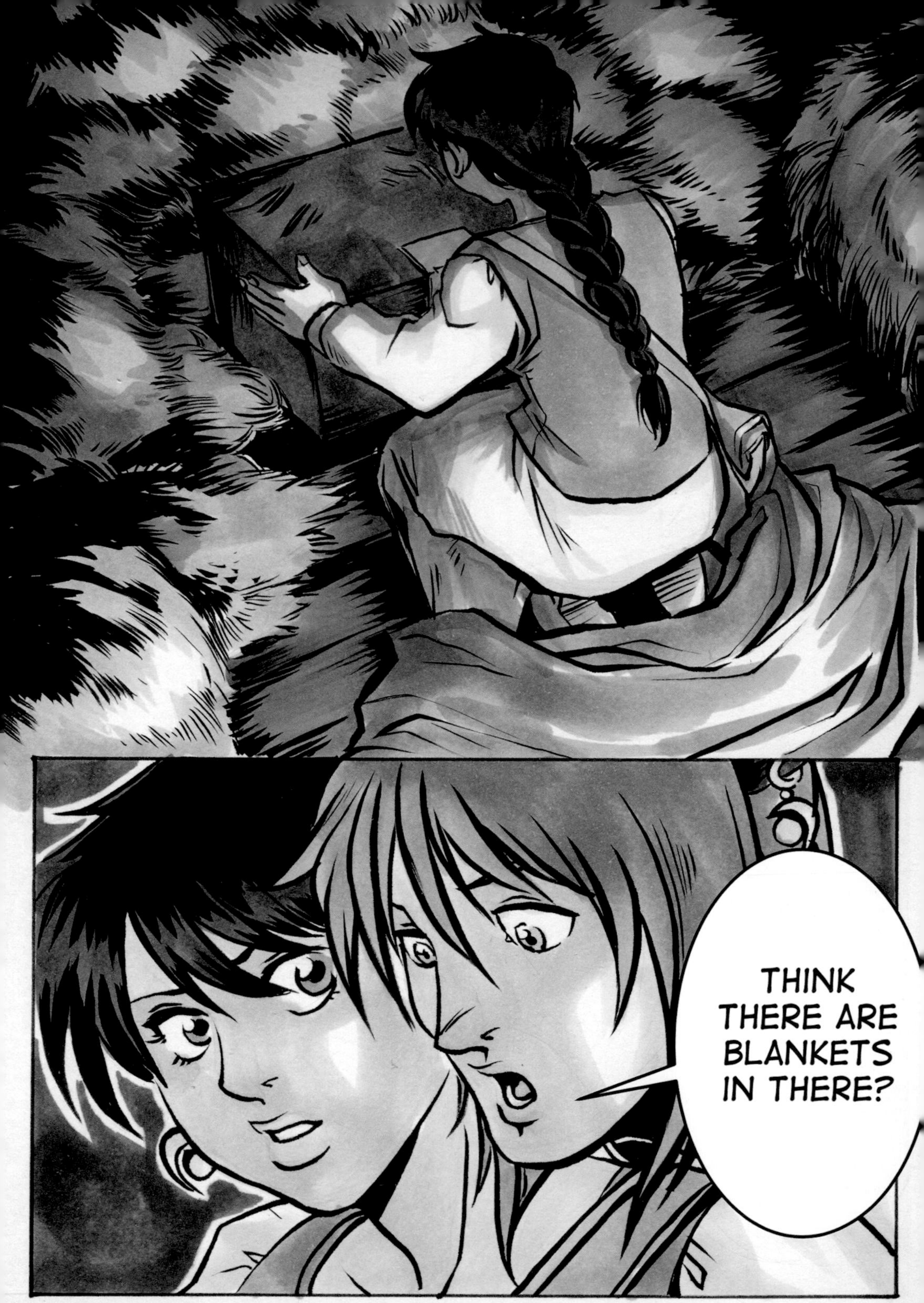
THINK THERE ARE BLANKETS IN THERE?

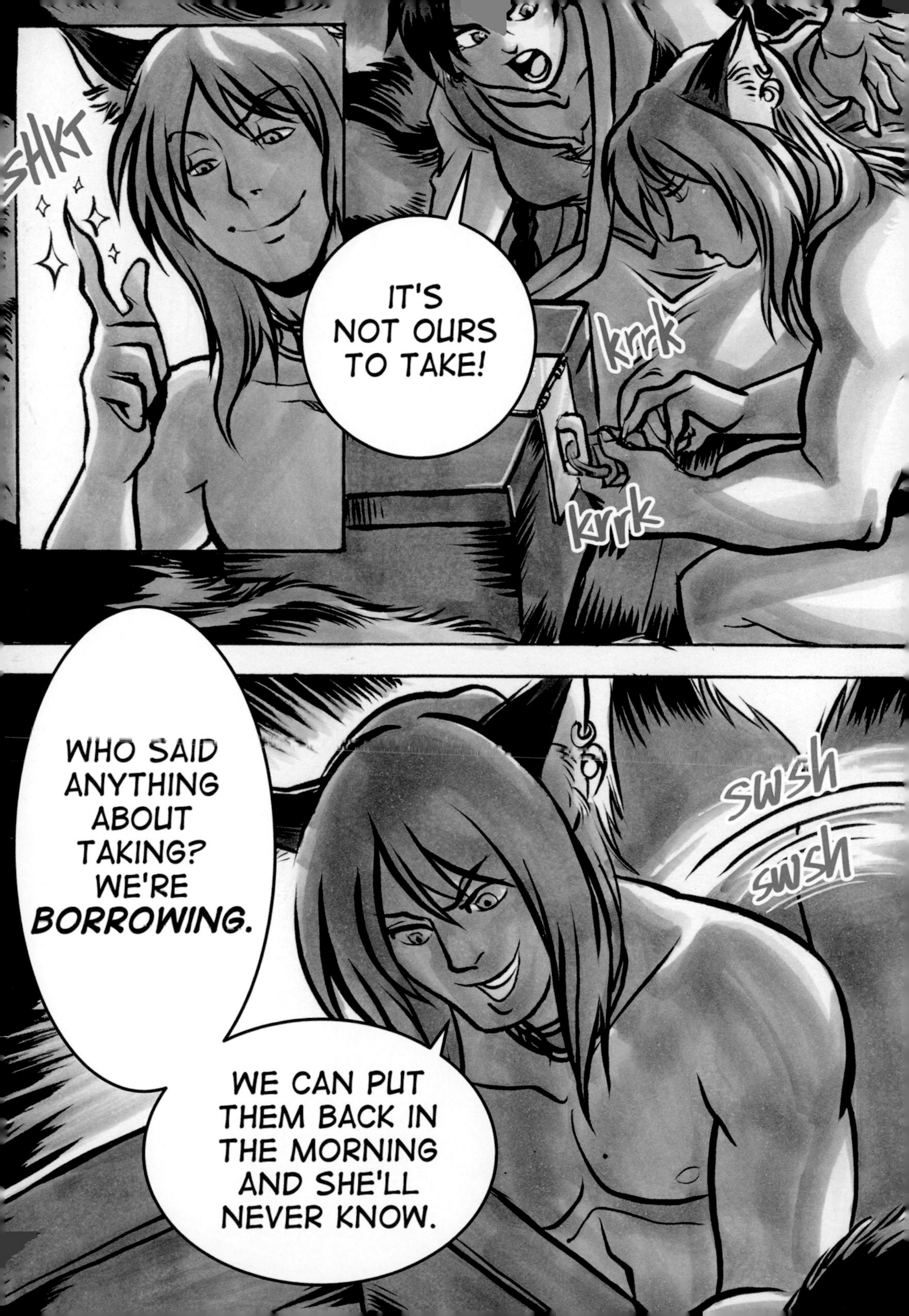
SHKT
IT'S NOT OURS TO TAKE!
krrk
krrk
WHO SAID ANYTHING ABOUT TAKING? WE'RE **BORROWING.**
swsh
swsh
WE CAN PUT THEM BACK IN THE MORNING AND SHE'LL NEVER KNOW.

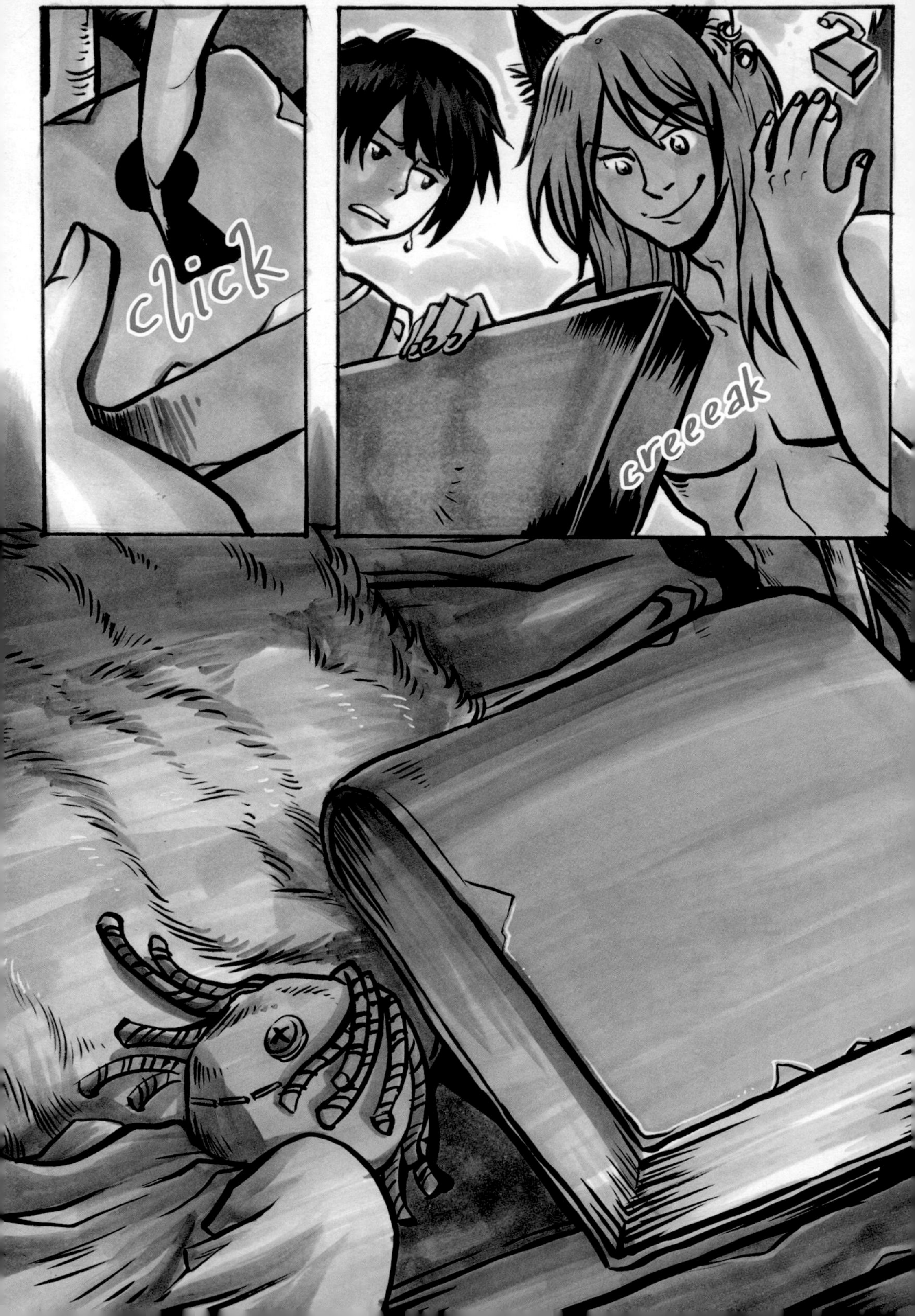
click
creeeak

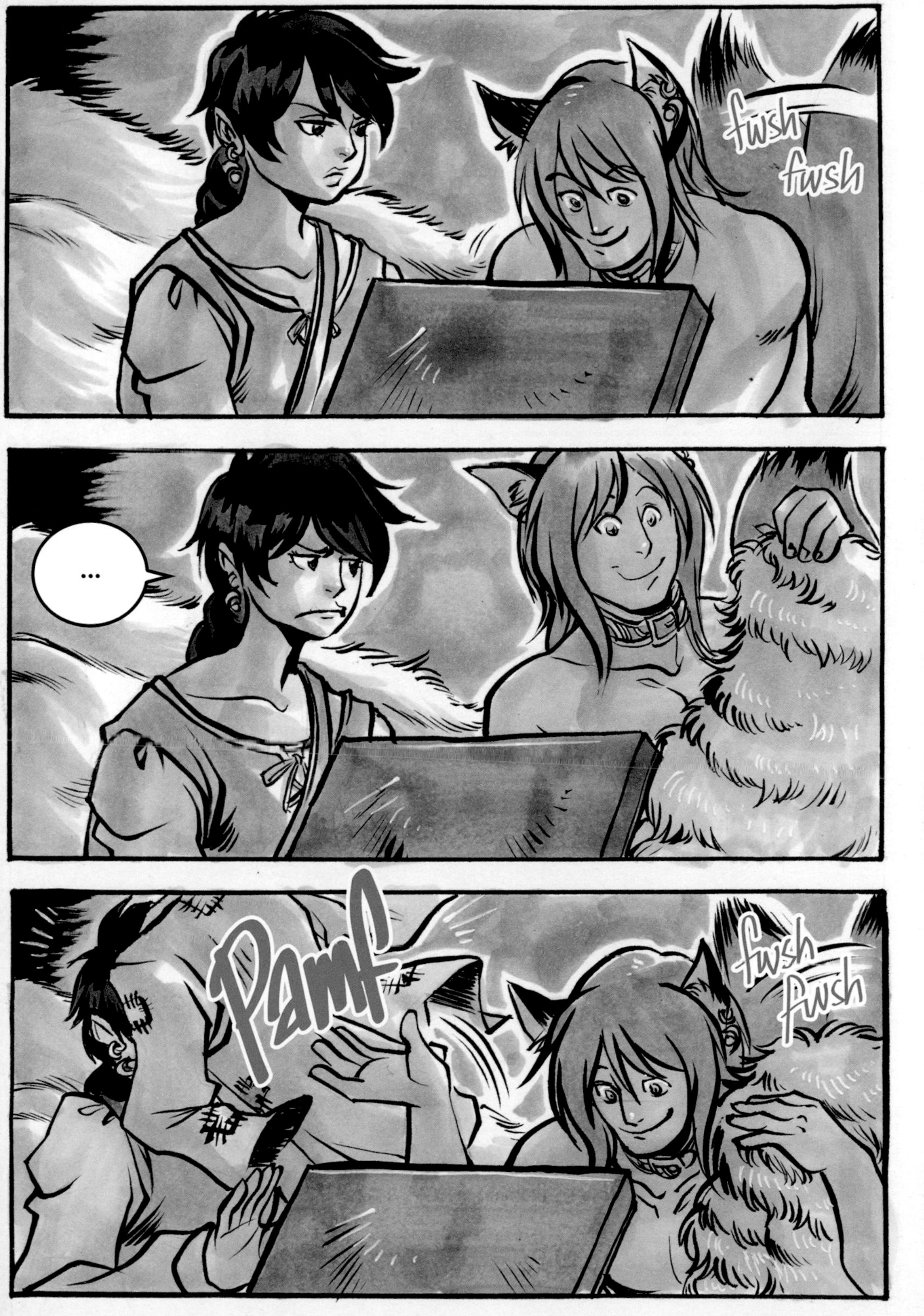
fwsh
fwsh
...
Pamf
fwsh
fwsh

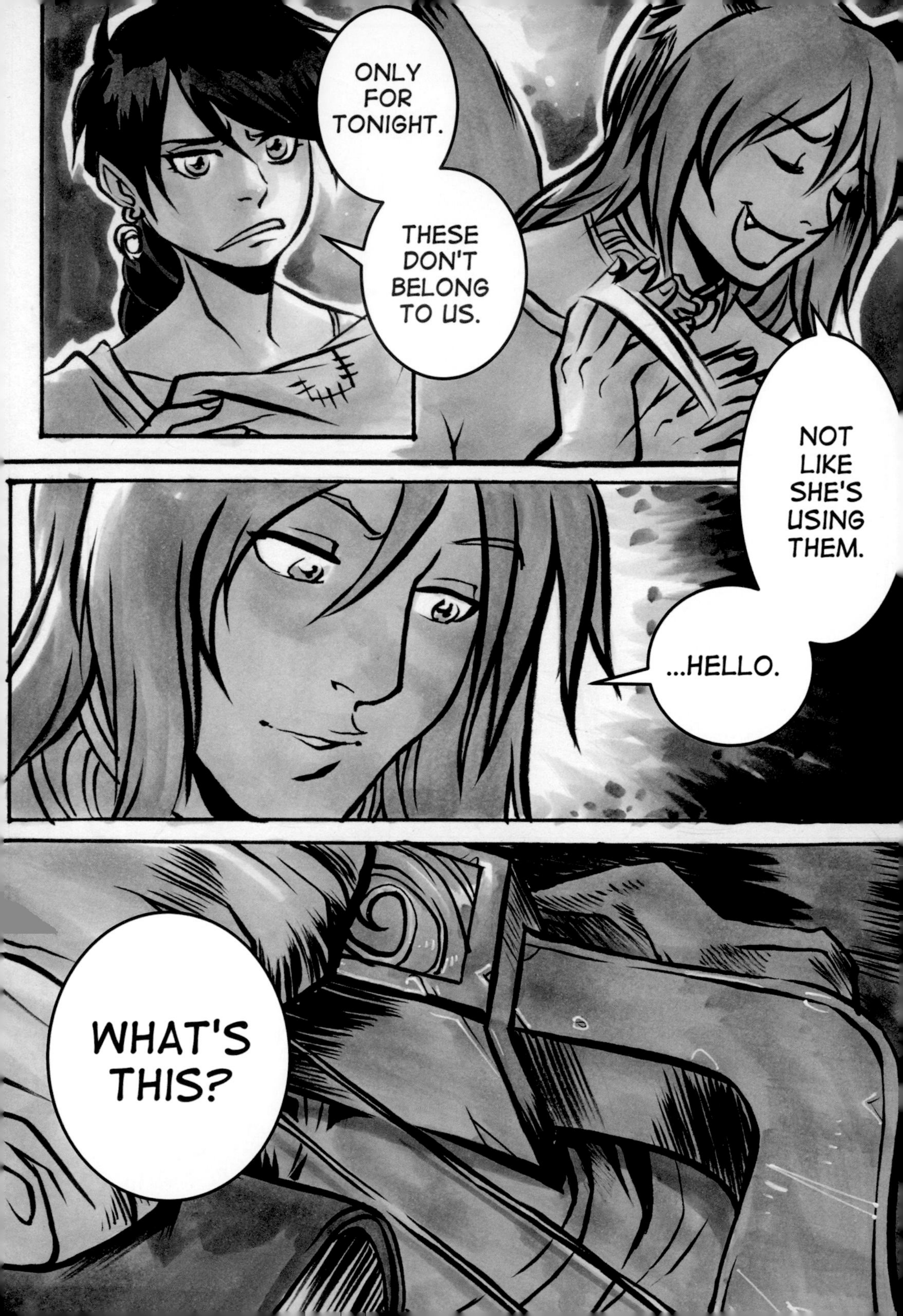
ONLY FOR TONIGHT.
THESE DON'T BELONG TO US.
NOT LIKE SHE'S USING THEM.
...HELLO.
WHAT'S THIS?

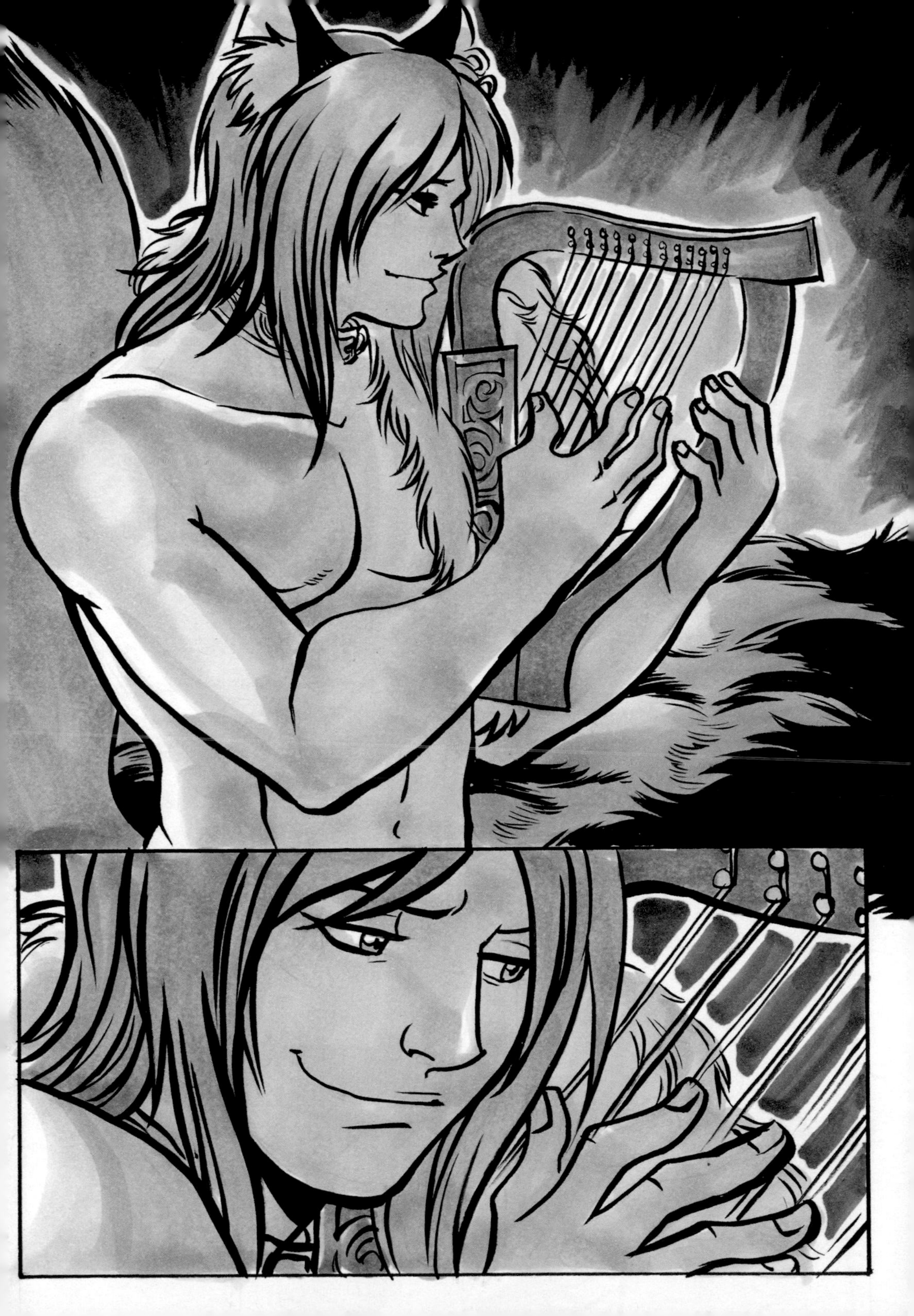

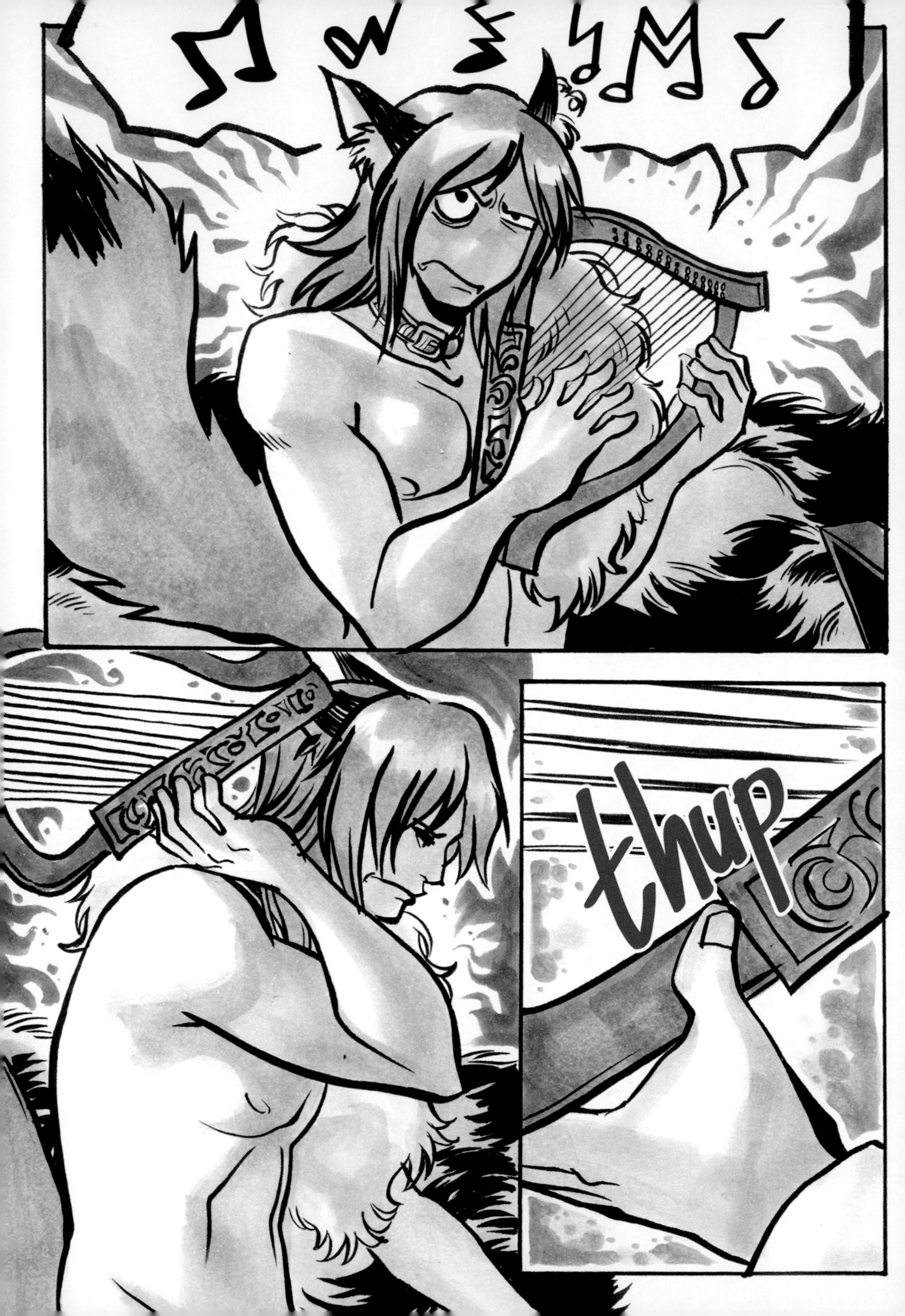
thup

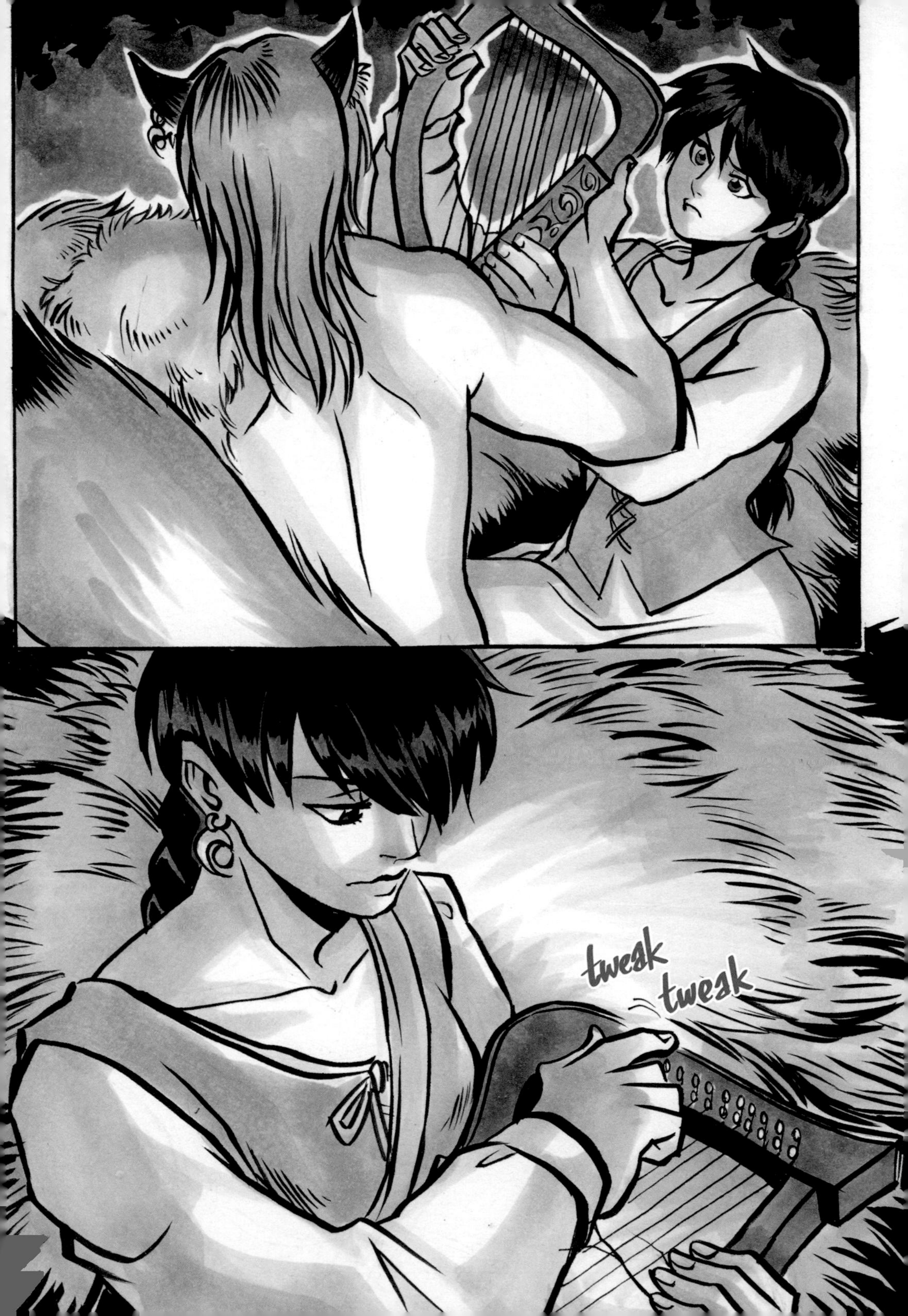
tweak
tweak

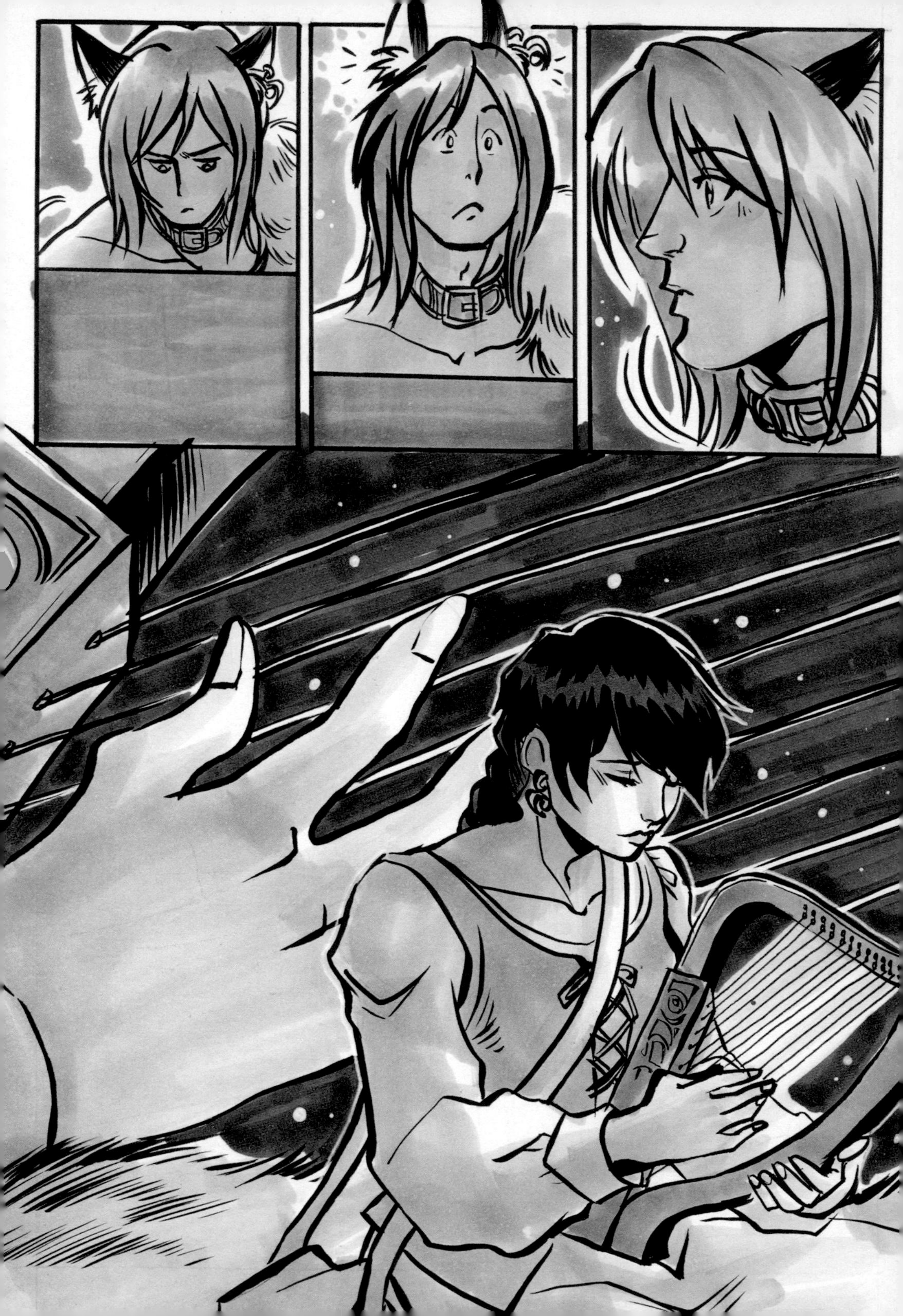

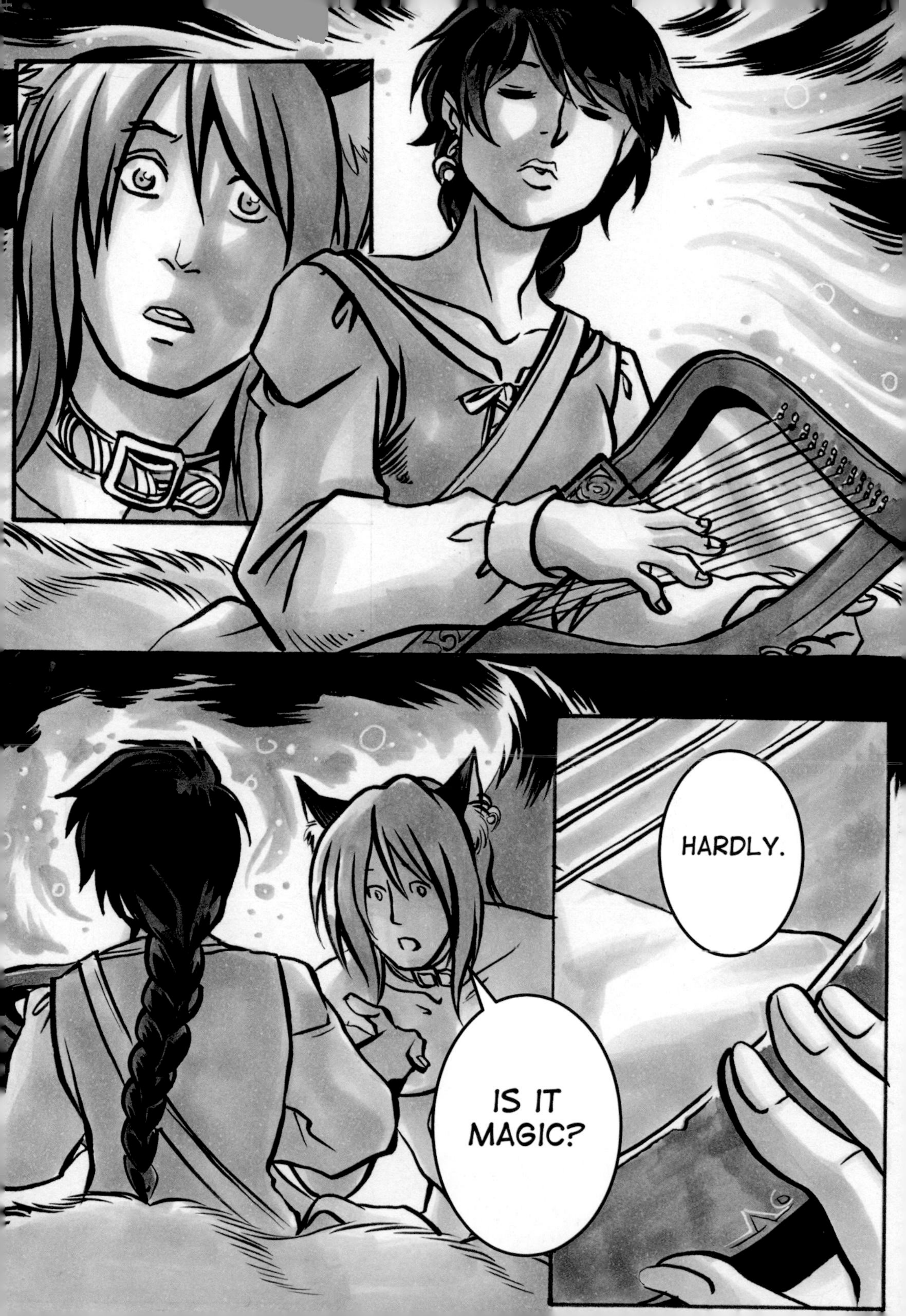
IS IT MAGIC?
HARDLY.

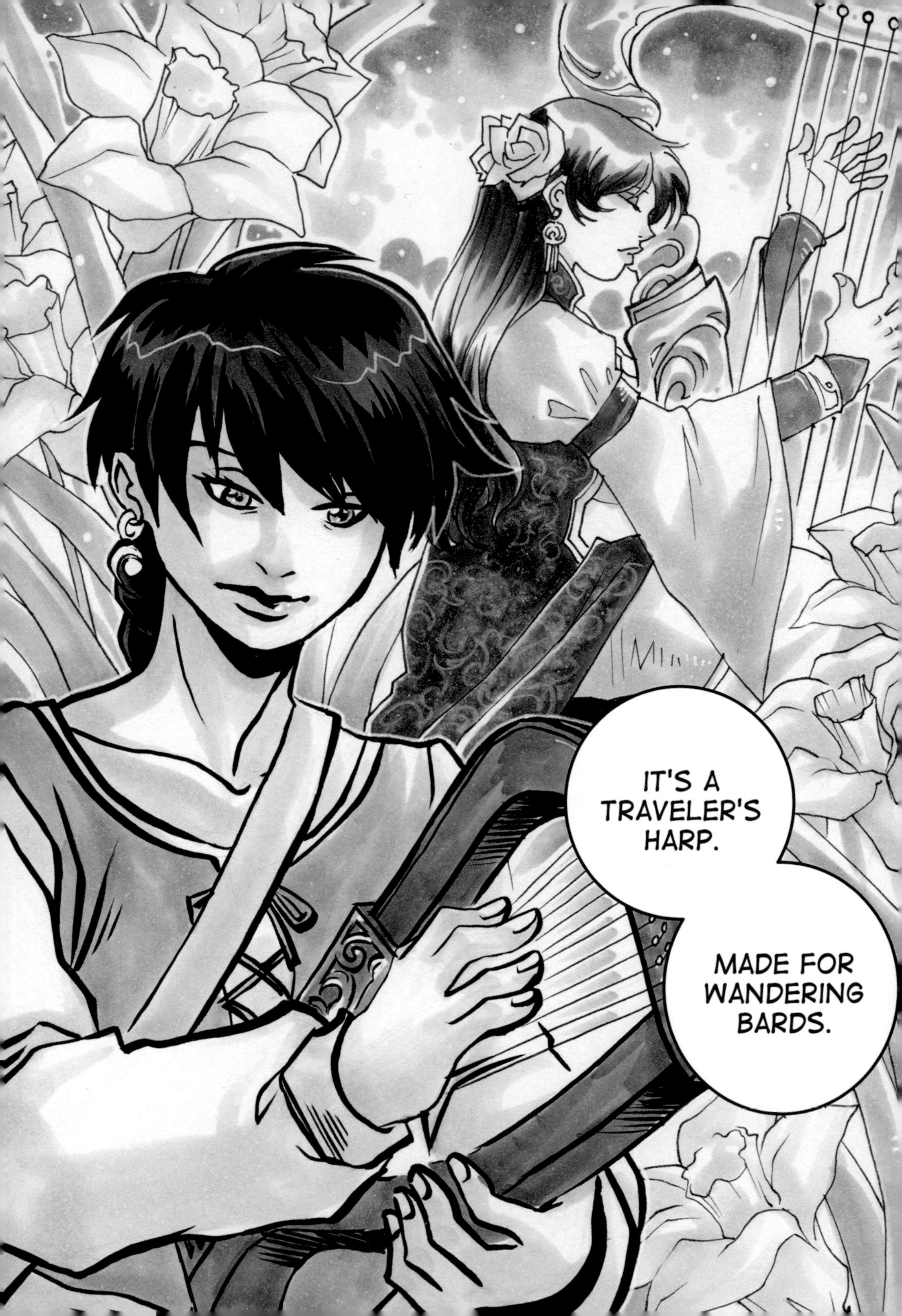
IT'S A TRAVELER'S HARP.
MADE FOR WANDERING BARDS.

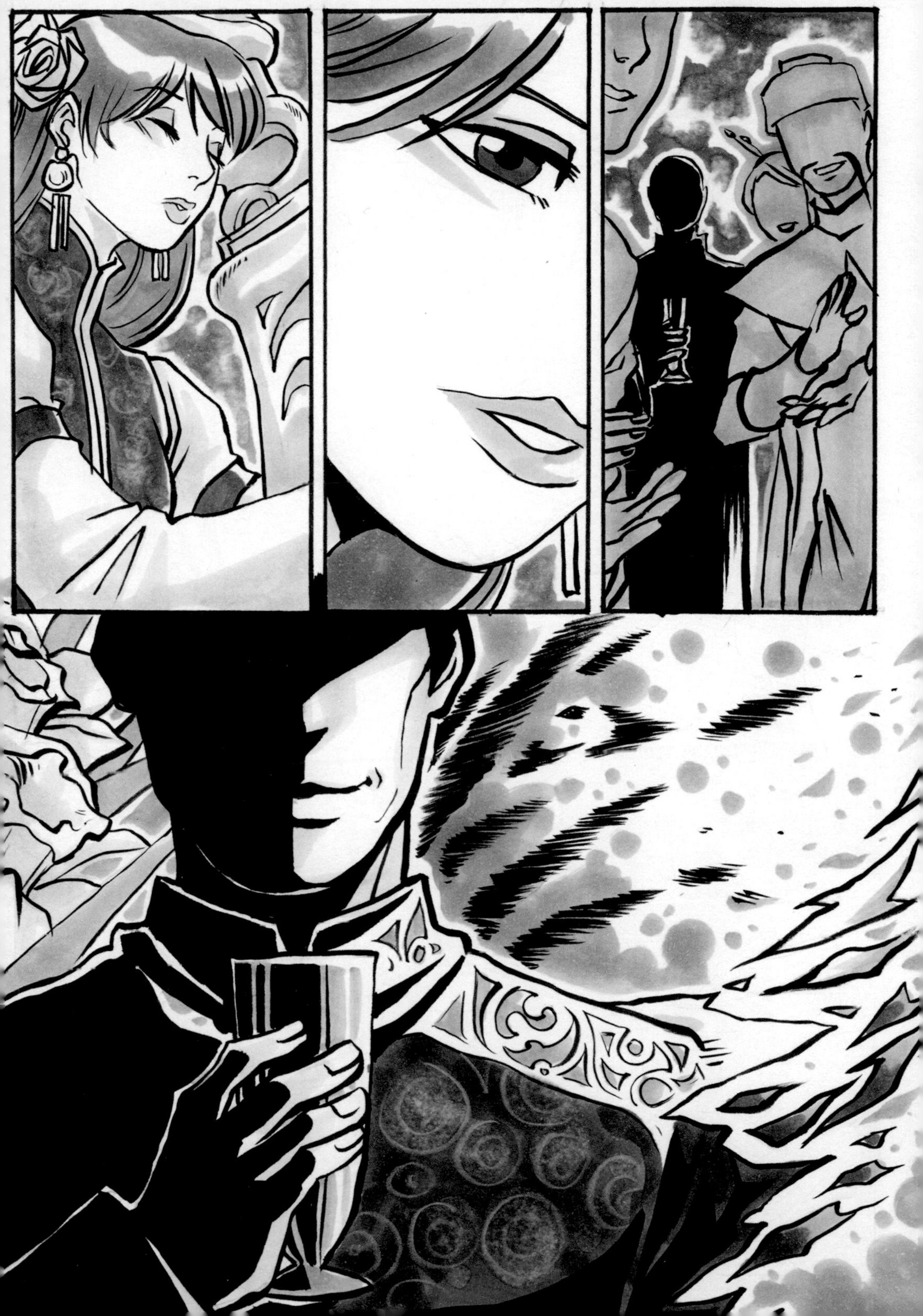

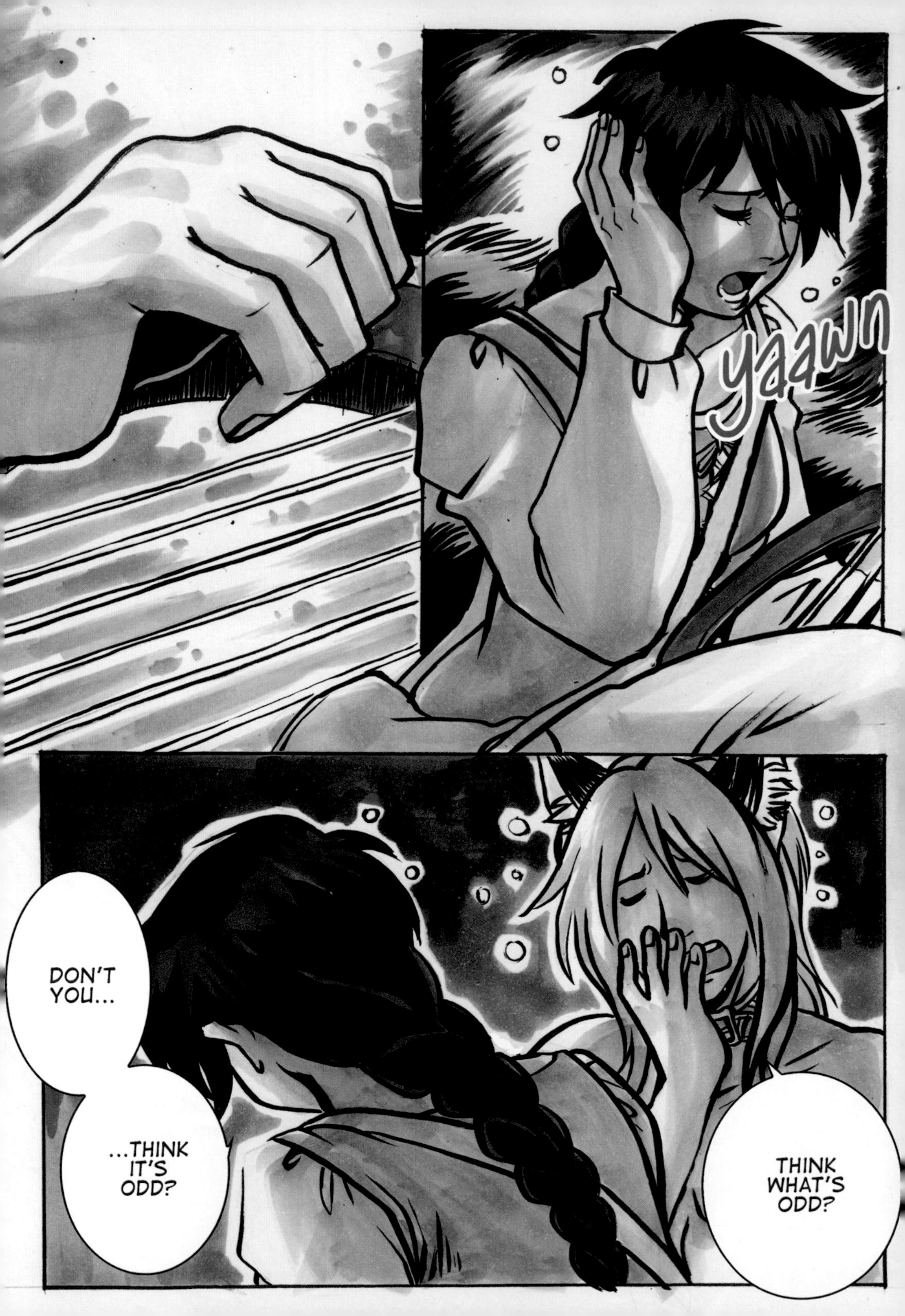
yaawn
DON'T YOU...
...THINK IT'S ODD?
THINK WHAT'S ODD?

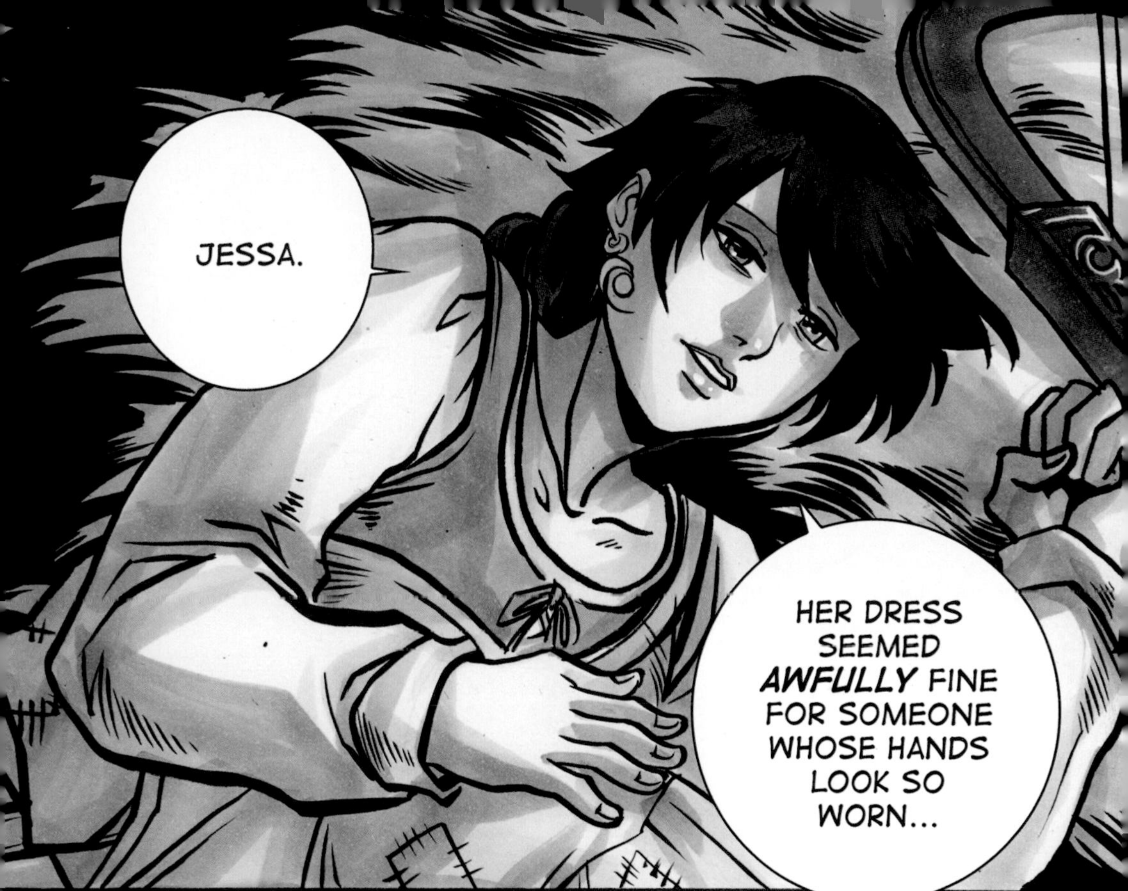
JESSA.
HER DRESS SEEMED AWFULLY FINE FOR SOMEONE WHOSE HANDS LOOK SO WORN...
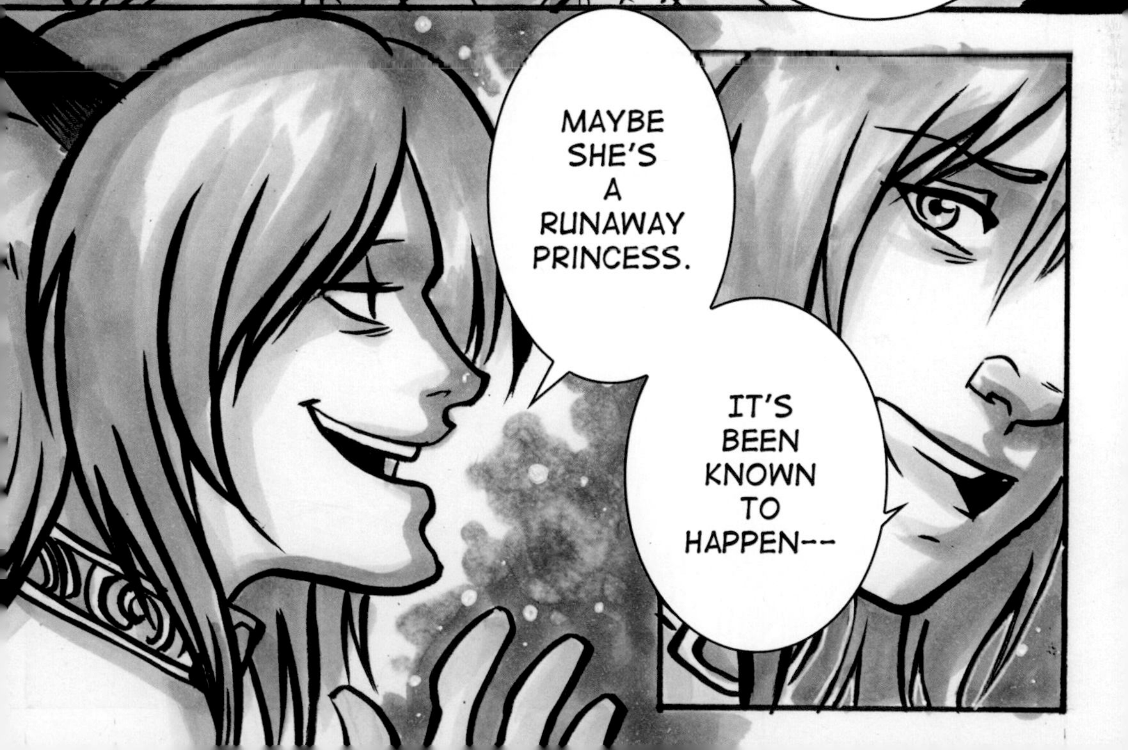
MAYBE SHE'S A RUNAWAY PRINCESS.
IT'S BEEN KNOWN TO HAPPEN--

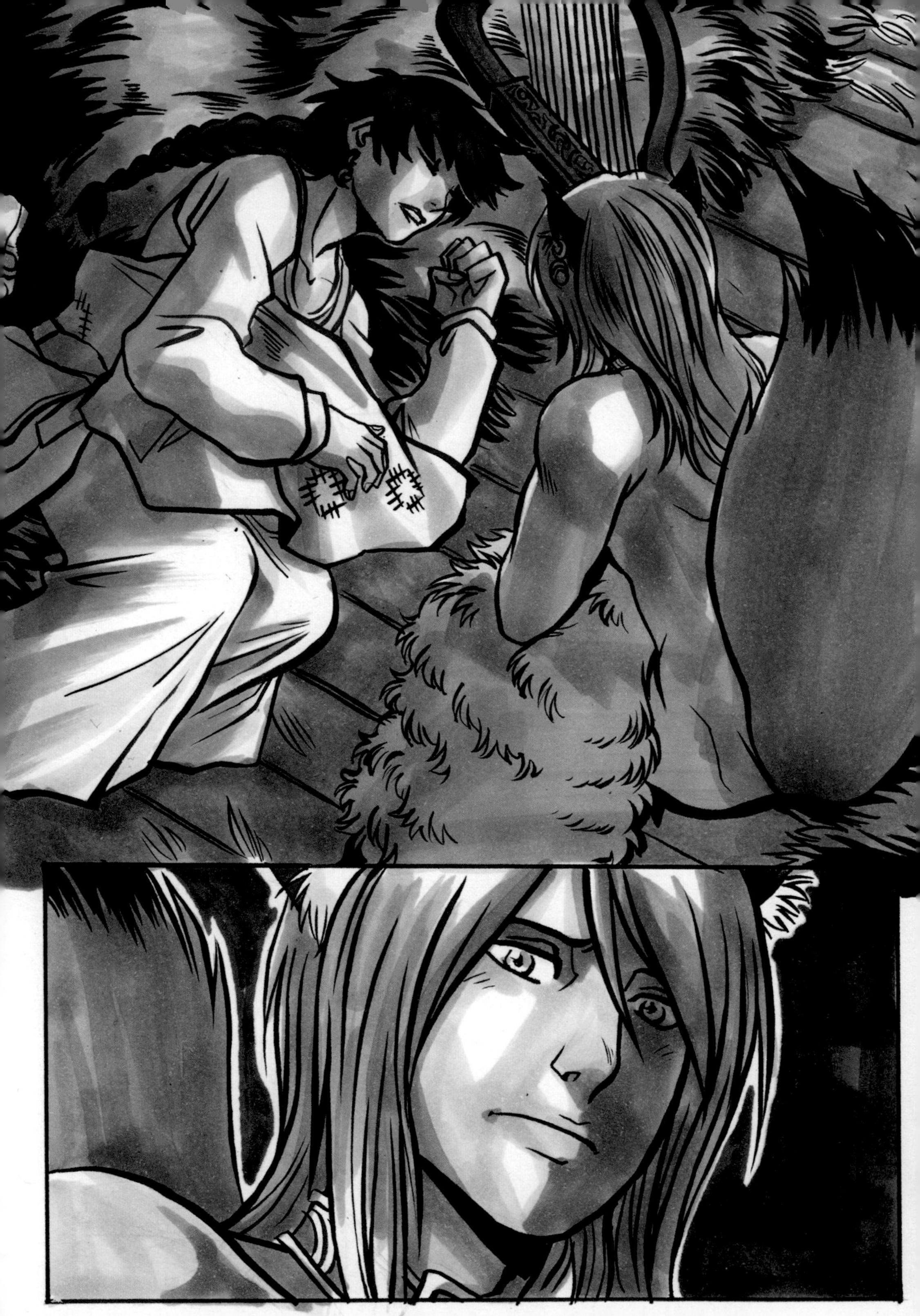

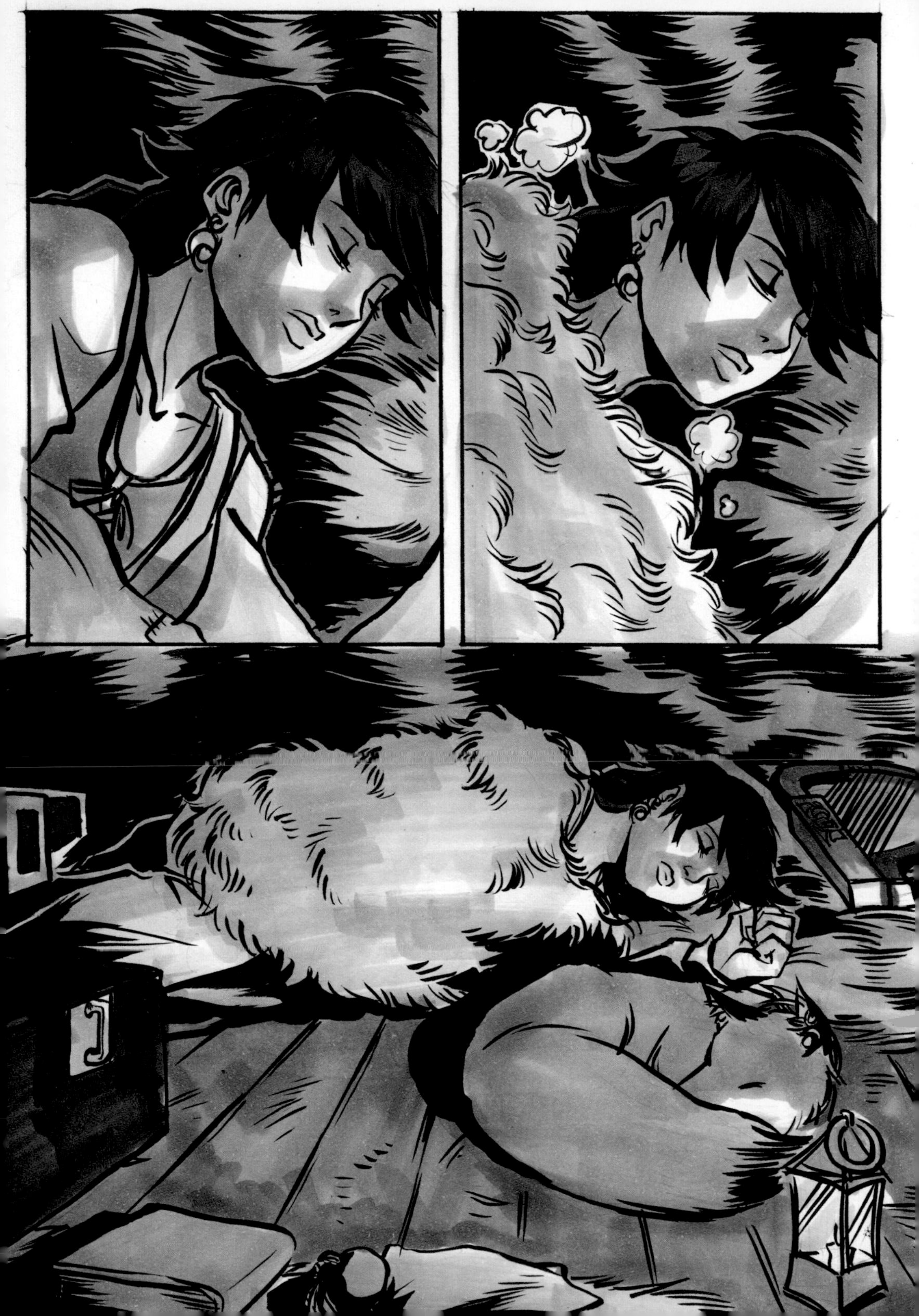

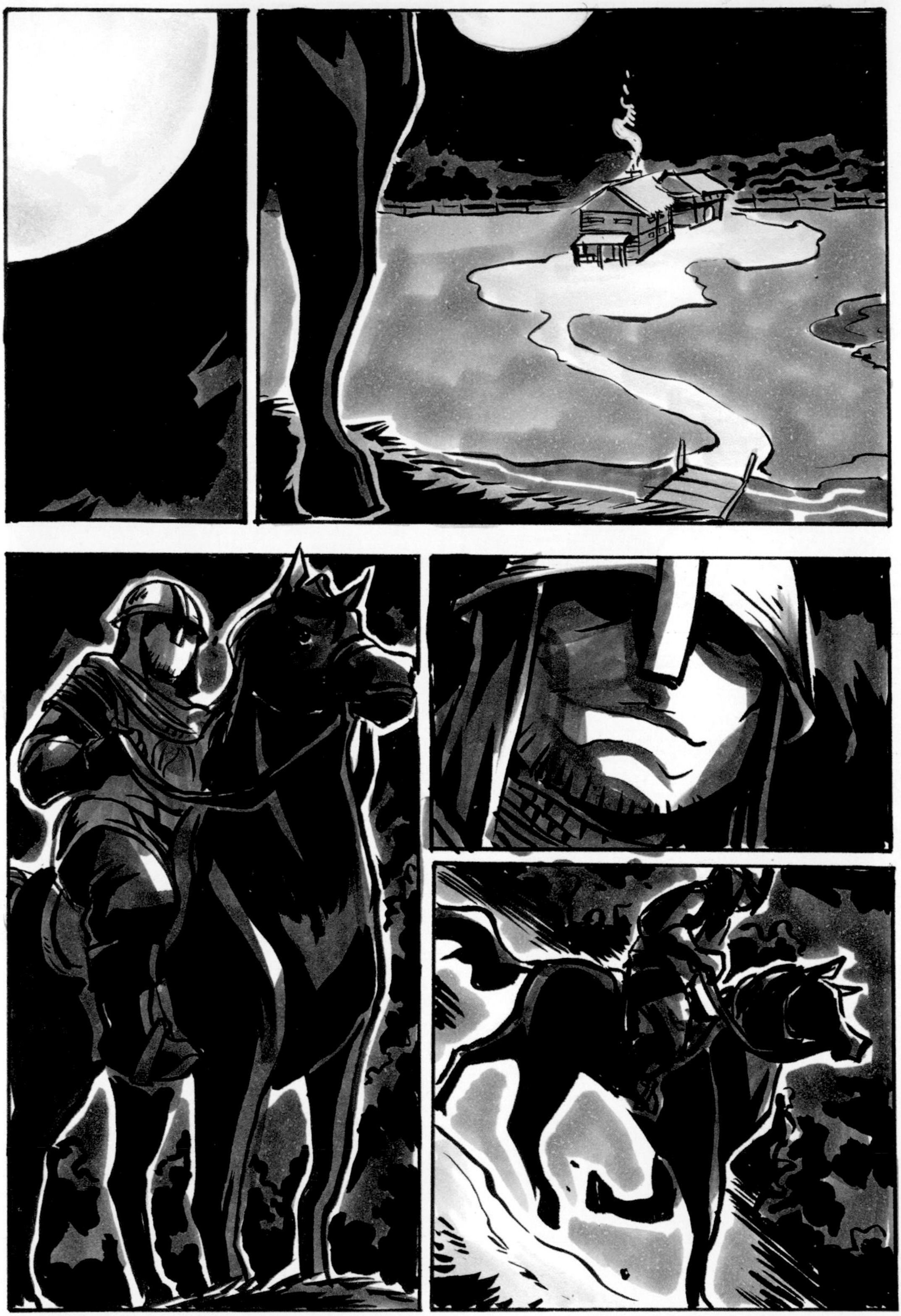

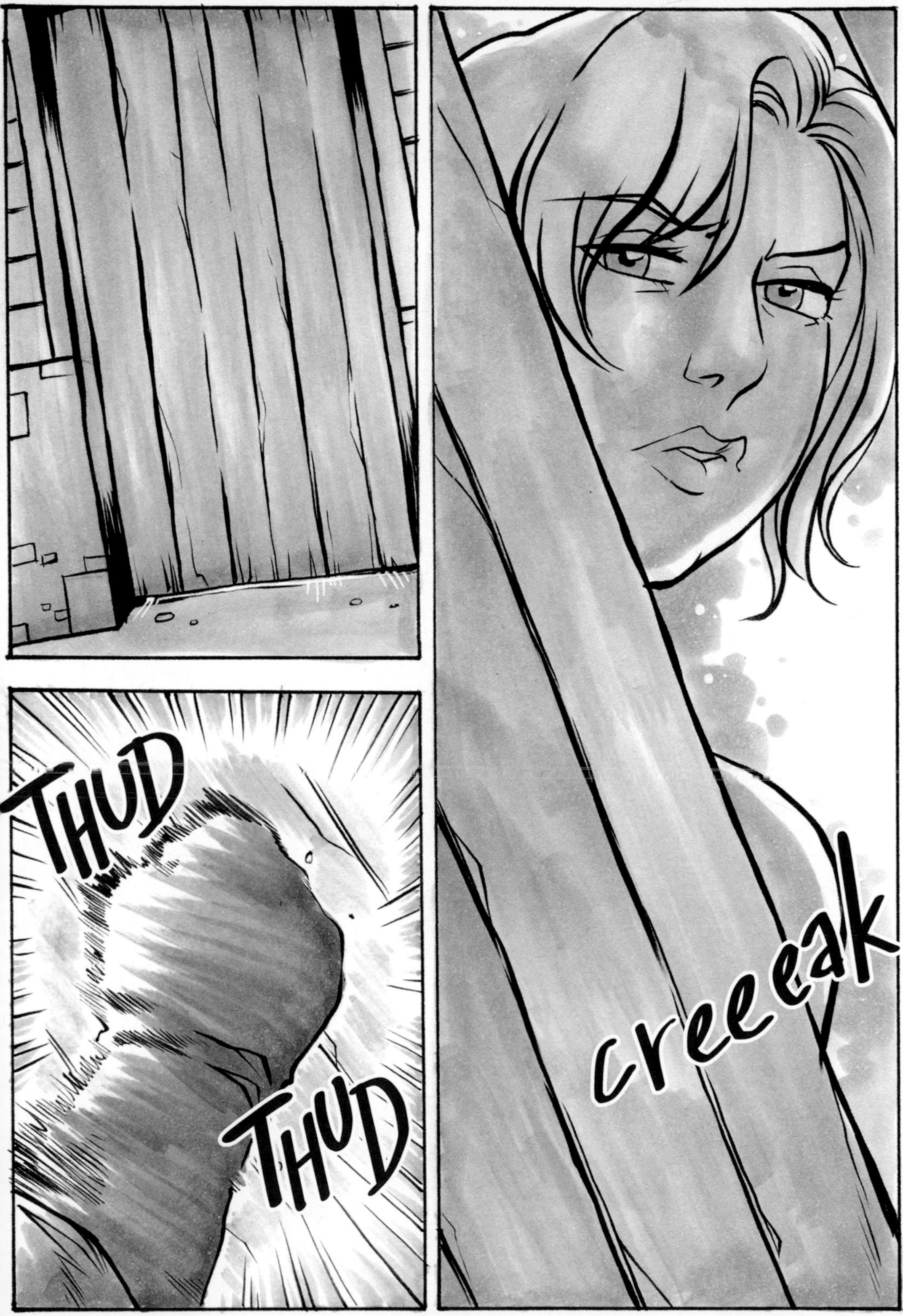
THUD
THUD
creeeak

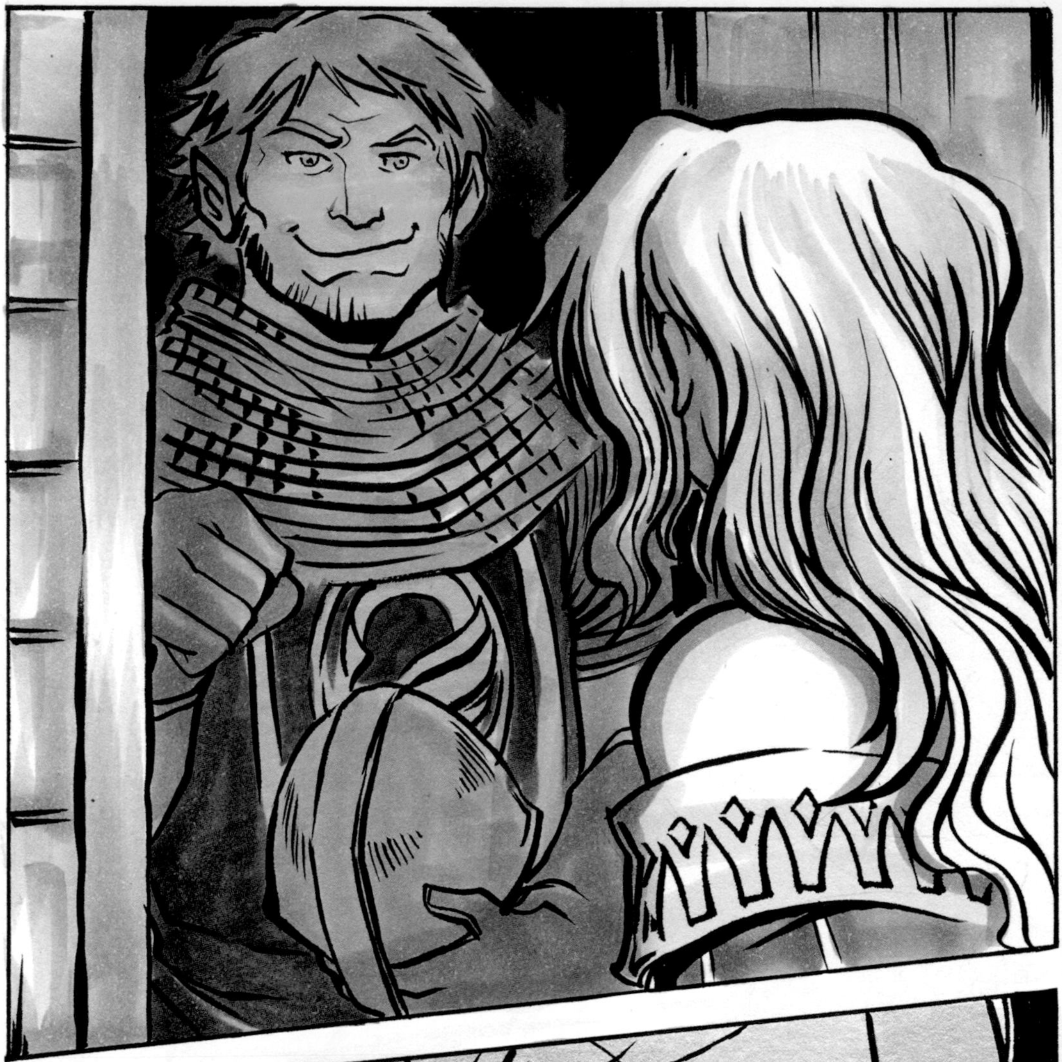
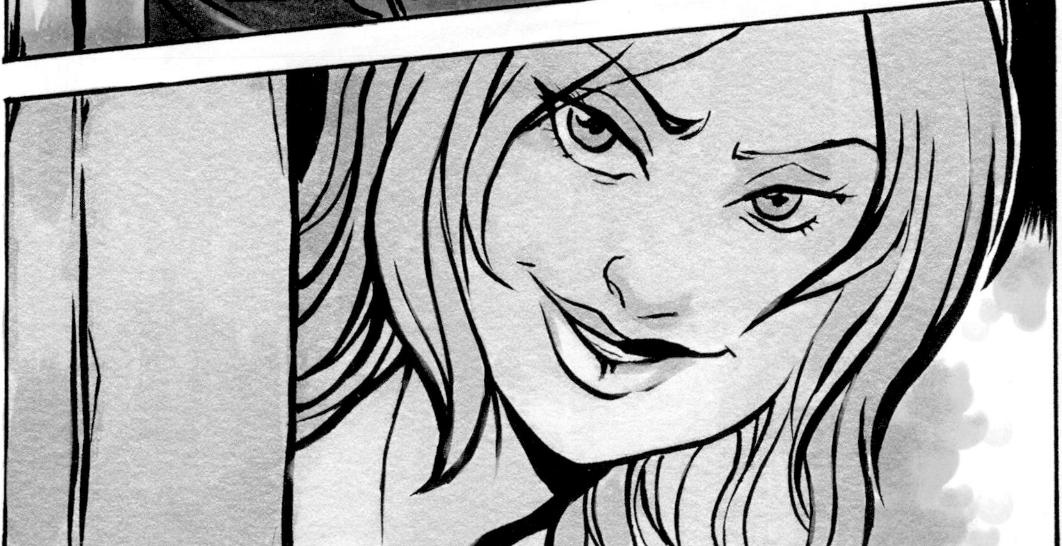

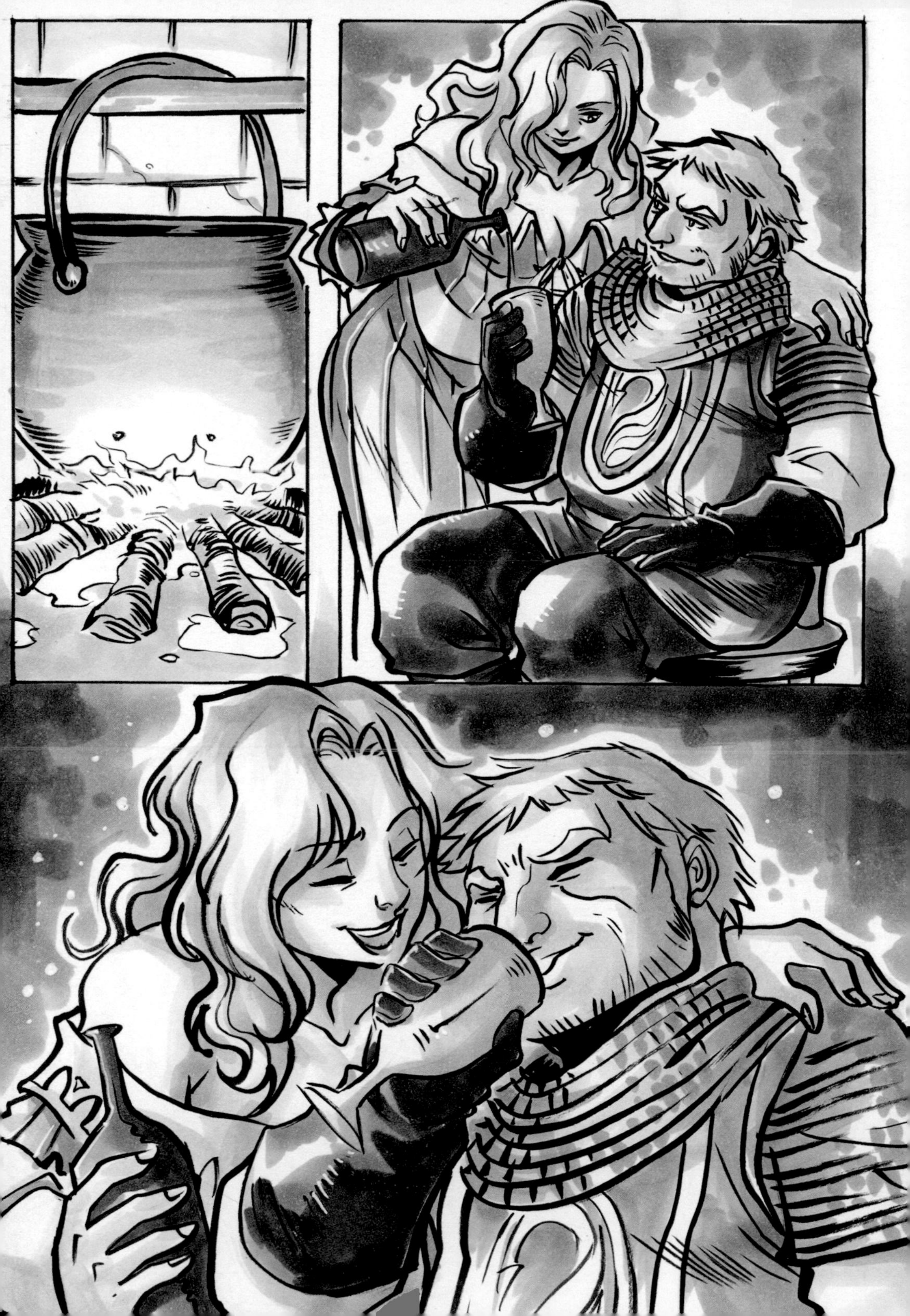

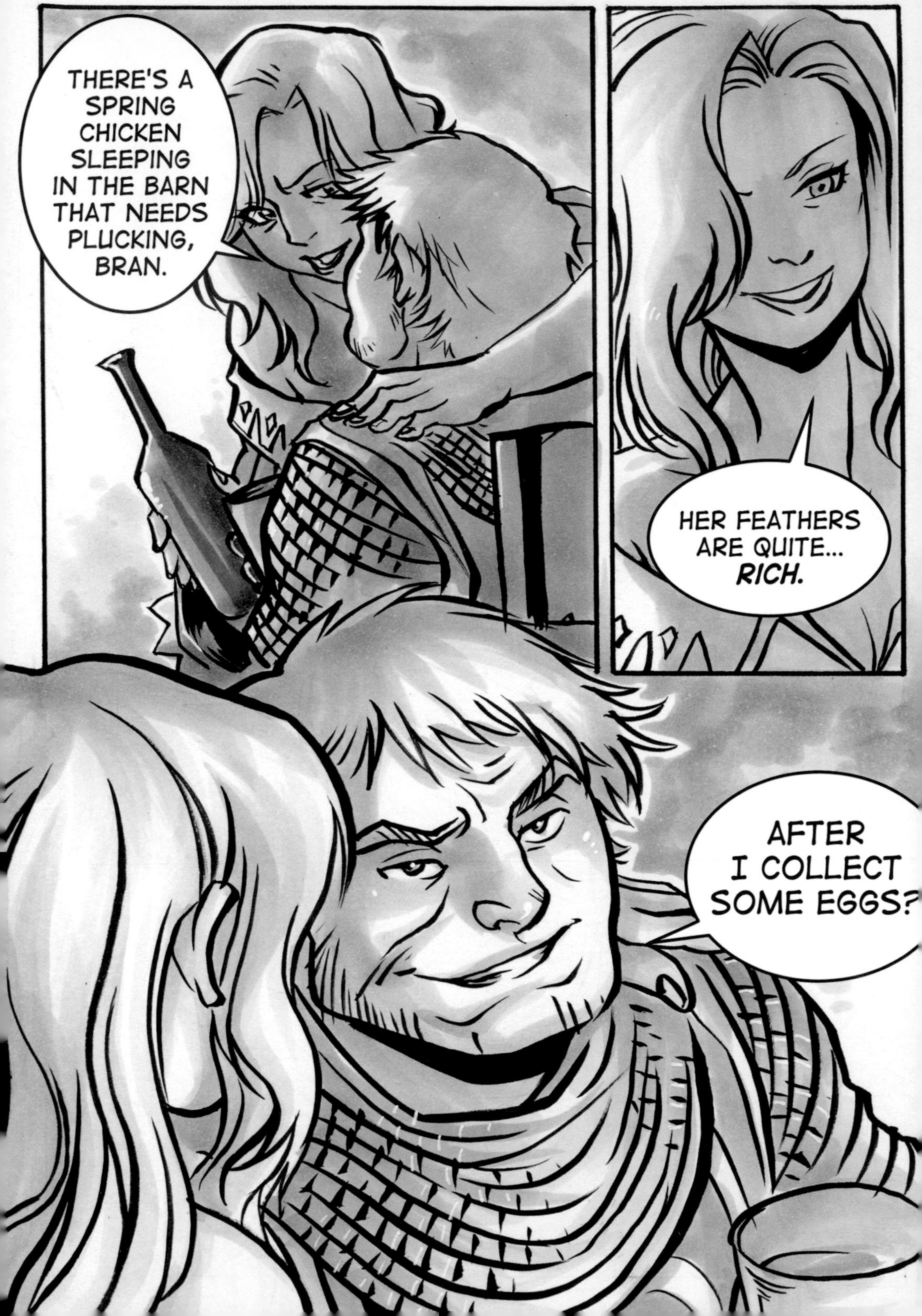
THERE'S A SPRING CHICKEN SLEEPING IN THE BARN THAT NEEDS PLUCKING, BRAN.
HER FEATHERS ARE QUITE... *RICH.*
AFTER I COLLECT SOME EGGS?

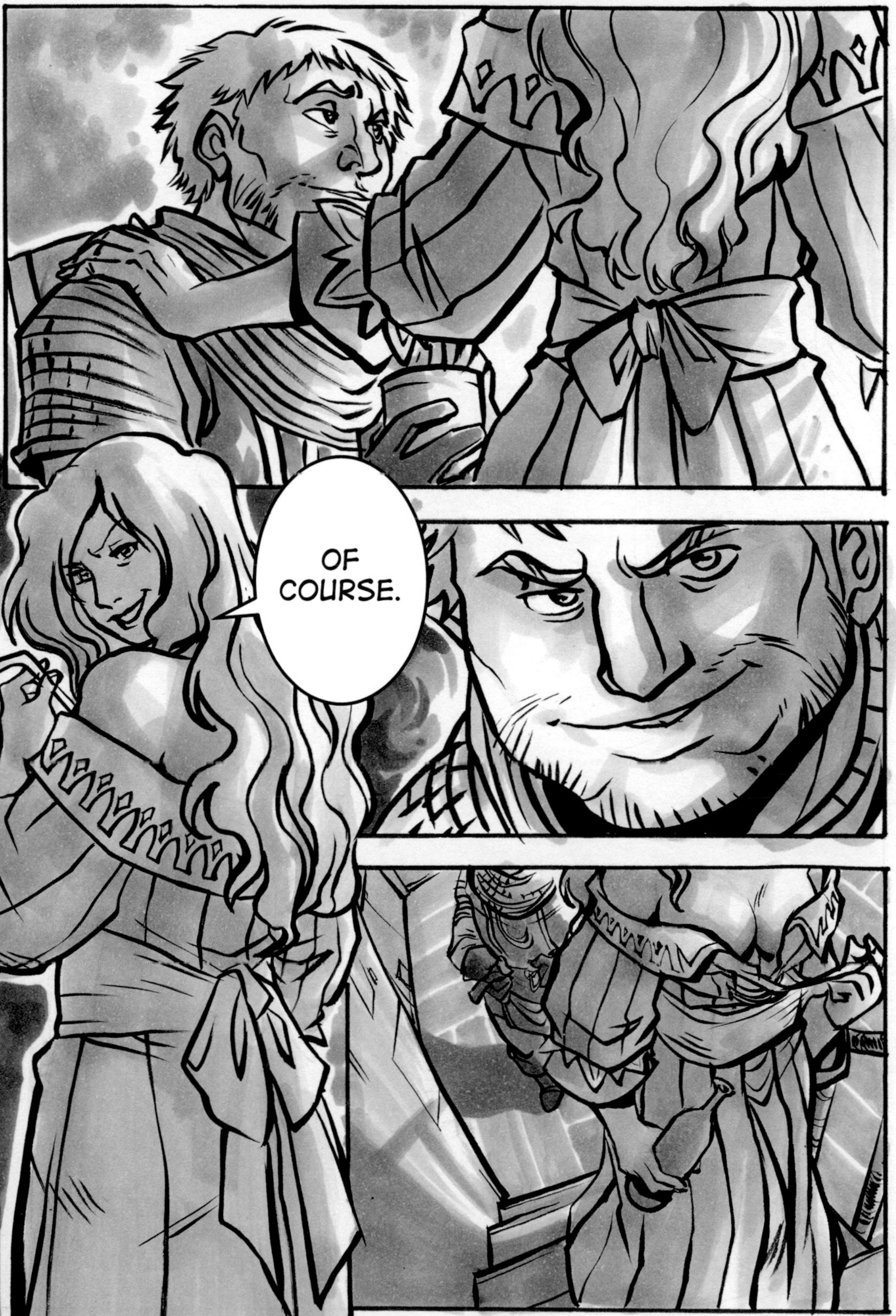
OF COURSE.

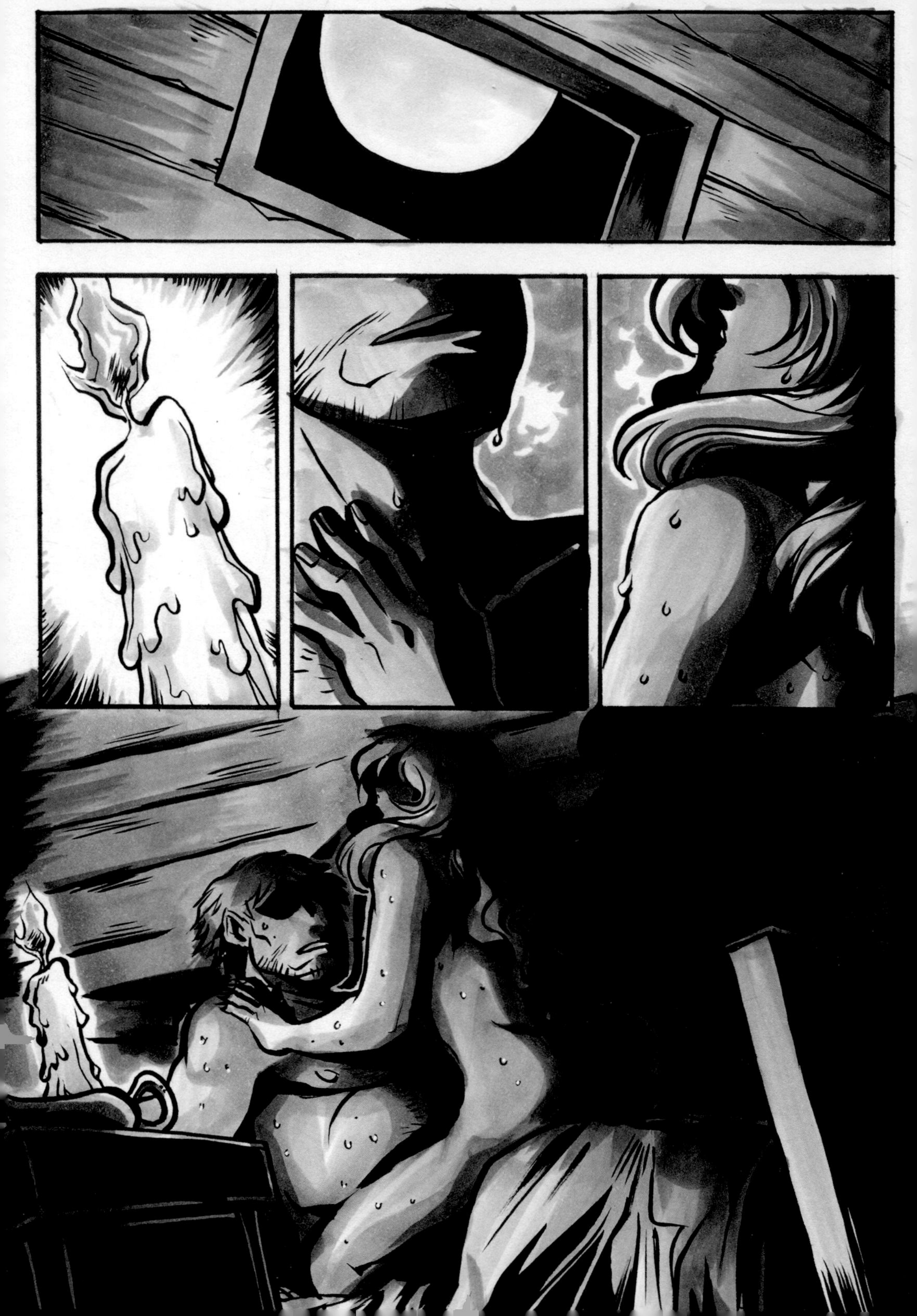

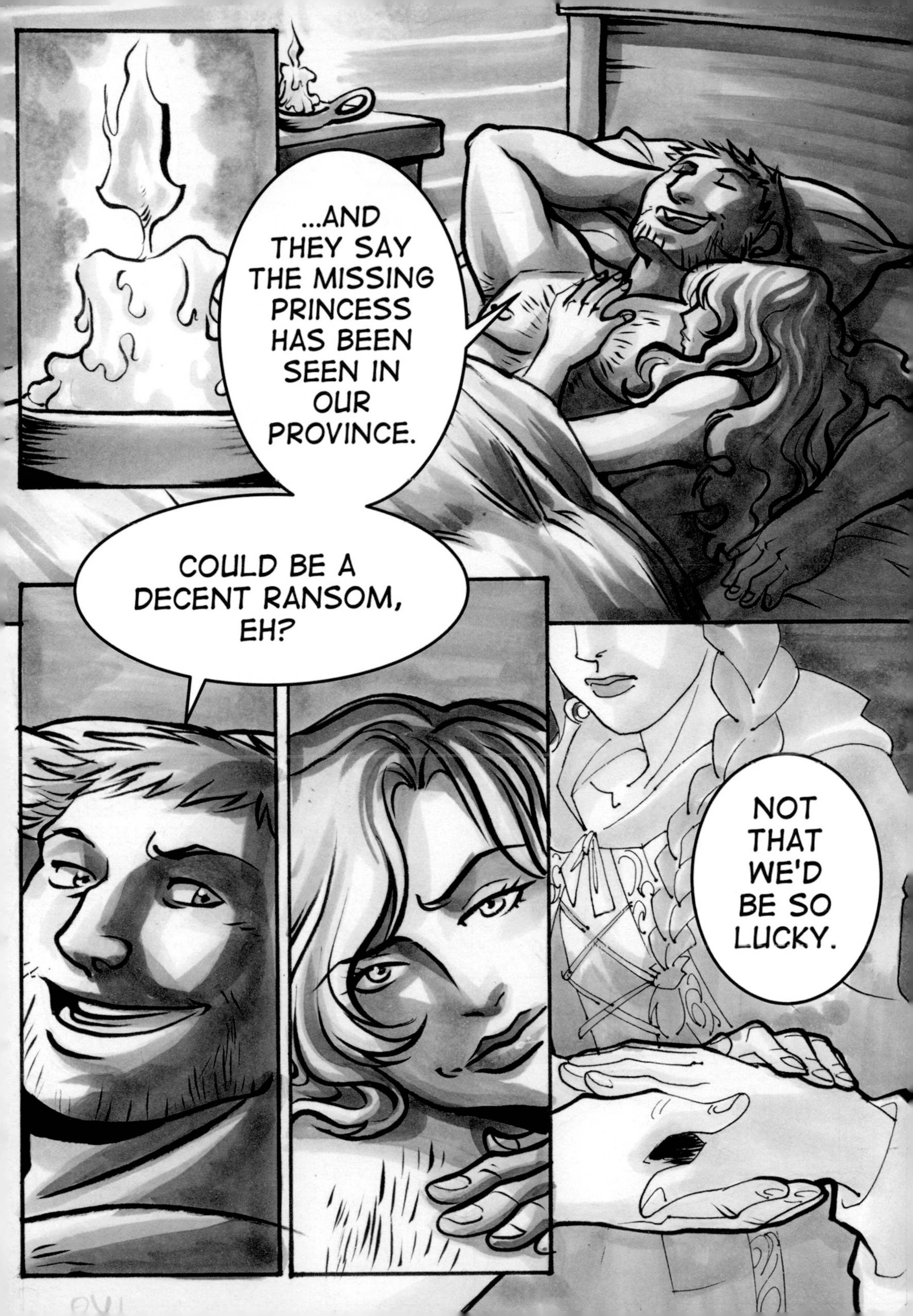
...AND THEY SAY THE MISSING PRINCESS HAS BEEN SEEN IN OUR PROVINCE.
COULD BE A DECENT RANSOM, EH?
NOT THAT WE'D BE SO LUCKY.

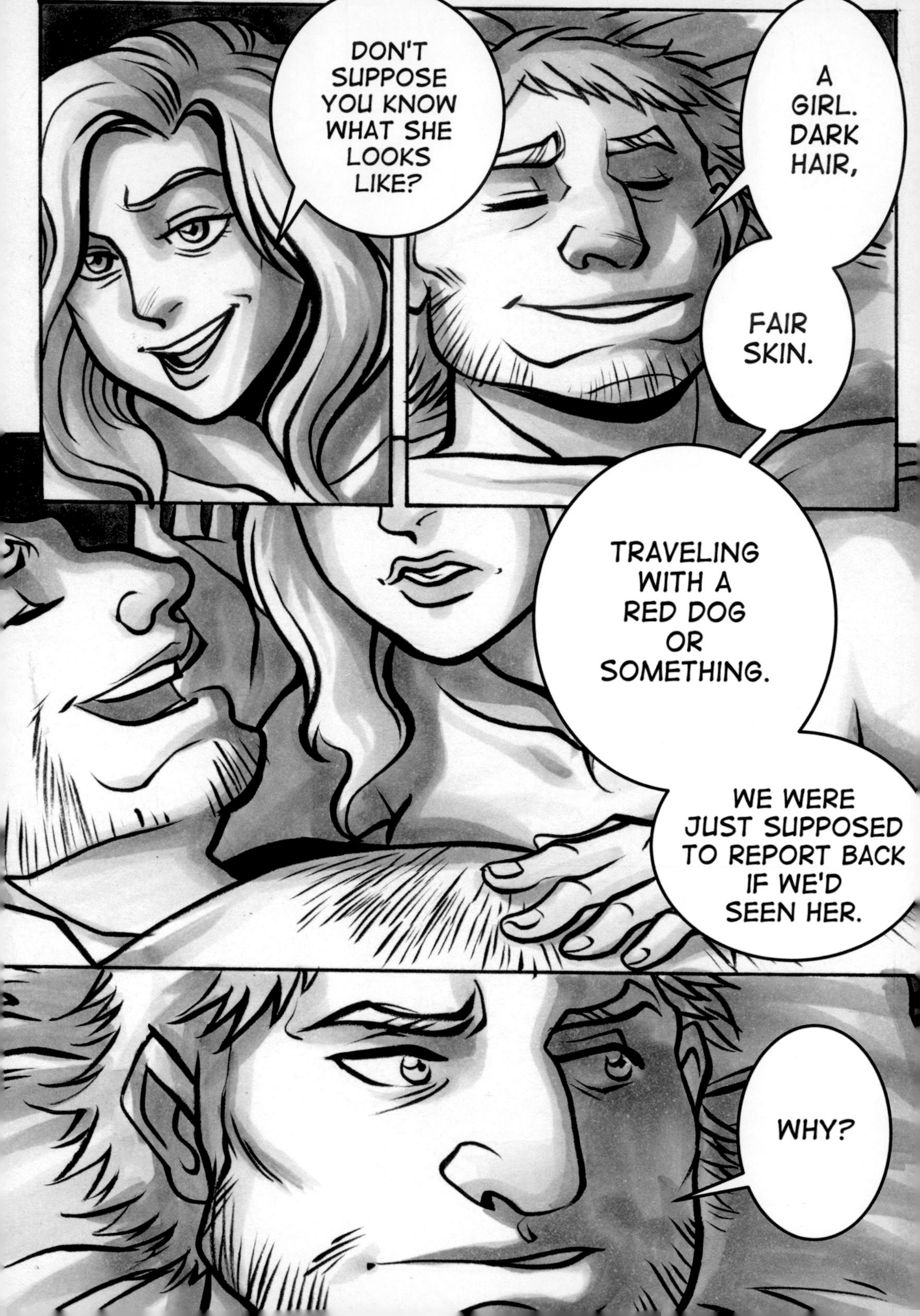
DON'T SUPPOSE YOU KNOW WHAT SHE LOOKS LIKE?
A GIRL. DARK HAIR,
FAIR SKIN.
TRAVELING WITH A RED DOG OR SOMETHING.
WE WERE JUST SUPPOSED TO REPORT BACK IF WE'D SEEN HER.
WHY?

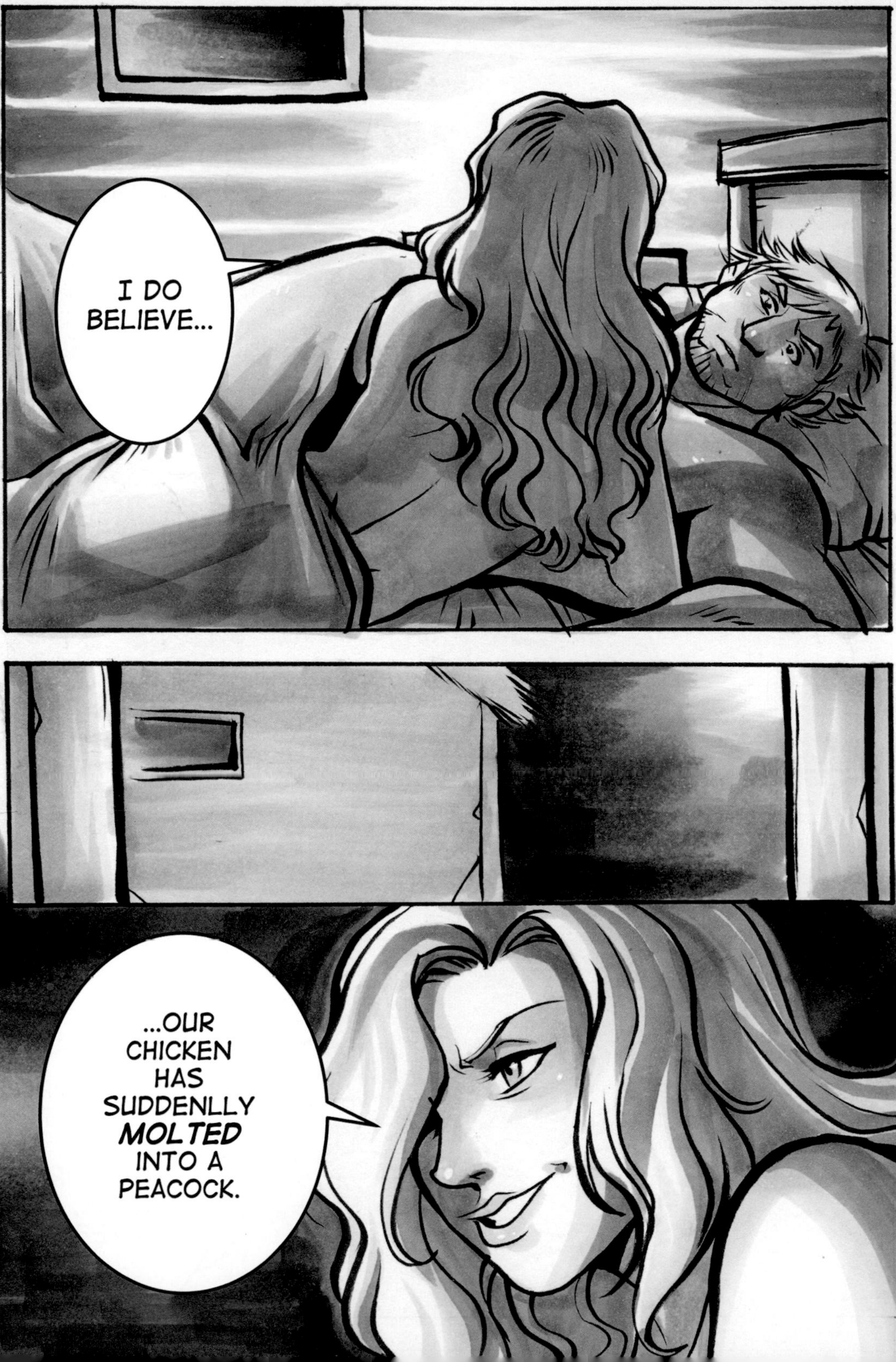
I DO BELIEVE...
...OUR CHICKEN HAS SUDDENLLY MOLTED INTO A PEACOCK.

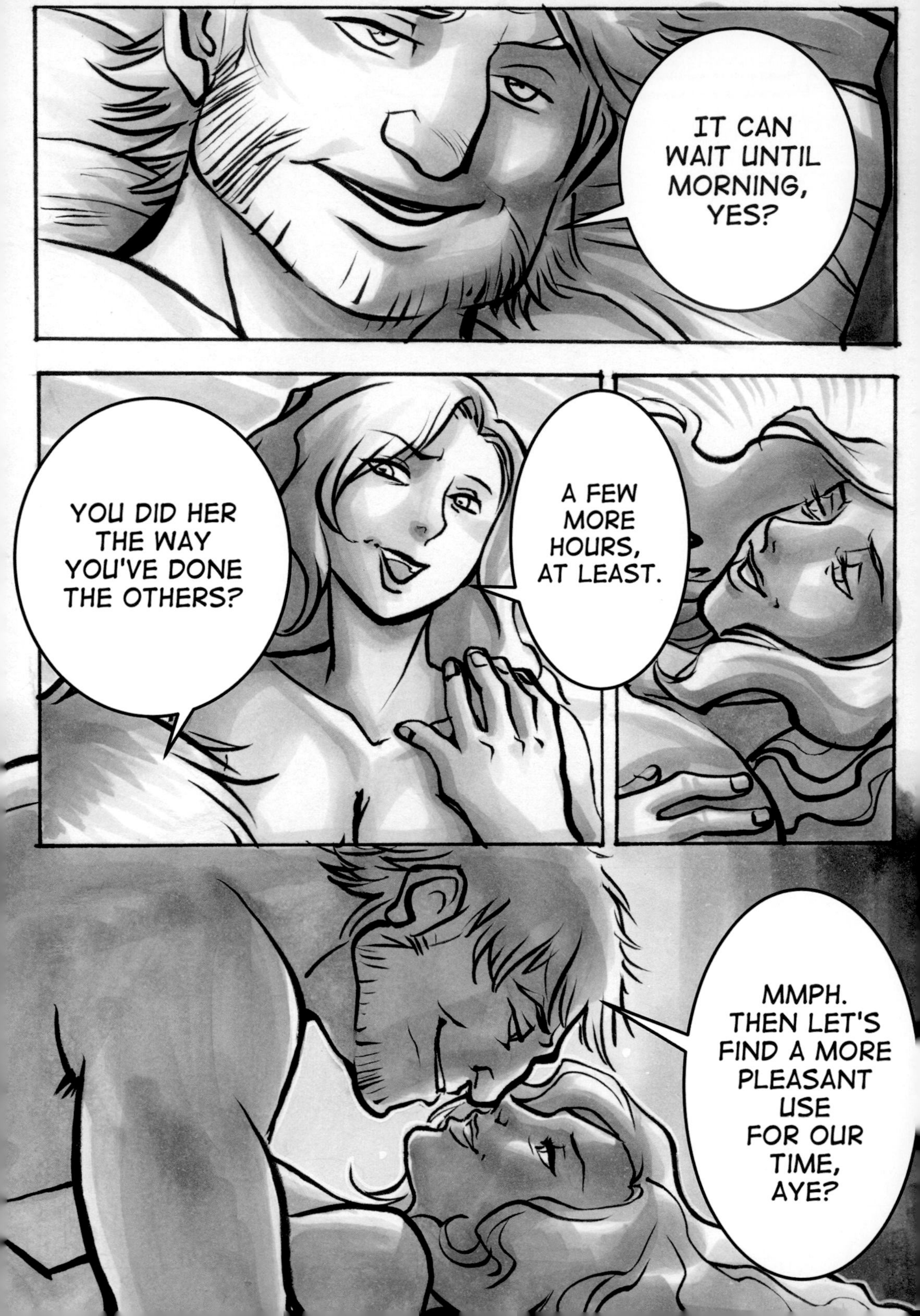
IT CAN WAIT UNTIL MORNING, YES?
YOU DID HER THE WAY YOU'VE DONE THE OTHERS?
A FEW MORE HOURS, AT LEAST.
MMPH. THEN LET'S FIND A MORE PLEASANT USE FOR OUR TIME, AYE?

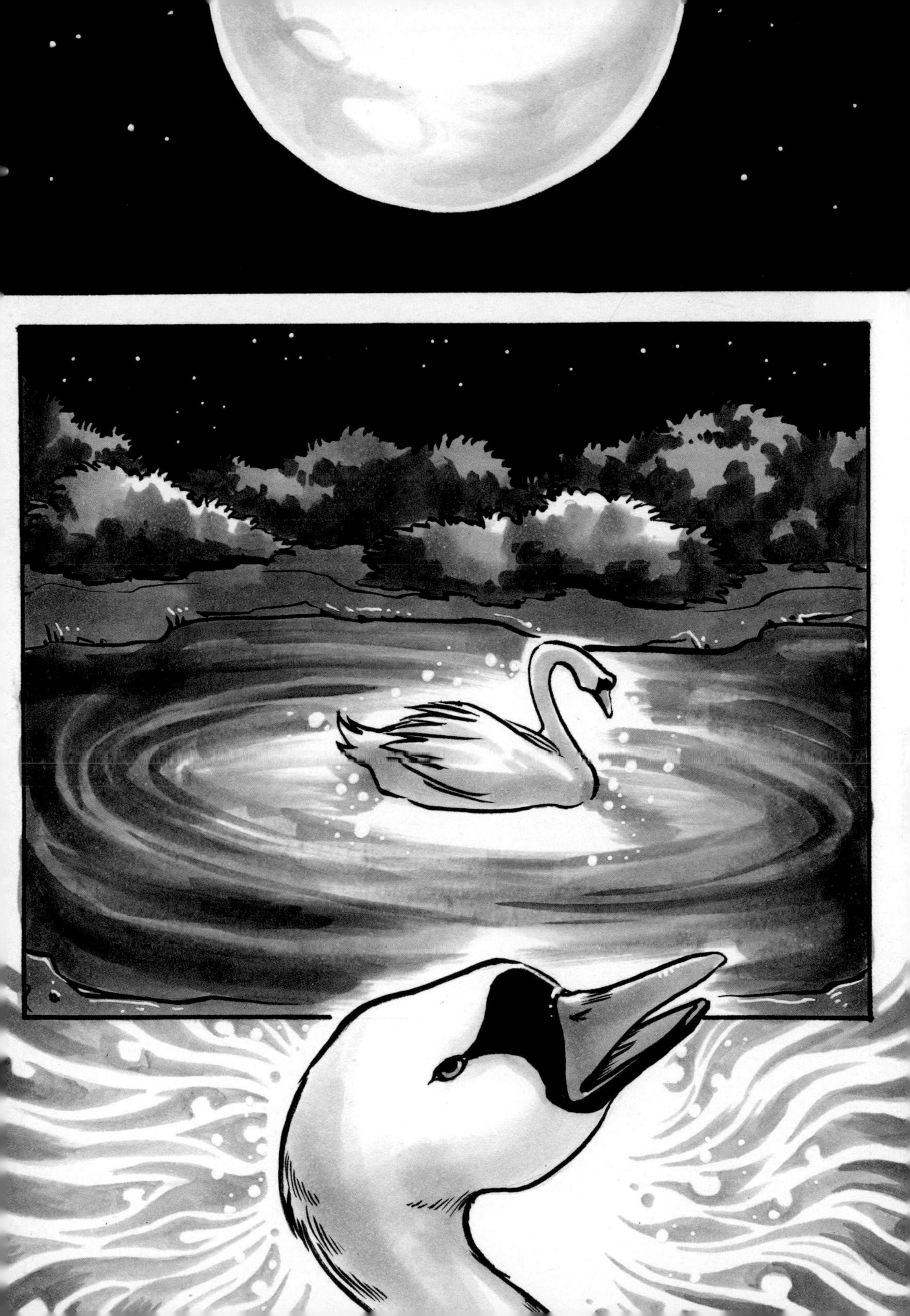

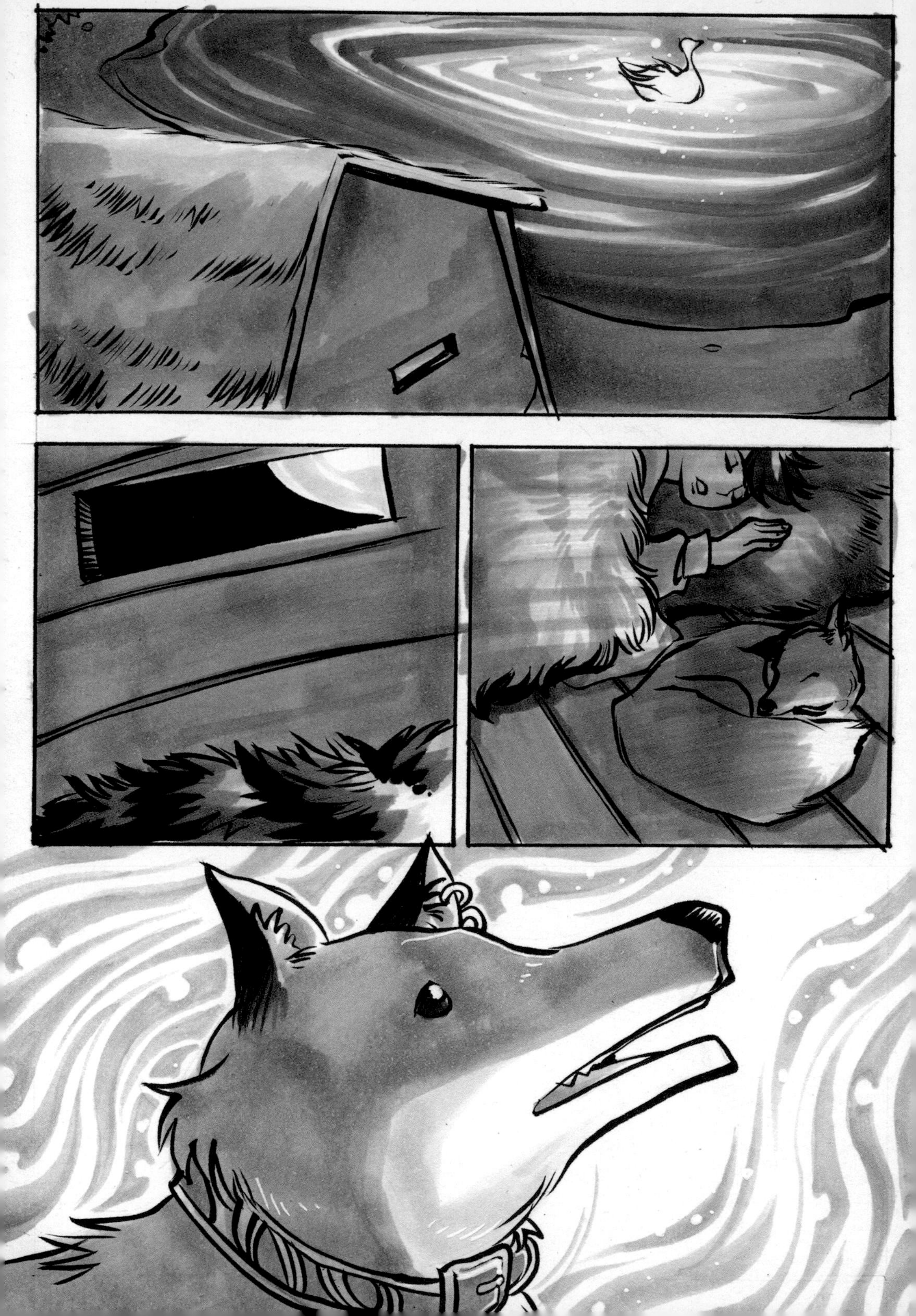

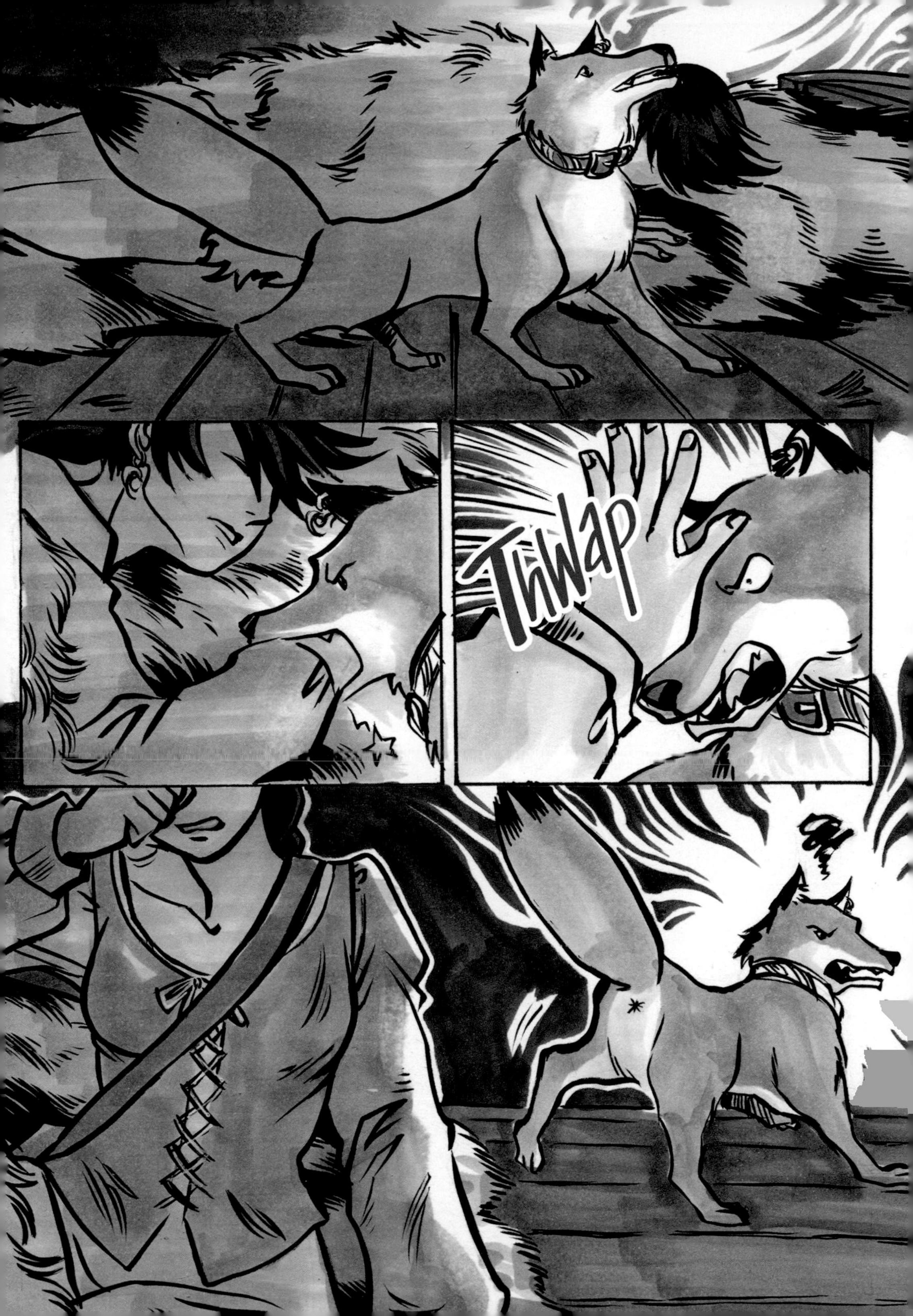
ThWap

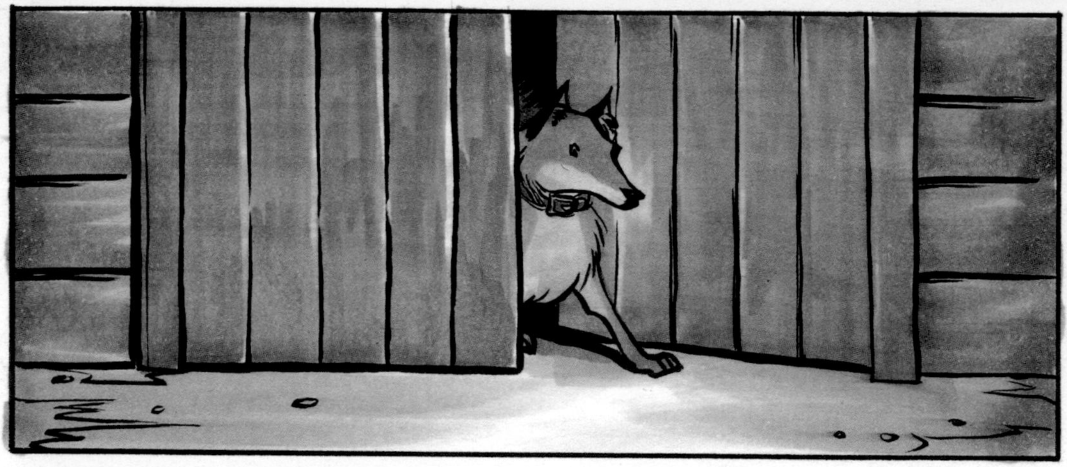
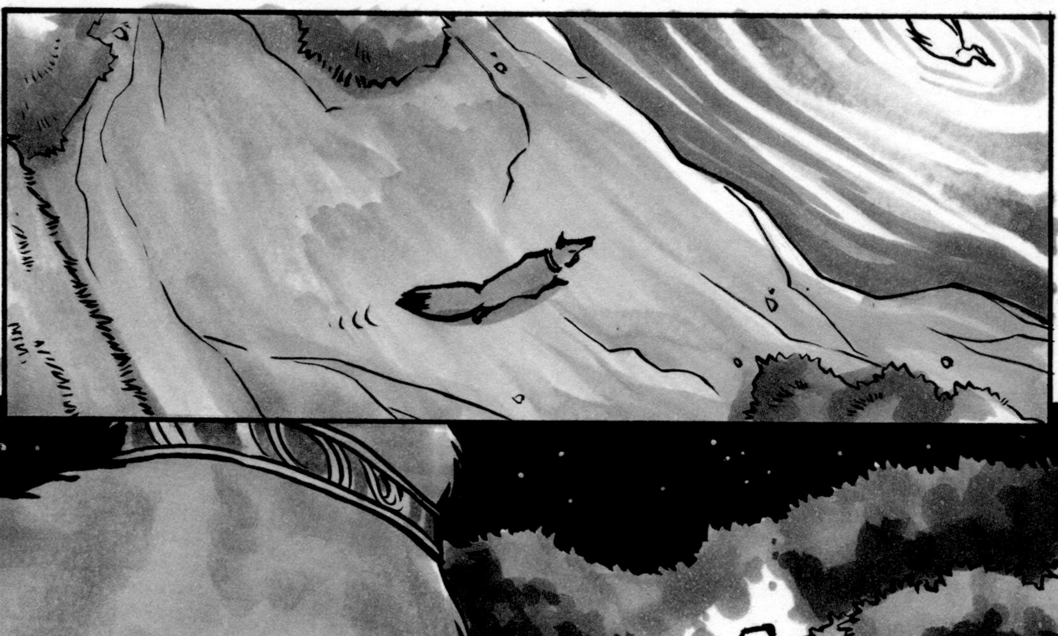
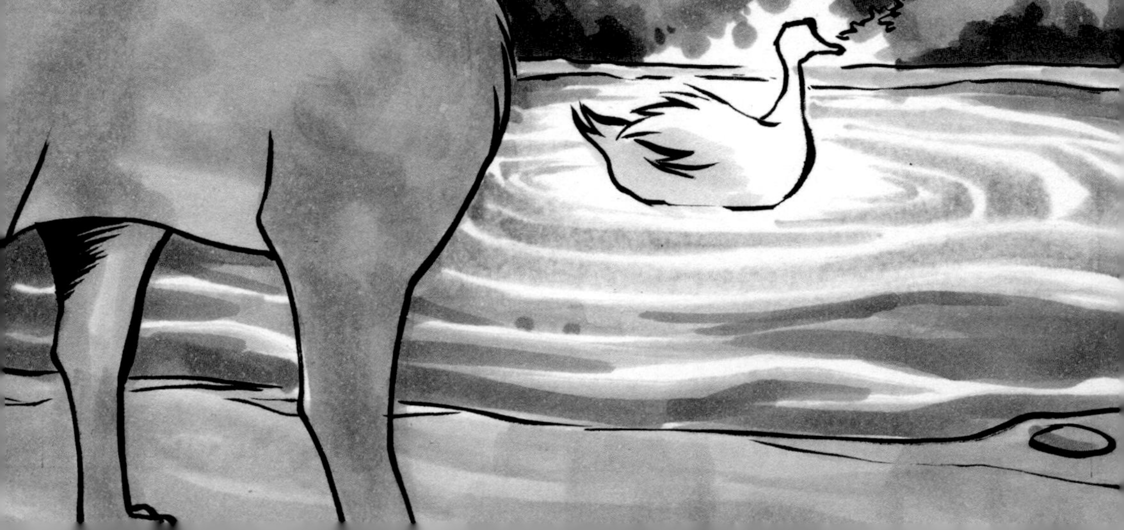

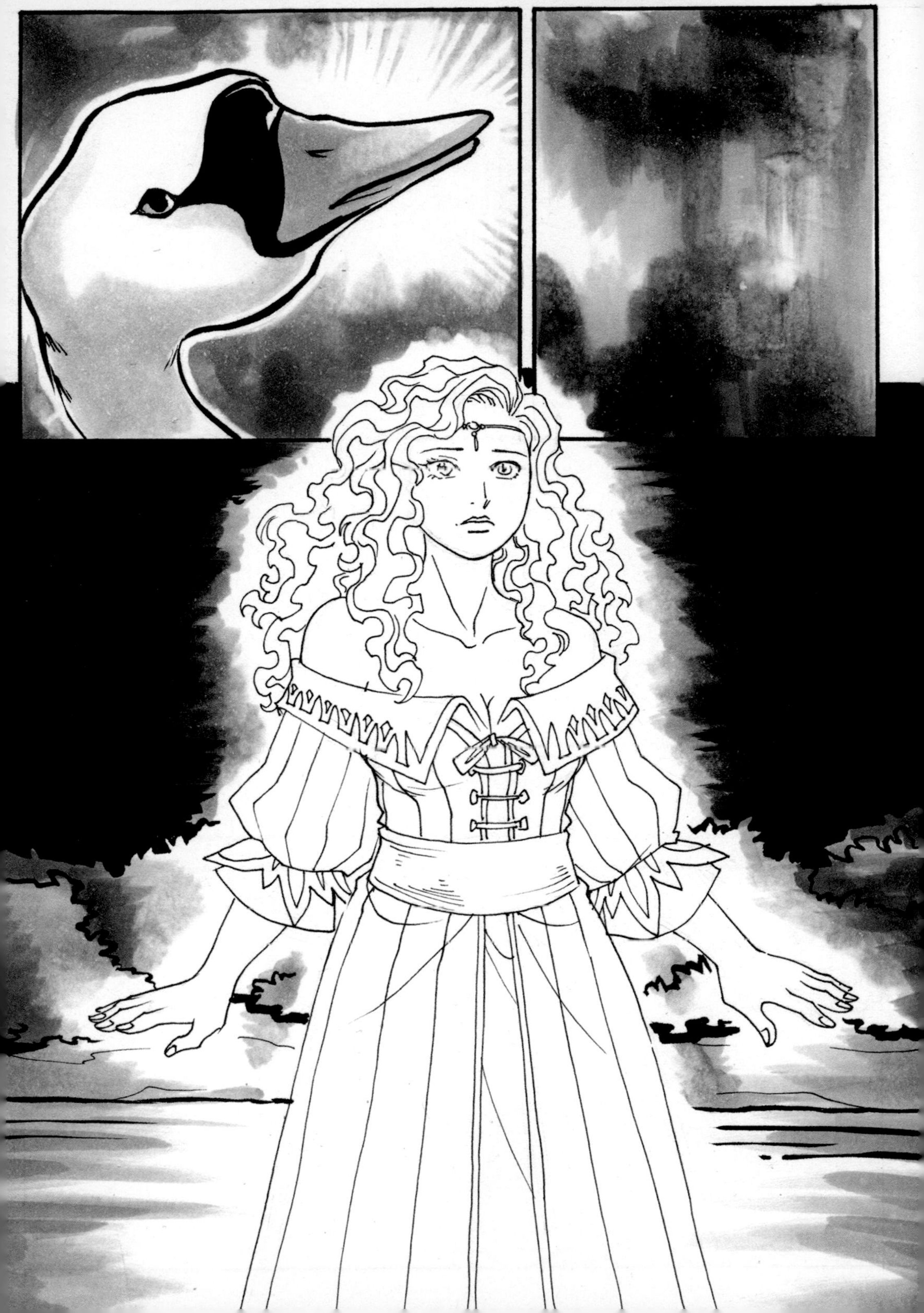

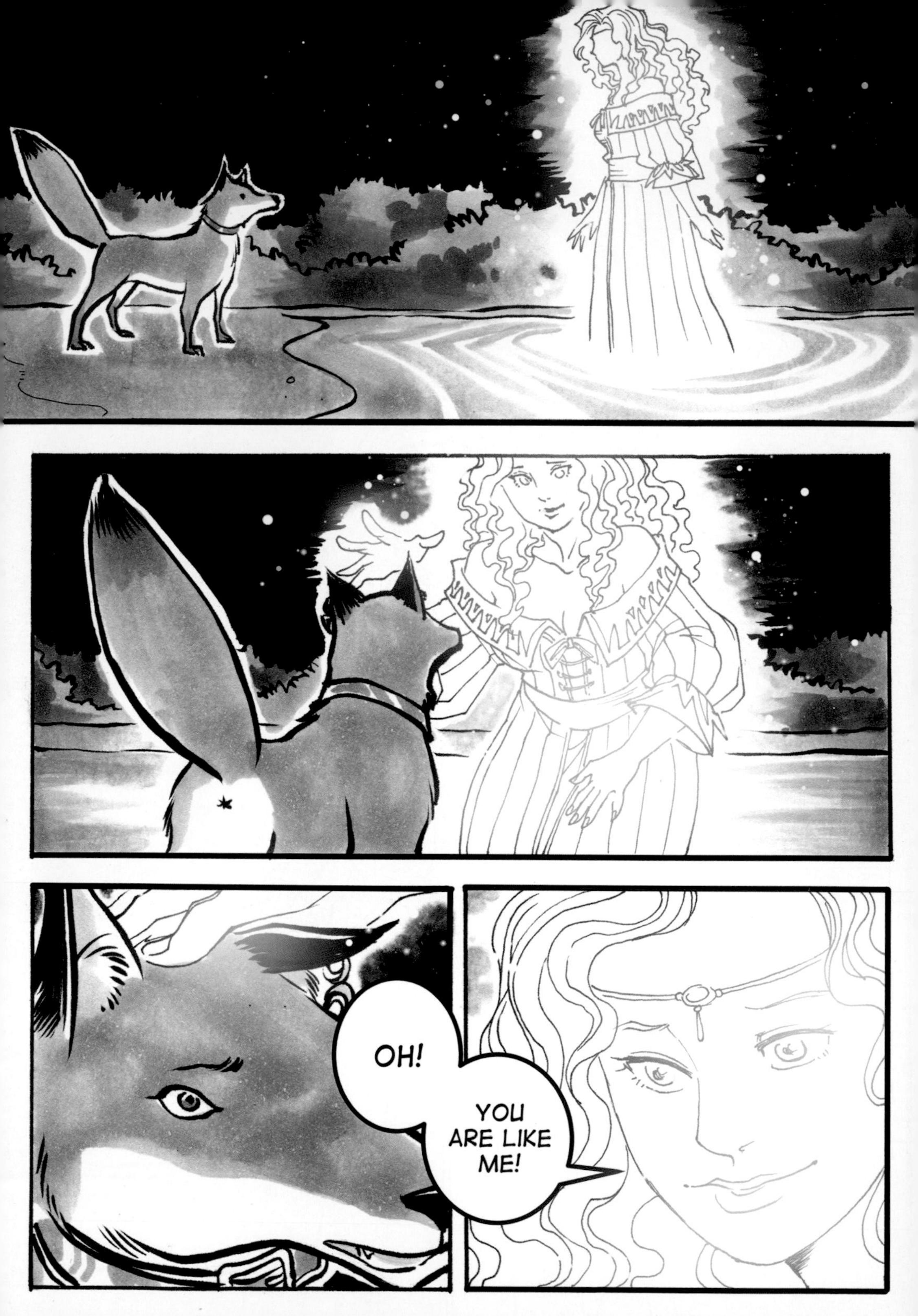
OH!
YOU ARE LIKE ME!

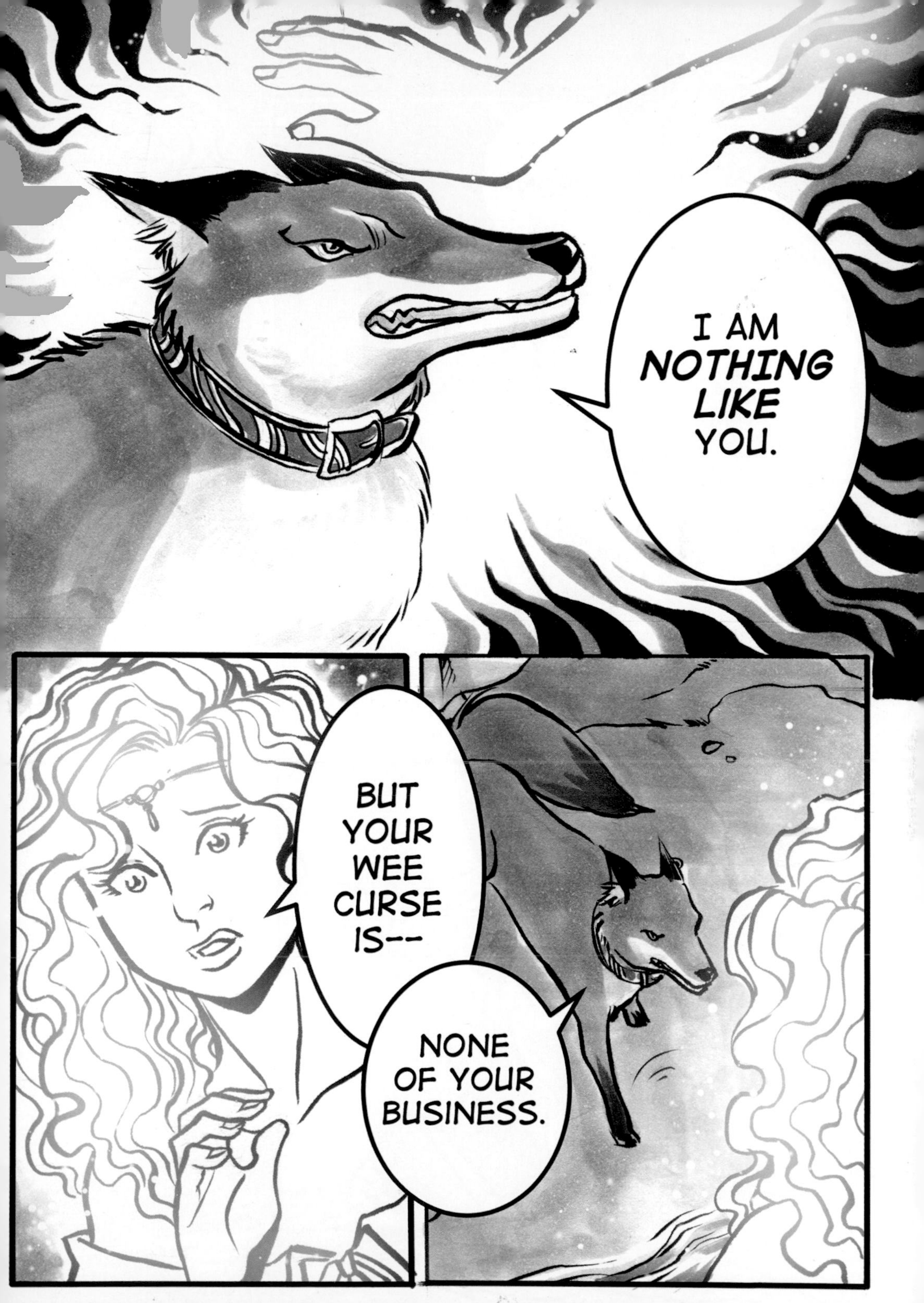
I AM *NOTHING LIKE* YOU.
BUT YOUR WEE CURSE IS--
NONE OF YOUR BUSINESS.

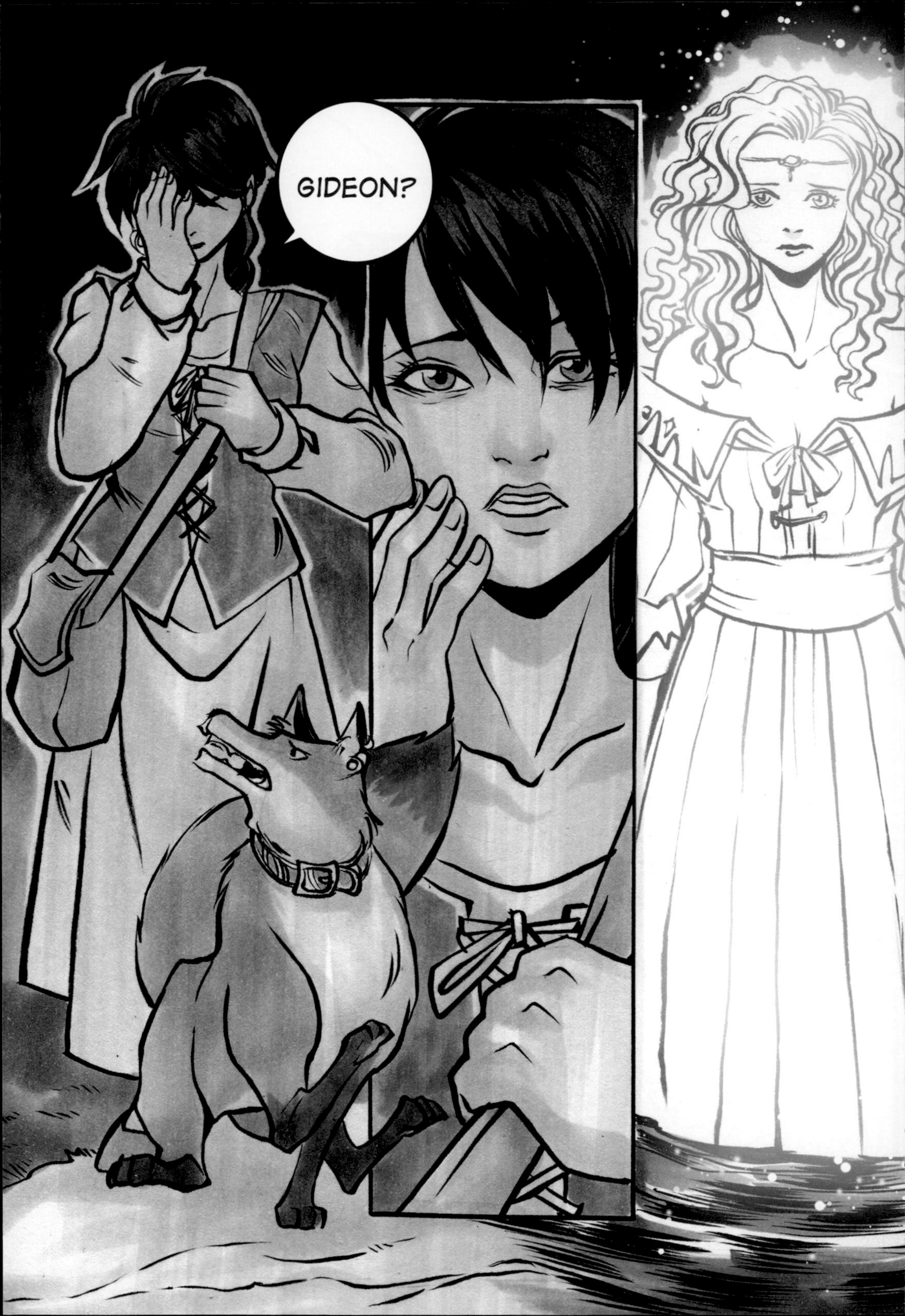
GIDEON?

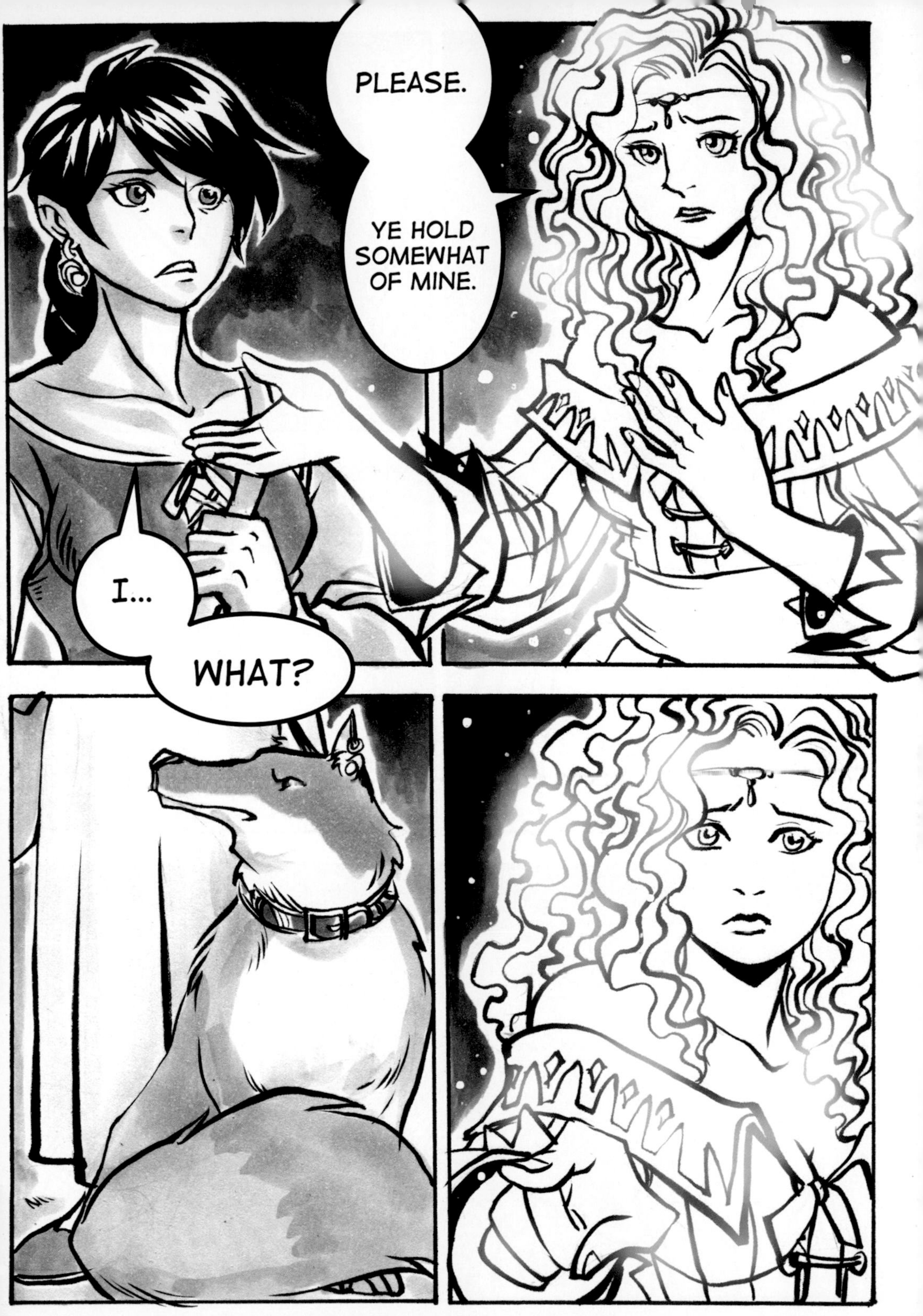
PLEASE.
YE HOLD SOMEWHAT OF MINE.
I...
WHAT?

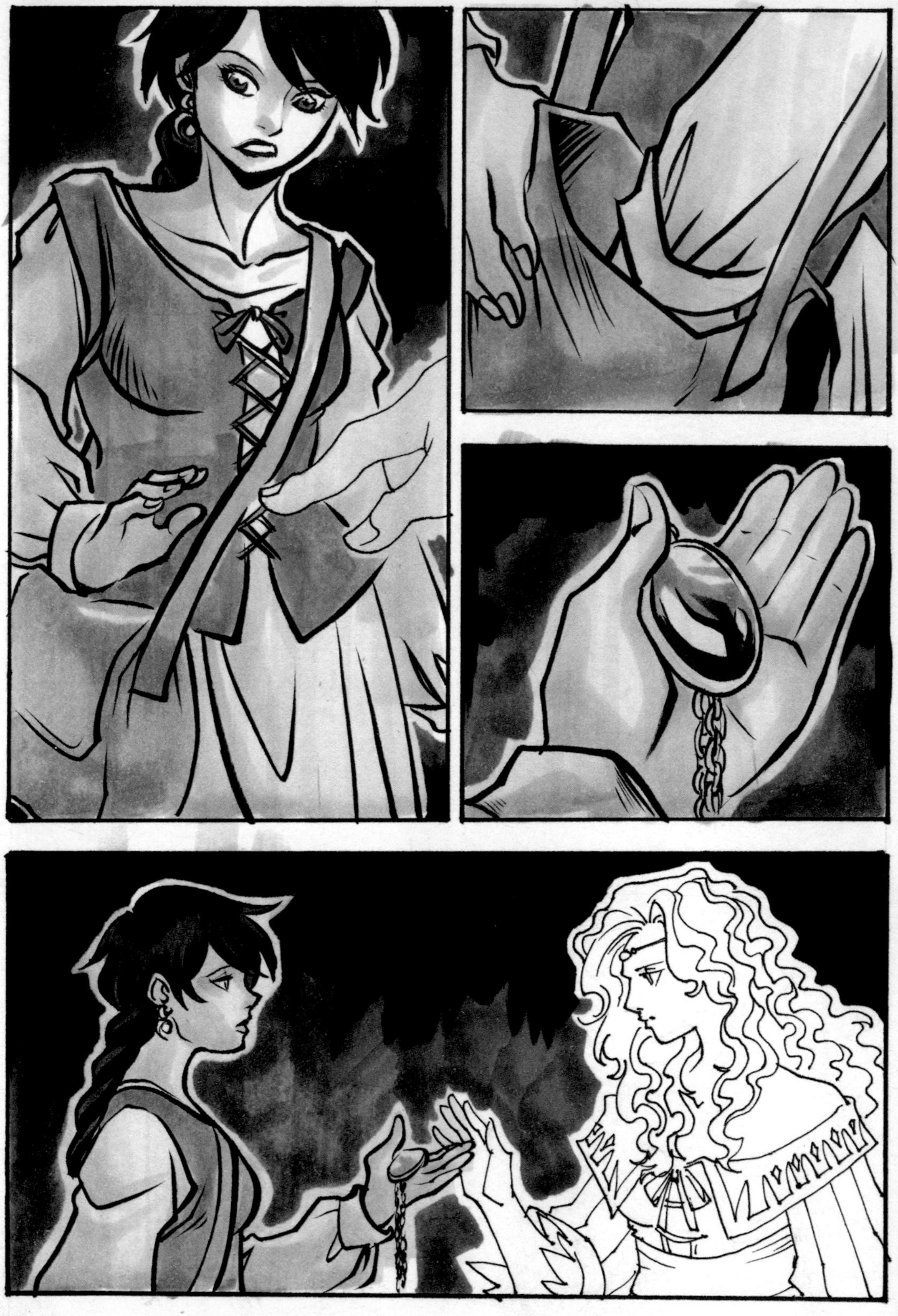

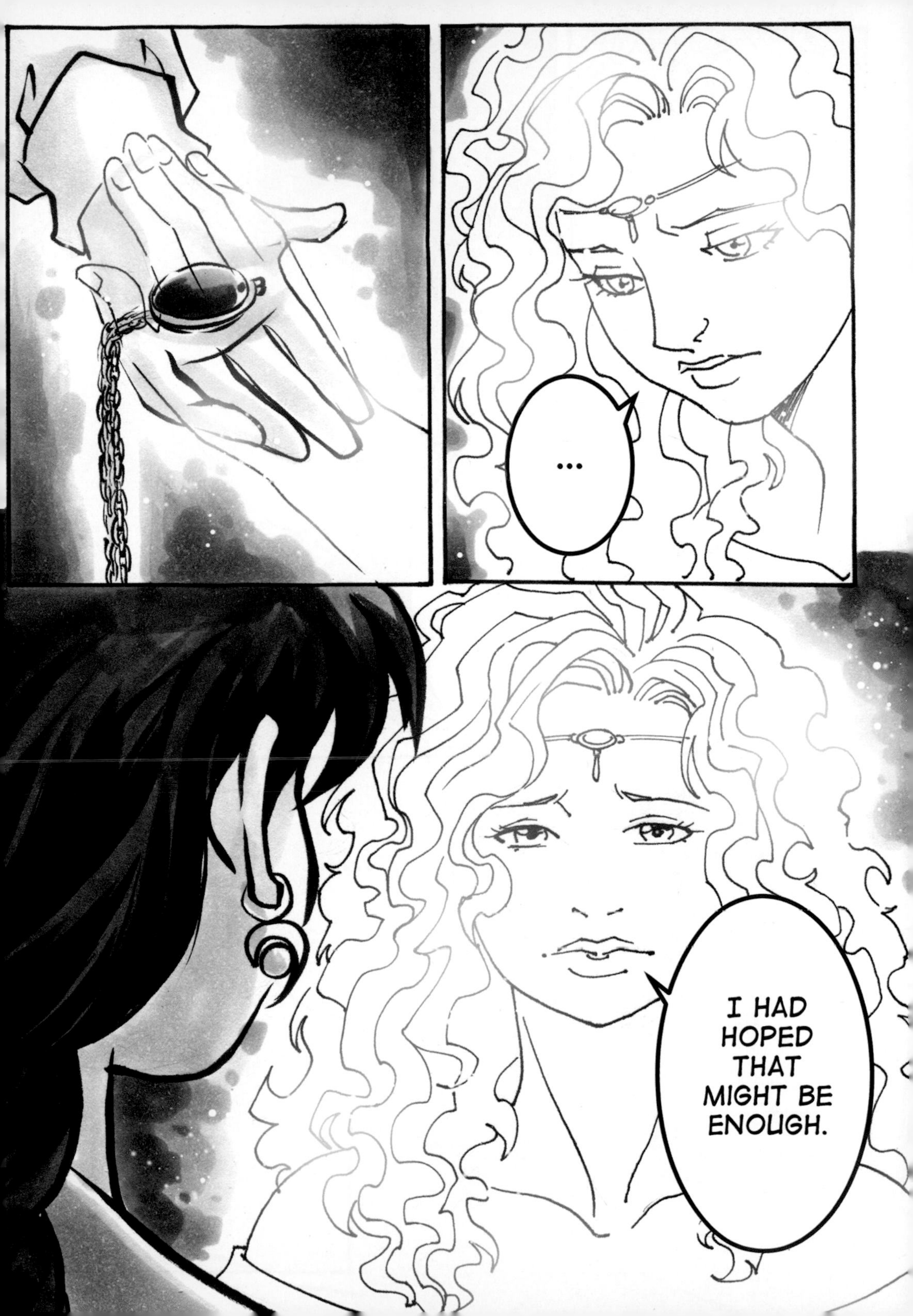
...
I HAD HOPED THAT MIGHT BE ENOUGH.

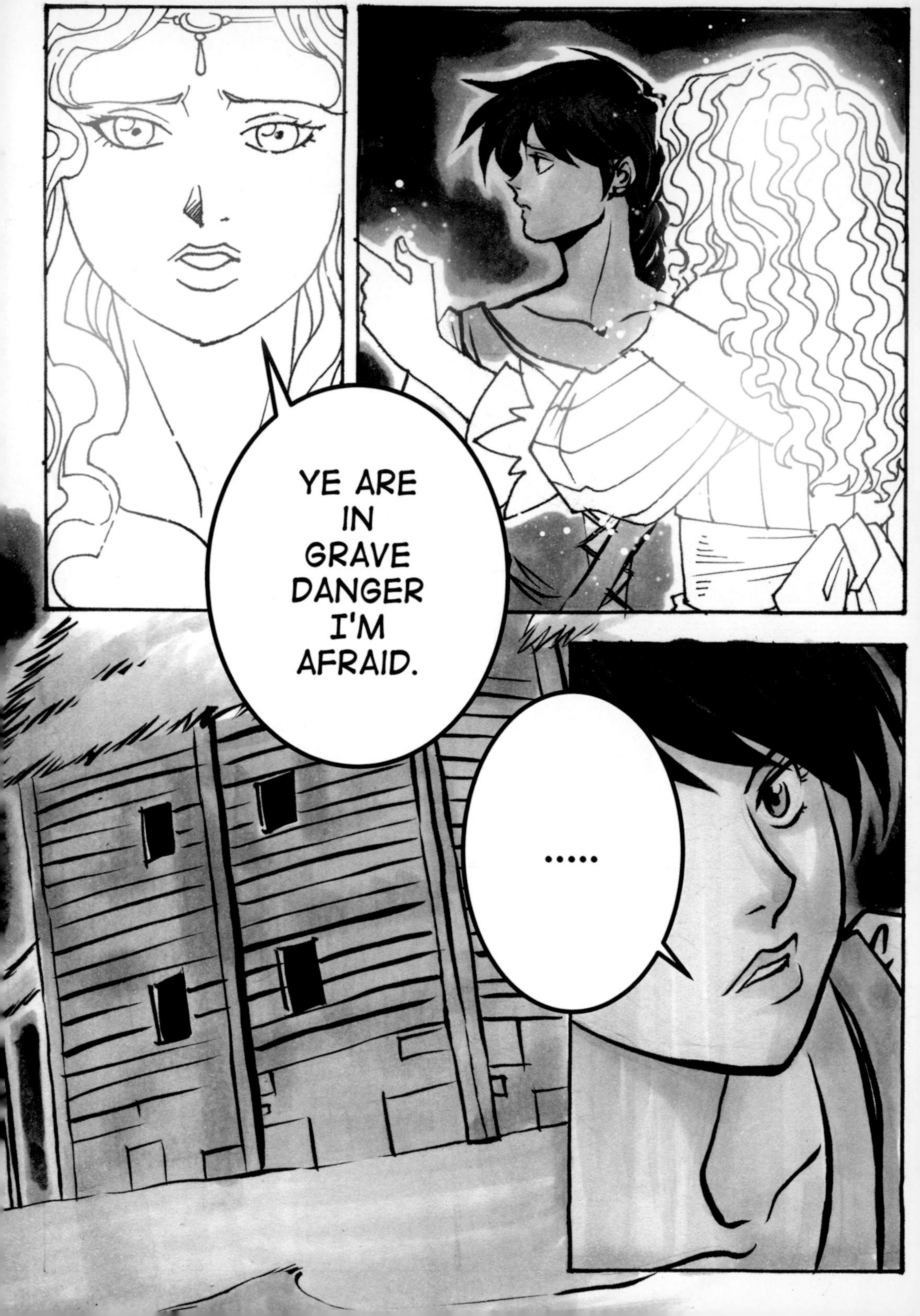
YE ARE IN GRAVE DANGER I'M AFRAID.
.....

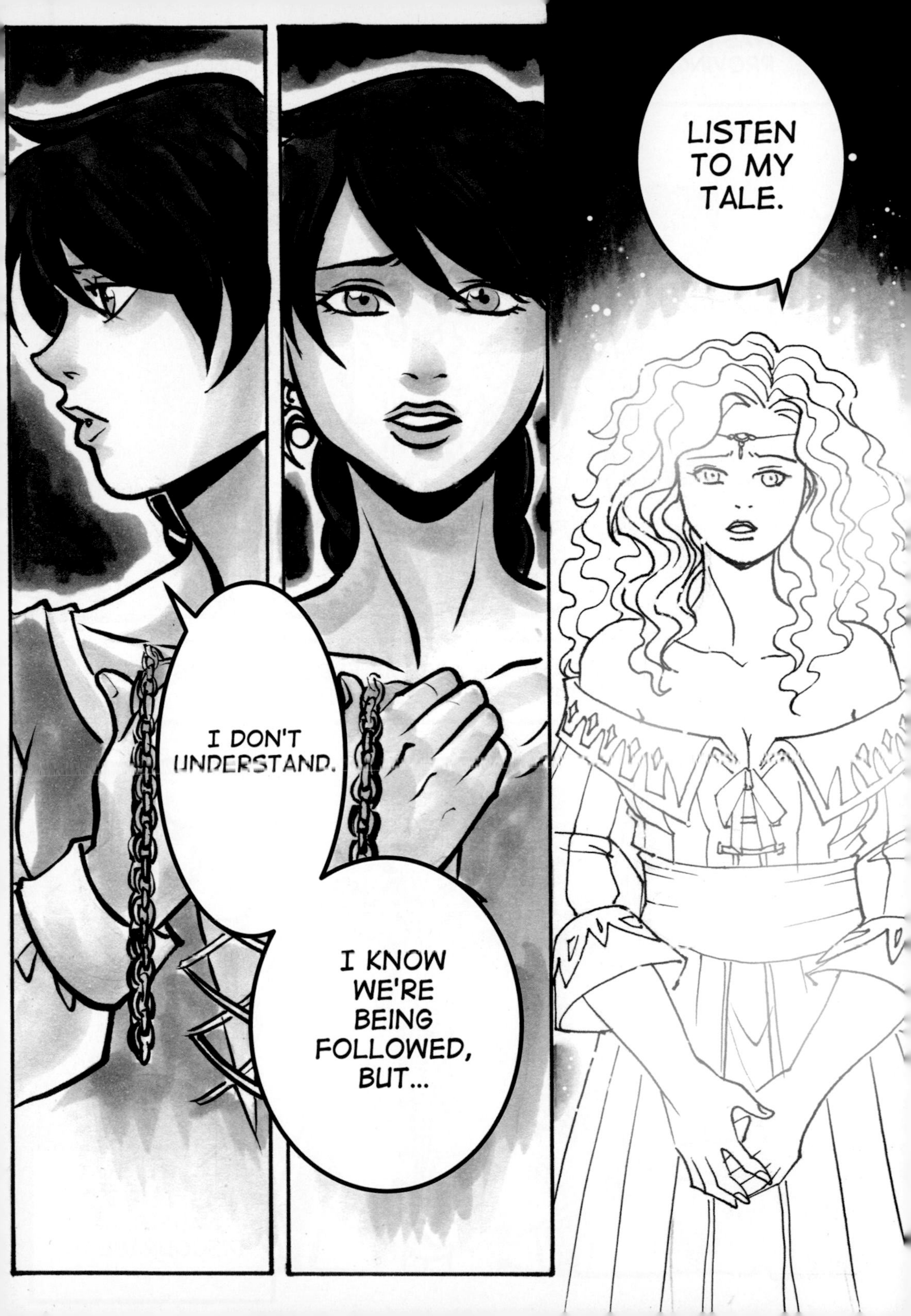
I DON'T UNDERSTAND.
I KNOW WE'RE BEING FOLLOWED, BUT...
LISTEN TO MY TALE.

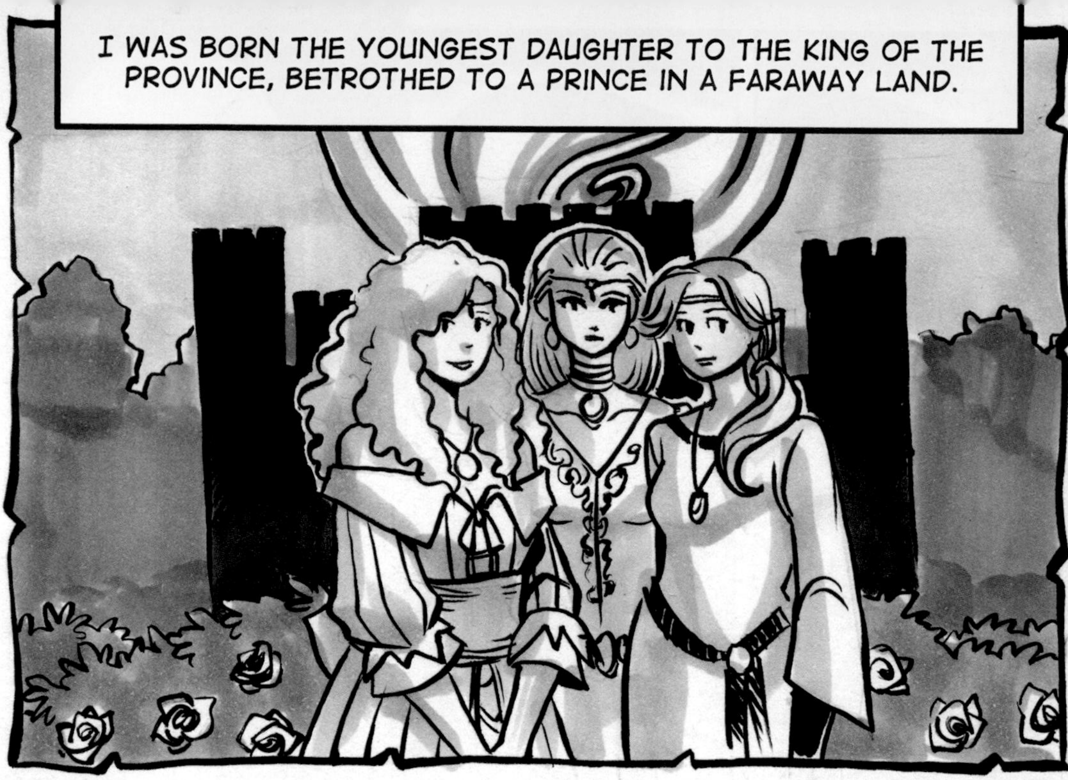
I WAS BORN THE YOUNGEST DAUGHTER TO THE KING OF THE PROVINCE, BETROTHED TO A PRINCE IN A FARAWAY LAND.

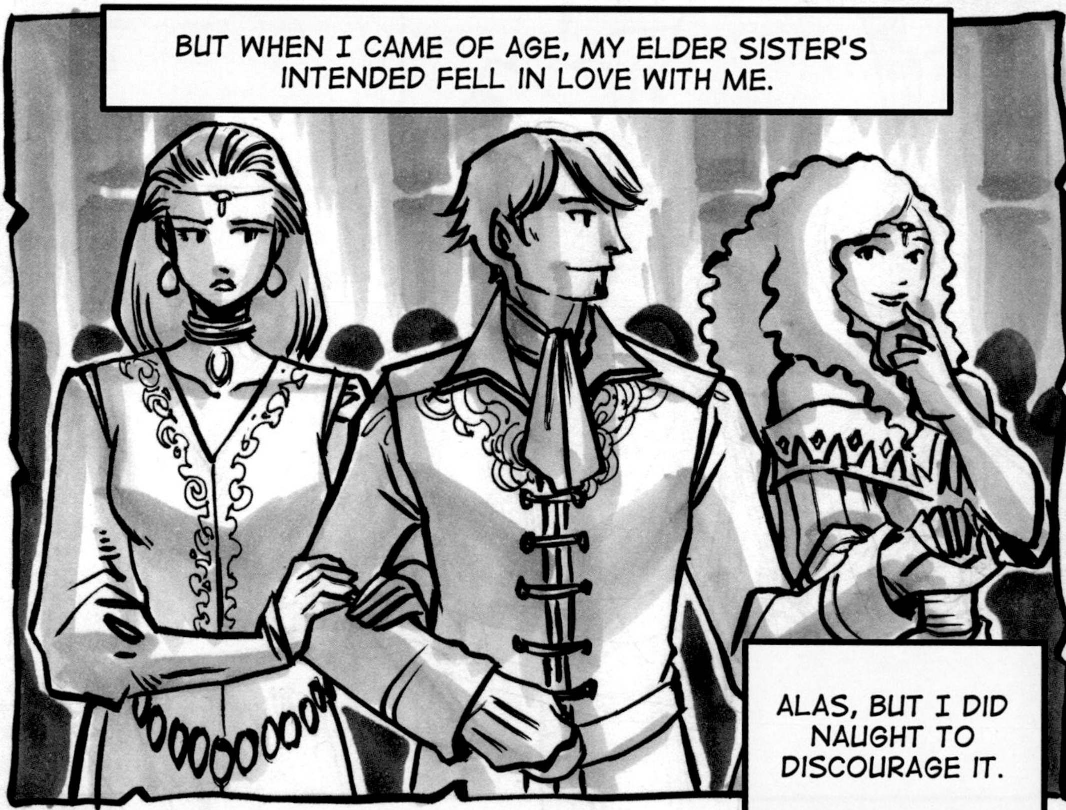
BUT WHEN I CAME OF AGE, MY ELDER SISTER'S INTENDED FELL IN LOVE WITH ME.
ALAS, BUT I DID NAUGHT TO DISCOURAGE IT.

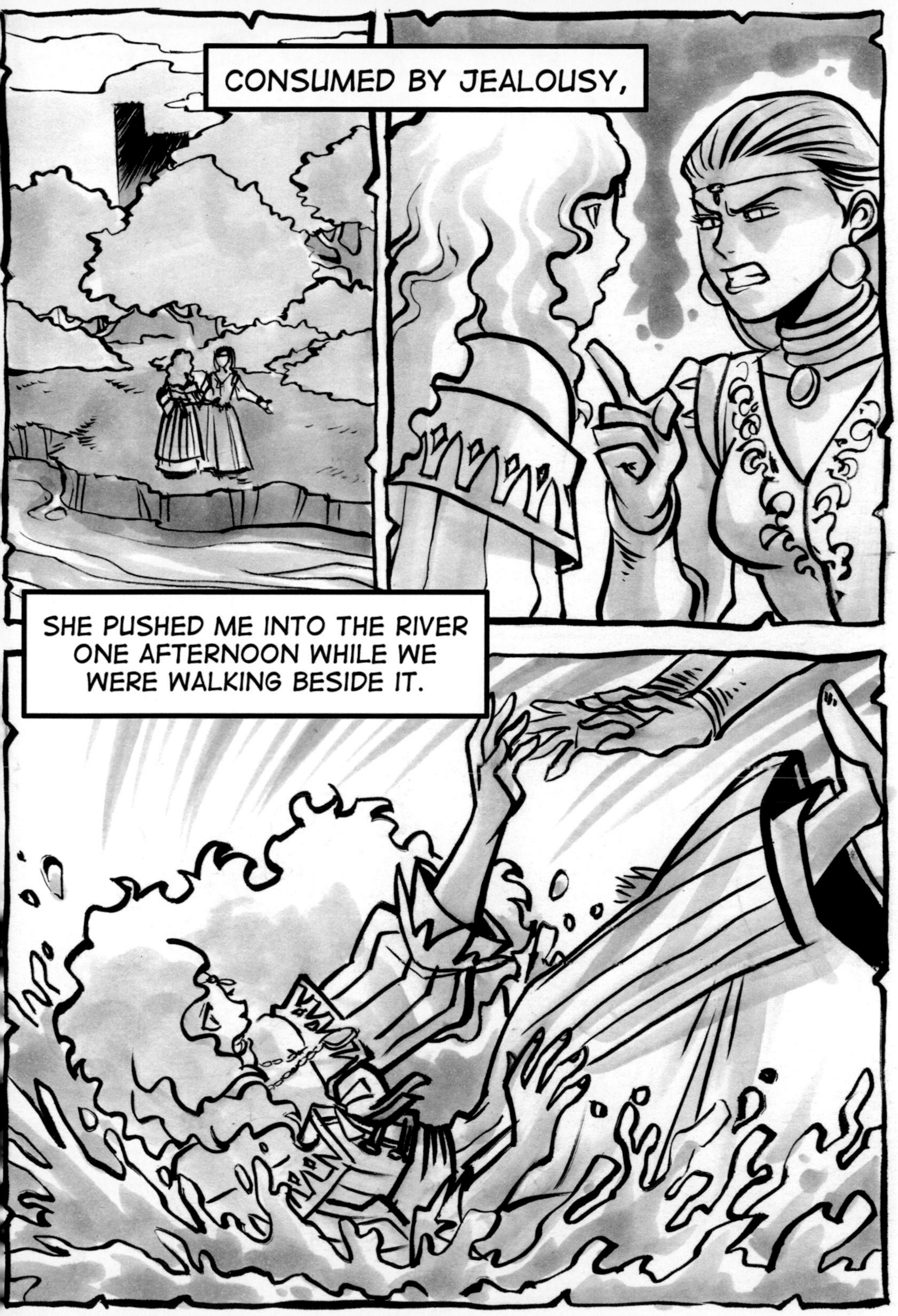
CONSUMED BY JEALOUSY,
SHE PUSHED ME INTO THE RIVER ONE AFTERNOON WHILE WE WERE WALKING BESIDE IT.

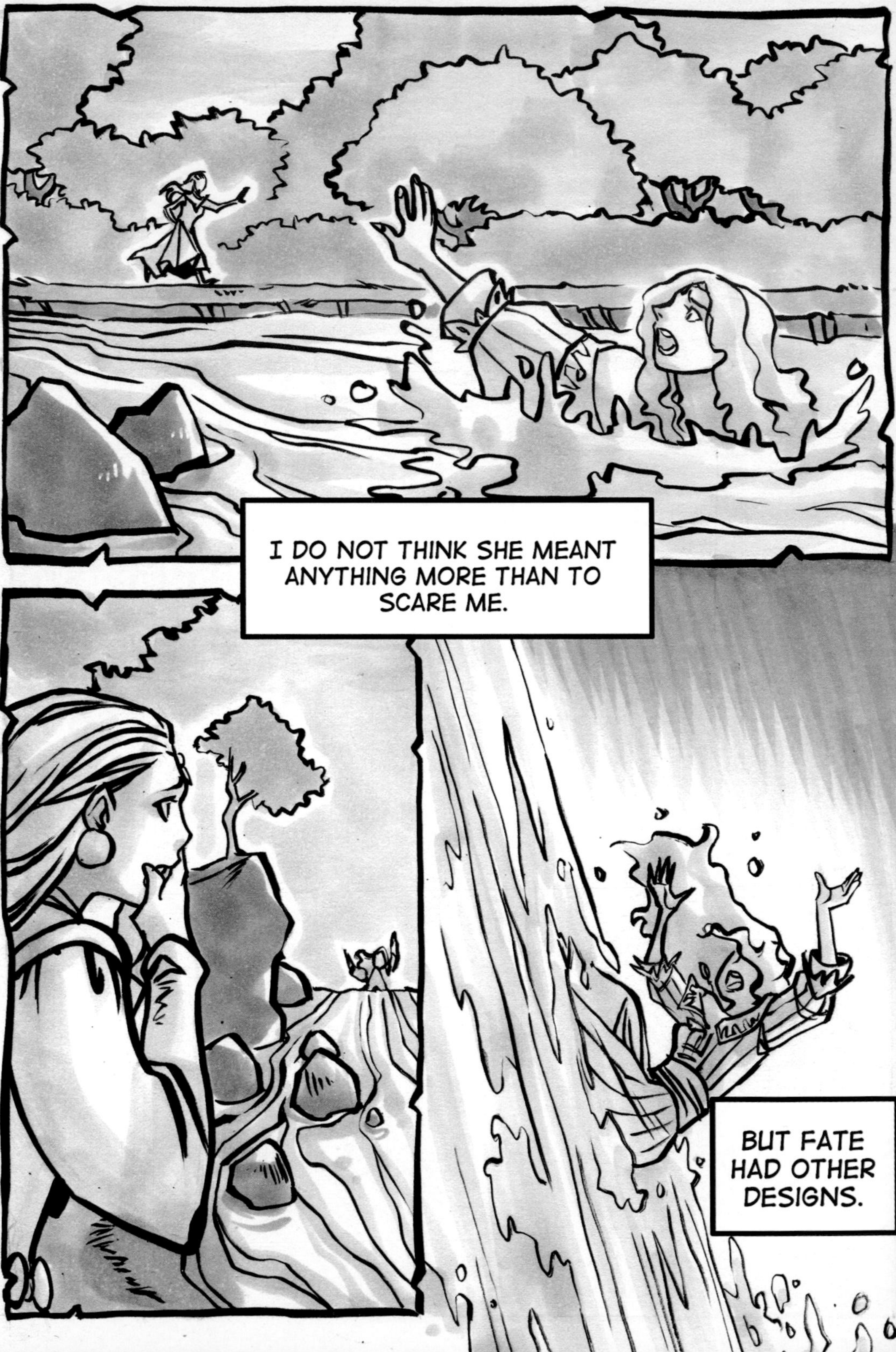
I DO NOT THINK SHE MEANT ANYTHING MORE THAN TO SCARE ME.
BUT FATE HAD OTHER DESIGNS.

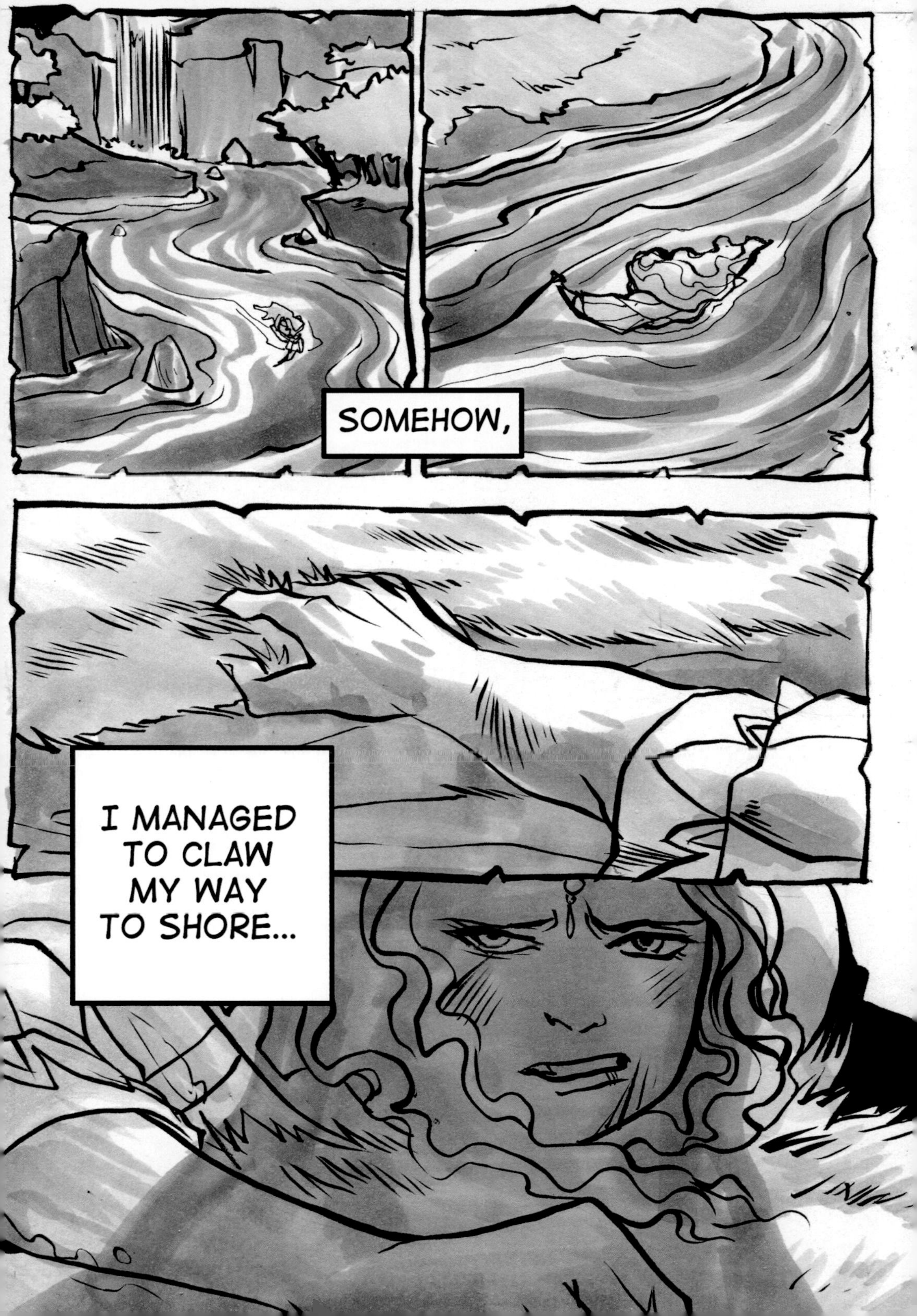
SOMEHOW,
I MANAGED TO CLAW MY WAY TO SHORE...

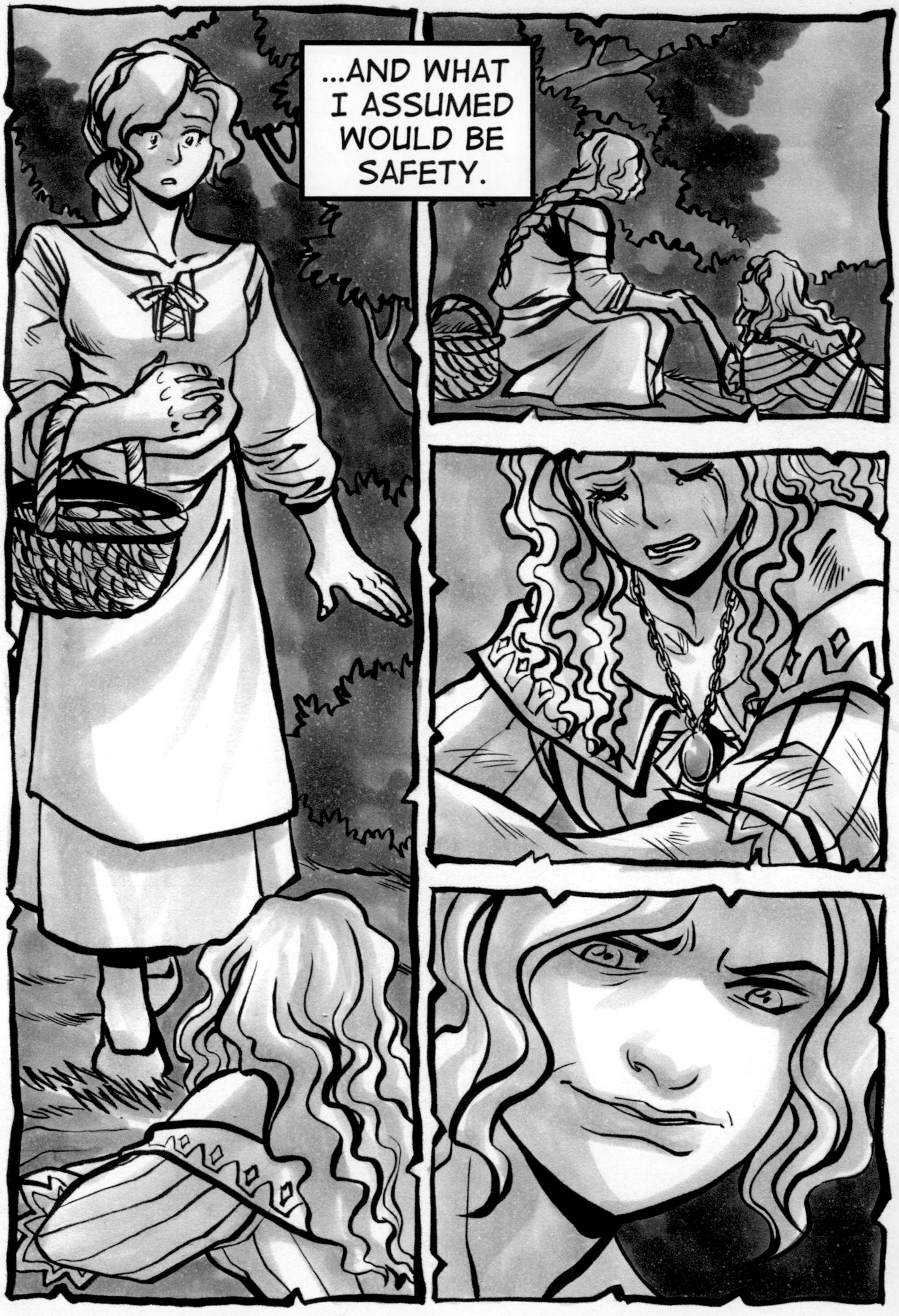
...AND WHAT I ASSUMED WOULD BE SAFETY.

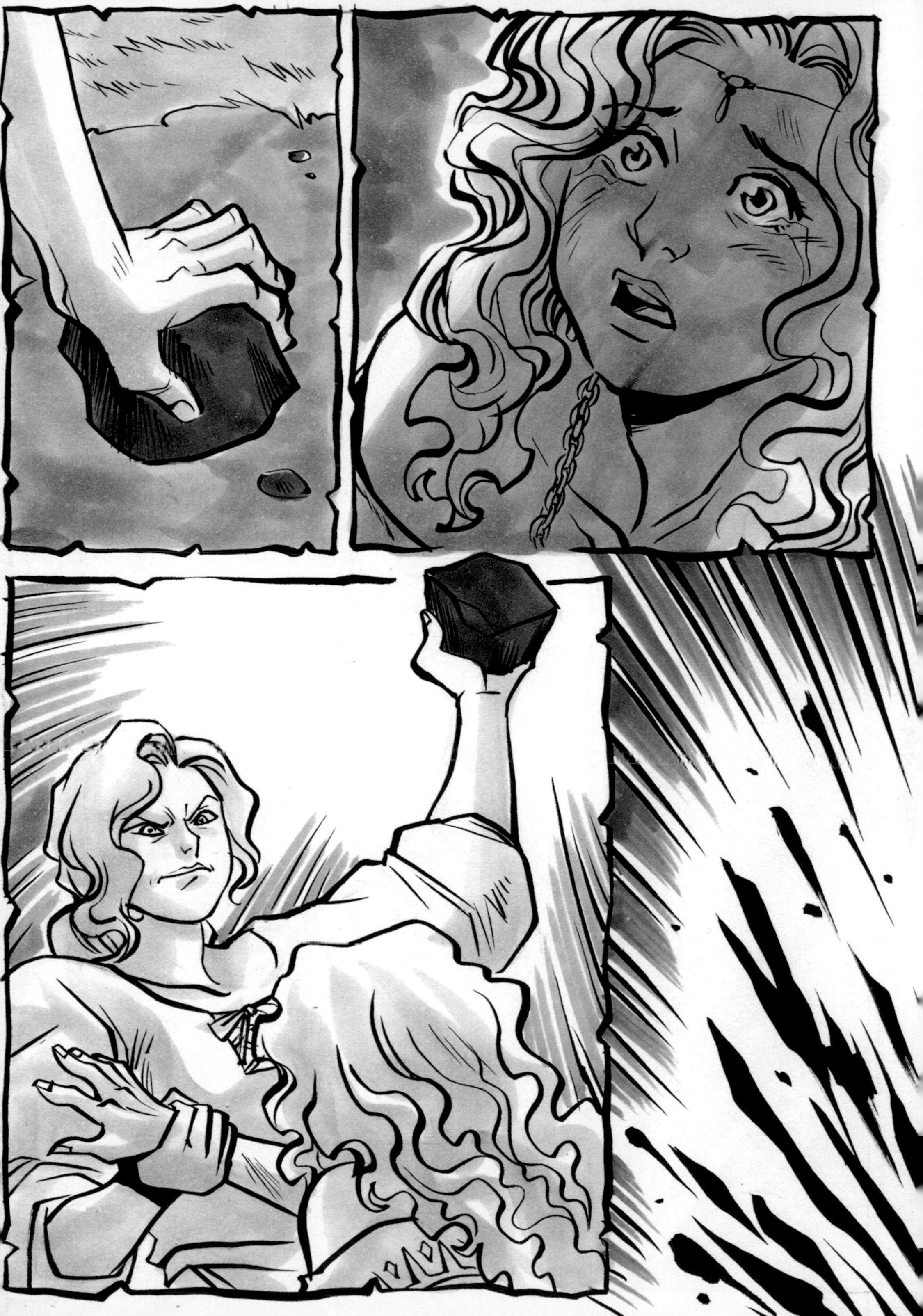

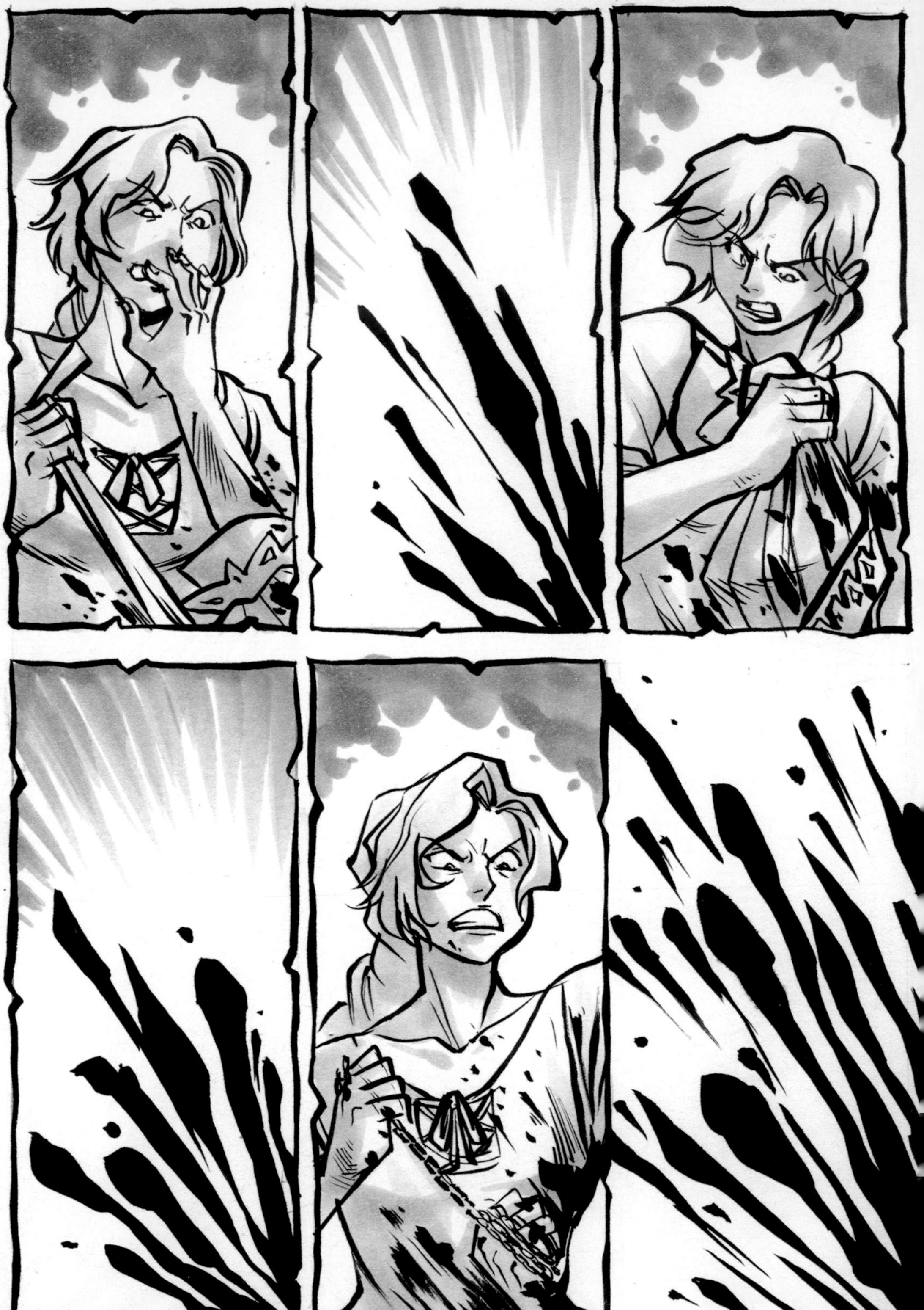

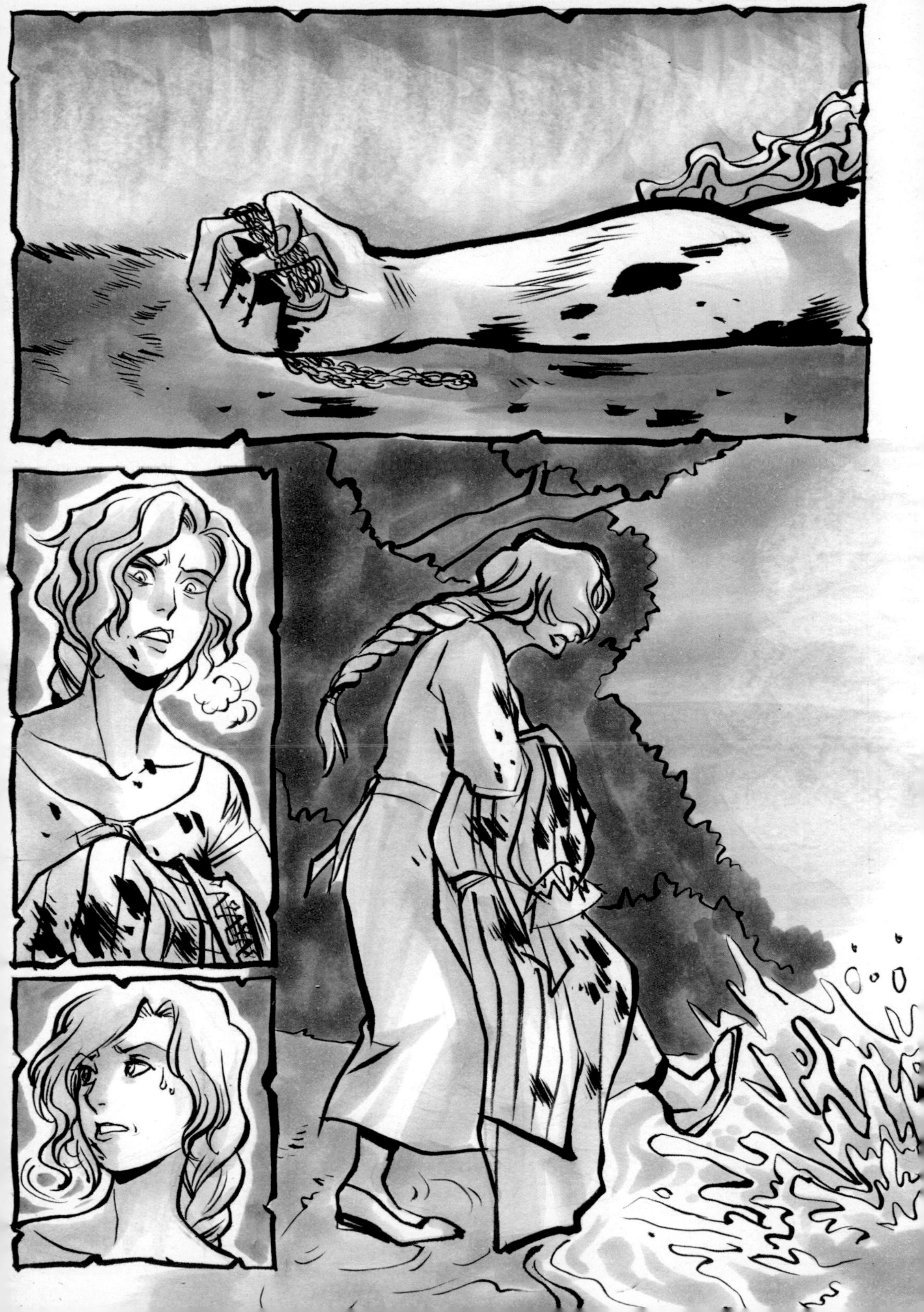

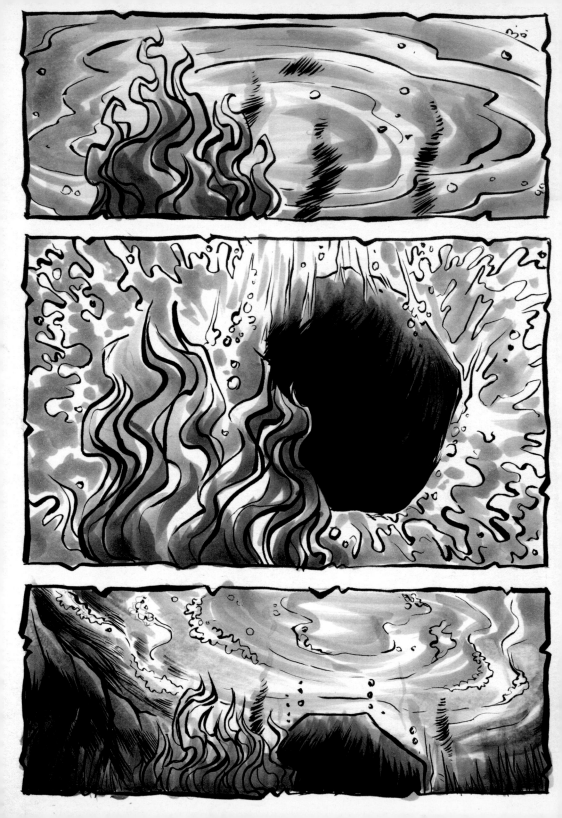

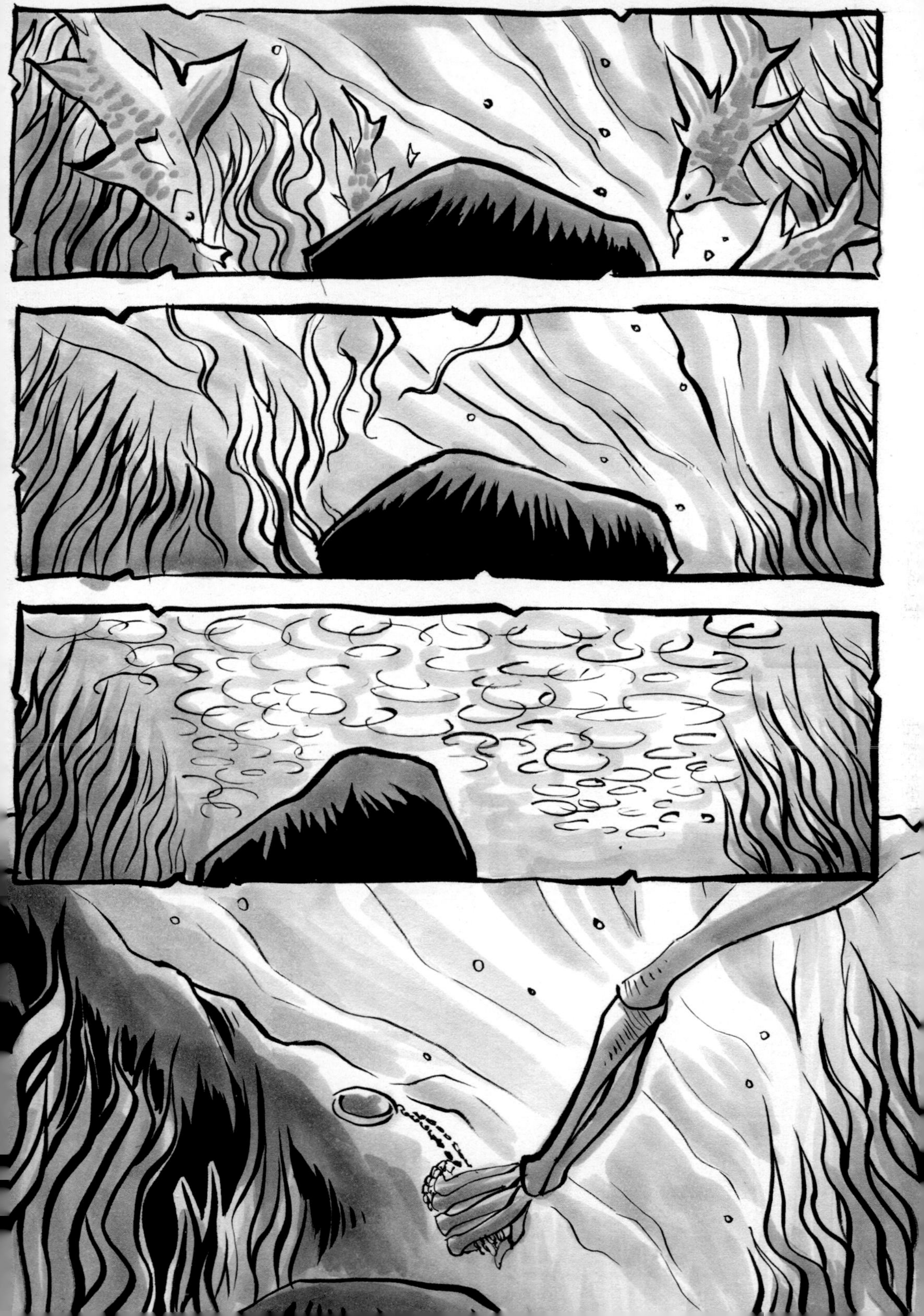

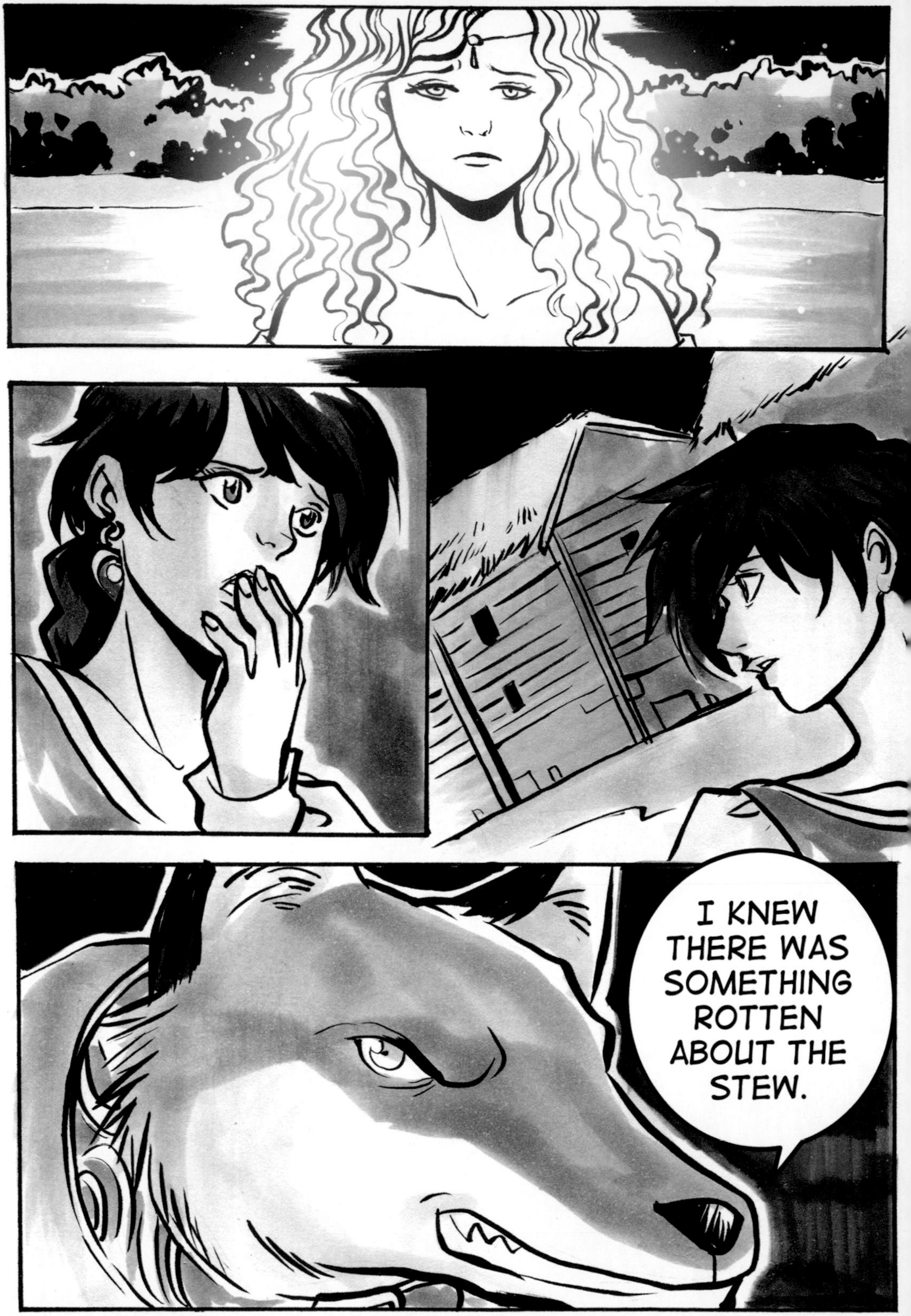
I KNEW THERE WAS SOMETHING ROTTEN ABOUT THE STEW.

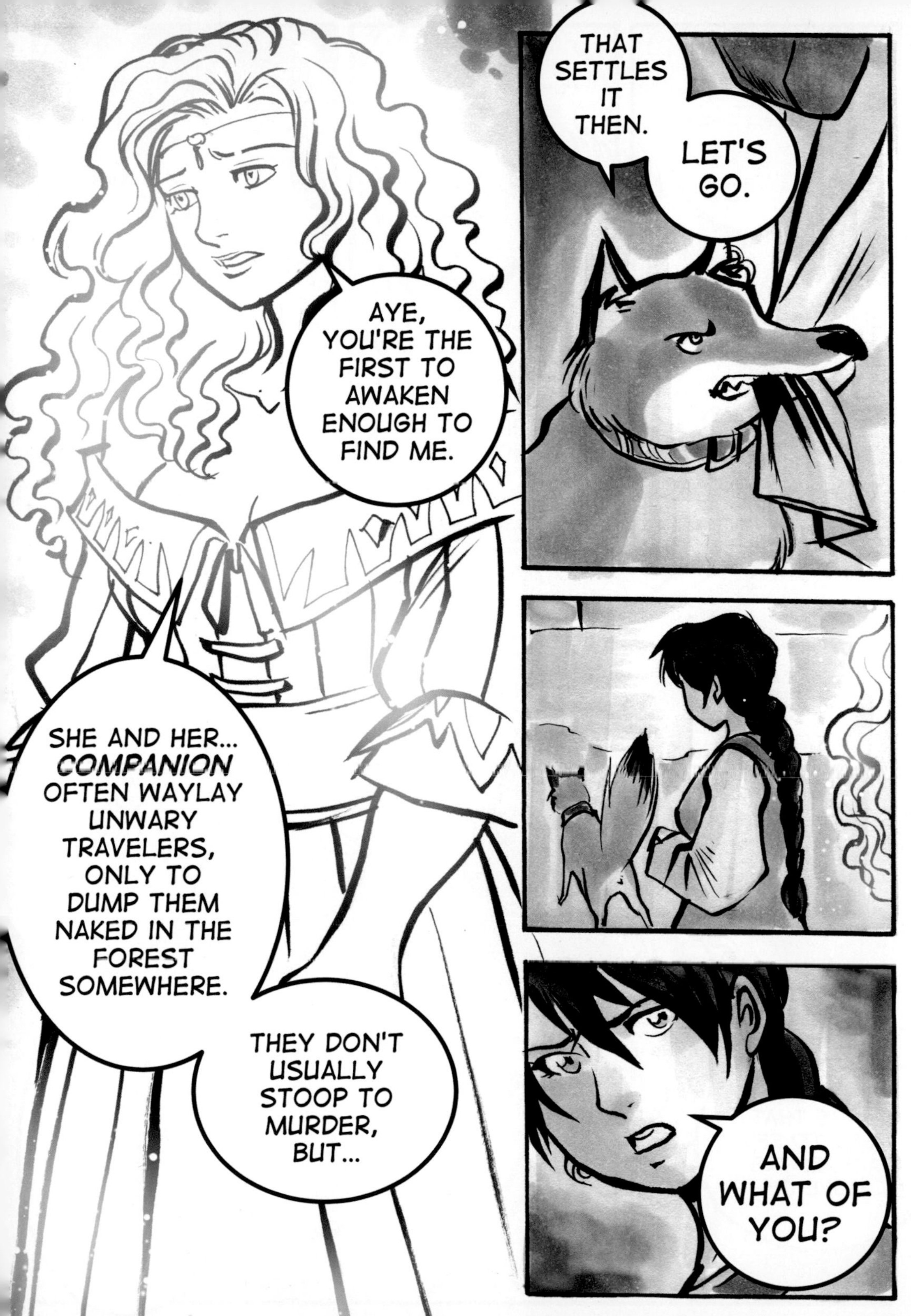

AYE, YOU'RE THE FIRST TO AWAKEN ENOUGH TO FIND ME.
SHE AND HER... *COMPANION* OFTEN WAYLAY UNWARY TRAVELERS, ONLY TO DUMP THEM NAKED IN THE FOREST SOMEWHERE.
THEY DON'T USUALLY STOOP TO MURDER, BUT...
THAT SETTLES IT THEN.
LET'S GO.
AND WHAT OF YOU?

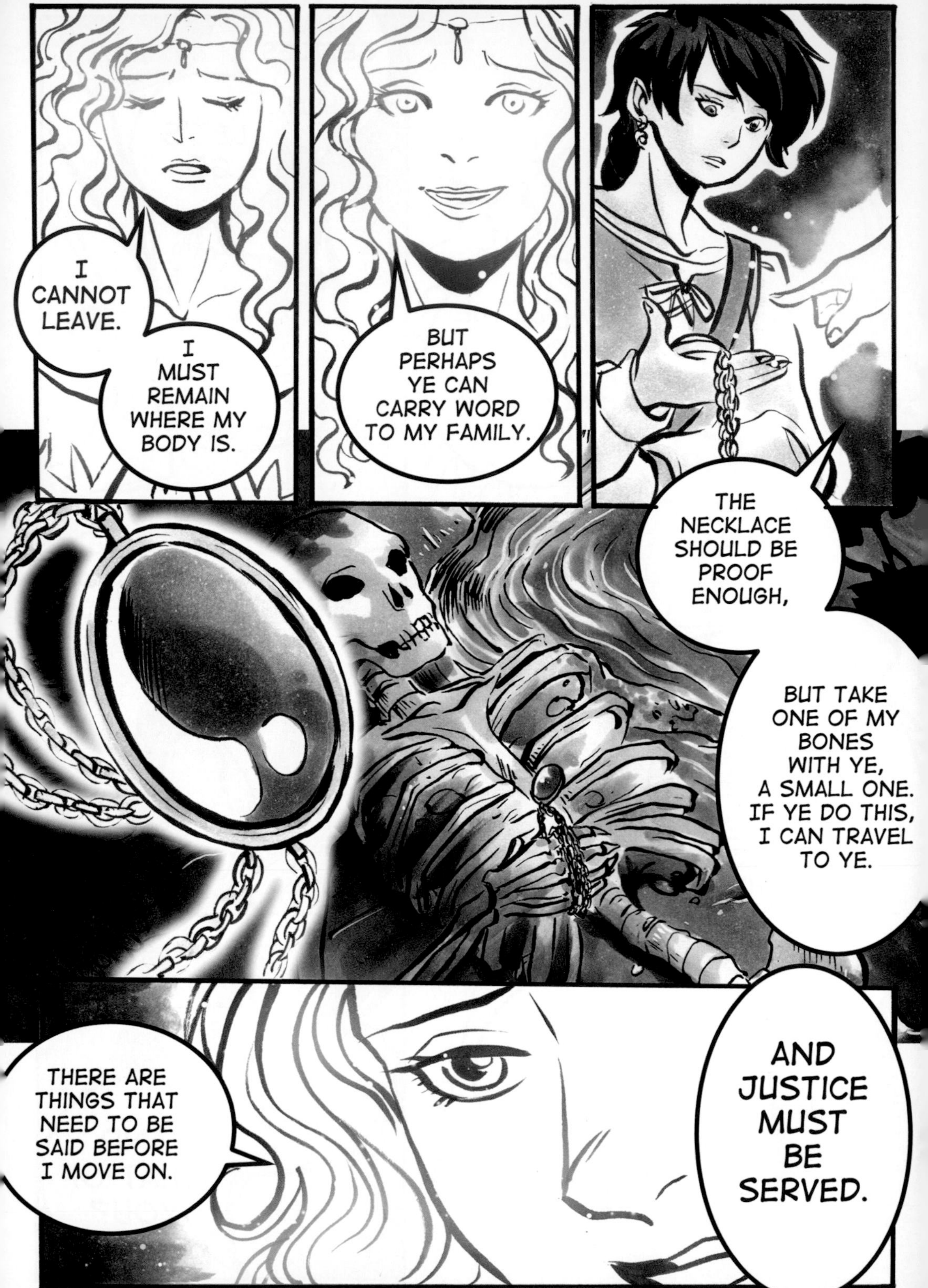
I CANNOT LEAVE.
I MUST REMAIN WHERE MY BODY IS.
BUT PERHAPS YE CAN CARRY WORD TO MY FAMILY.
THE NECKLACE SHOULD BE PROOF ENOUGH,
BUT TAKE ONE OF MY BONES WITH YE, A SMALL ONE. IF YE DO THIS, I CAN TRAVEL TO YE.
THERE ARE THINGS THAT NEED TO BE SAID BEFORE I MOVE ON.
AND JUSTICE MUST BE SERVED.

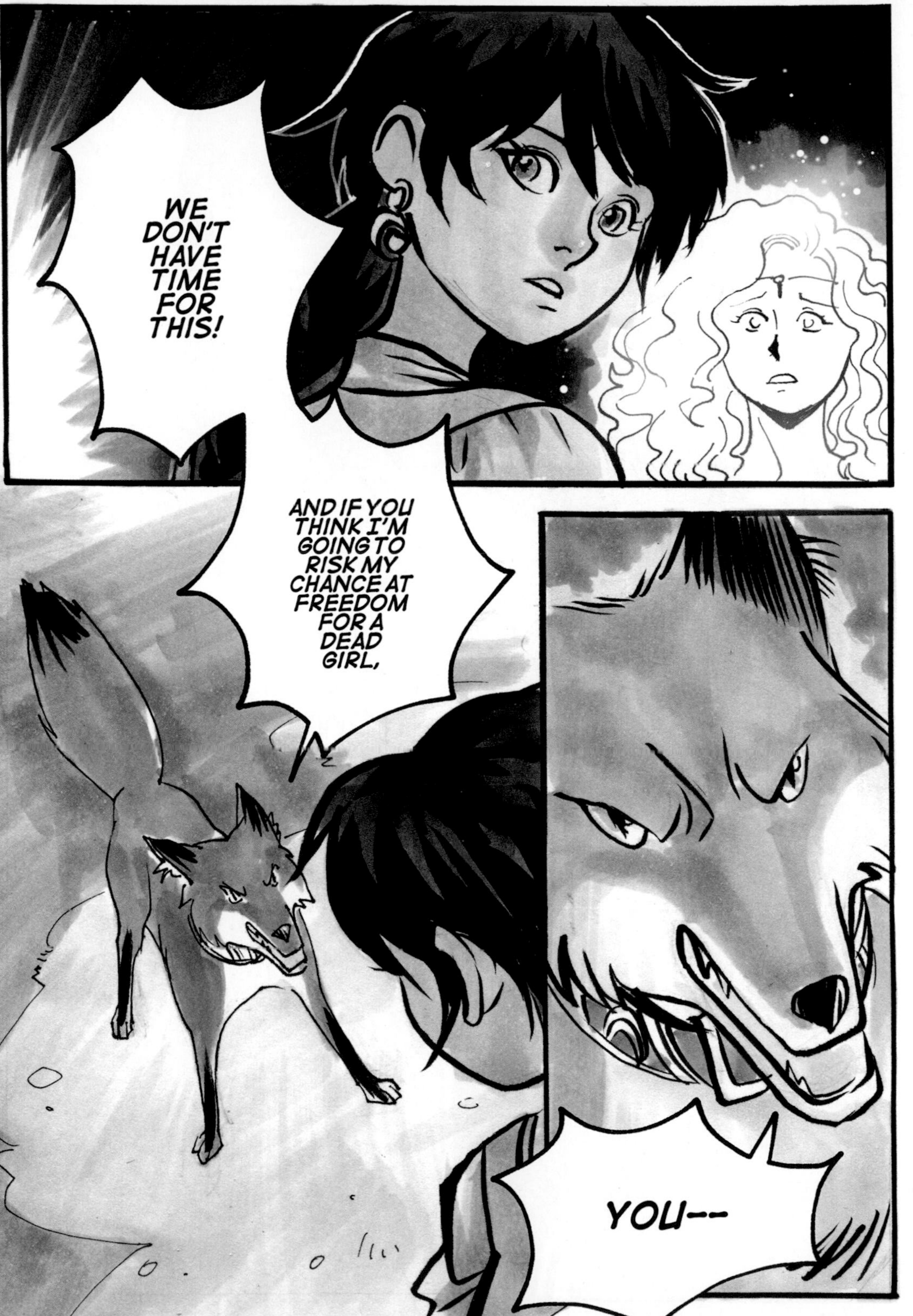
WE DON'T HAVE TIME FOR THIS!
AND IF YOU THINK I'M GOING TO RISK MY CHANCE AT FREEDOM FOR A DEAD GIRL,
YOU--

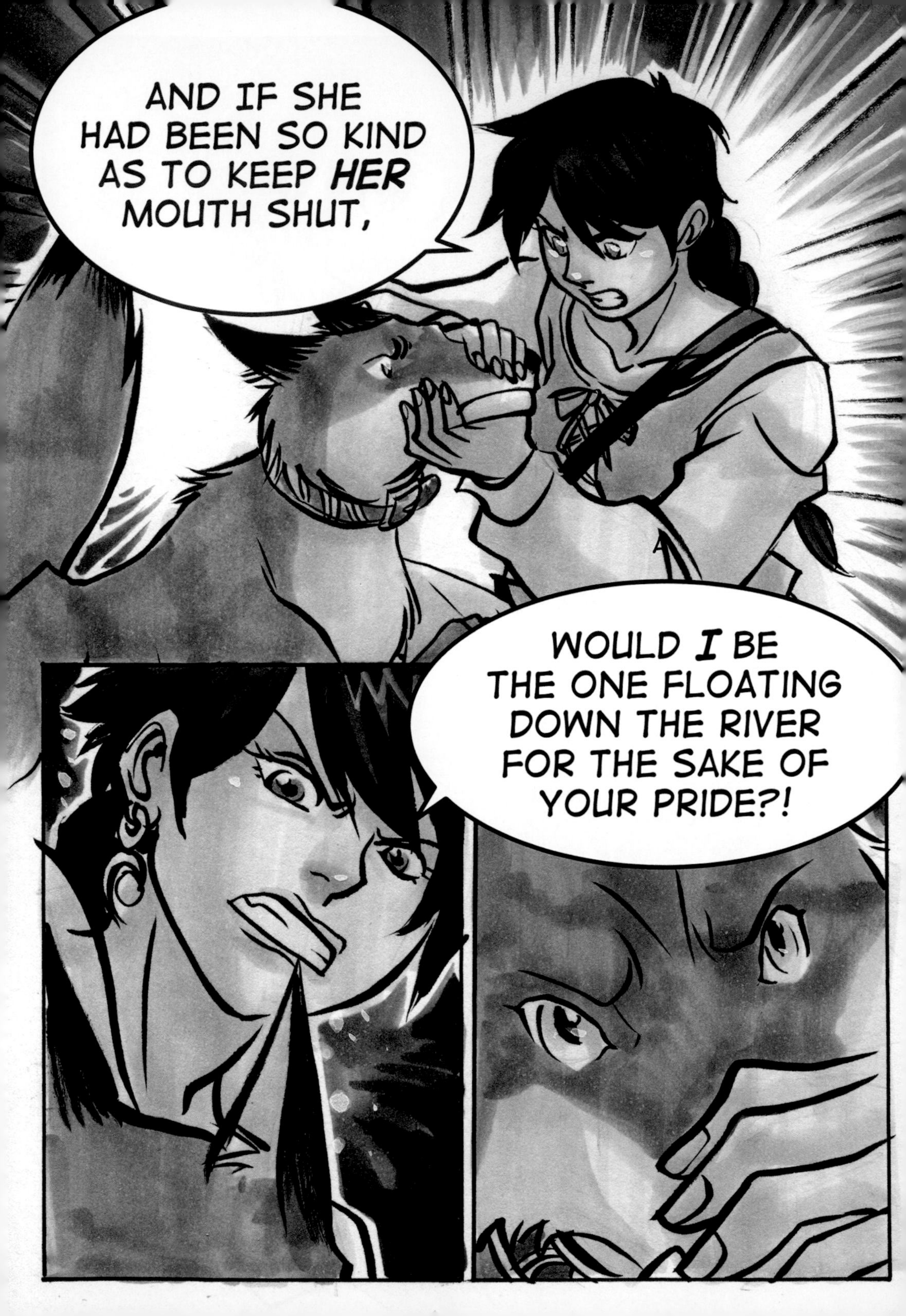
AND IF SHE HAD BEEN SO KIND AS TO KEEP **HER** MOUTH SHUT,
WOULD **I** BE THE ONE FLOATING DOWN THE RIVER FOR THE SAKE OF YOUR PRIDE?!

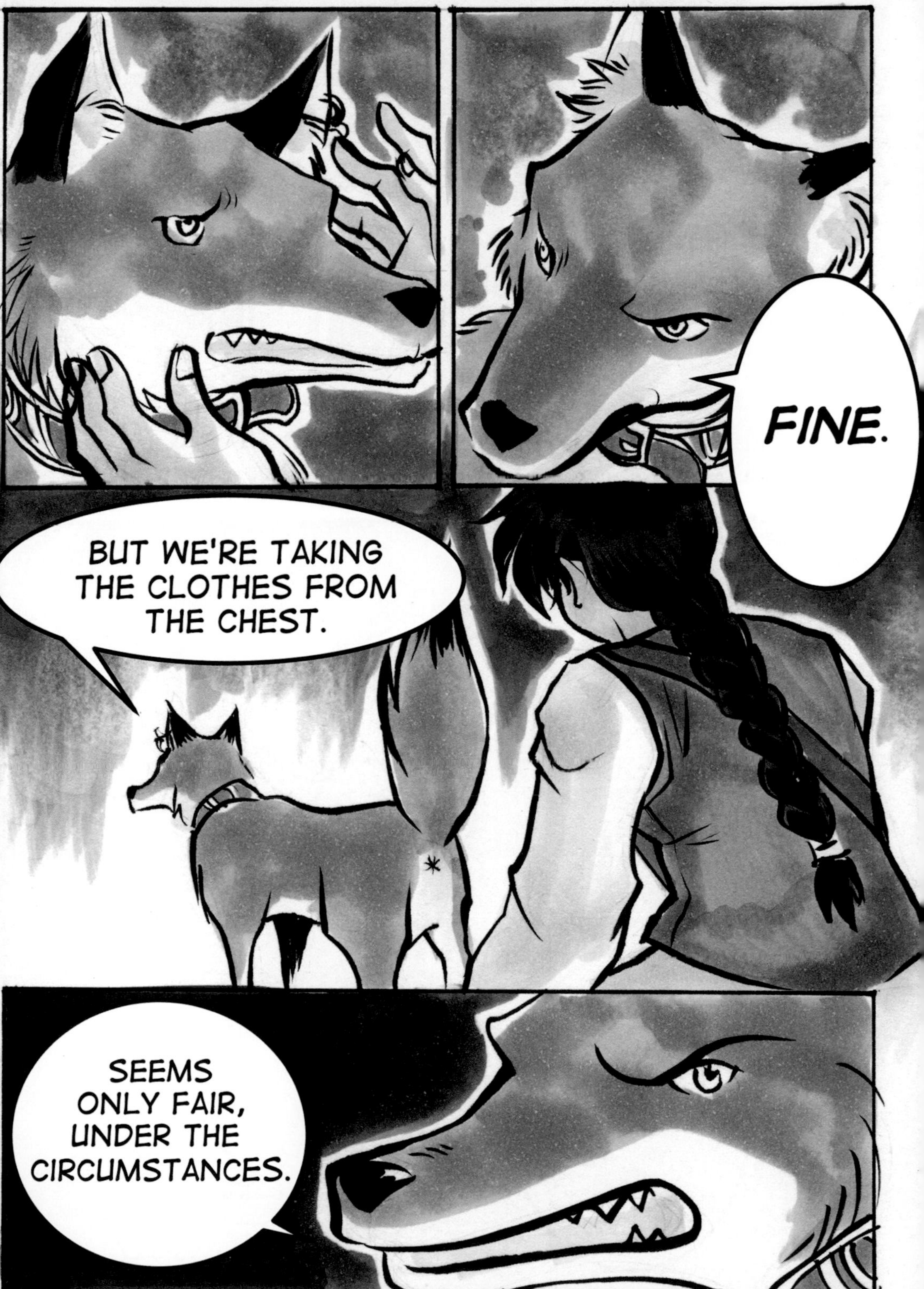
FINE.
BUT WE'RE TAKING THE CLOTHES FROM THE CHEST.
SEEMS ONLY FAIR, UNDER THE CIRCUMSTANCES.

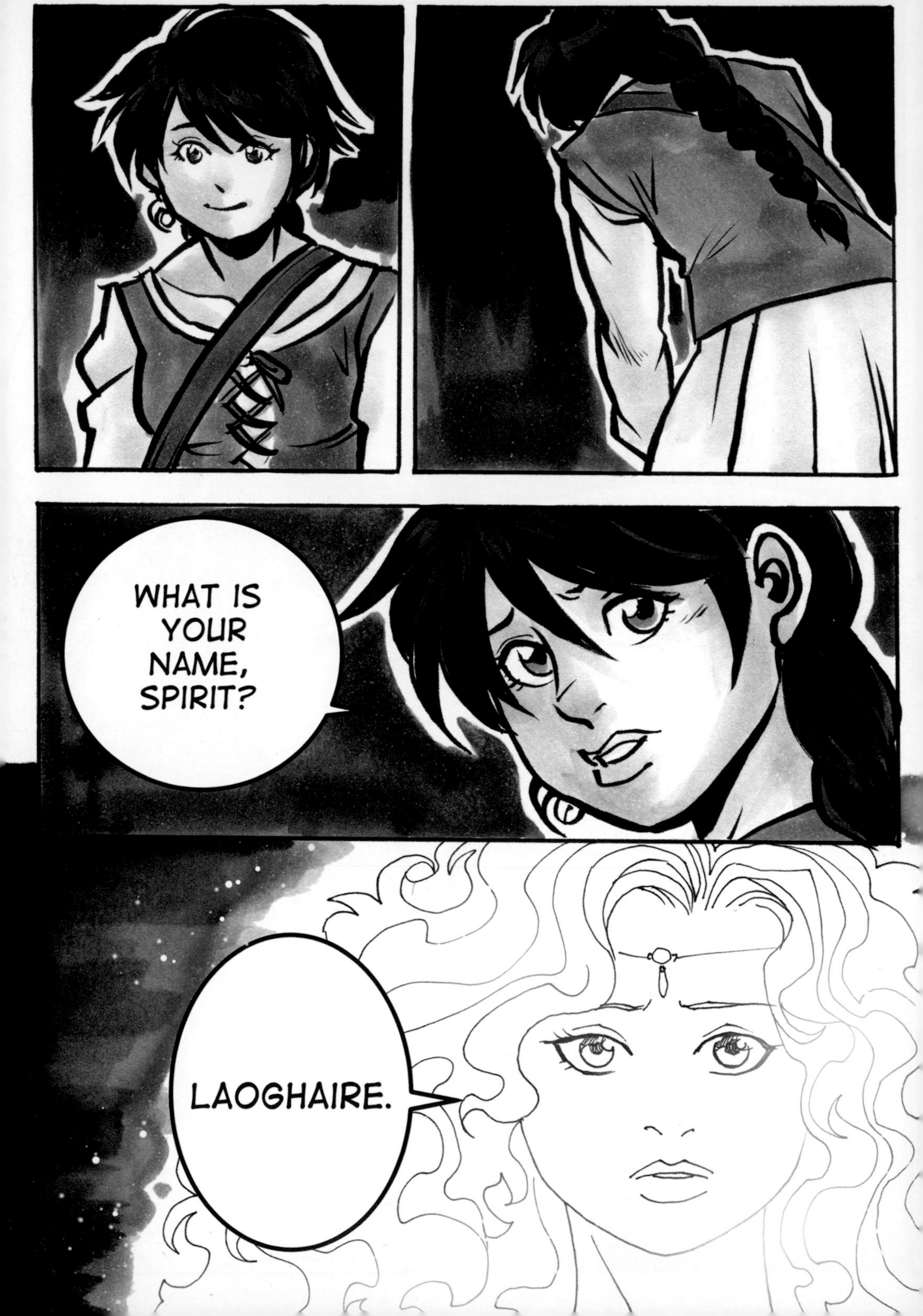
WHAT IS YOUR NAME, SPIRIT?
LAOGHAIRE.

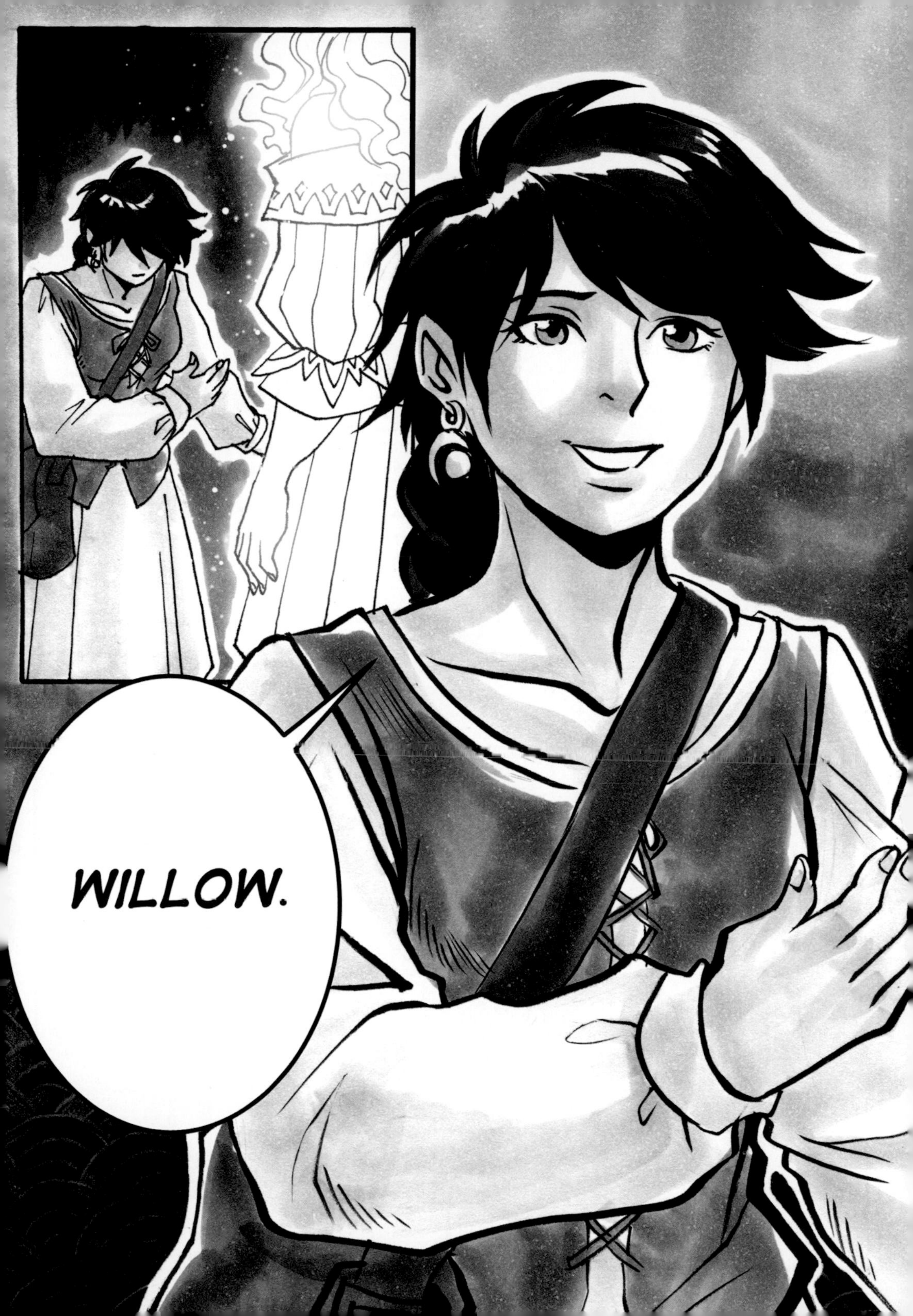
WILLOW.

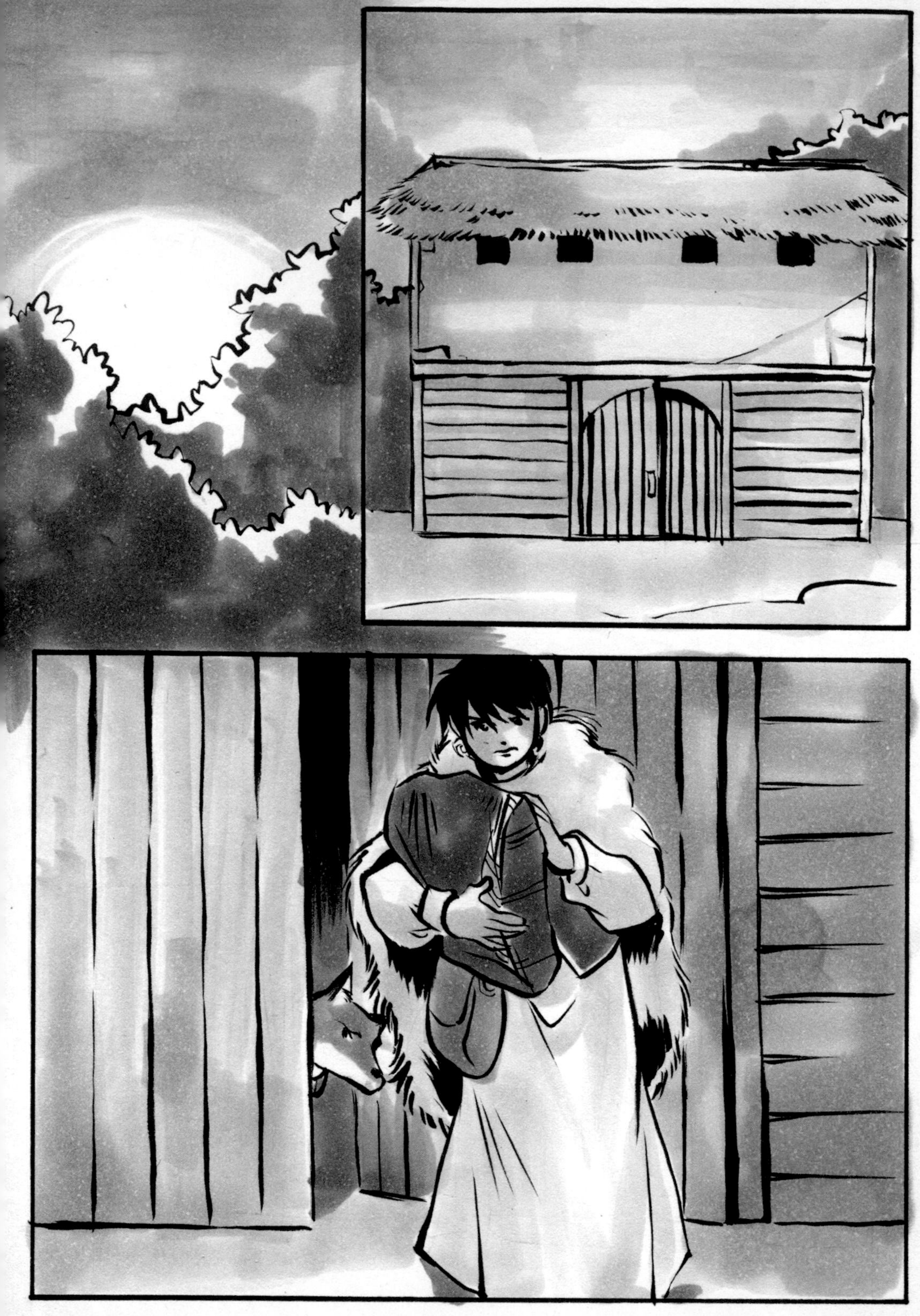

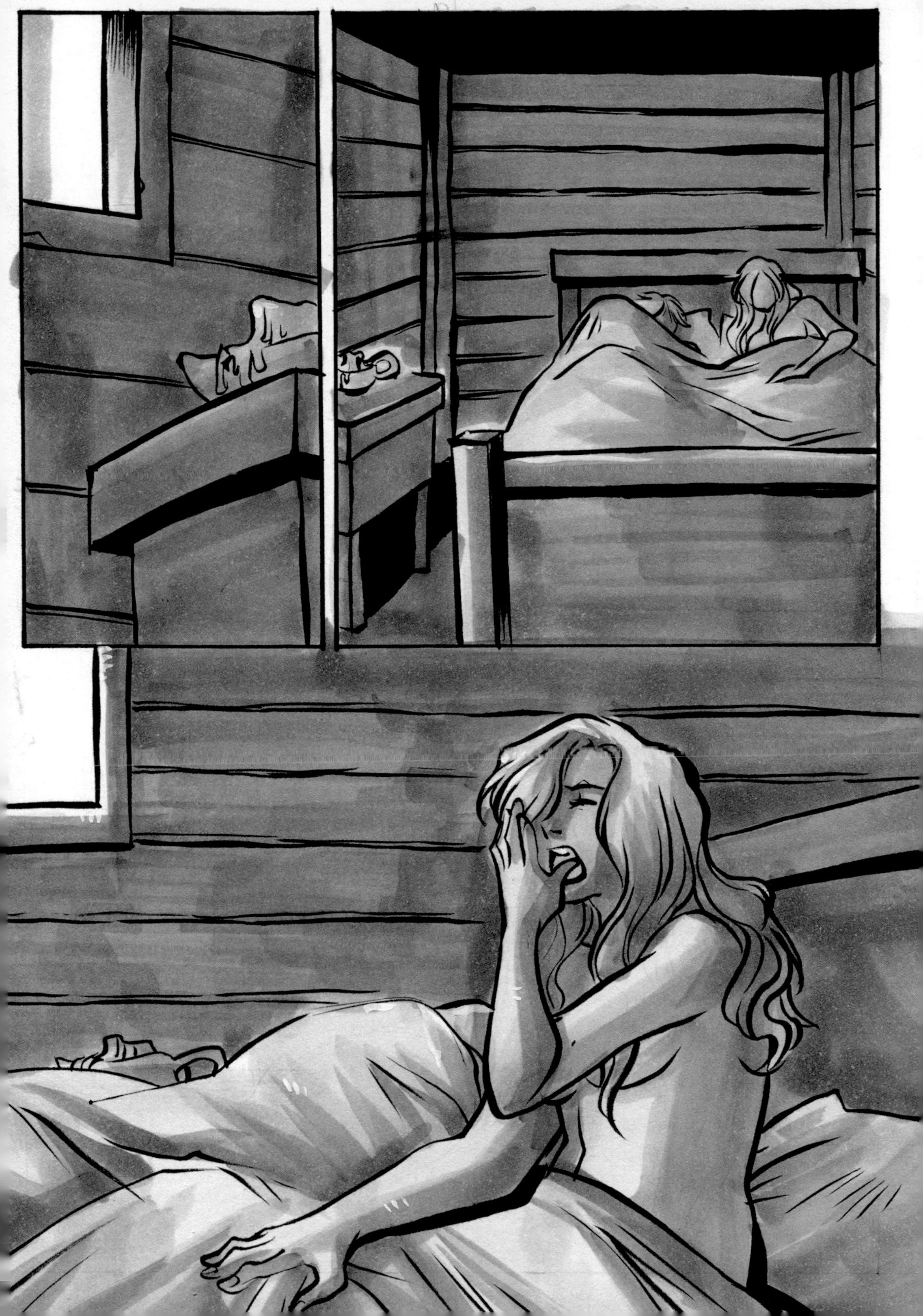

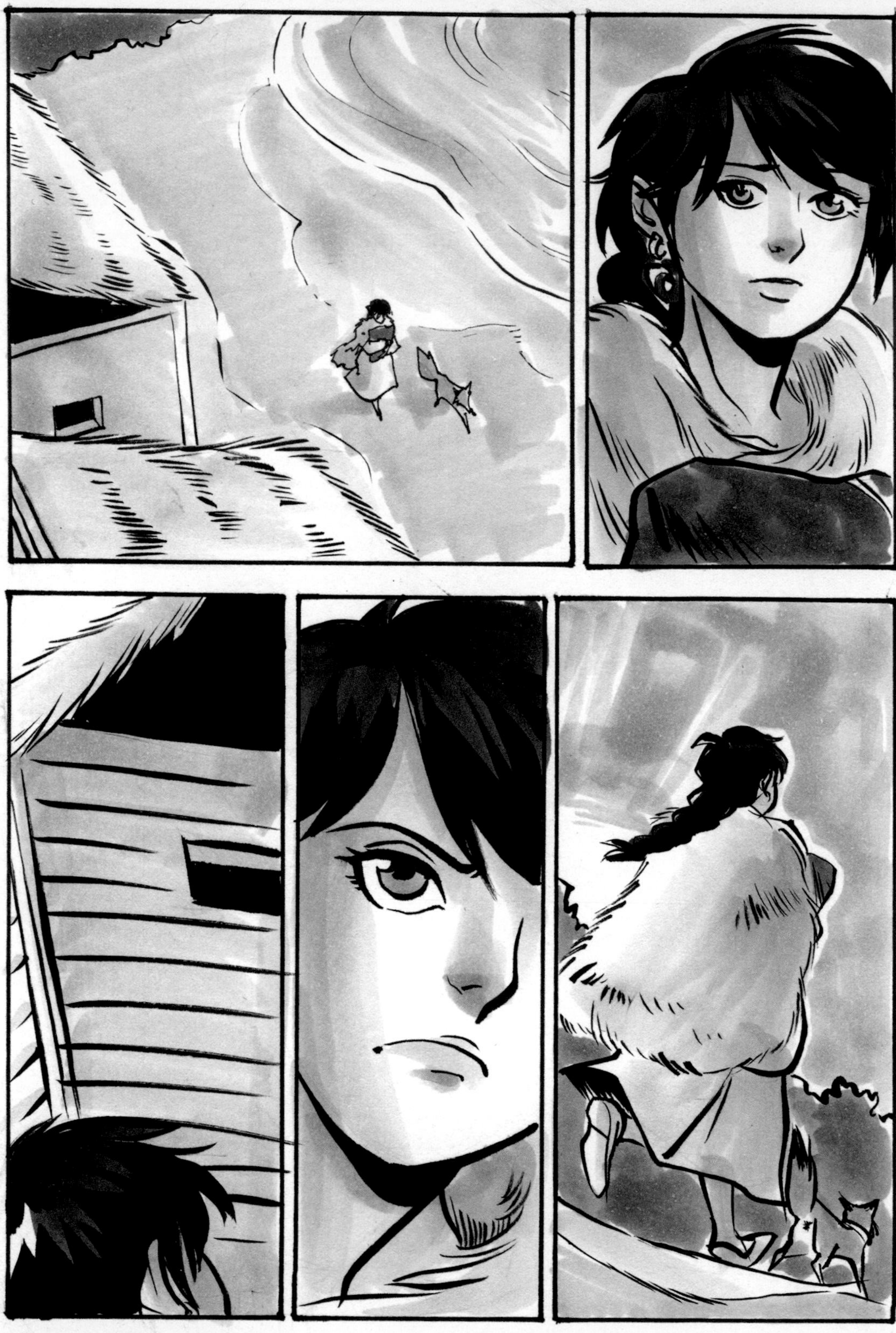

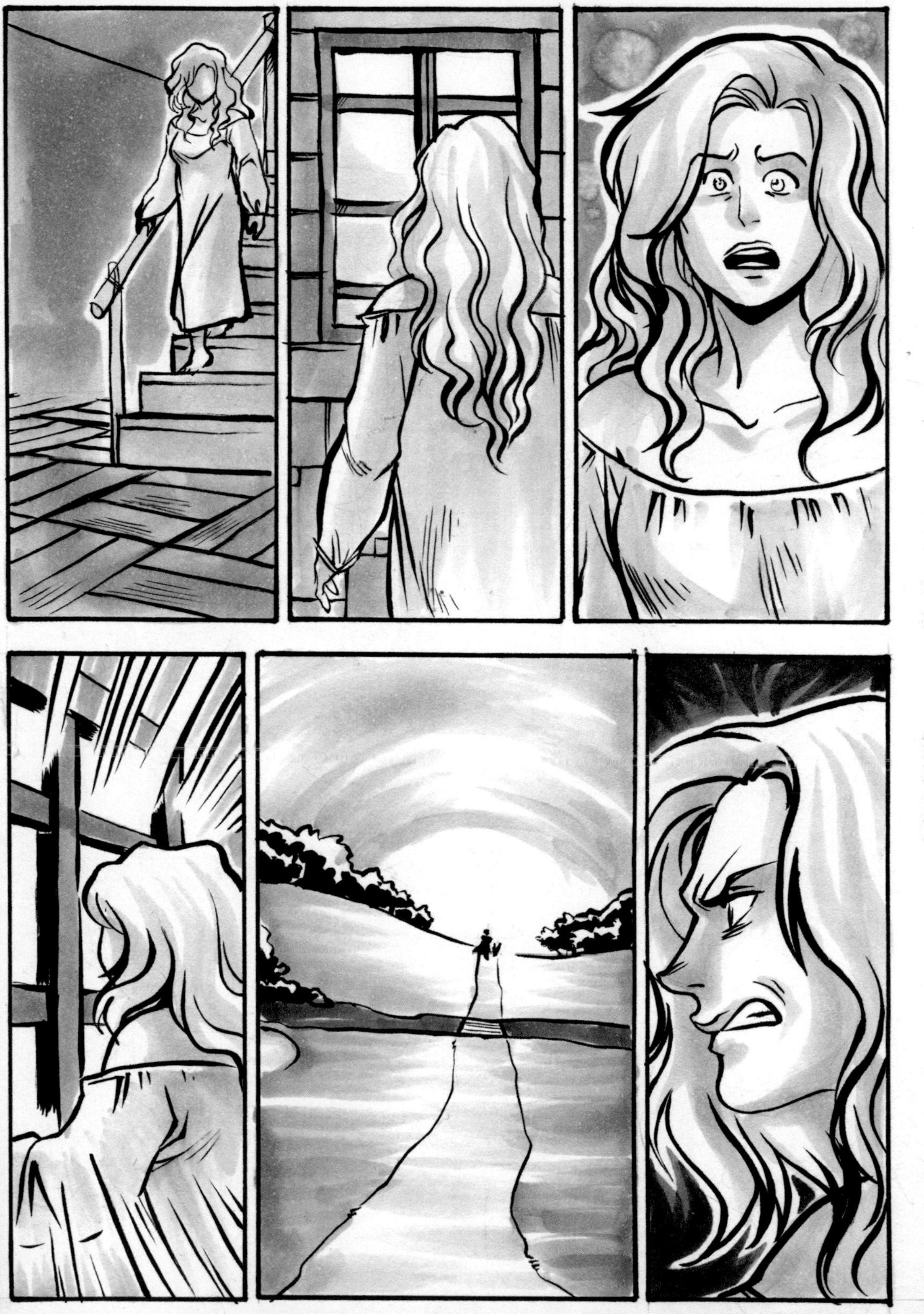

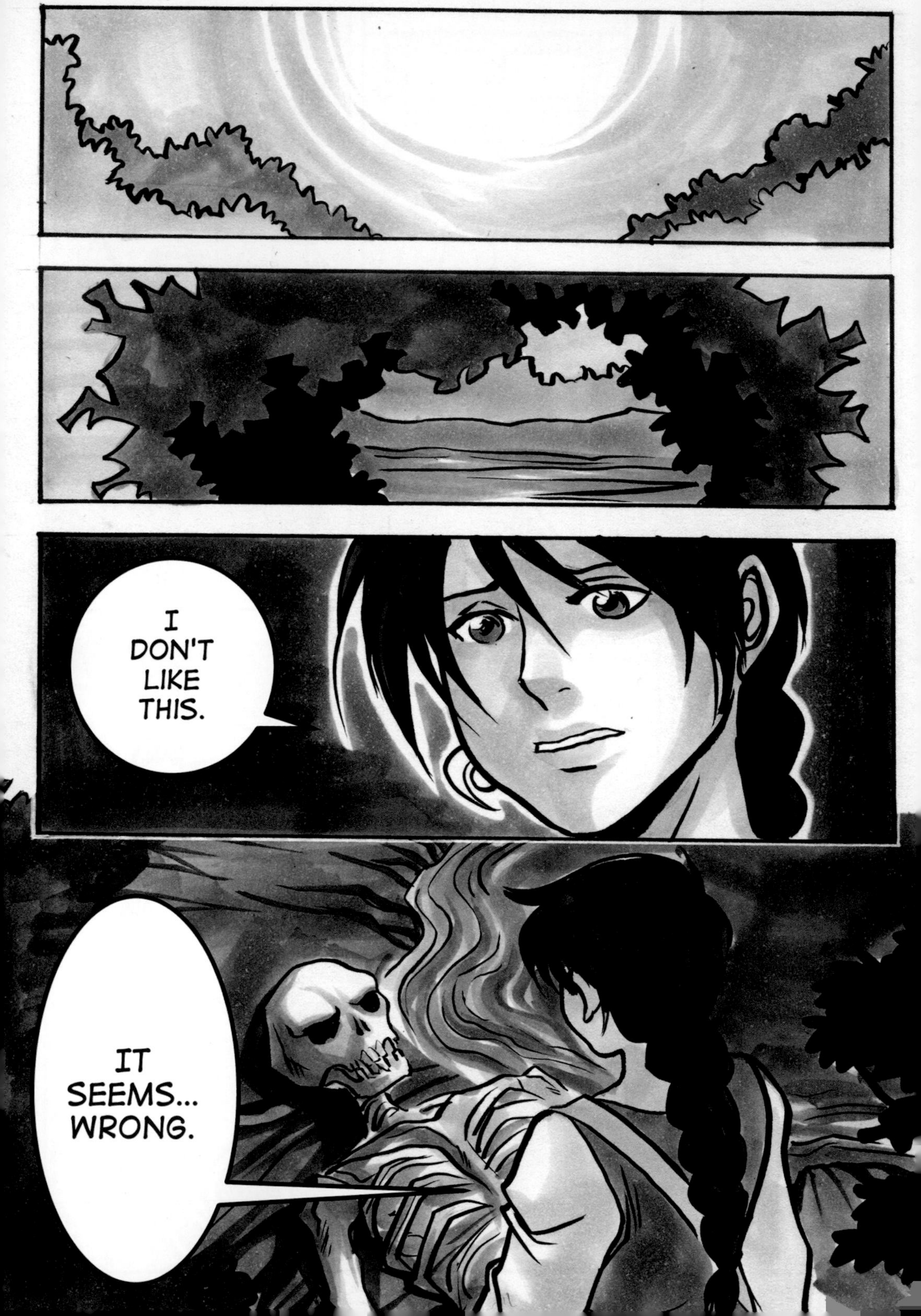
I DON'T LIKE THIS.
IT SEEMS... WRONG.

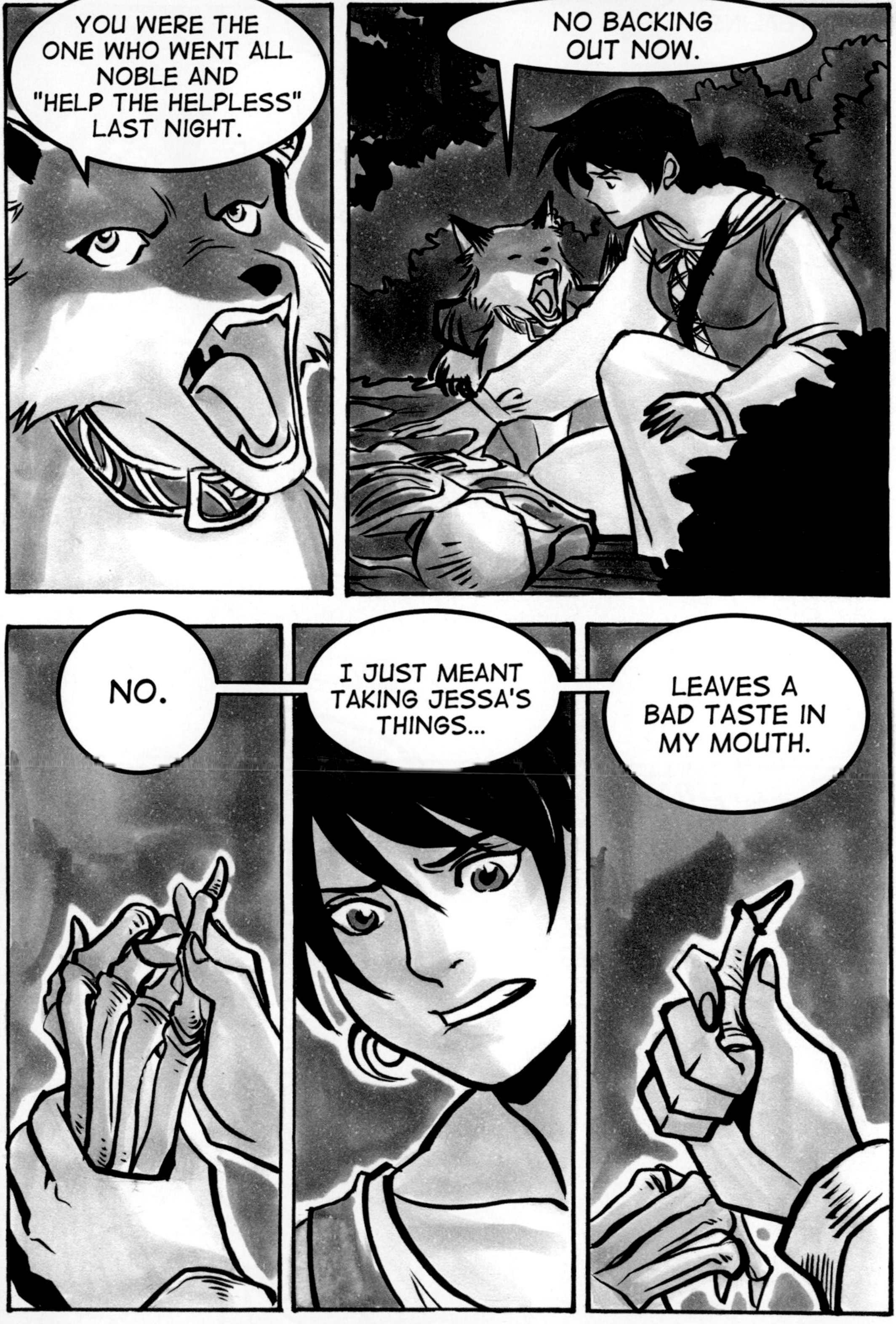
YOU WERE THE ONE WHO WENT ALL NOBLE AND "HELP THE HELPLESS" LAST NIGHT.
NO BACKING OUT NOW.
NO.
I JUST MEANT TAKING JESSA'S THINGS...
LEAVES A BAD TASTE IN MY MOUTH.

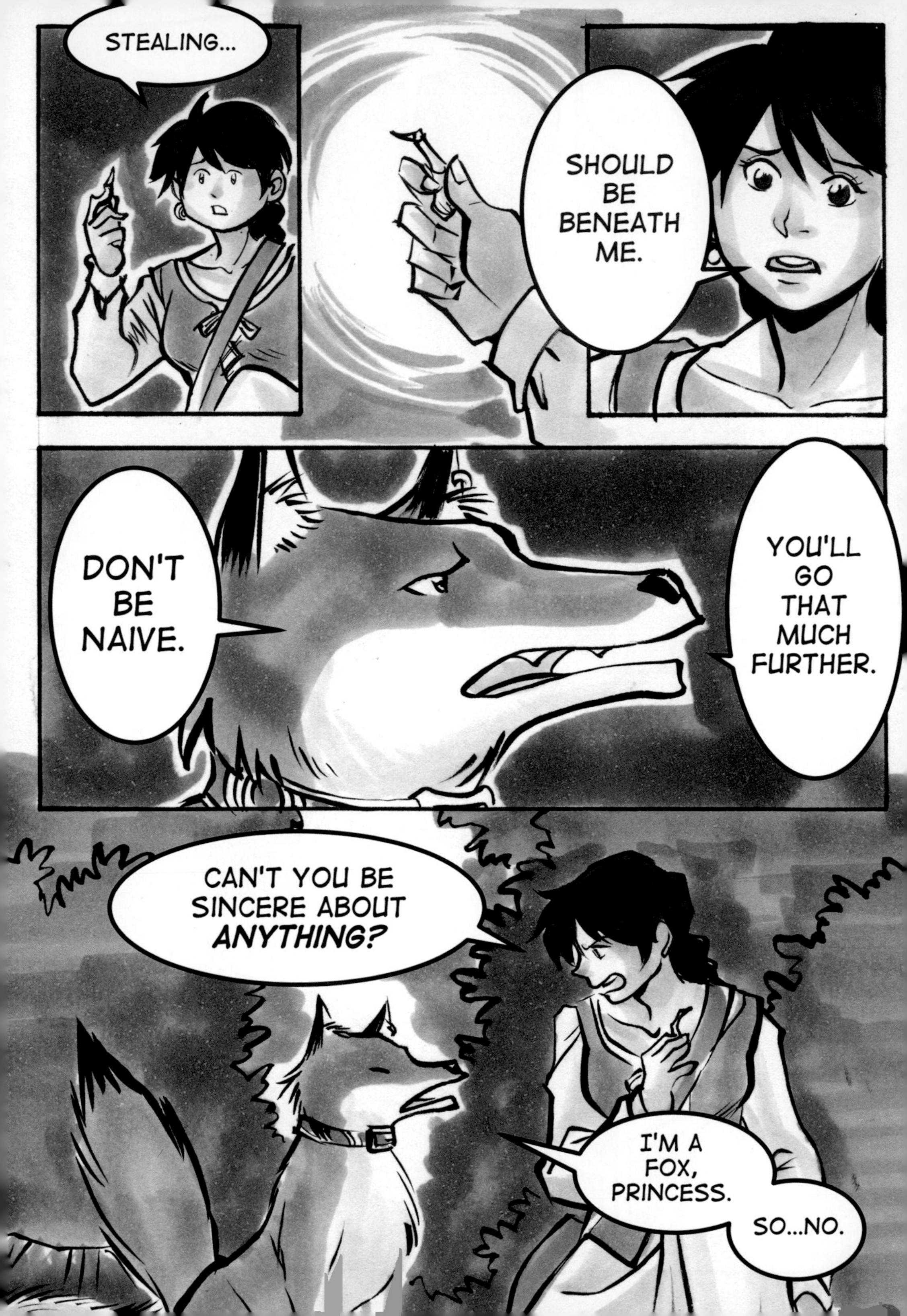
STEALING...
SHOULD BE BENEATH ME.
DON'T BE NAIVE.
YOU'LL GO THAT MUCH FURTHER.
CAN'T YOU BE SINCERE ABOUT *ANYTHING?*
I'M A FOX, PRINCESS.
SO...NO.

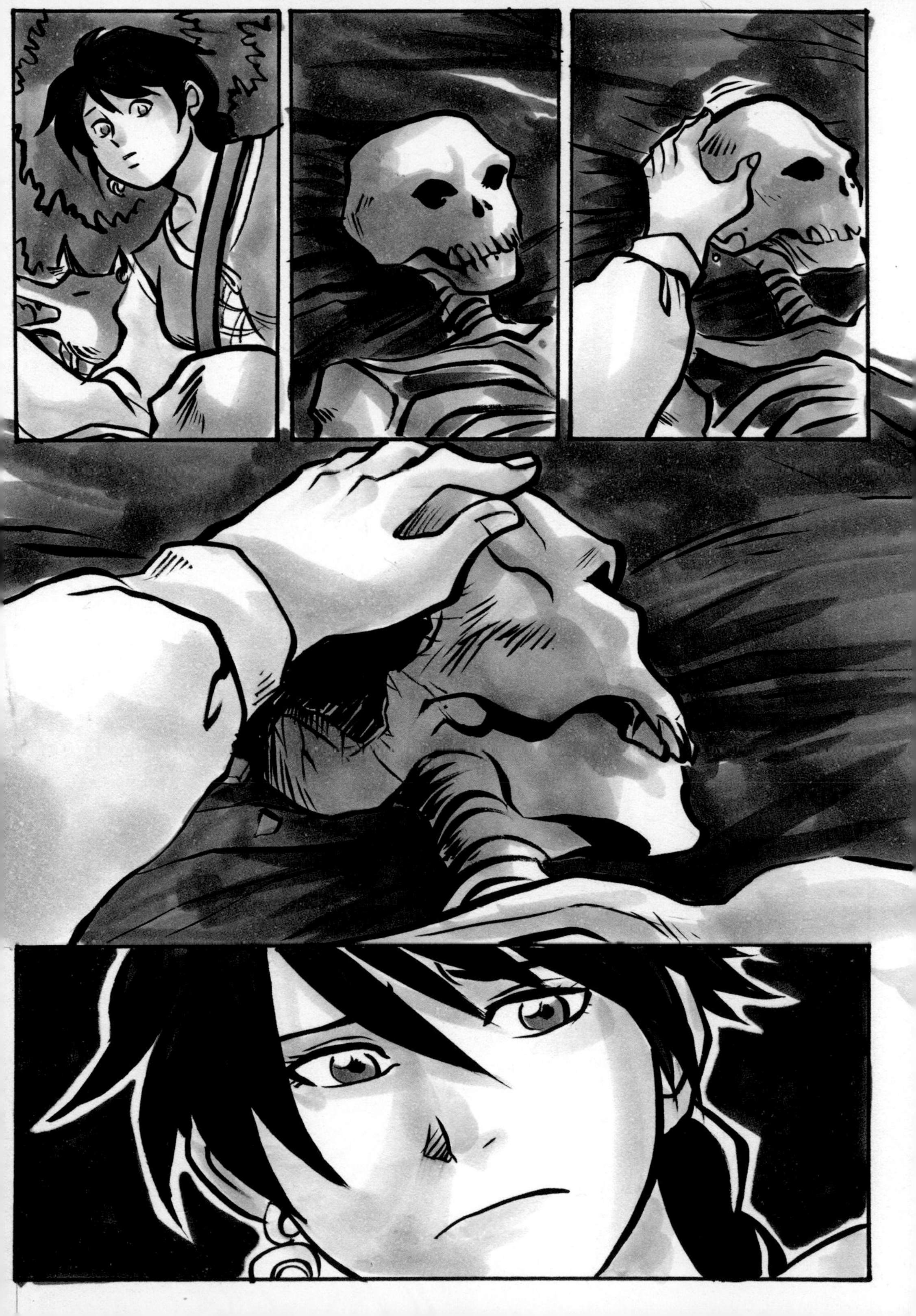

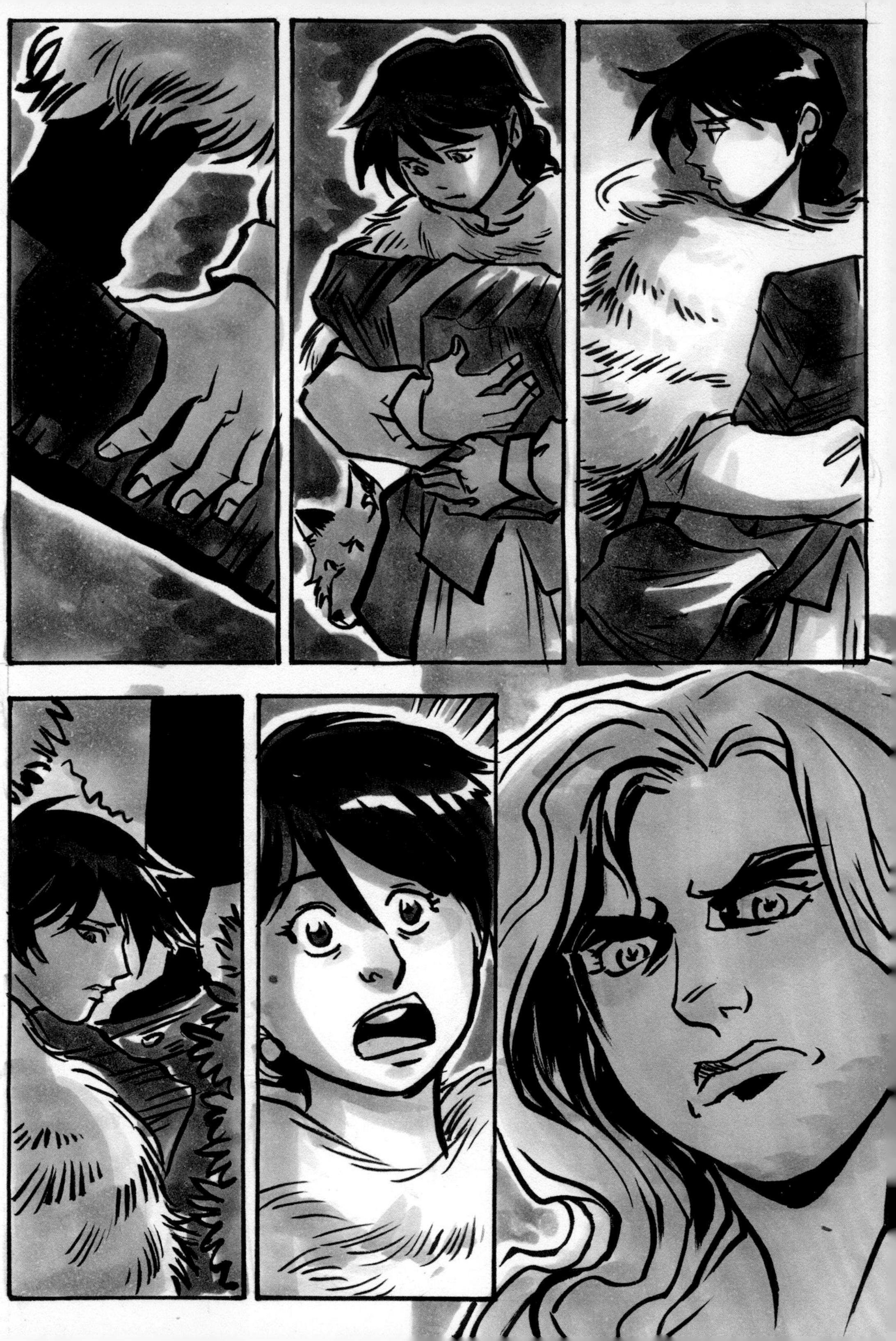

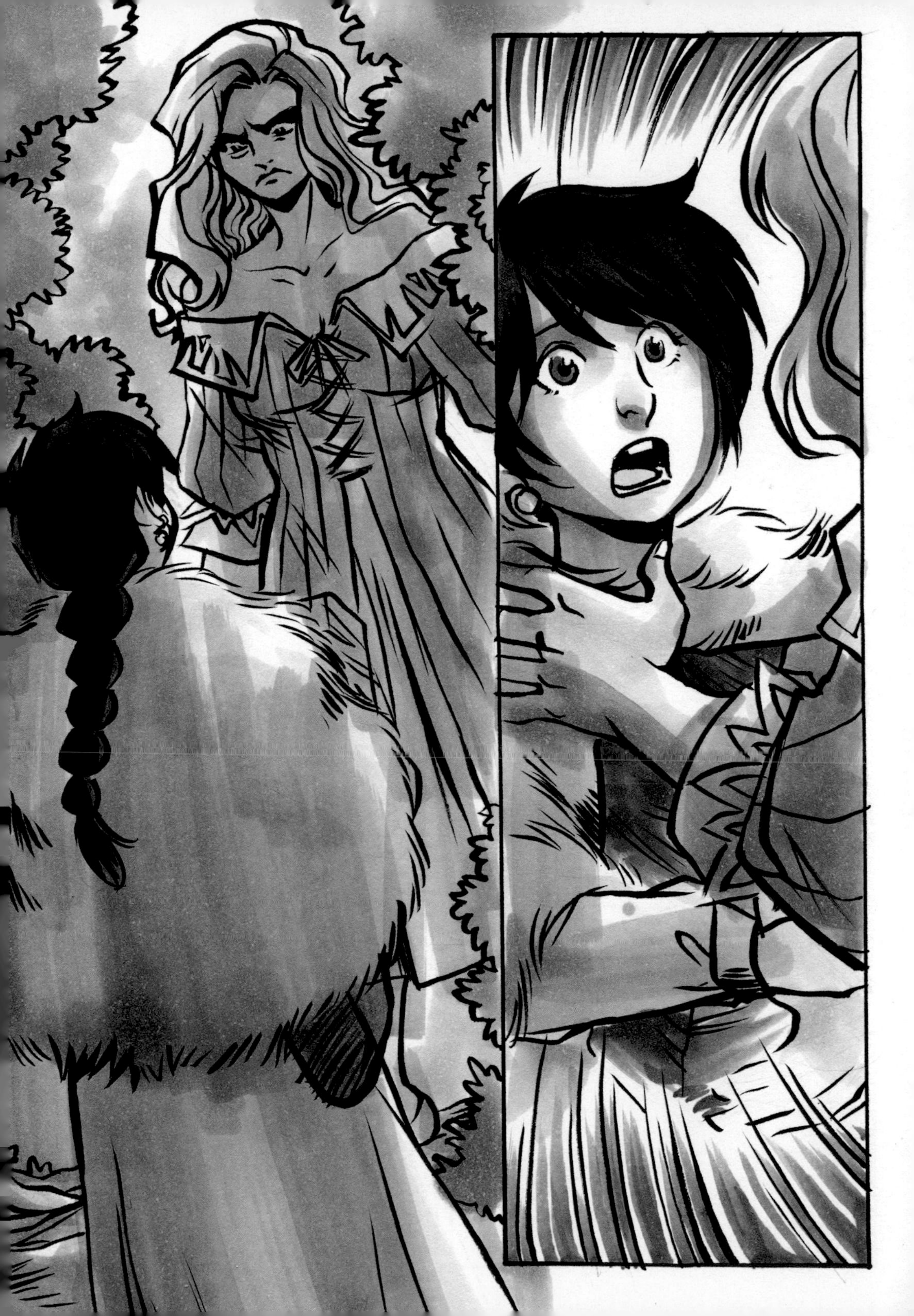

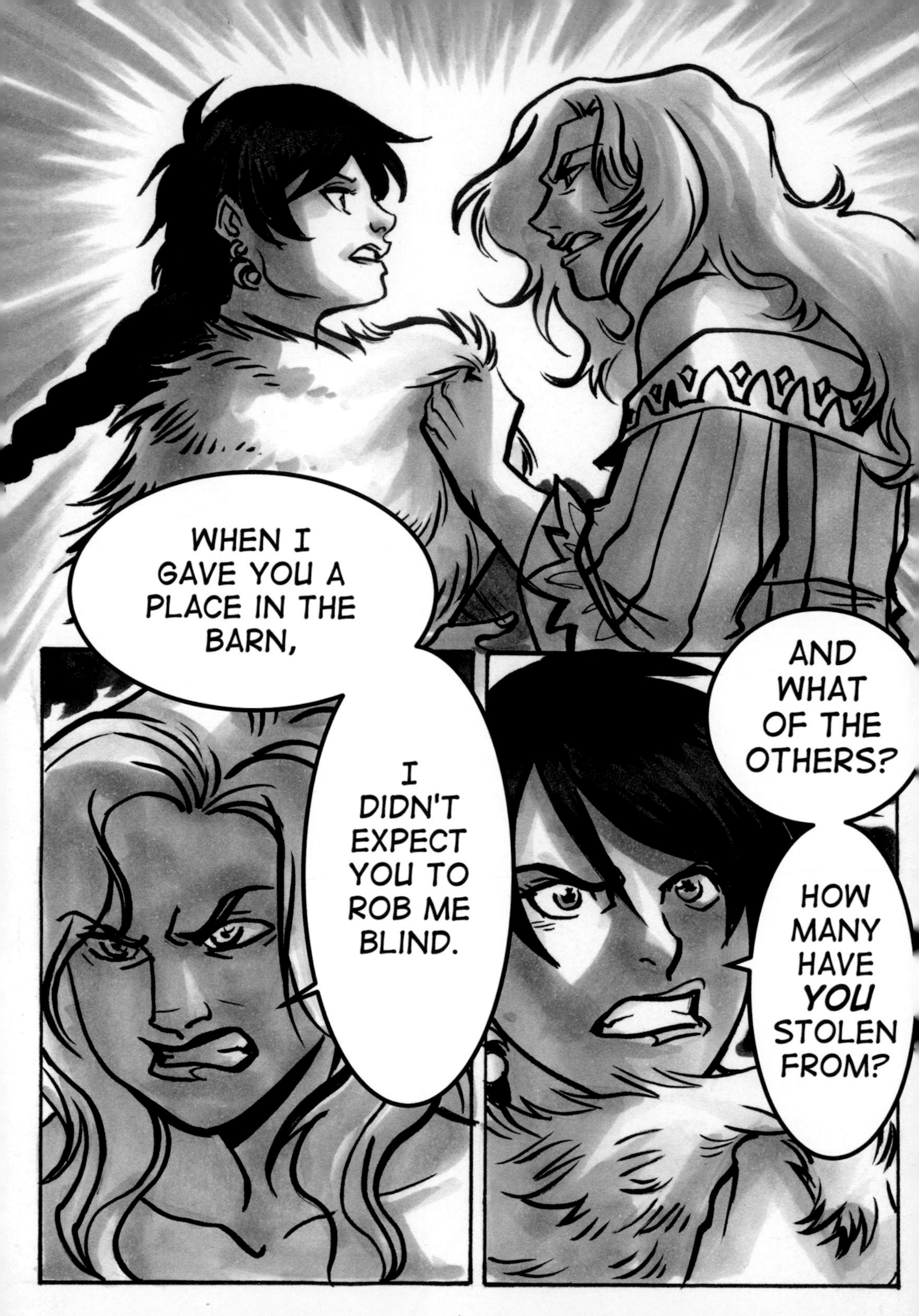
WHEN I GAVE YOU A PLACE IN THE BARN,
I DIDN'T EXPECT YOU TO ROB ME BLIND.
AND WHAT OF THE OTHERS?
HOW MANY HAVE *YOU* STOLEN FROM?

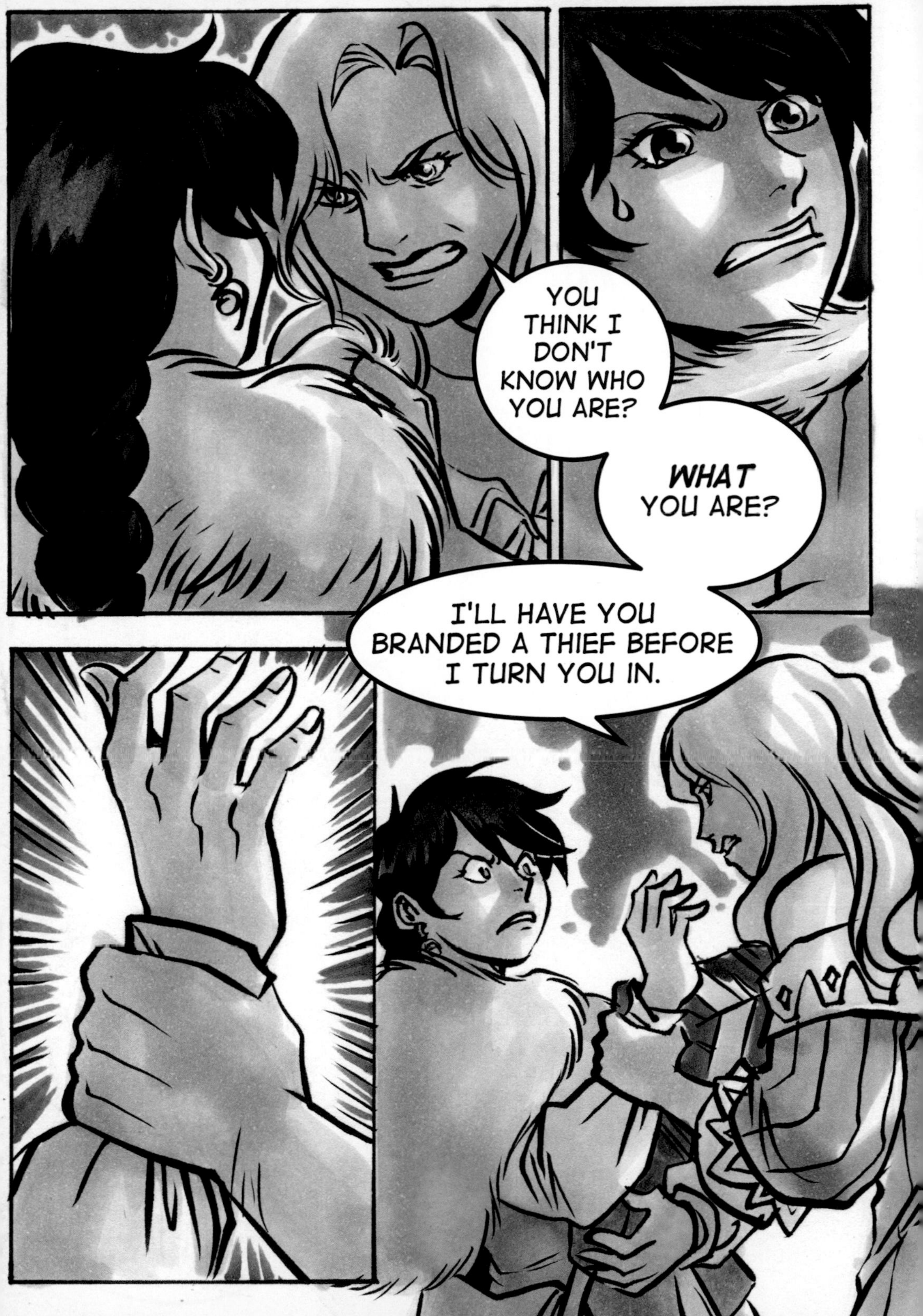
YOU THINK I DON'T KNOW WHO YOU ARE?
WHAT YOU ARE?
I'LL HAVE YOU BRANDED A THIEF BEFORE I TURN YOU IN.

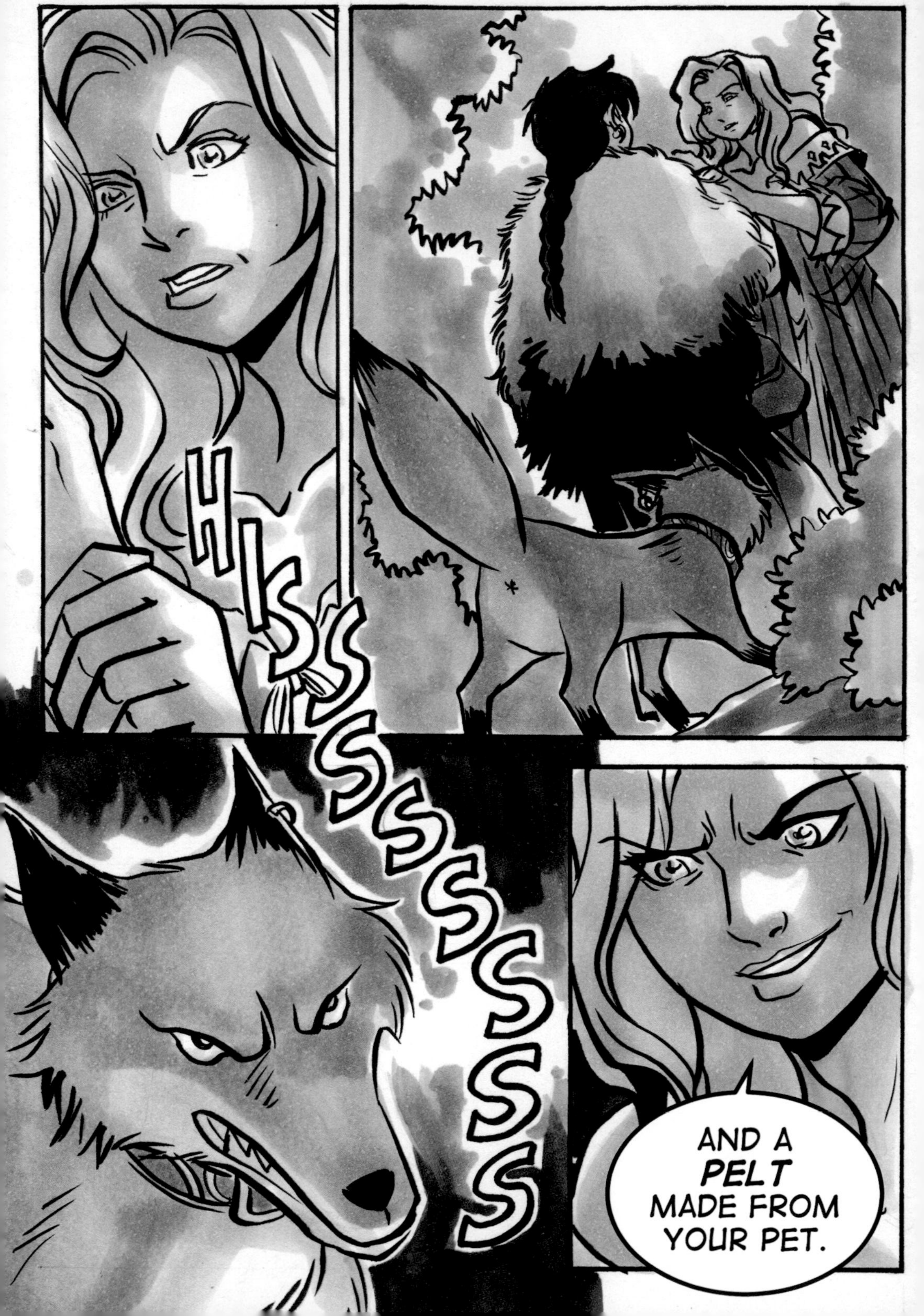
HISSSSSSSSSS
AND A PELT MADE FROM YOUR PET.

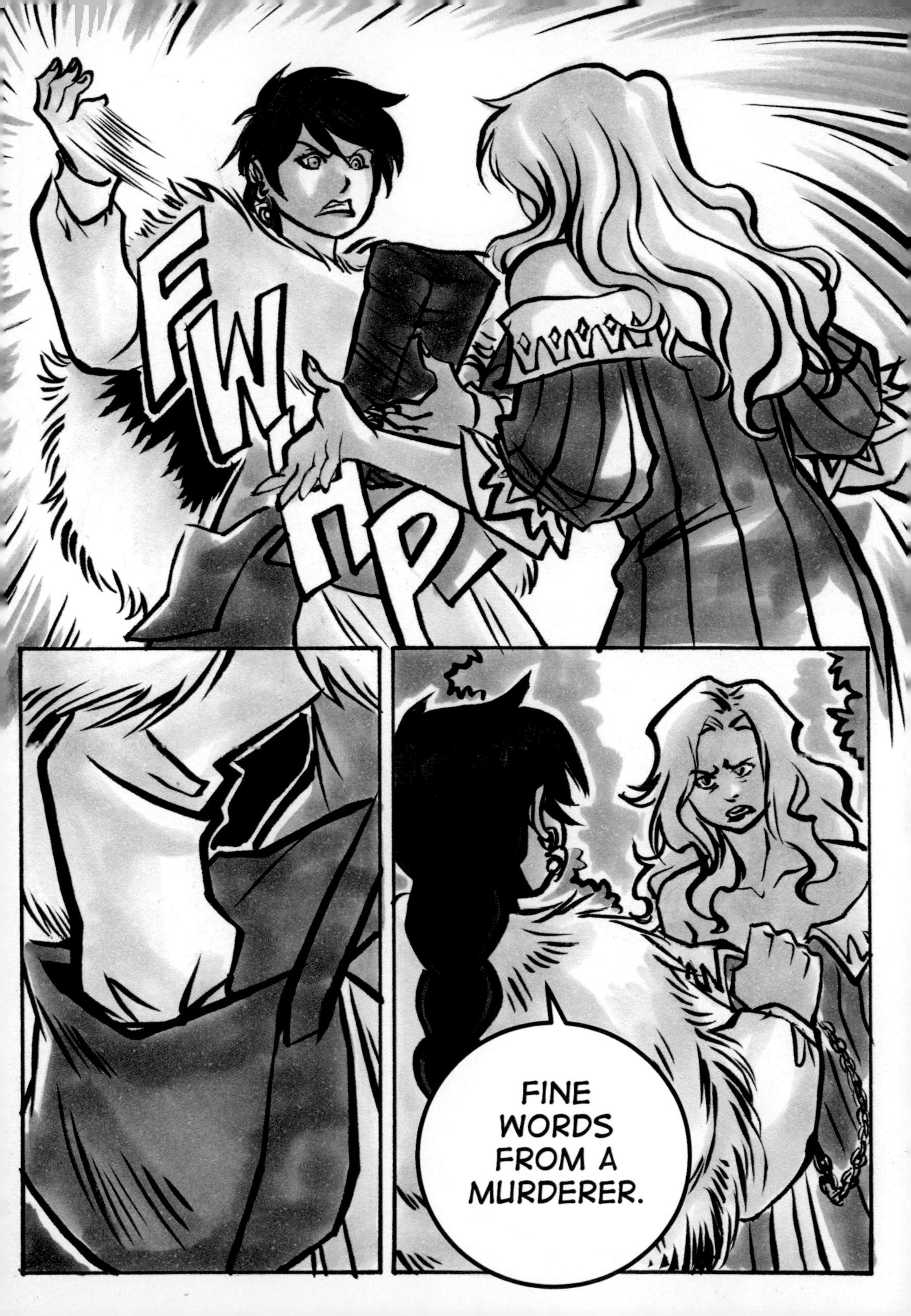
FWNP
FINE WORDS FROM A MURDERER.

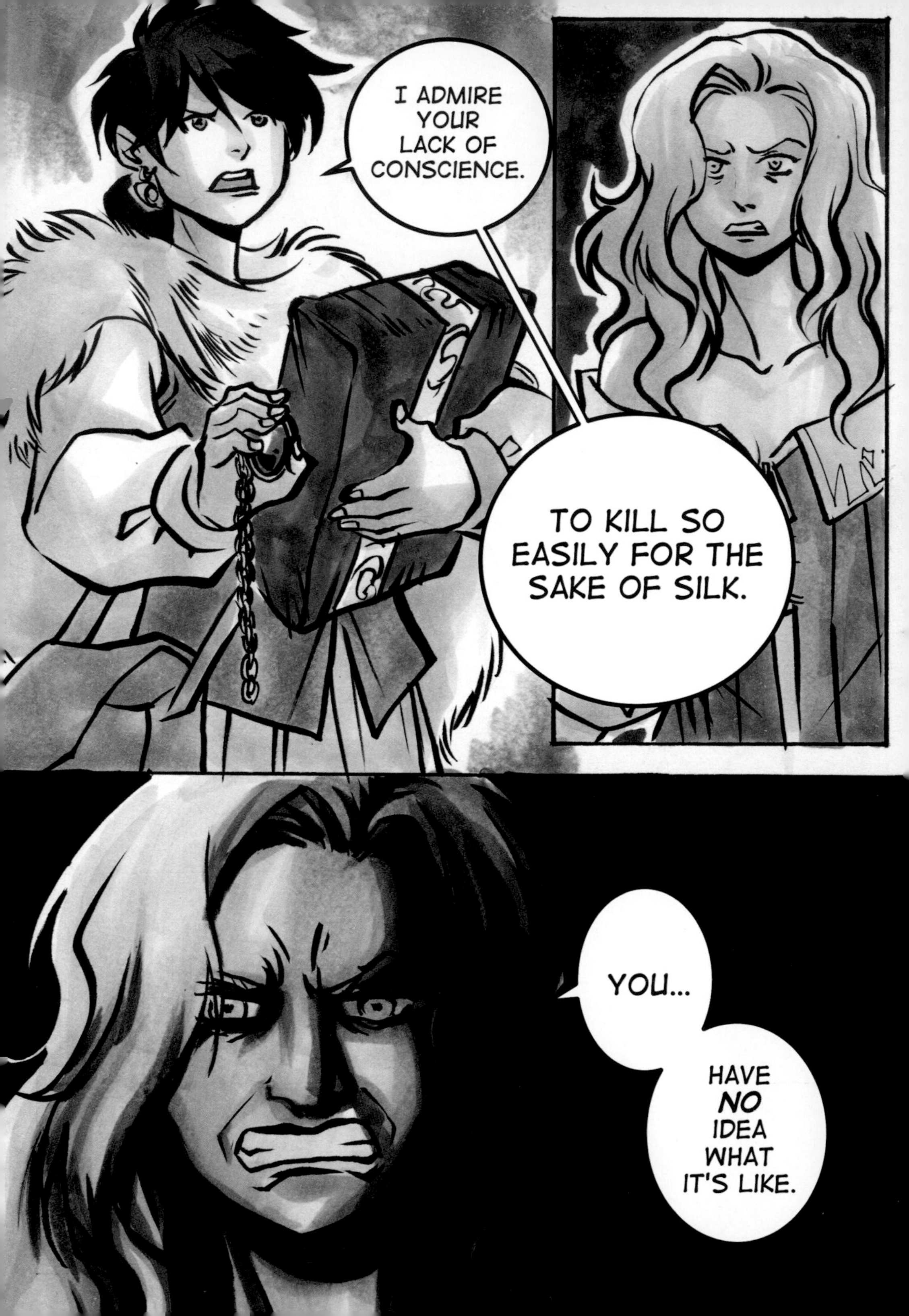
I ADMIRE YOUR LACK OF CONSCIENCE.
TO KILL SO EASILY FOR THE SAKE OF SILK.
YOU...
HAVE *NO* IDEA WHAT IT'S LIKE.

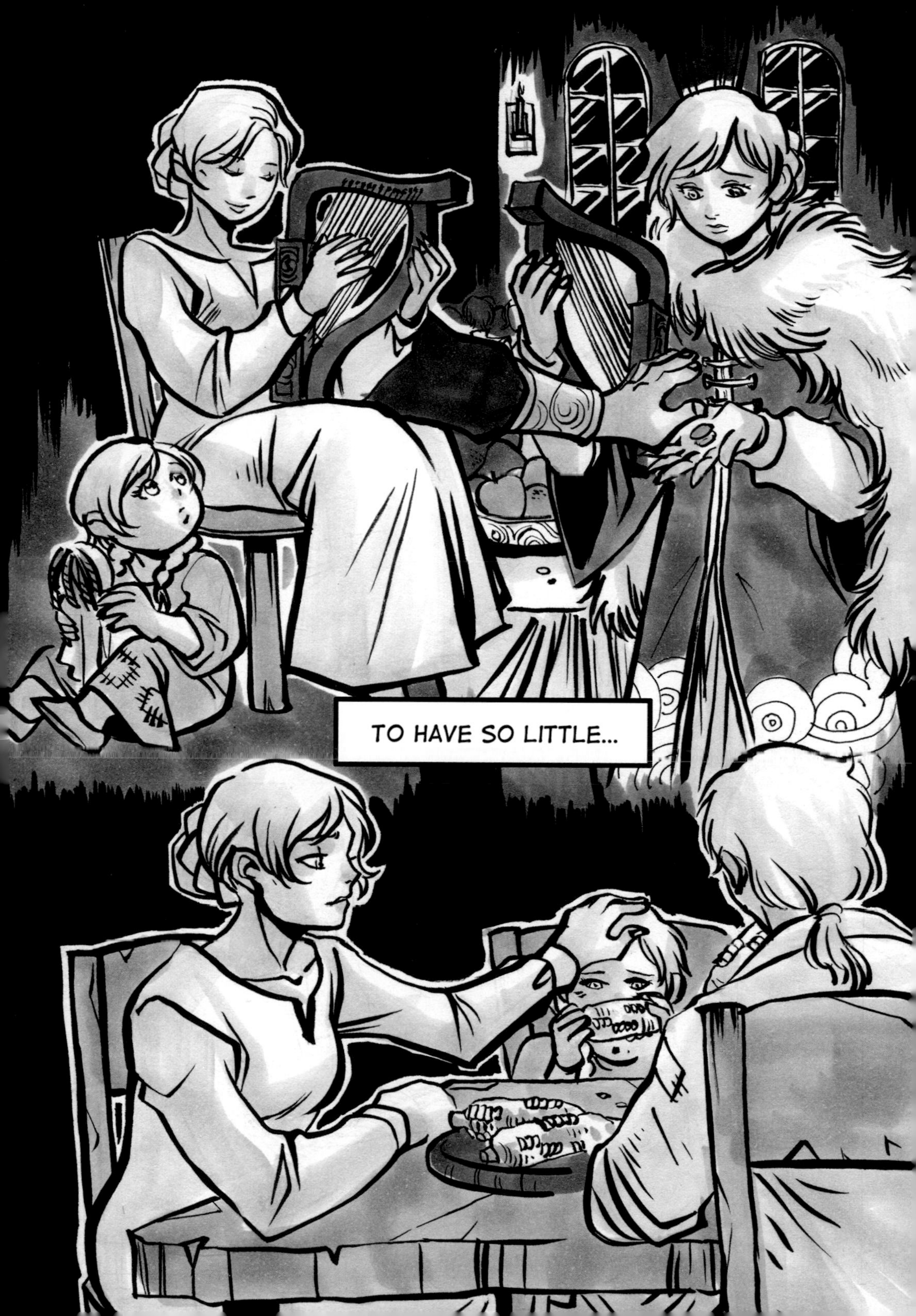
TO HAVE SO LITTLE...

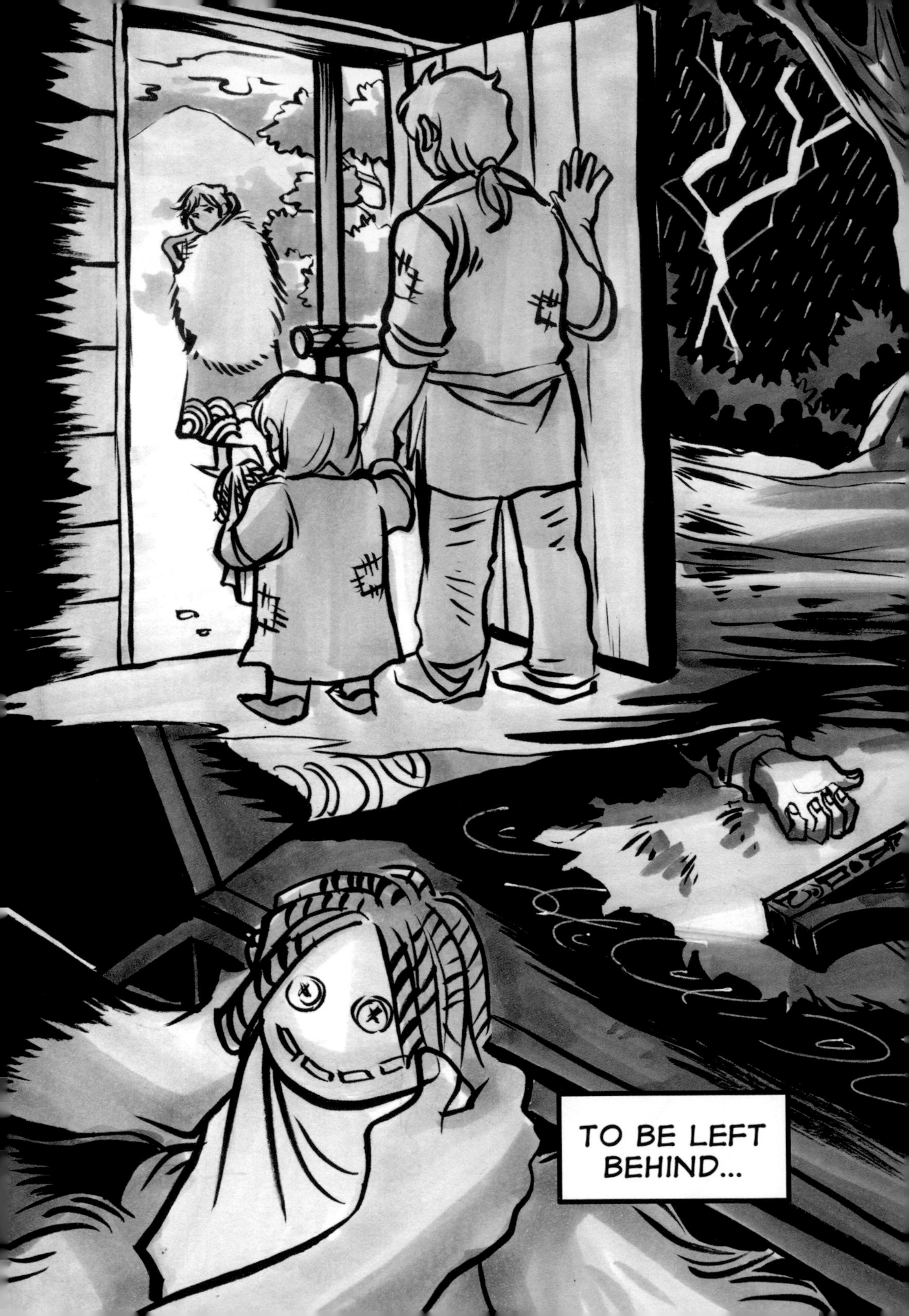
TO BE LEFT BEHIND...

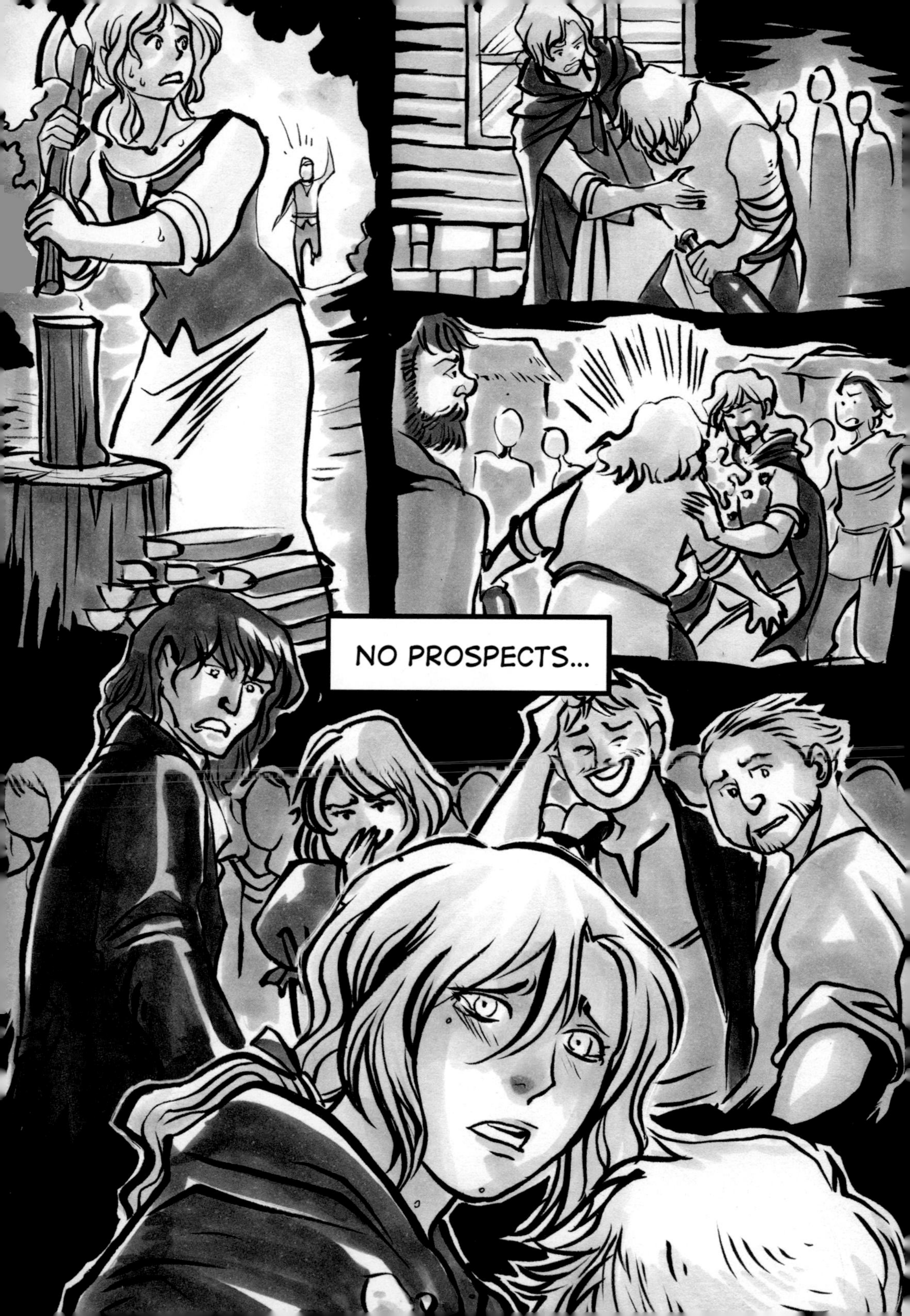
NO PROSPECTS...

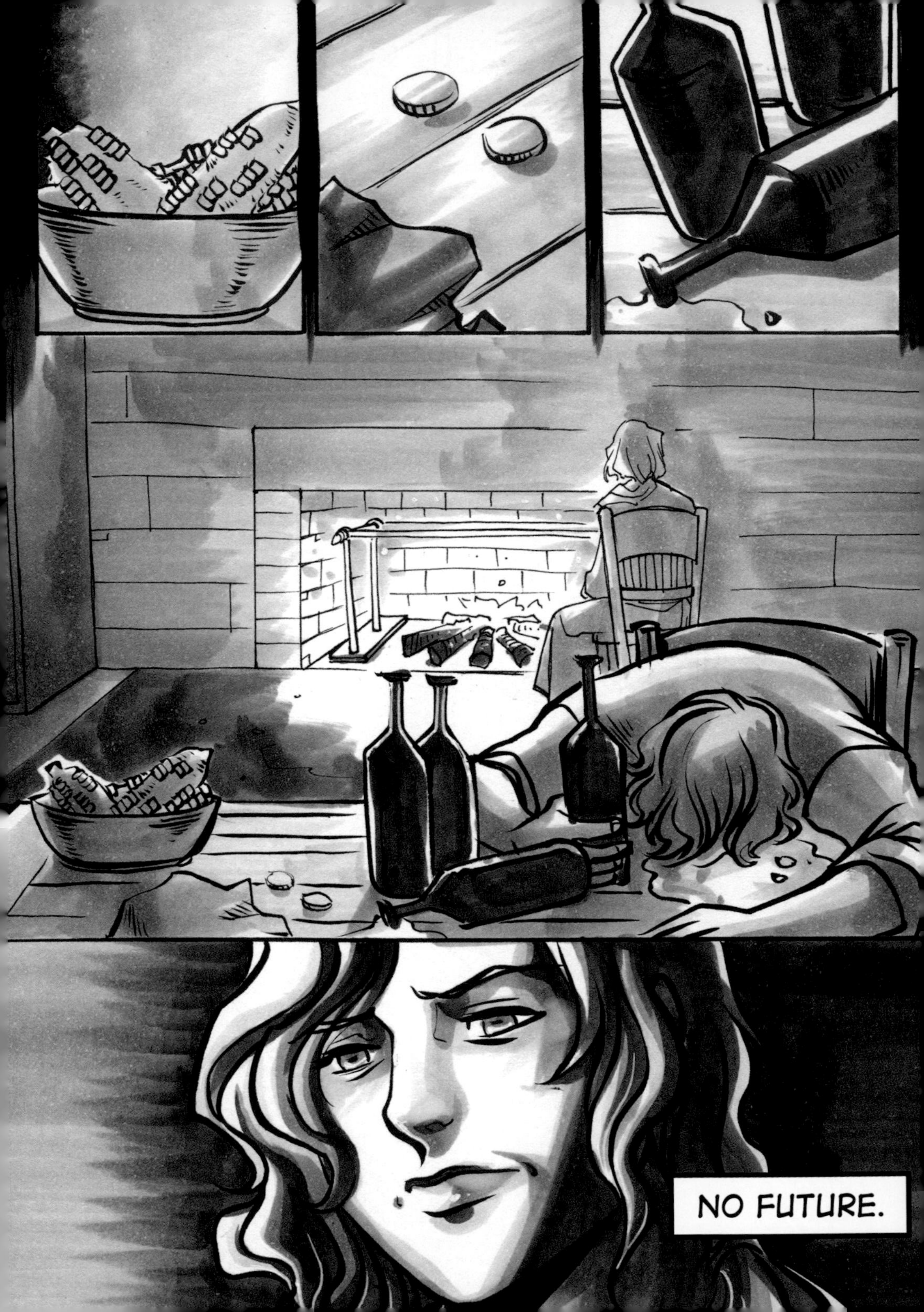
NO FUTURE.

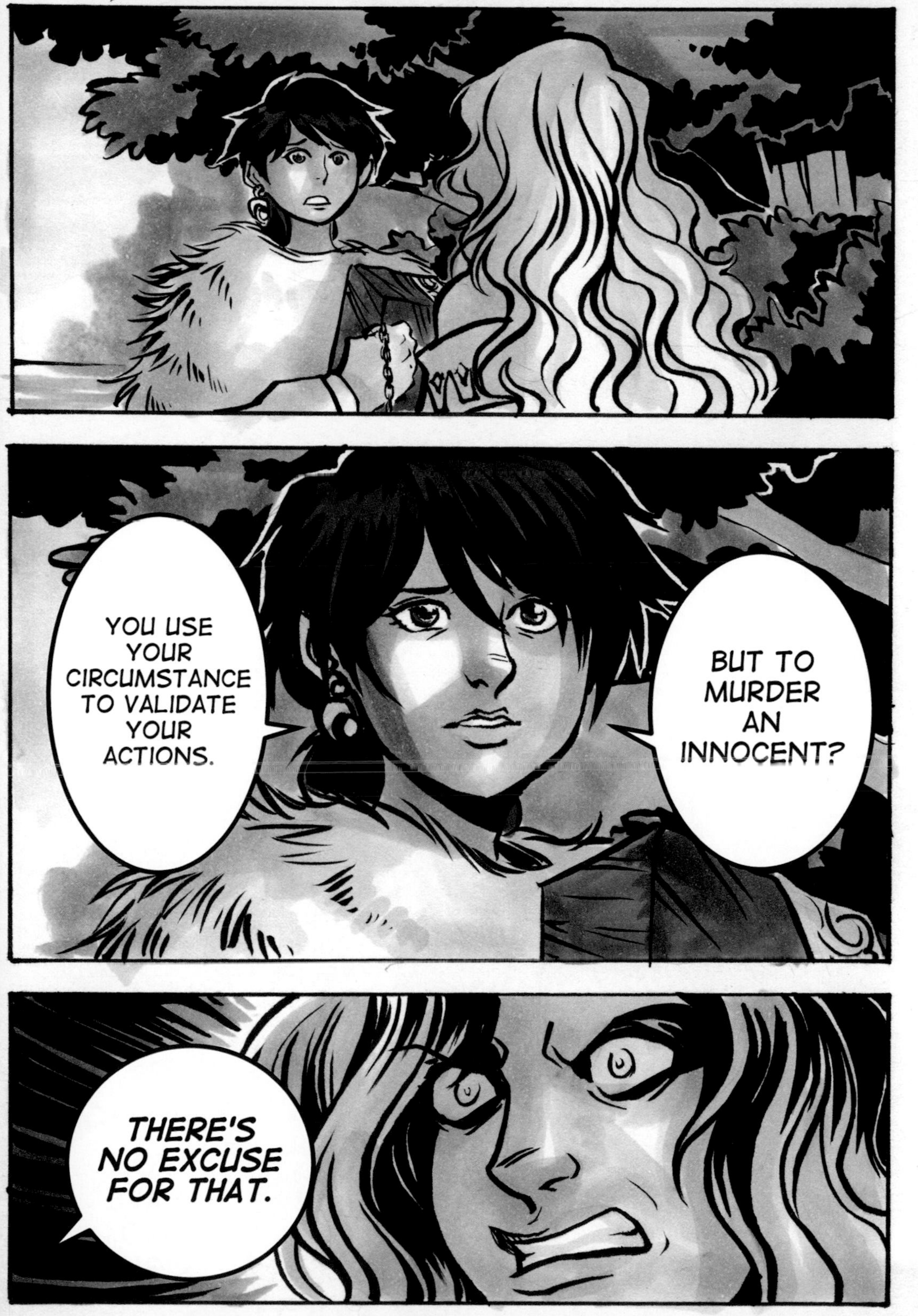
YOU USE YOUR CIRCUMSTANCE TO VALIDATE YOUR ACTIONS.
BUT TO MURDER AN INNOCENT?
THERE'S NO EXCUSE FOR THAT.

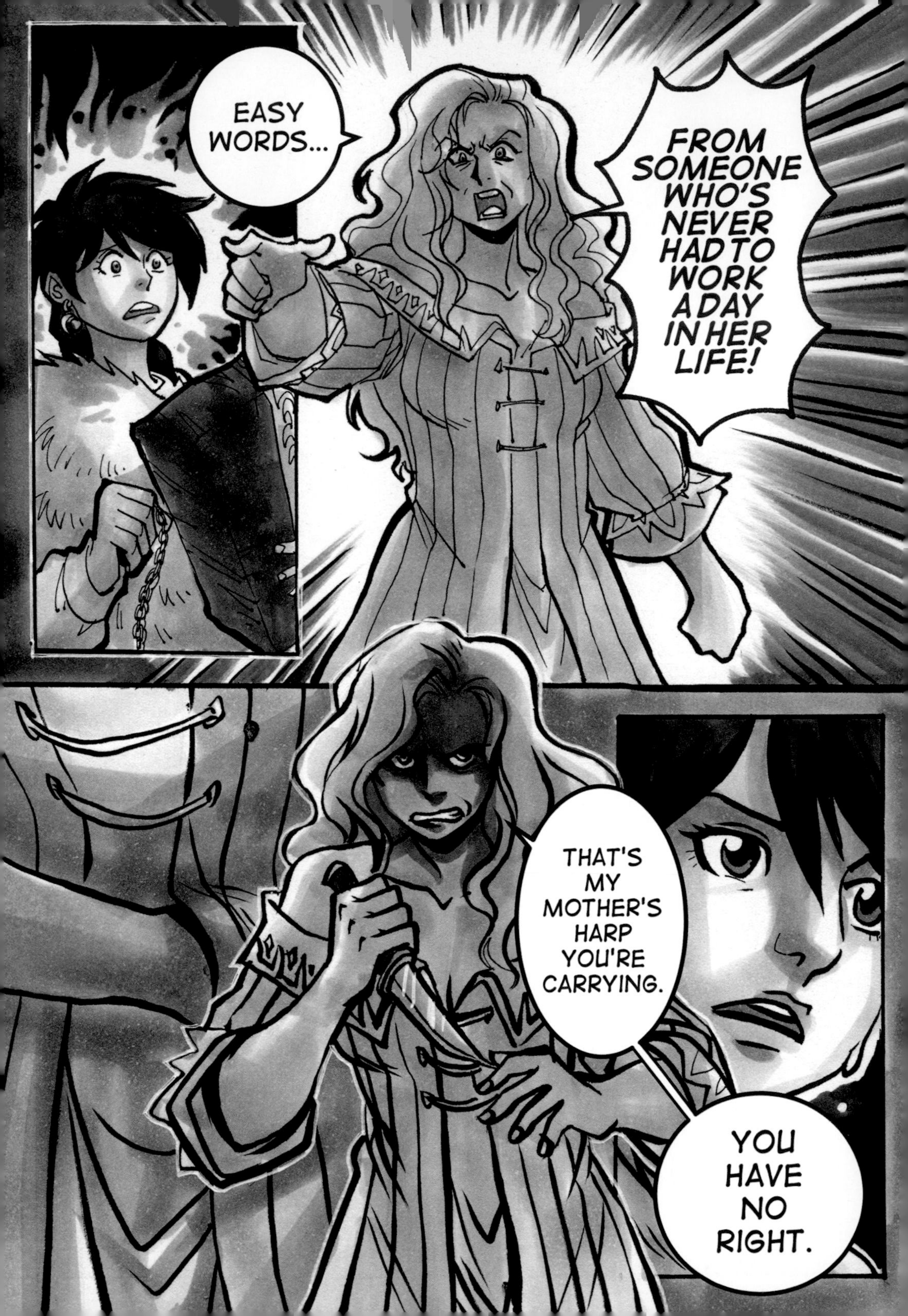
EASY WORDS...
FROM SOMEONE WHO'S NEVER HAD TO WORK A DAY IN HER LIFE!
THAT'S MY MOTHER'S HARP YOU'RE CARRYING.
YOU HAVE NO RIGHT.

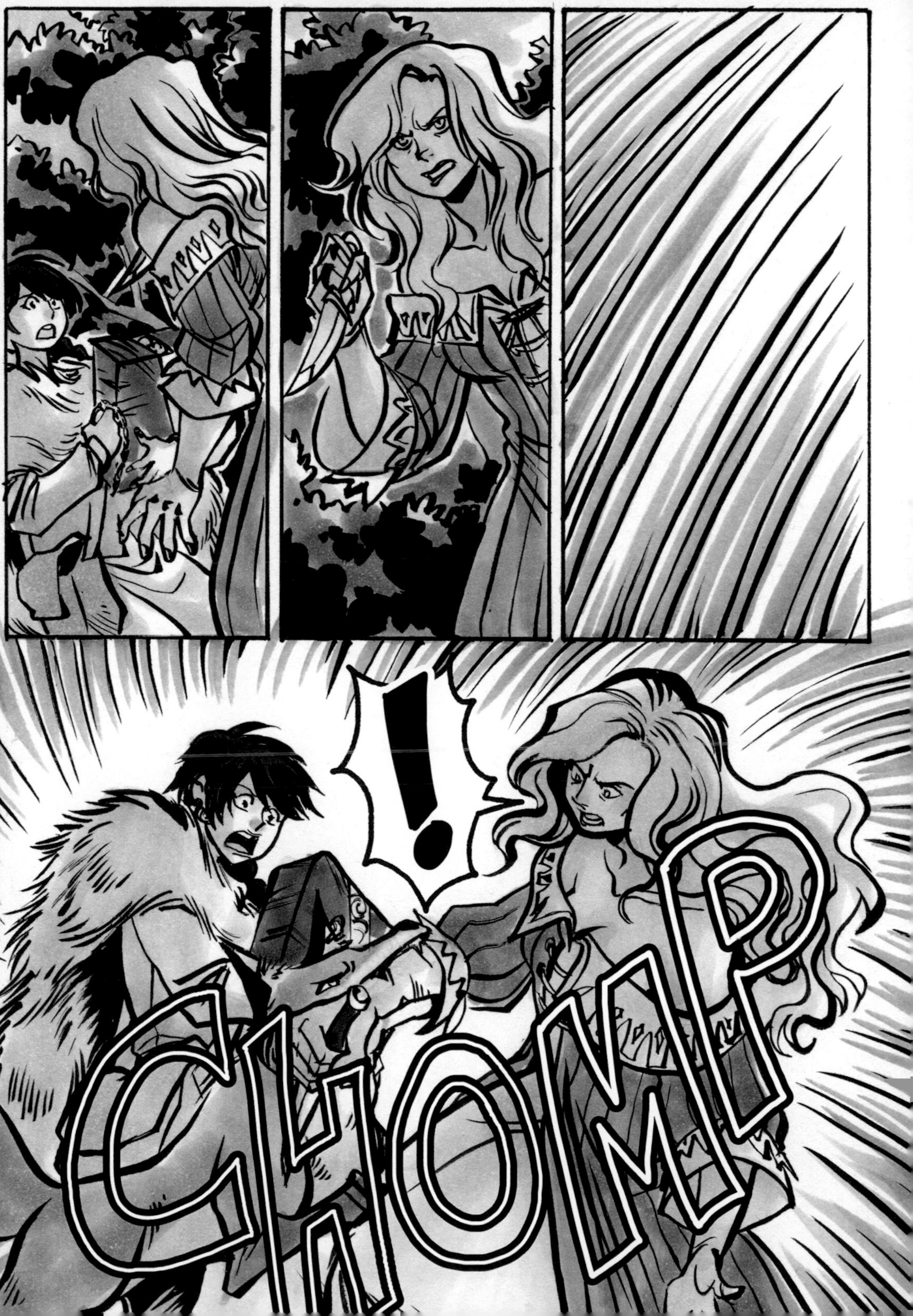
!
CHOMP

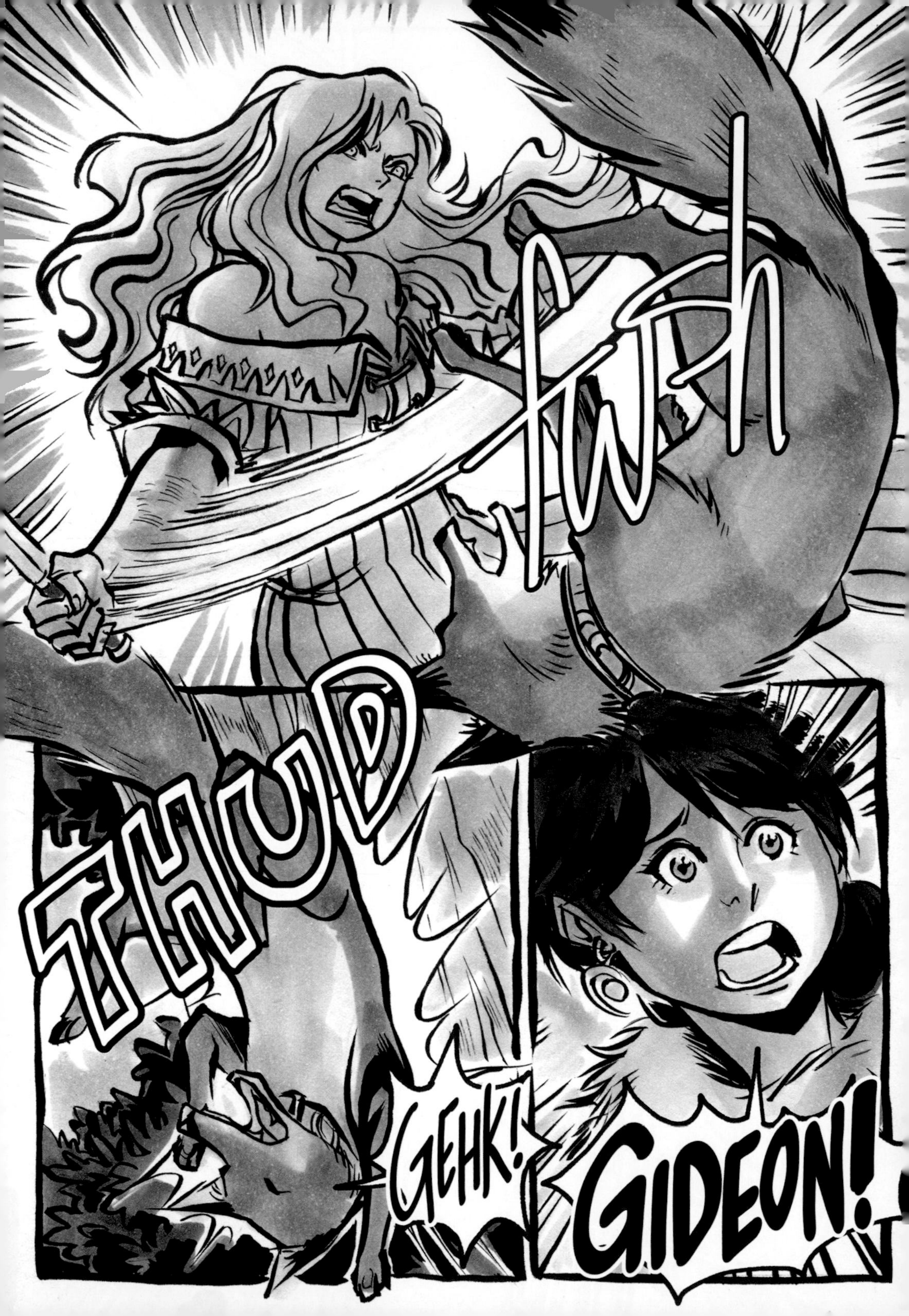
fwish
THUD
GEHK!
GIDEON!

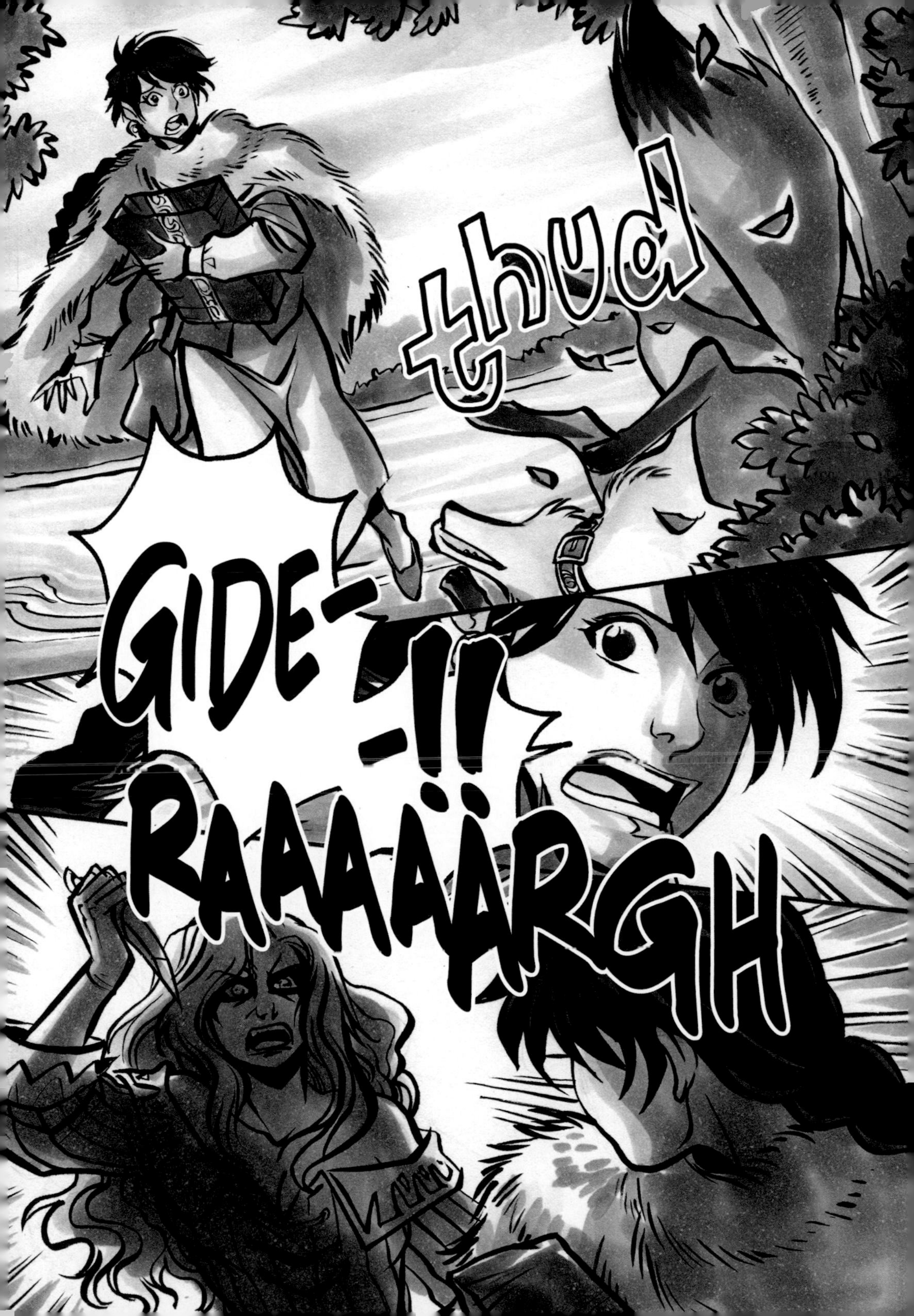
thud
GIDE--!!
RAAAAÄRGH

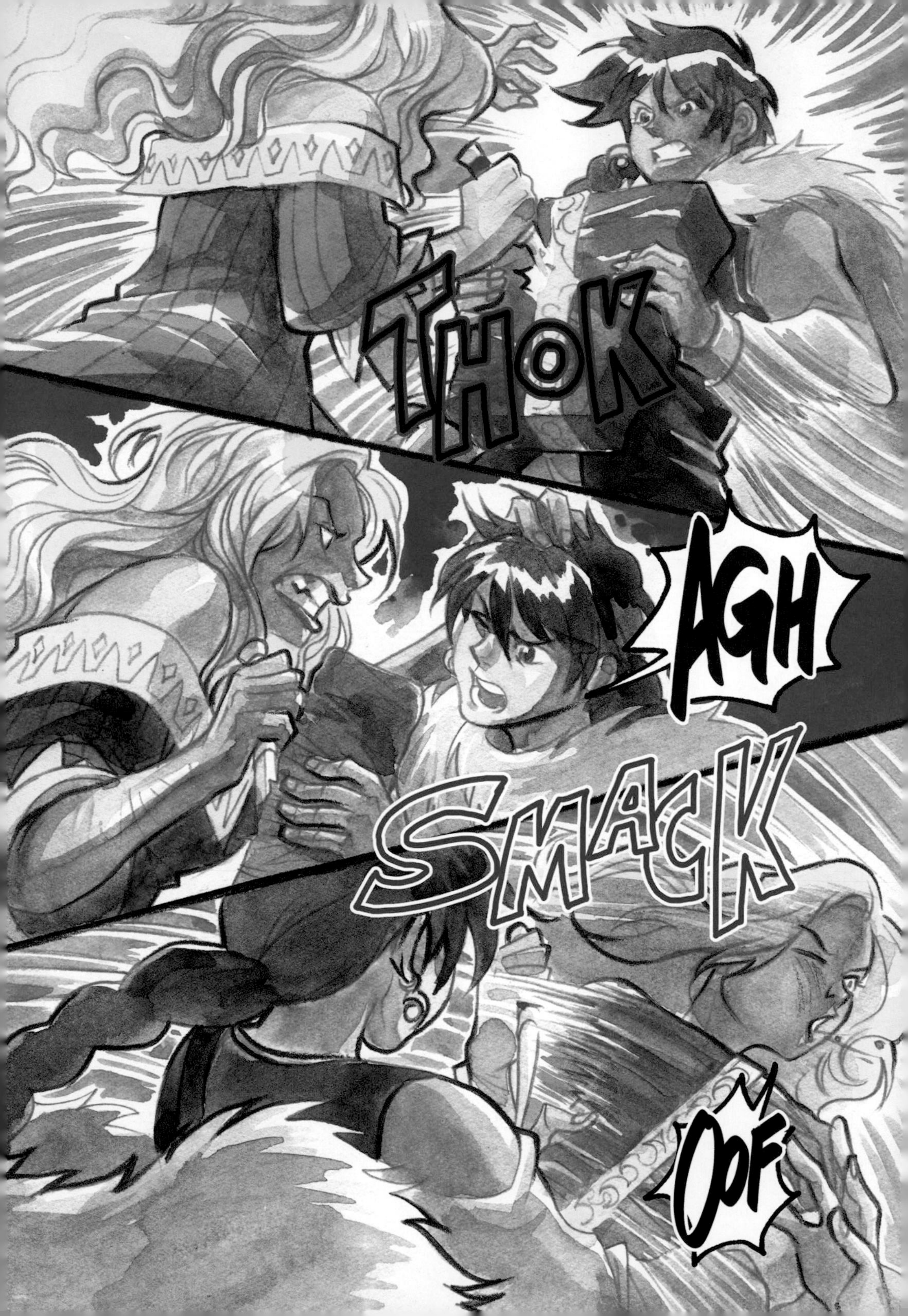
THOK
AGH
SMACK
OOF

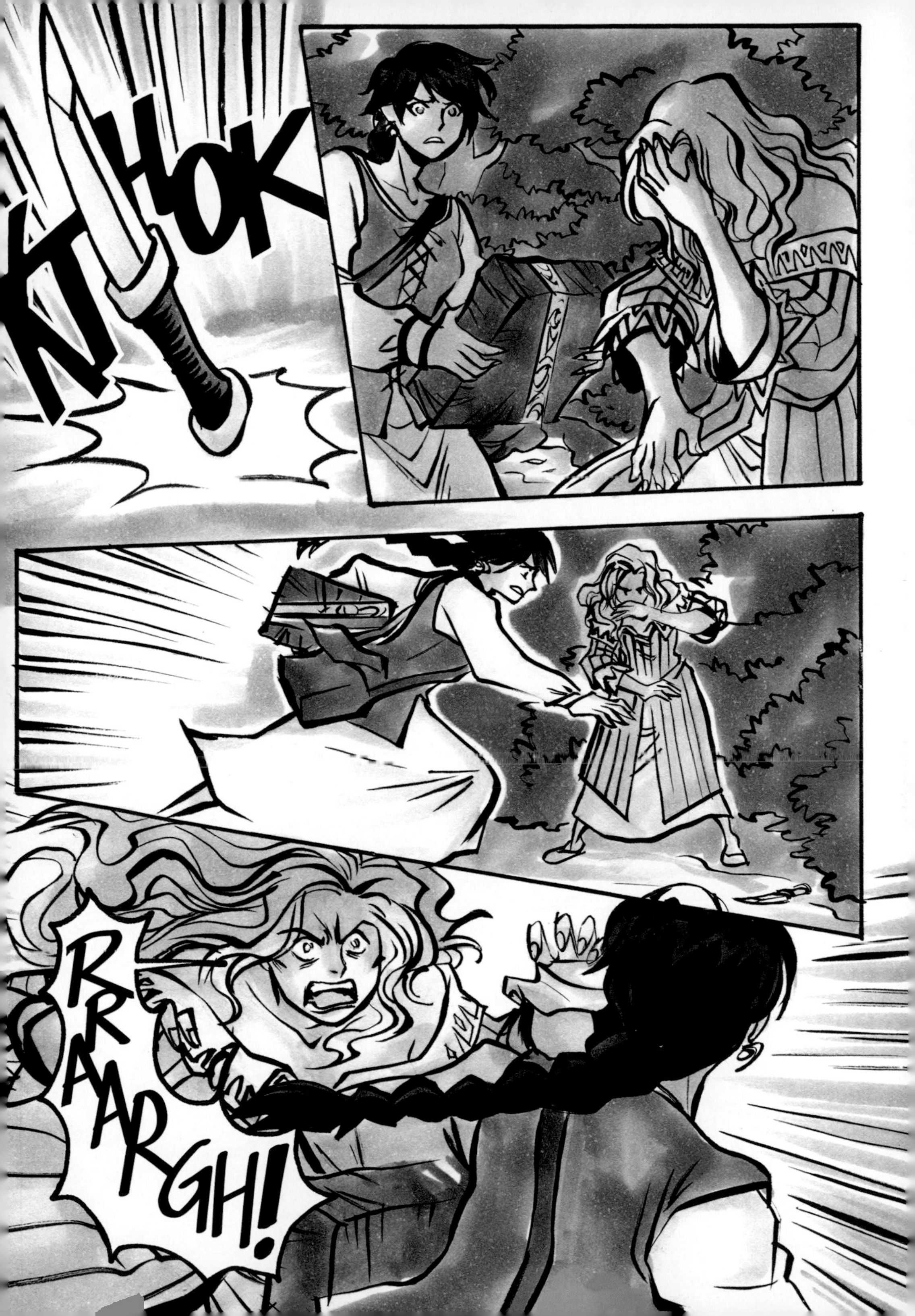

KTHOK
RRRAARGH!

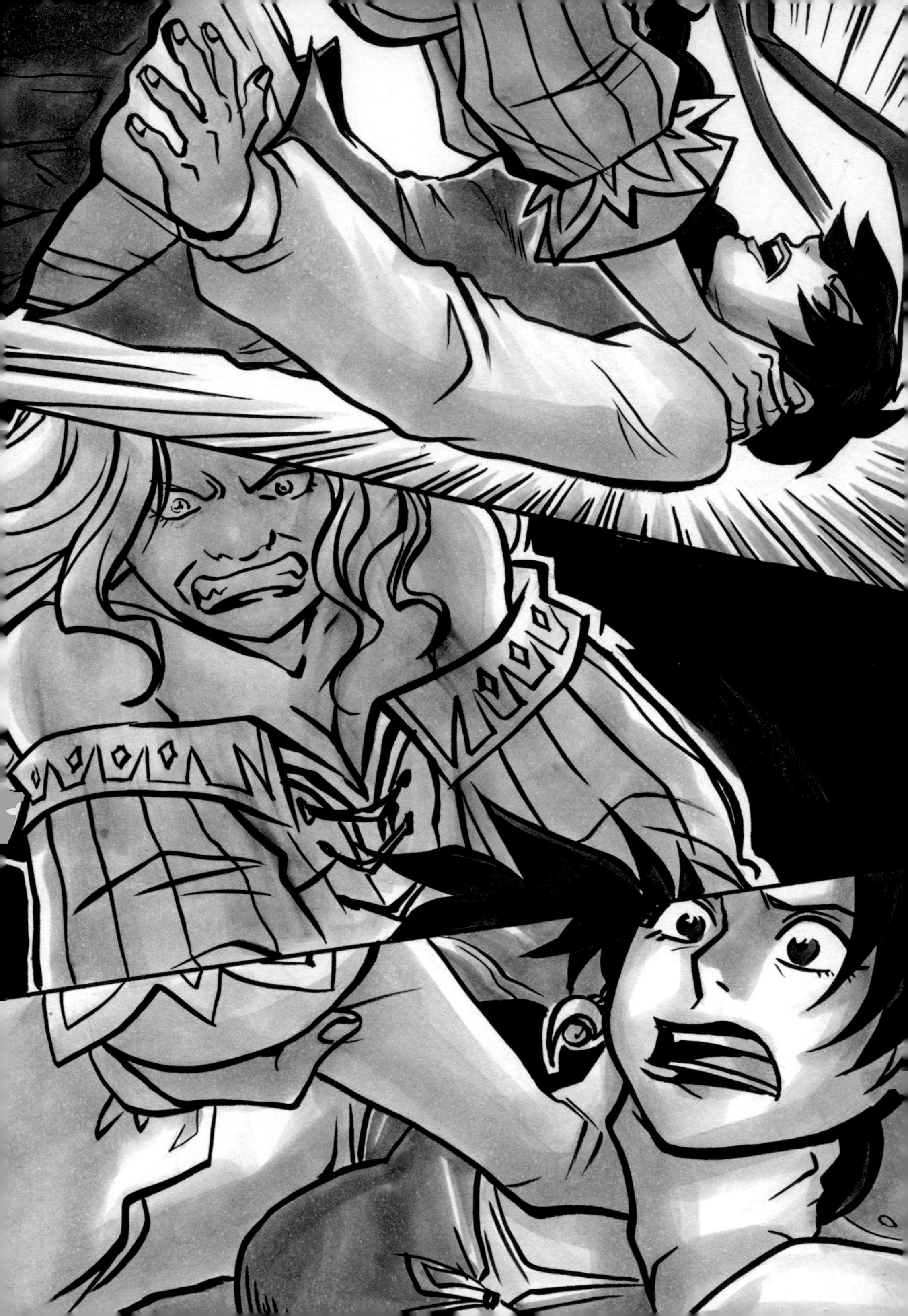

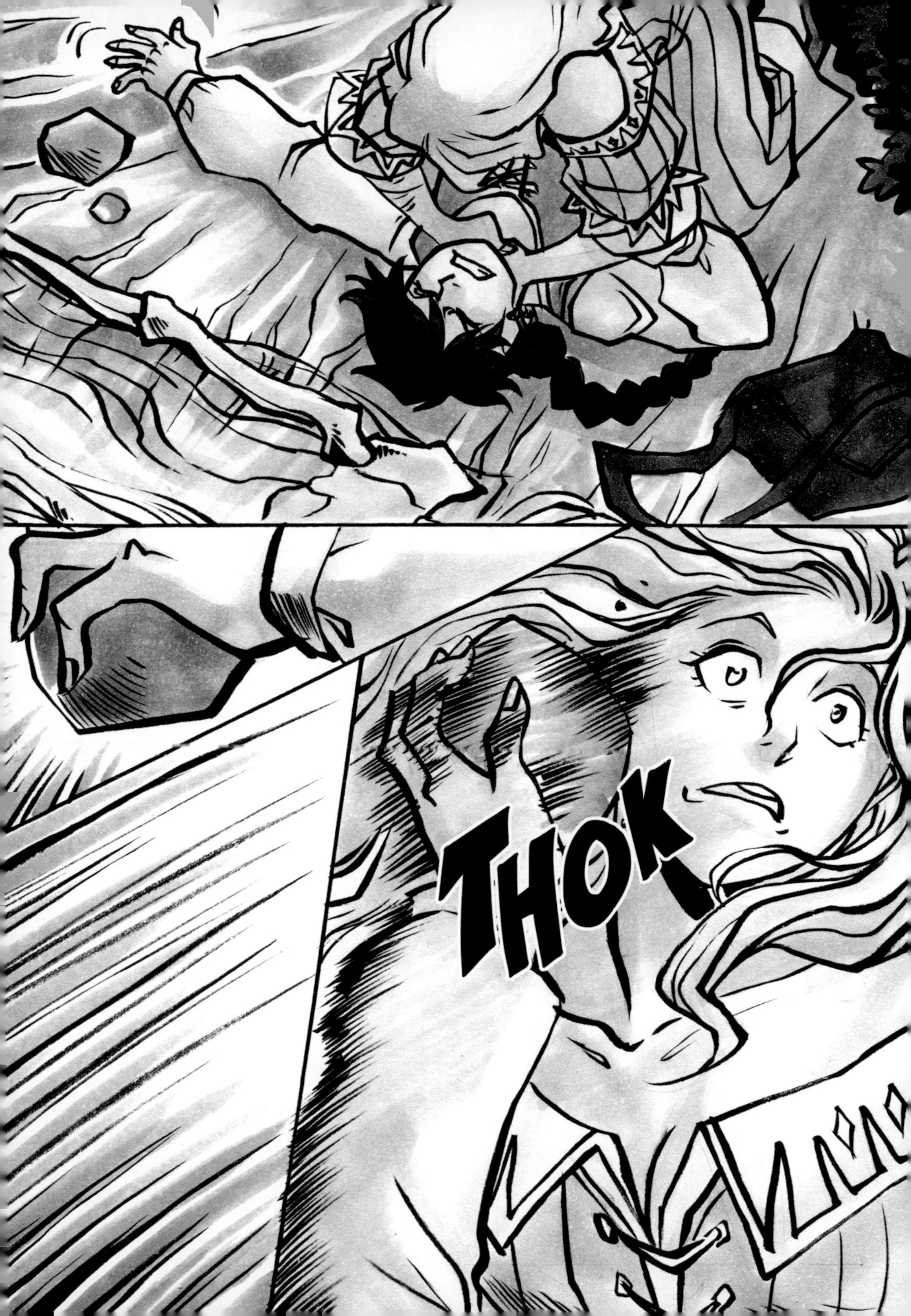
THOK

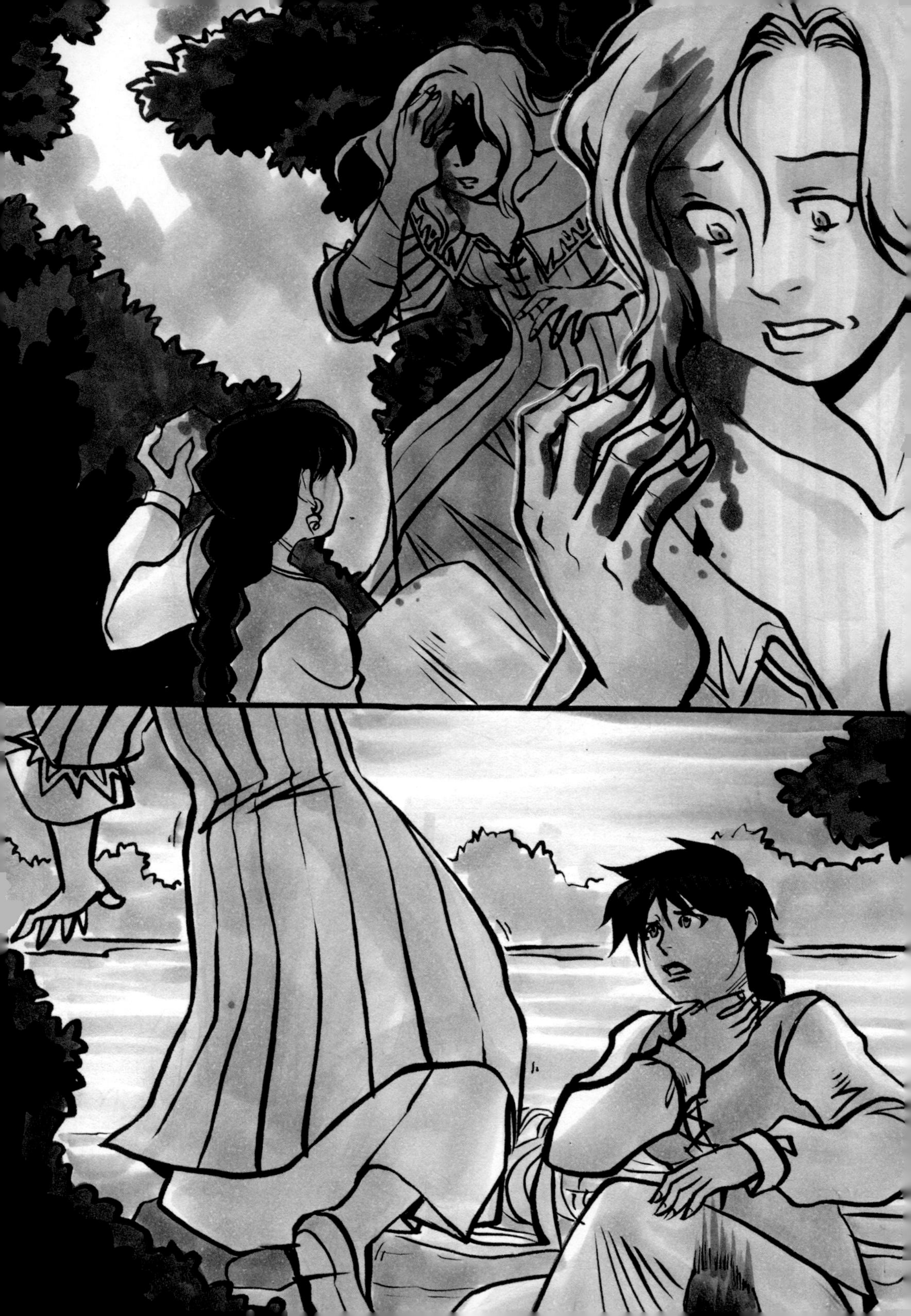

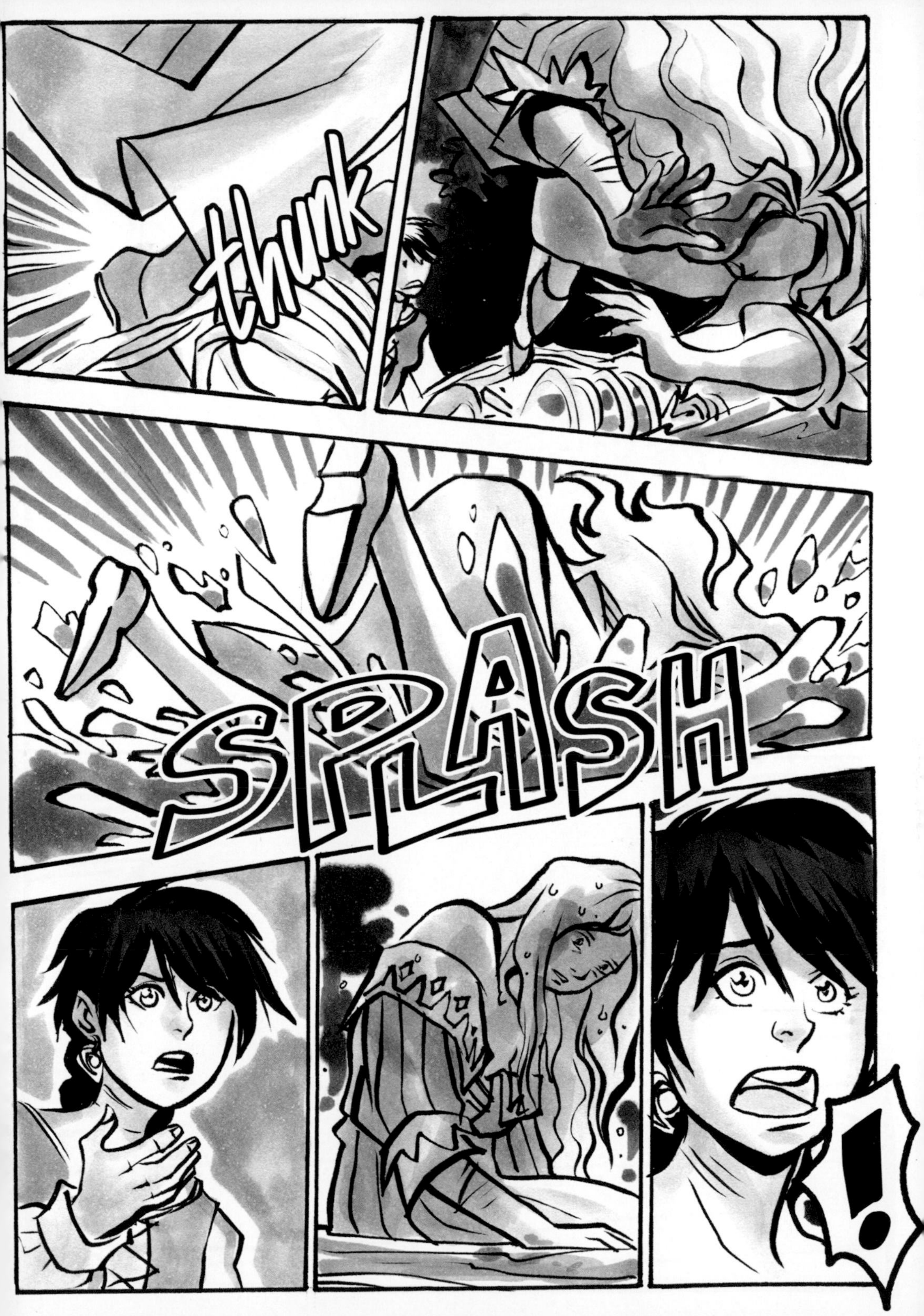
thunk
SPLASH
!

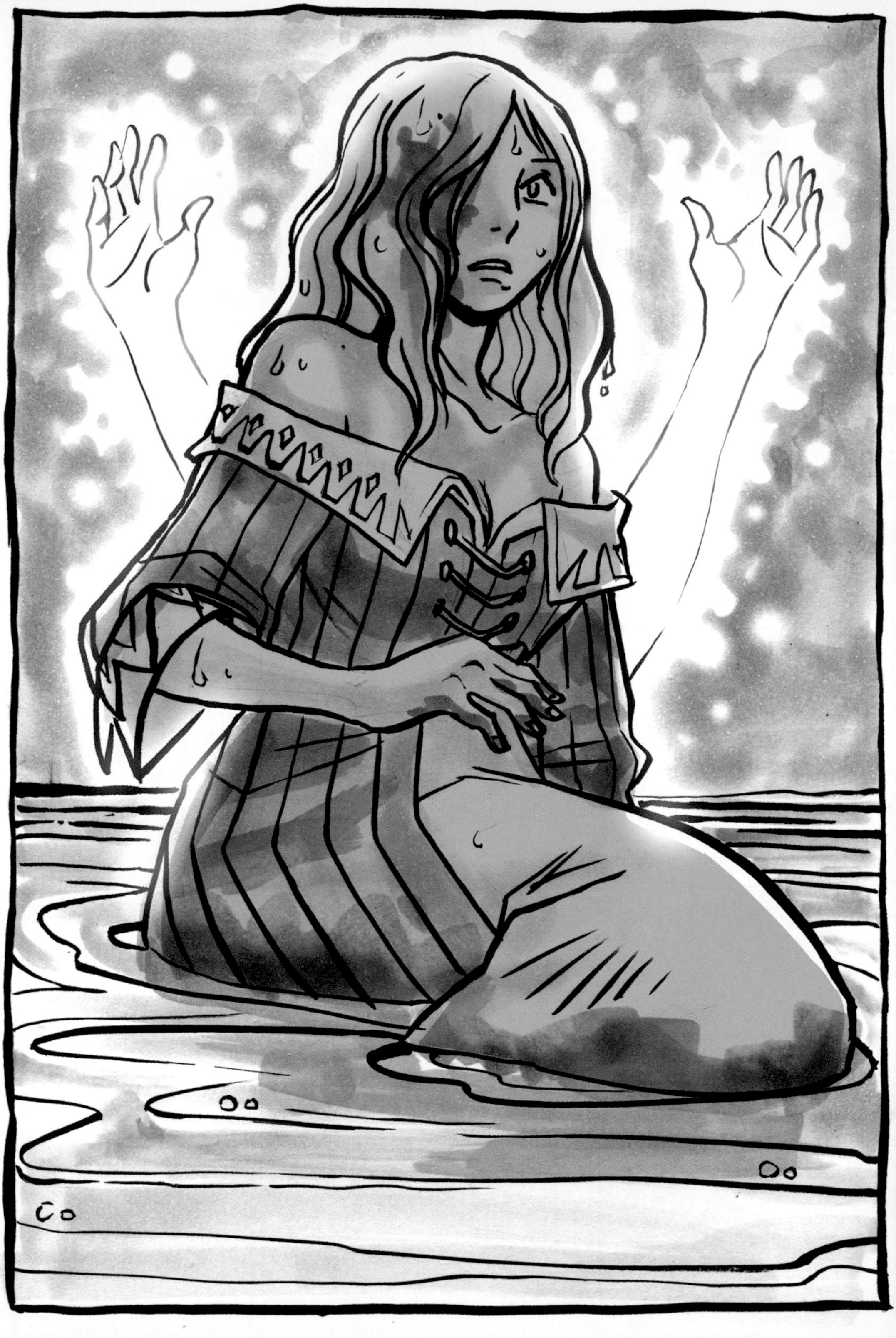

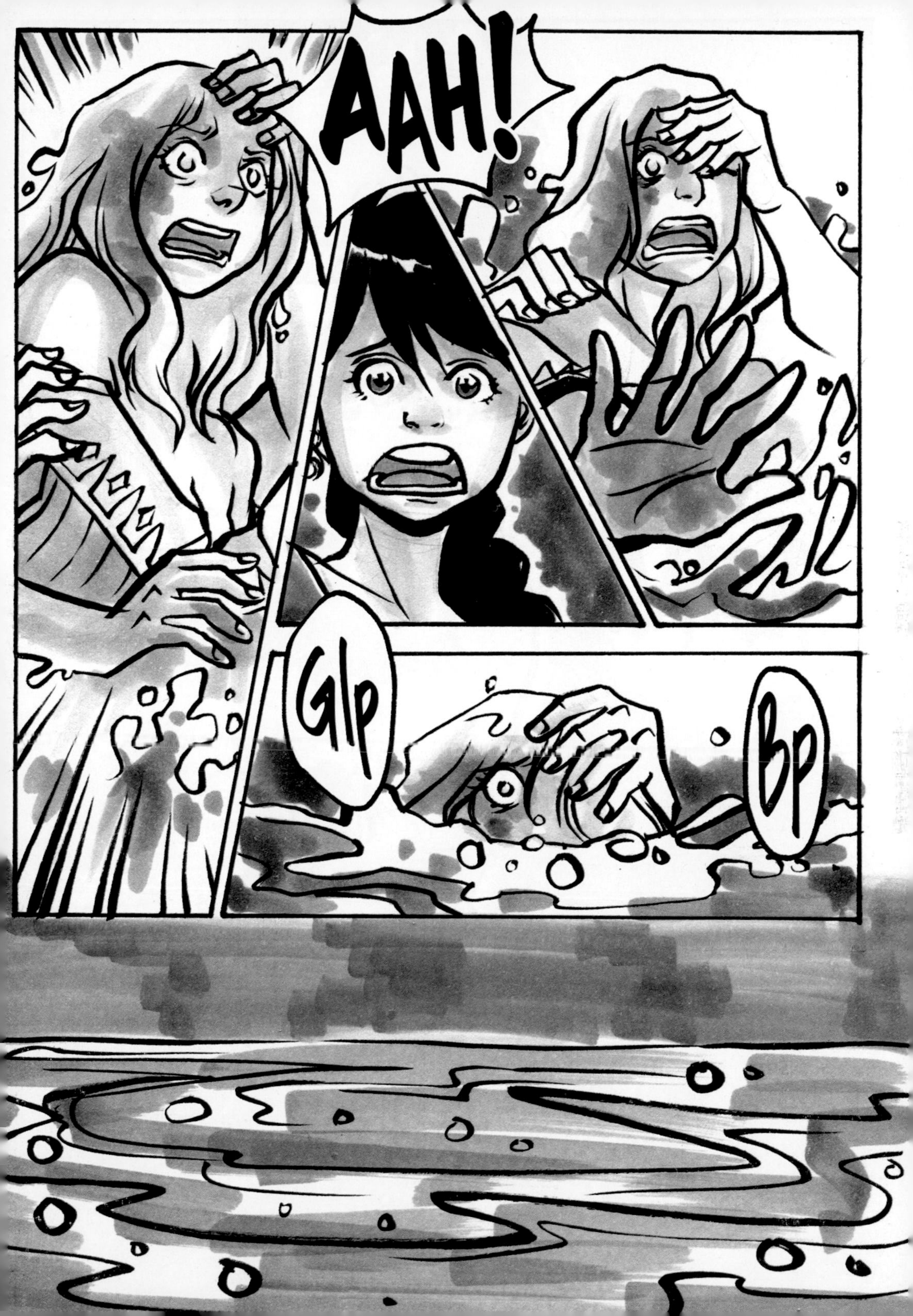
AAH!
Glp
Bp

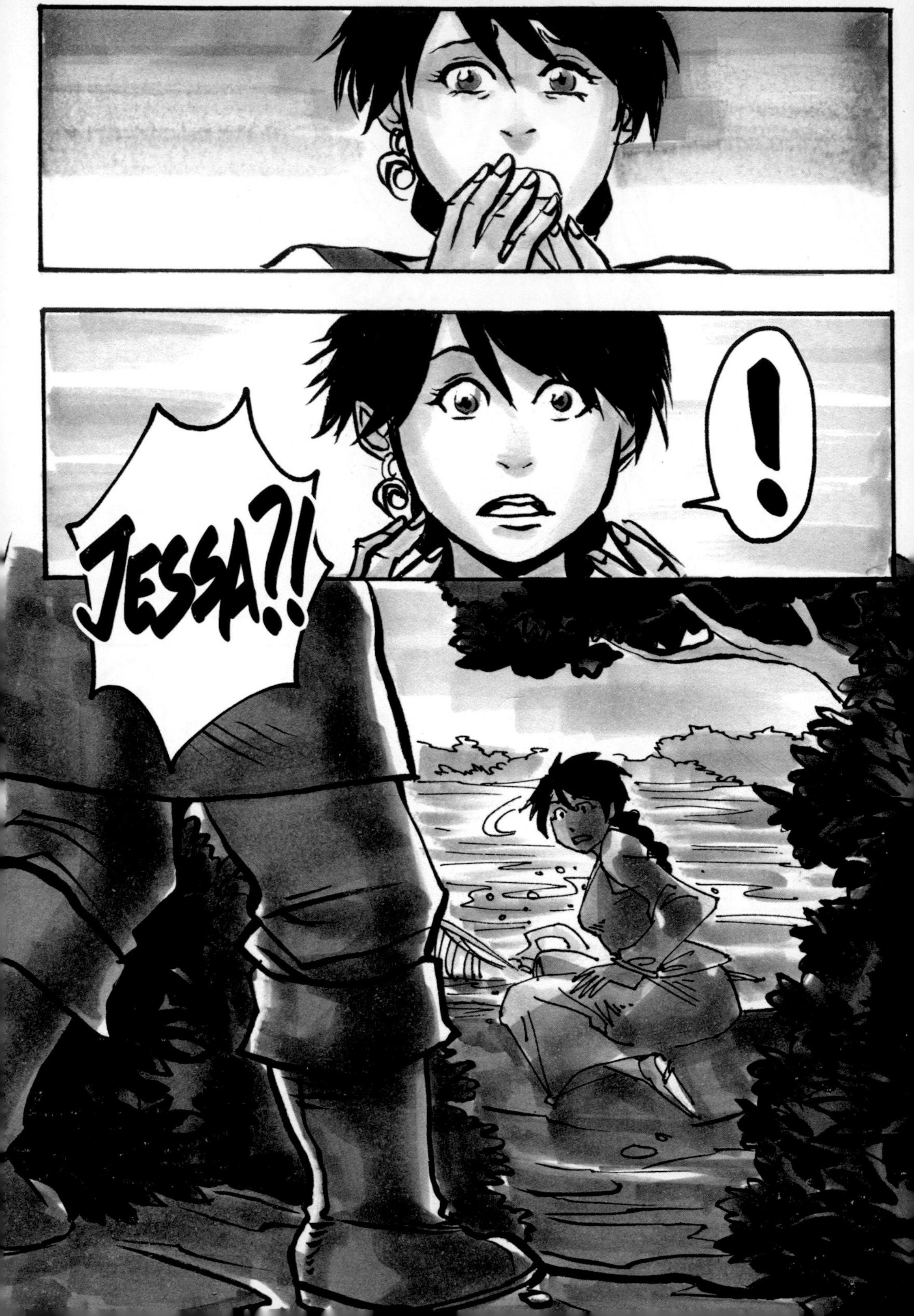
!
JESSA?!

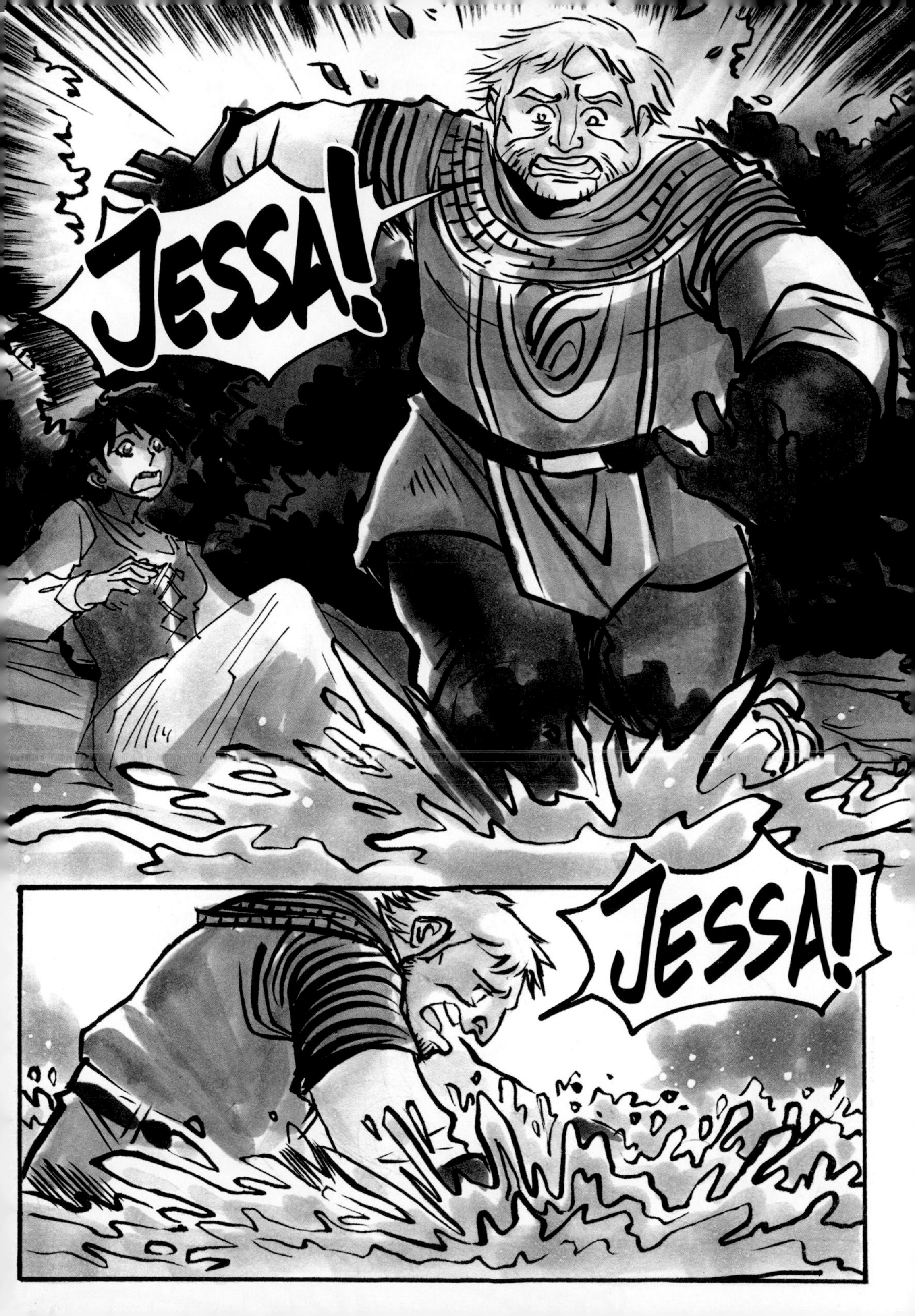
JESSA!
JESSA!

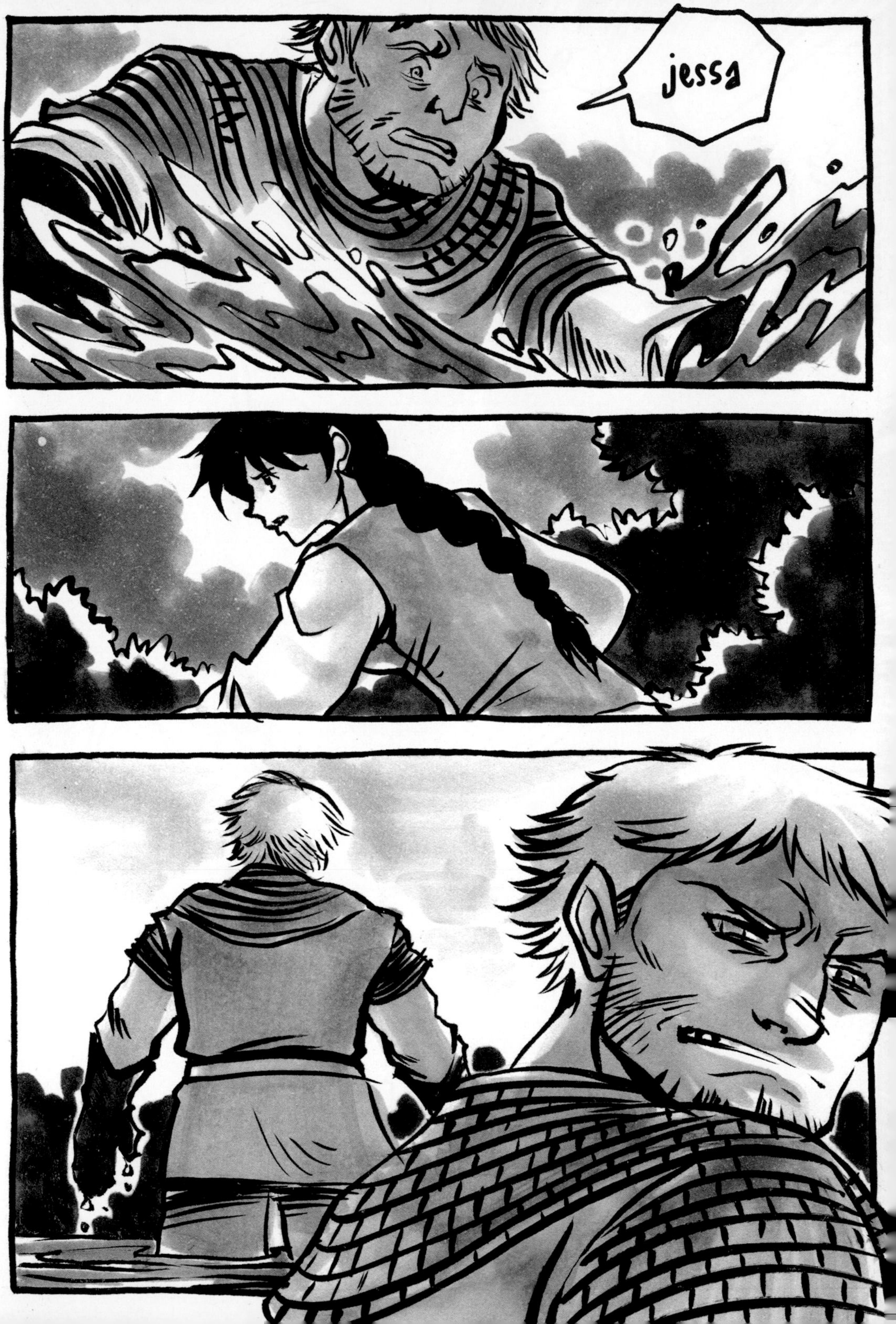
jessa

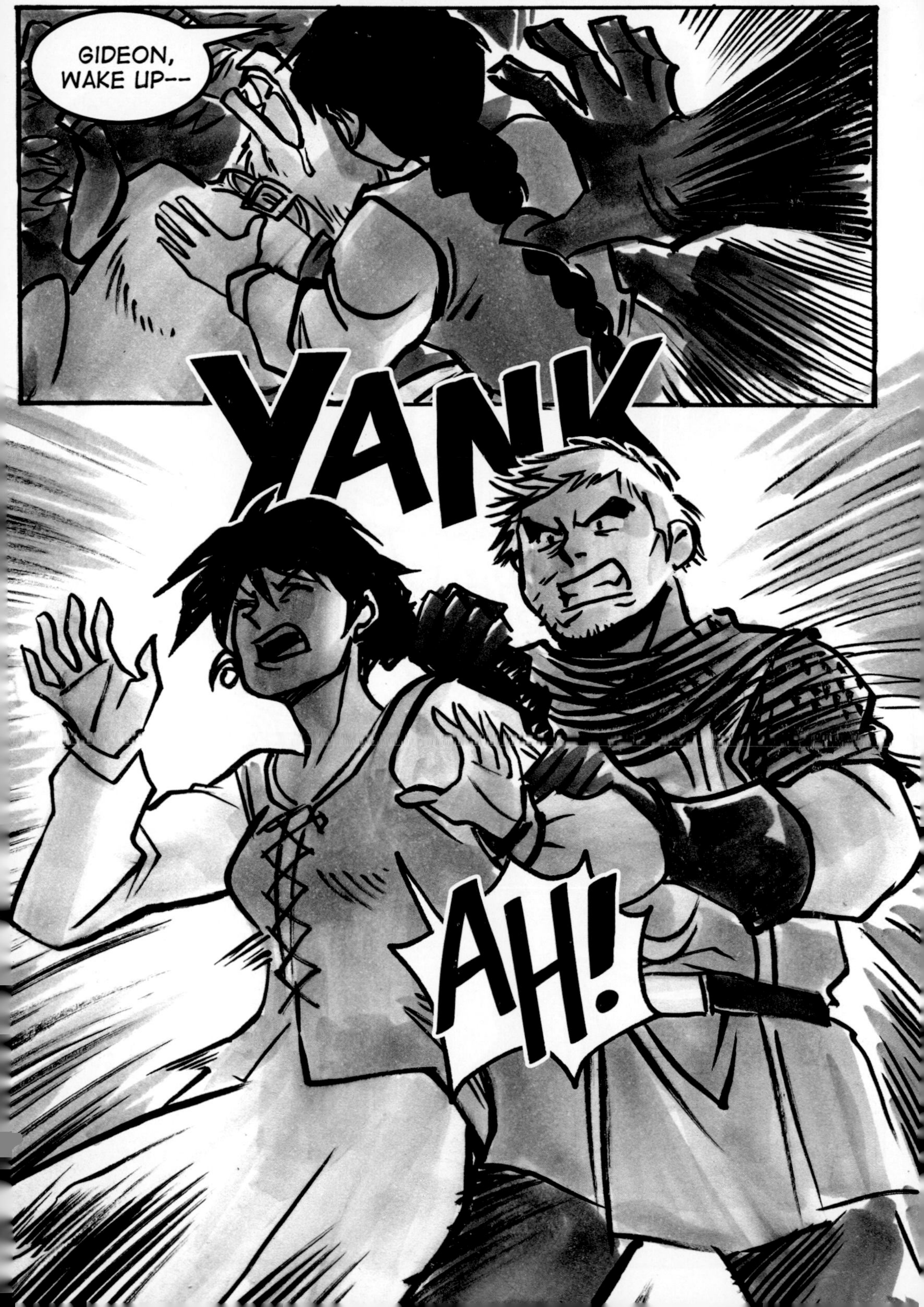
GIDEON, WAKE UP--
YANK
AH!

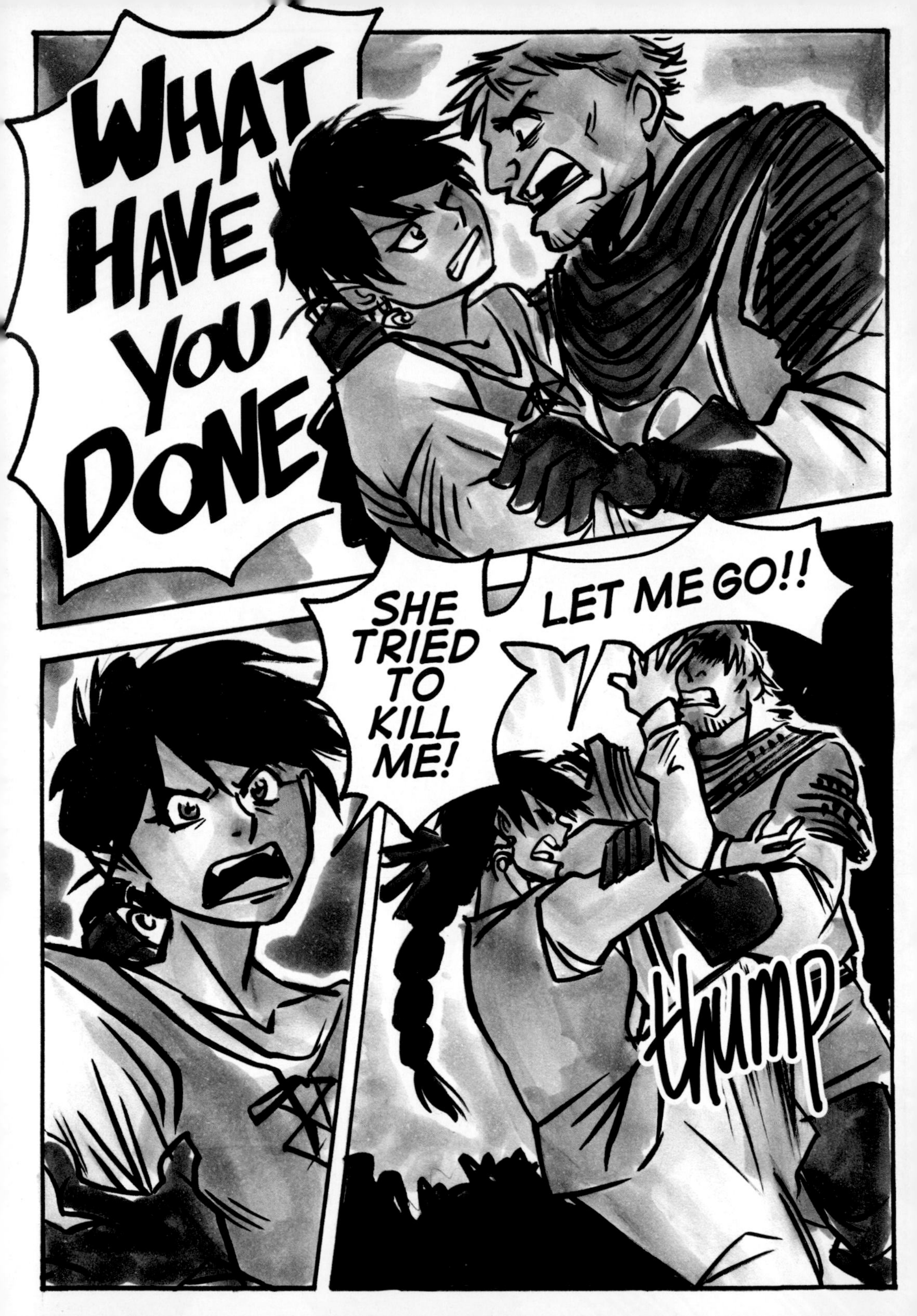
WHAT HAVE YOU DONE
SHE TRIED TO KILL ME!
LET ME GO!!
thump

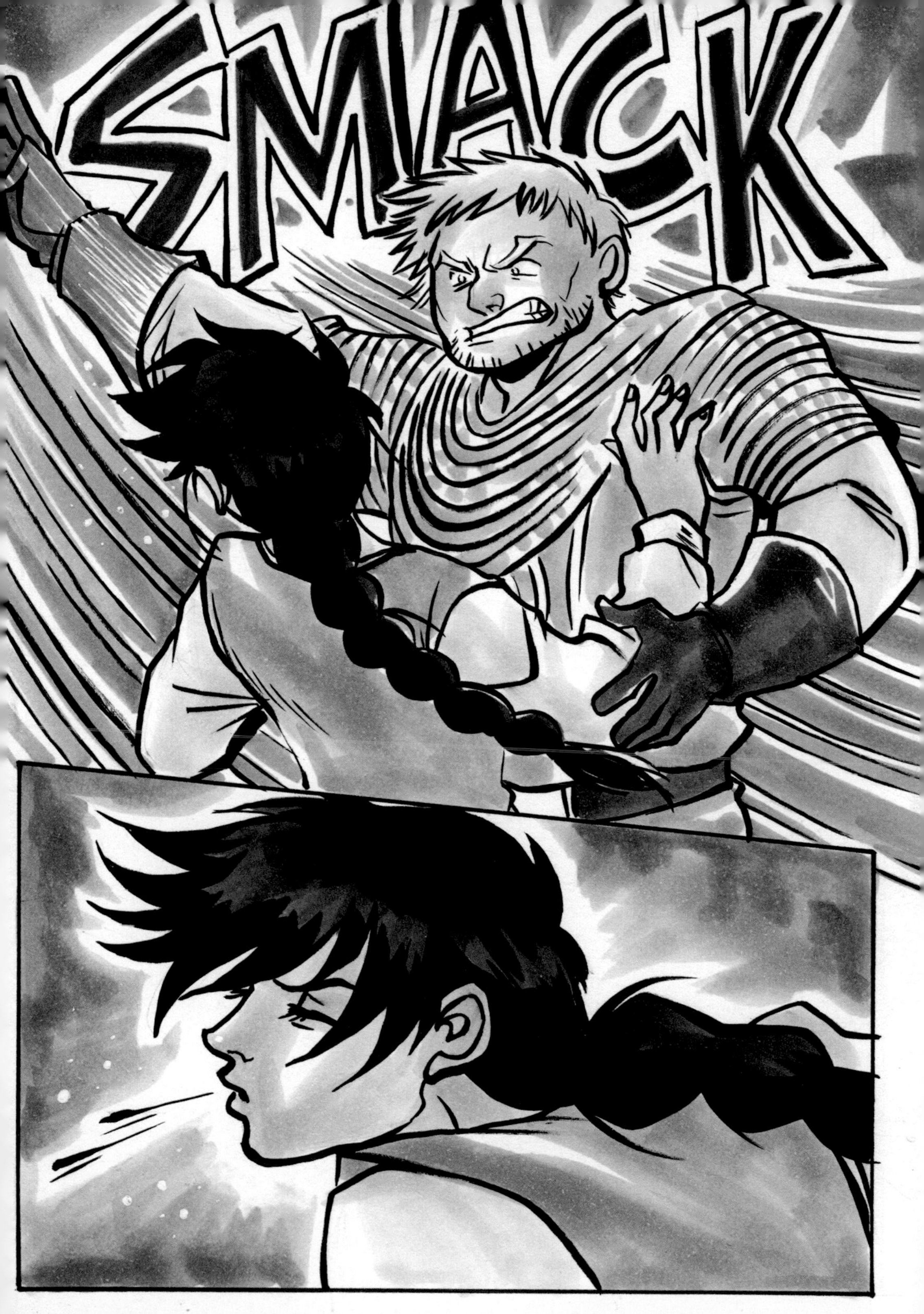
SMACK

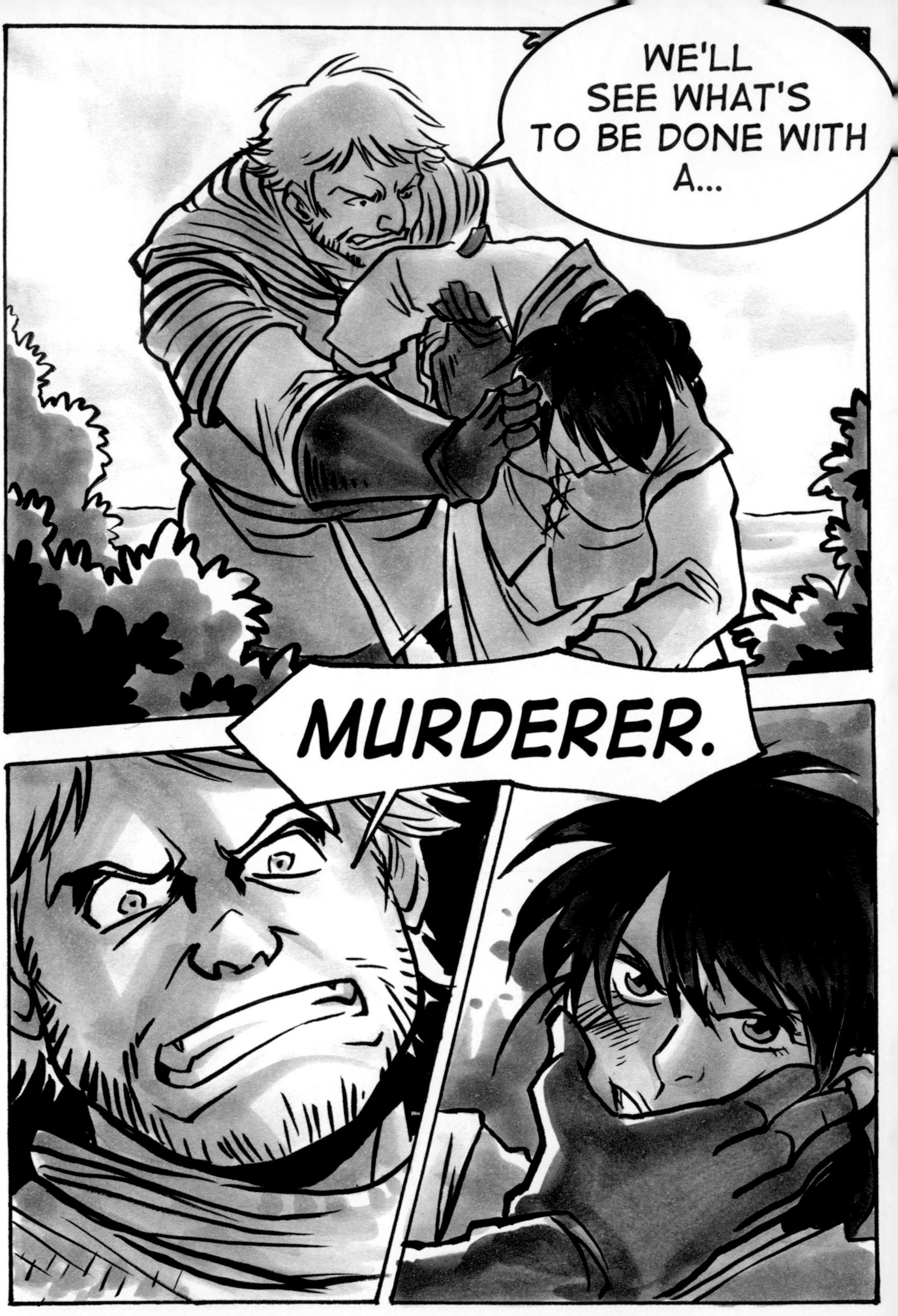
WE'LL SEE WHAT'S TO BE DONE WITH A...
MURDERER.

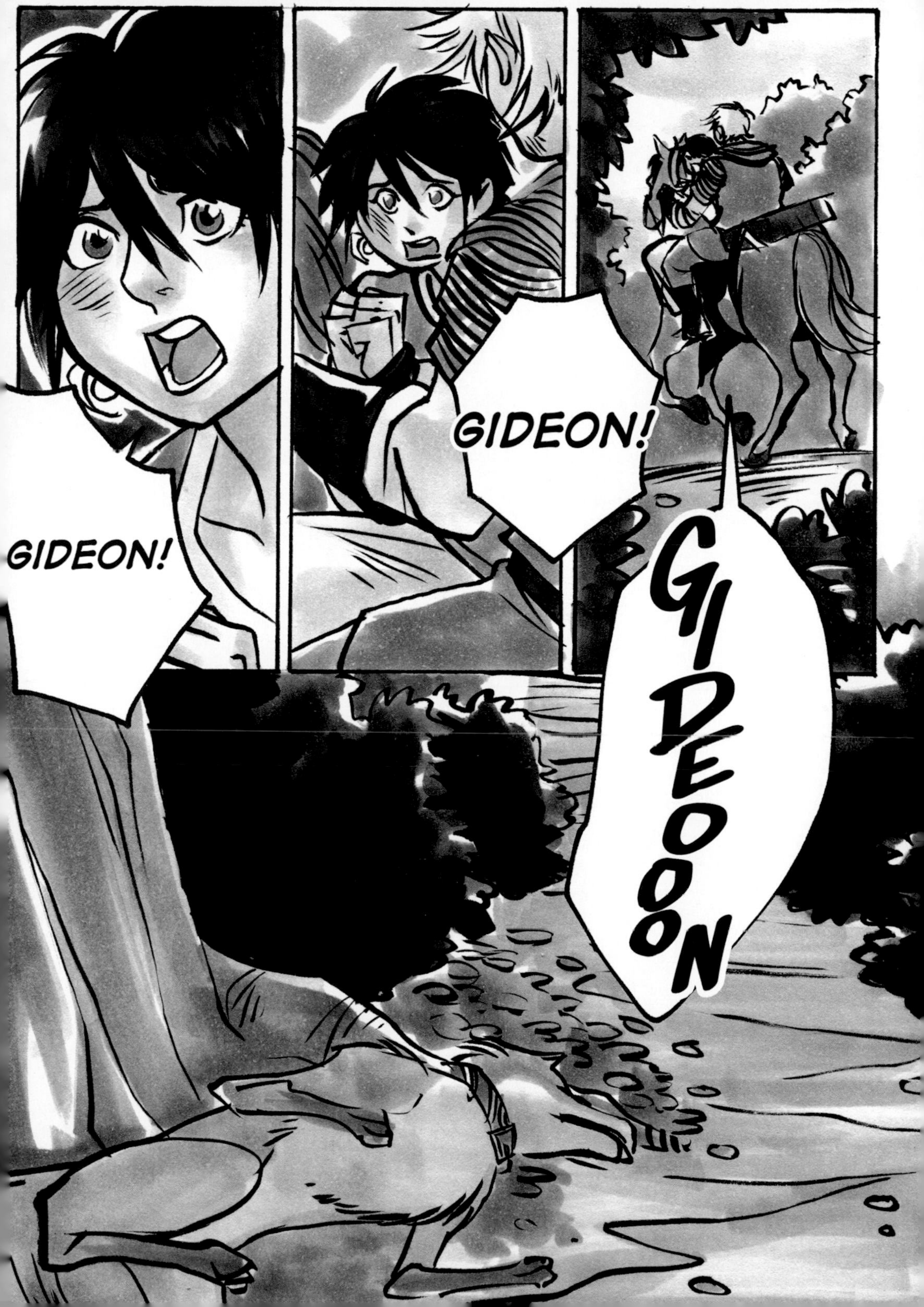
GIDEON!
GIDEON!
GIDEOOON

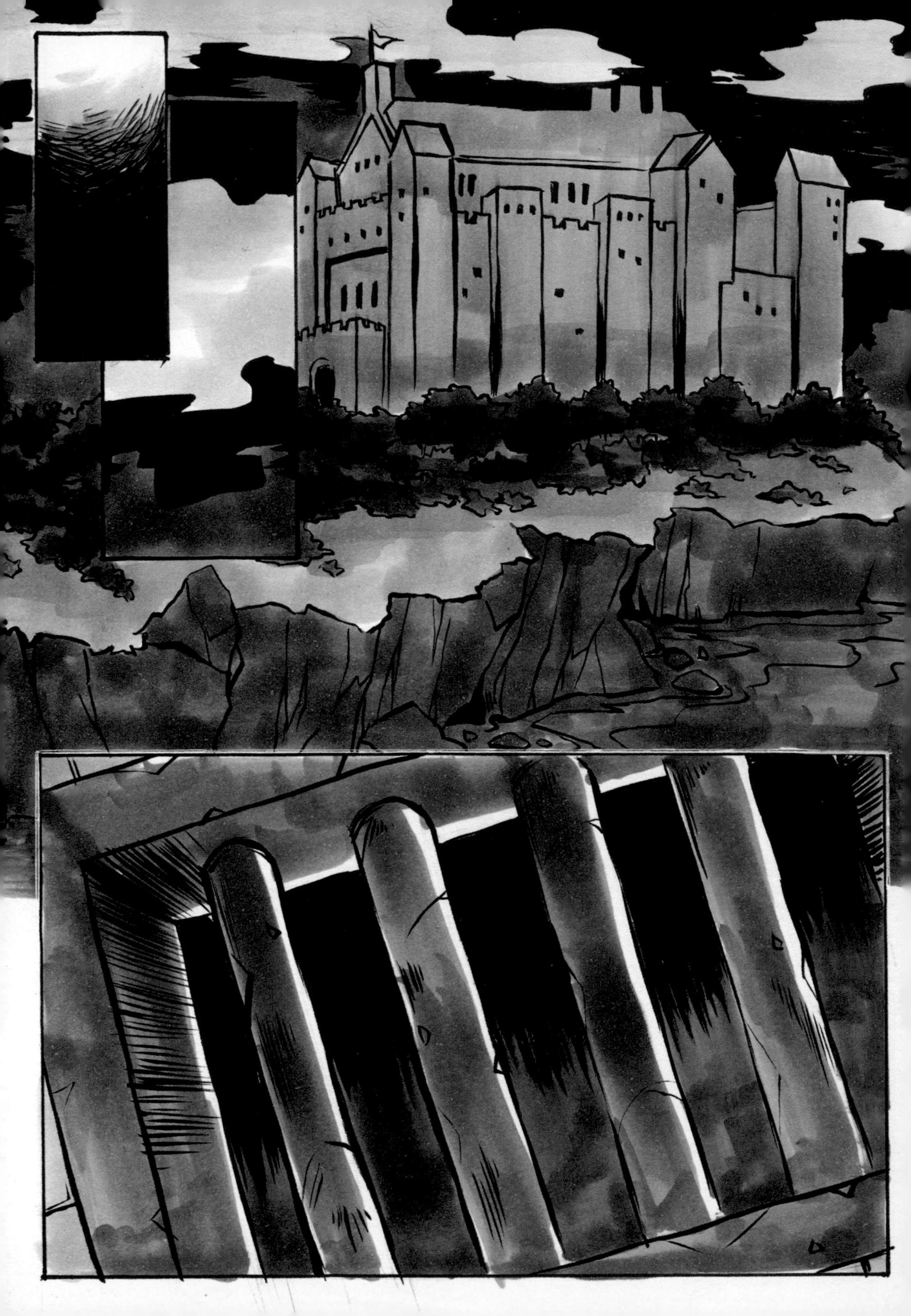

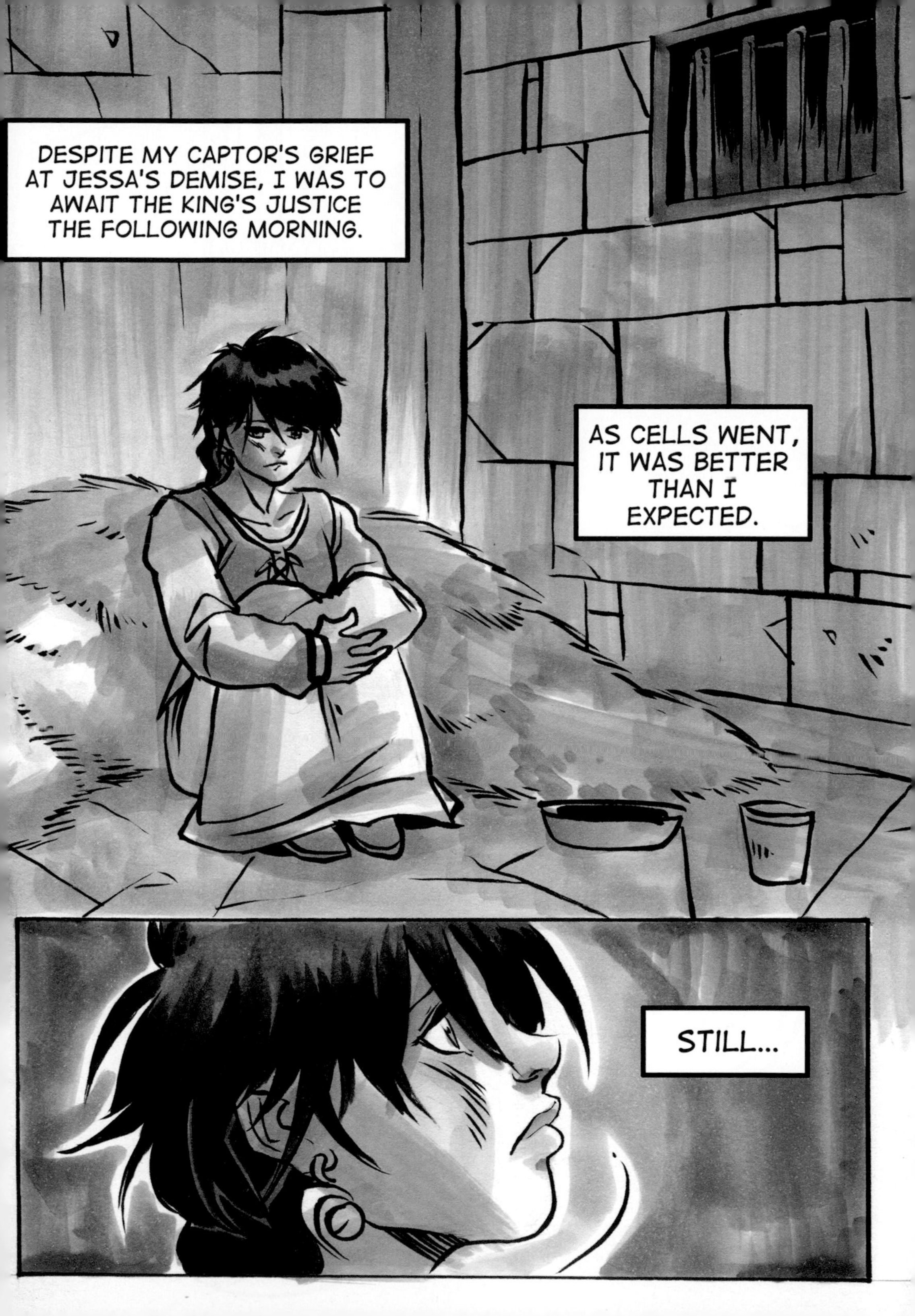
DESPITE MY CAPTOR'S GRIEF AT JESSA'S DEMISE, I WAS TO AWAIT THE KING'S JUSTICE THE FOLLOWING MORNING.
AS CELLS WENT, IT WAS BETTER THAN I EXPECTED.
STILL...

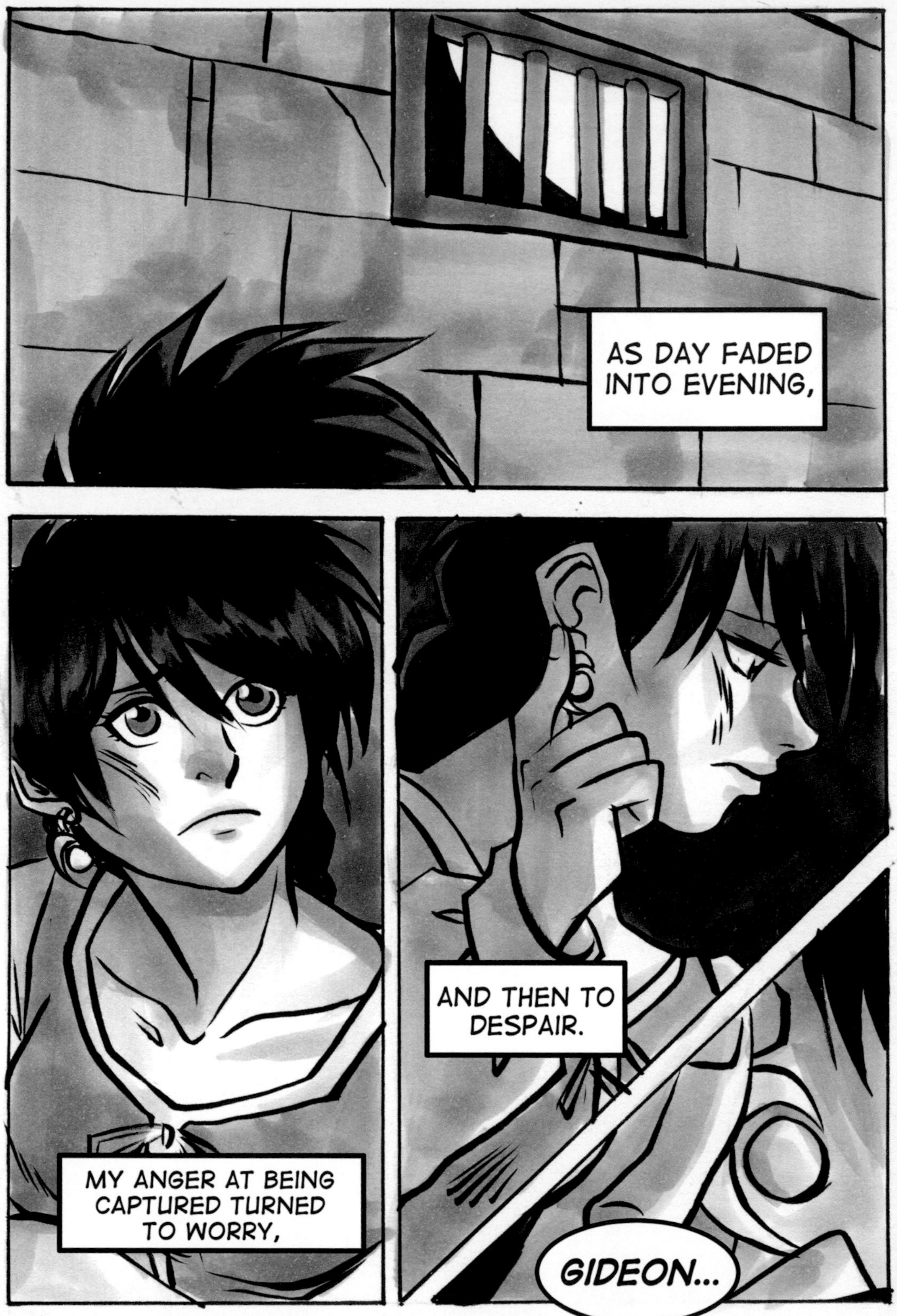
AS DAY FADED INTO EVENING,
MY ANGER AT BEING CAPTURED TURNED TO WORRY,
AND THEN TO DESPAIR.
GIDEON...

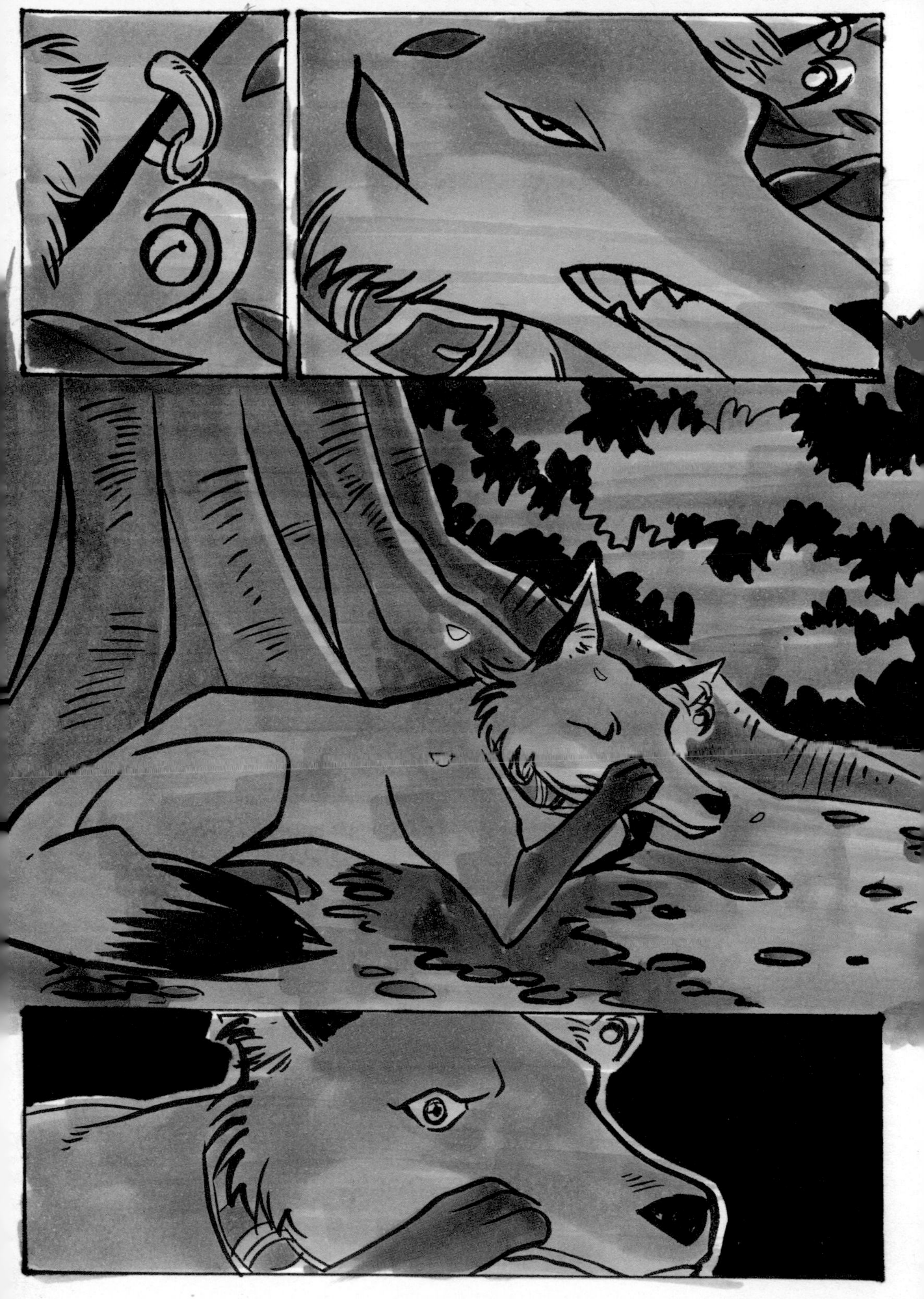

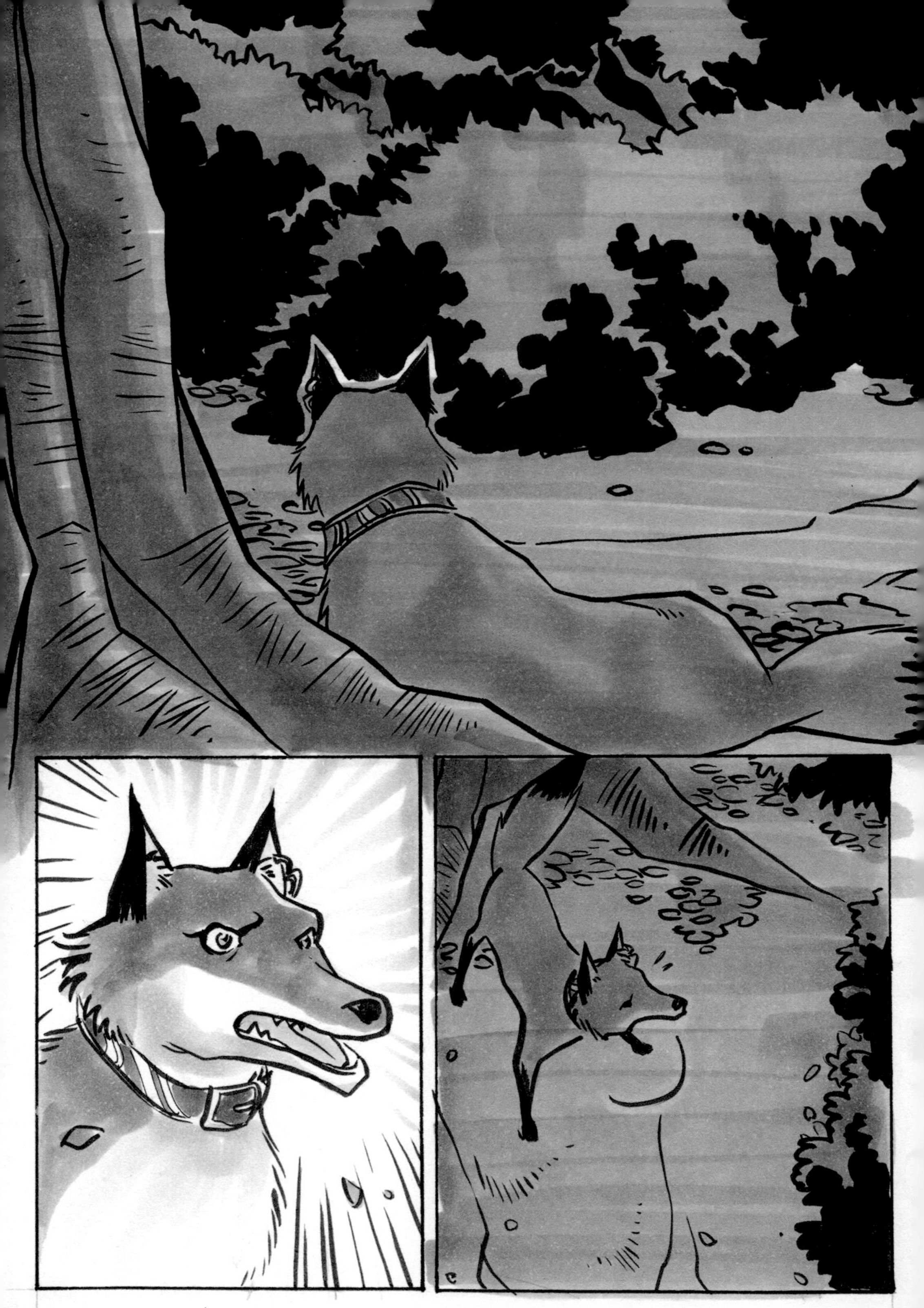

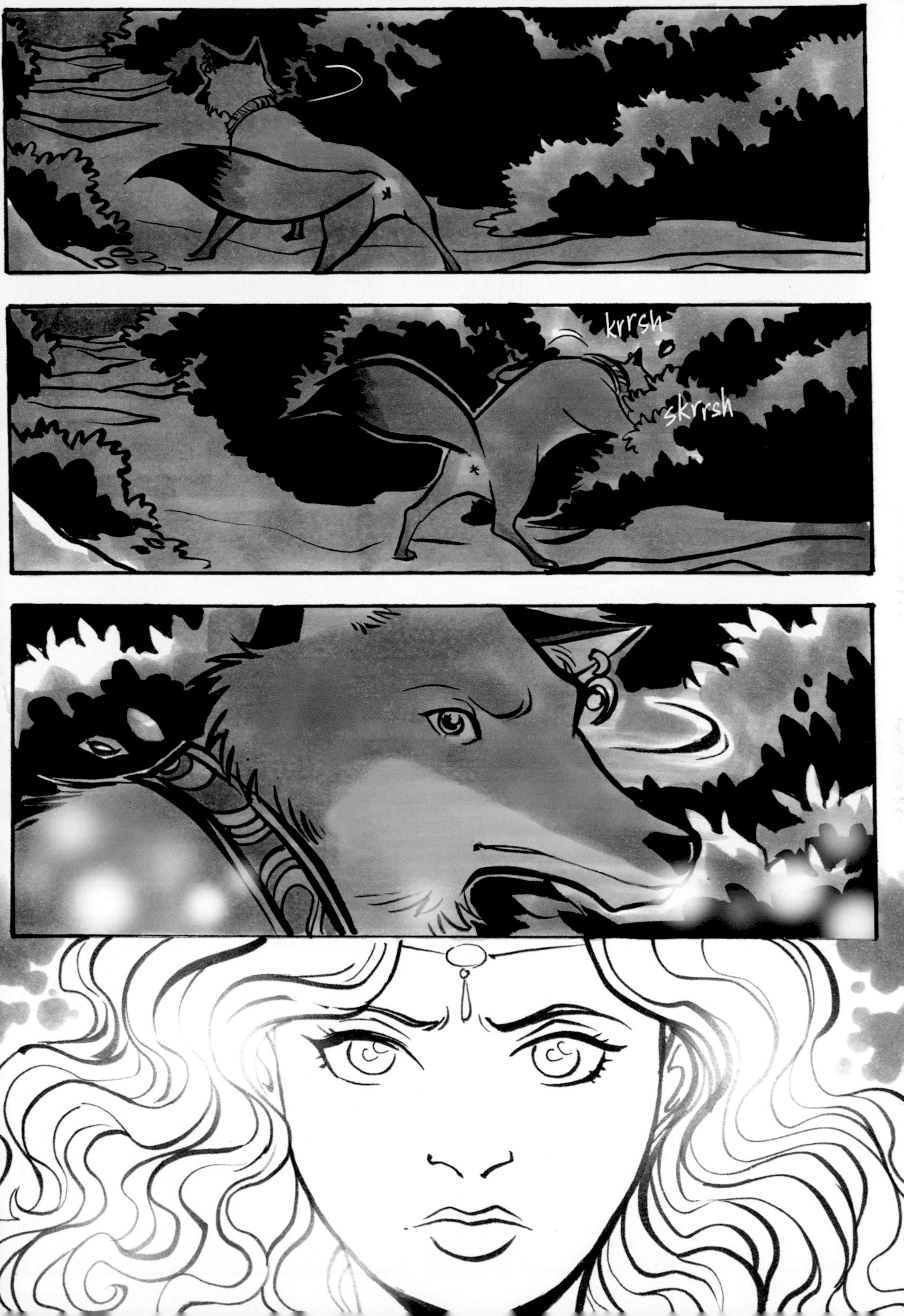
krrsh
skrrsh

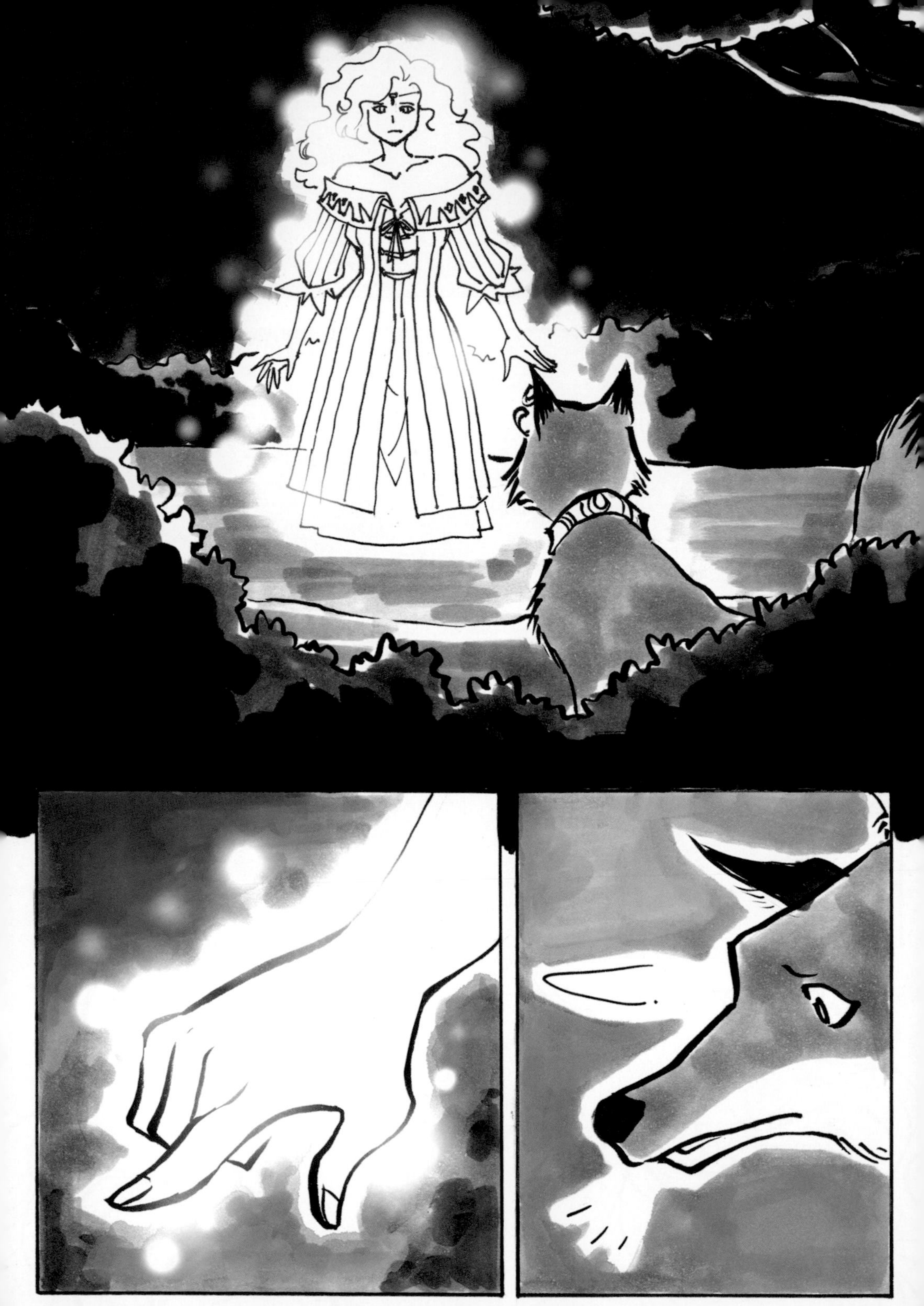

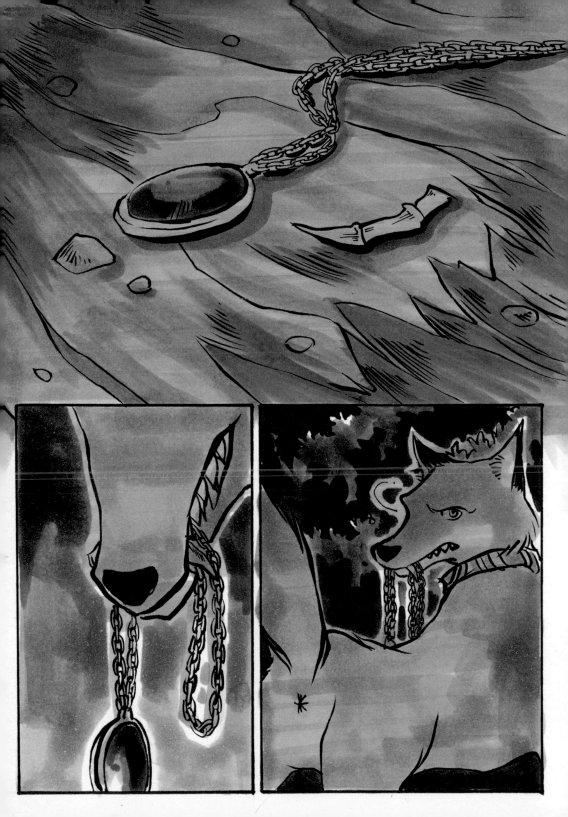

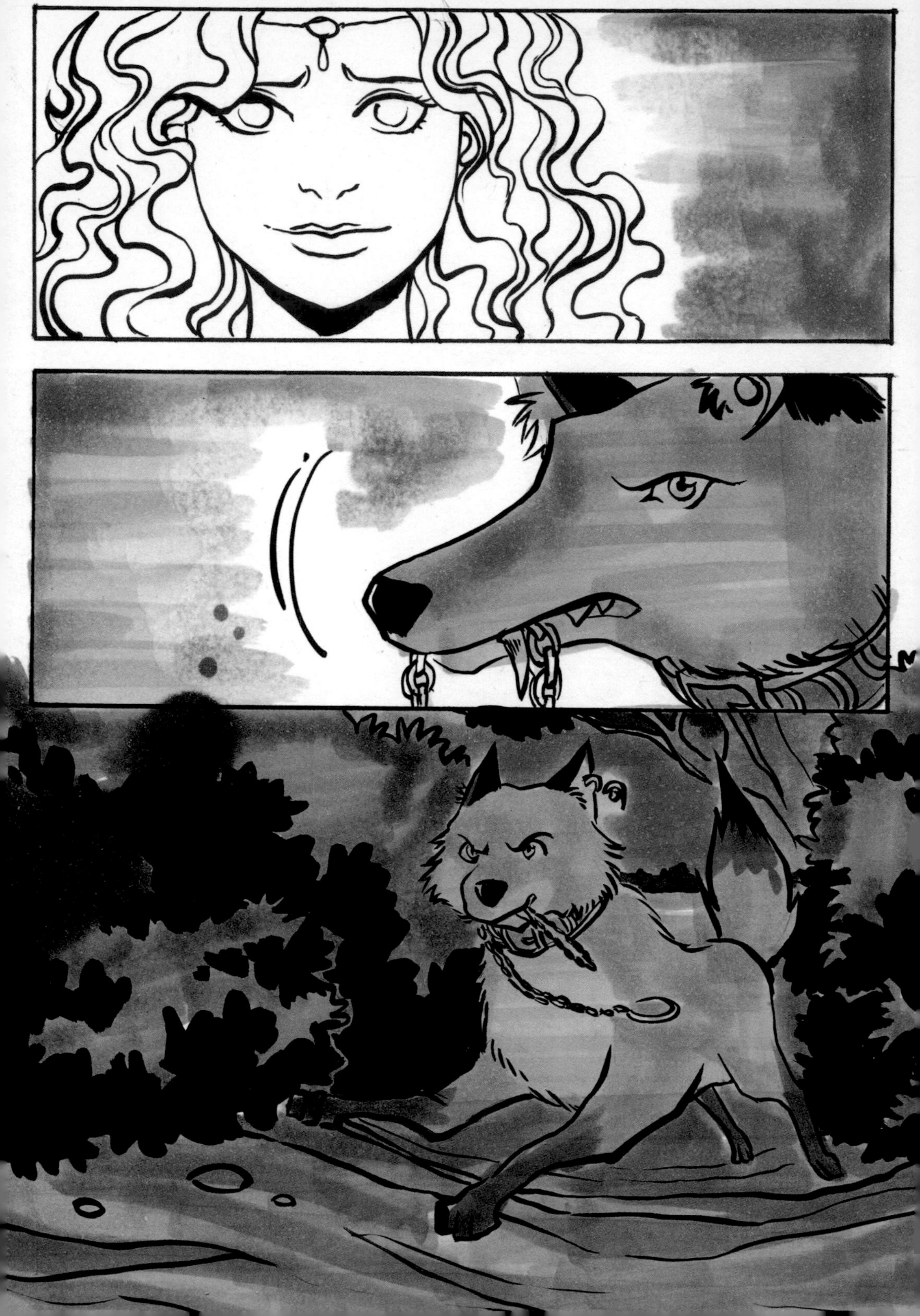

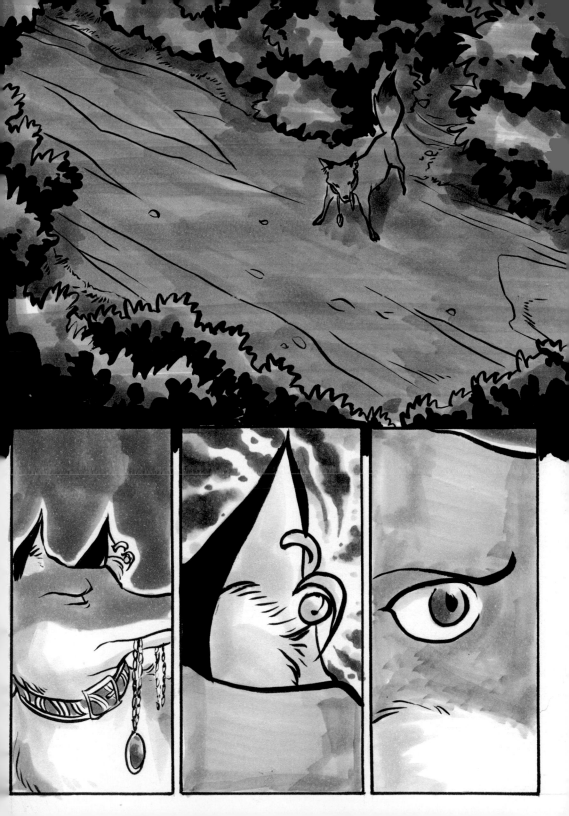

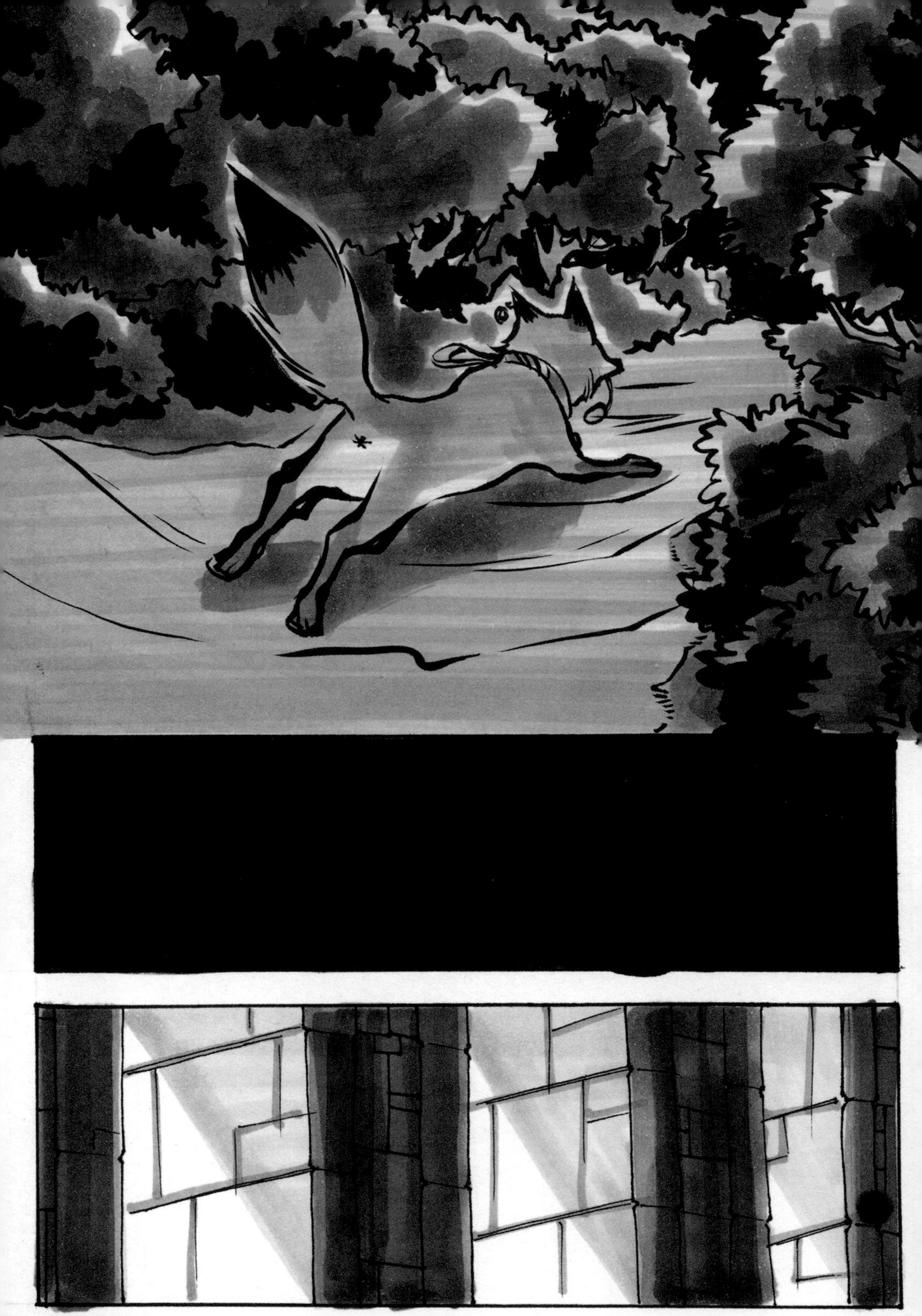

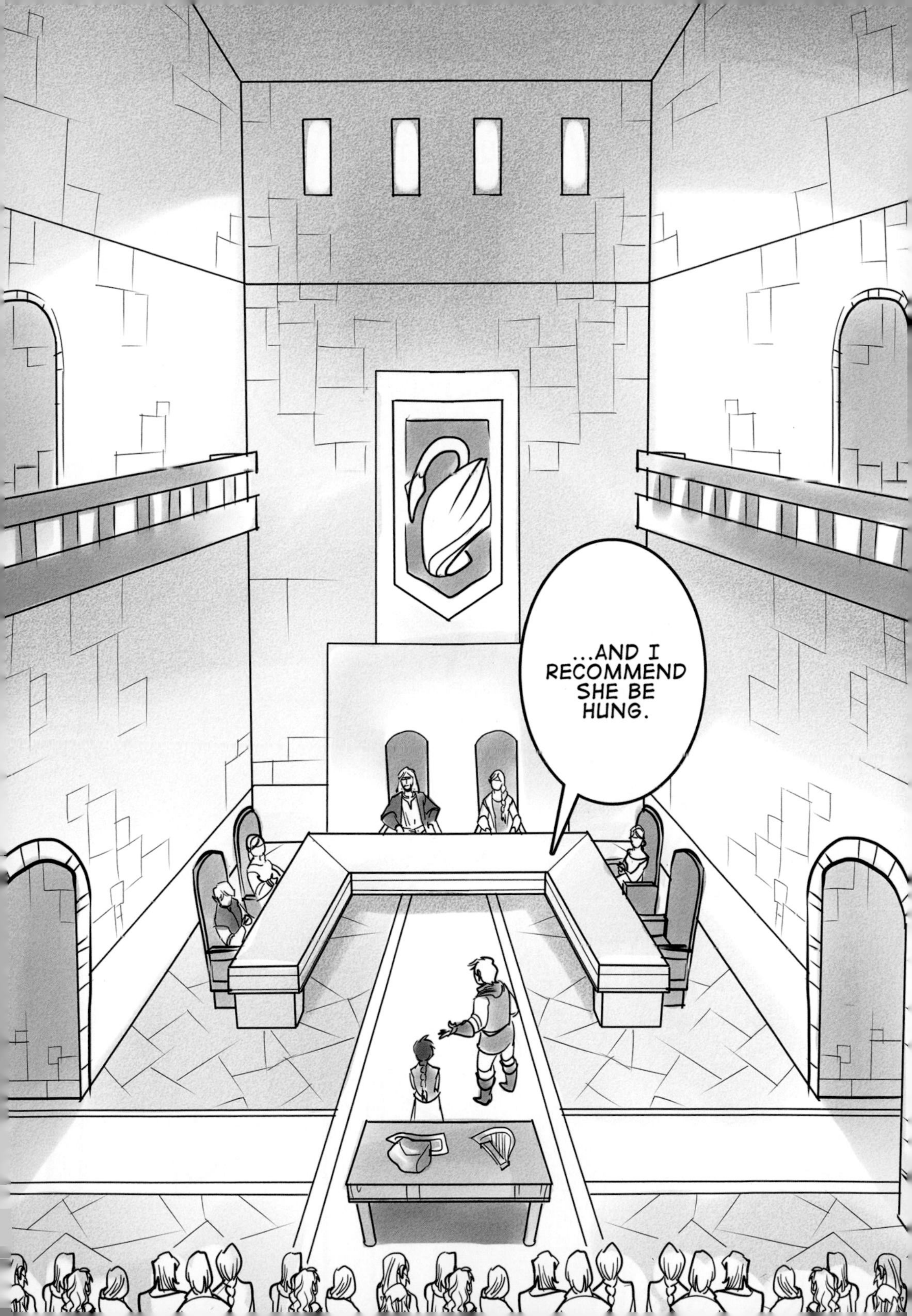
...AND I RECOMMEND SHE BE HUNG.

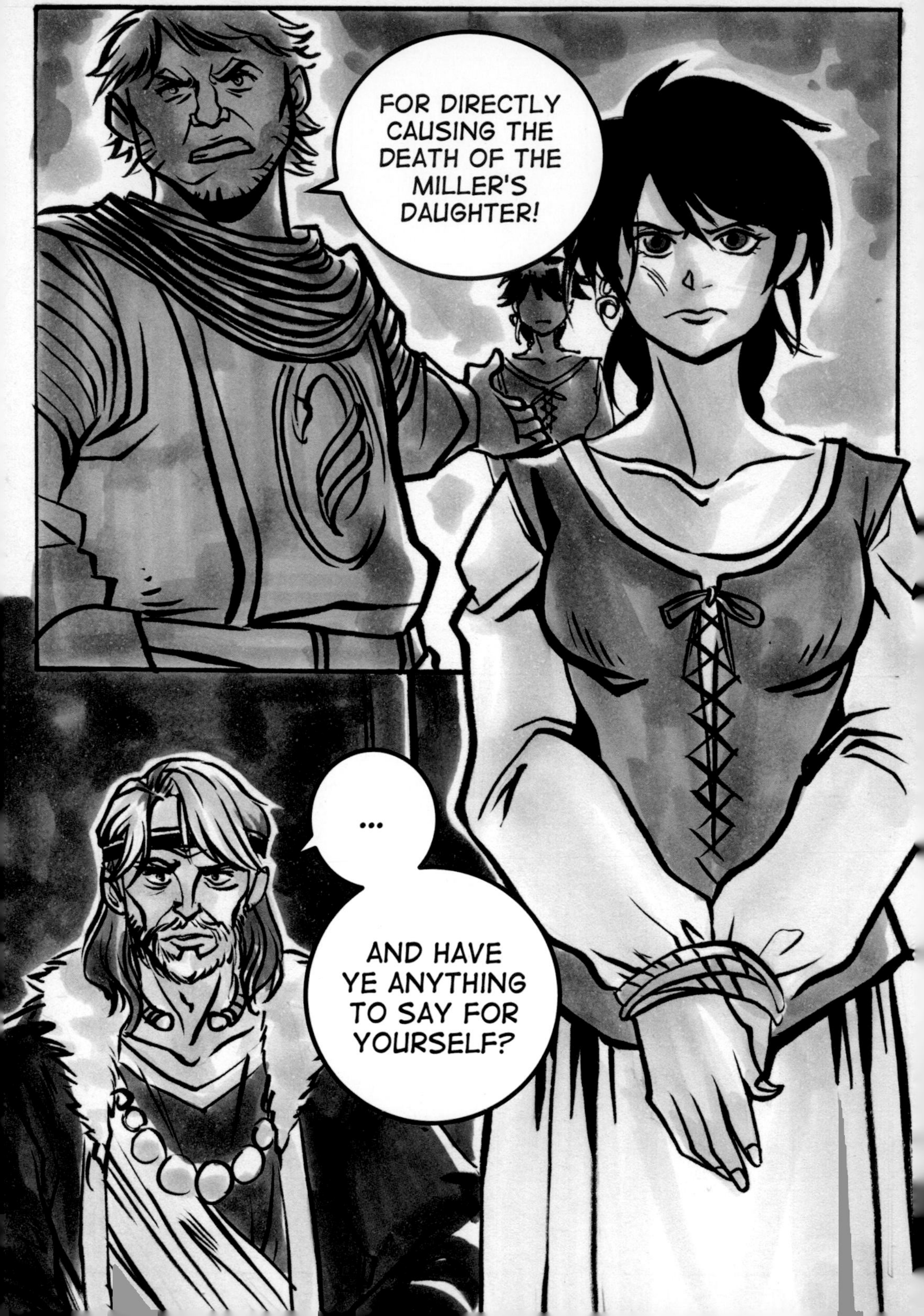
FOR DIRECTLY CAUSING THE DEATH OF THE MILLER'S DAUGHTER!
...
AND HAVE YE ANYTHING TO SAY FOR YOURSELF?

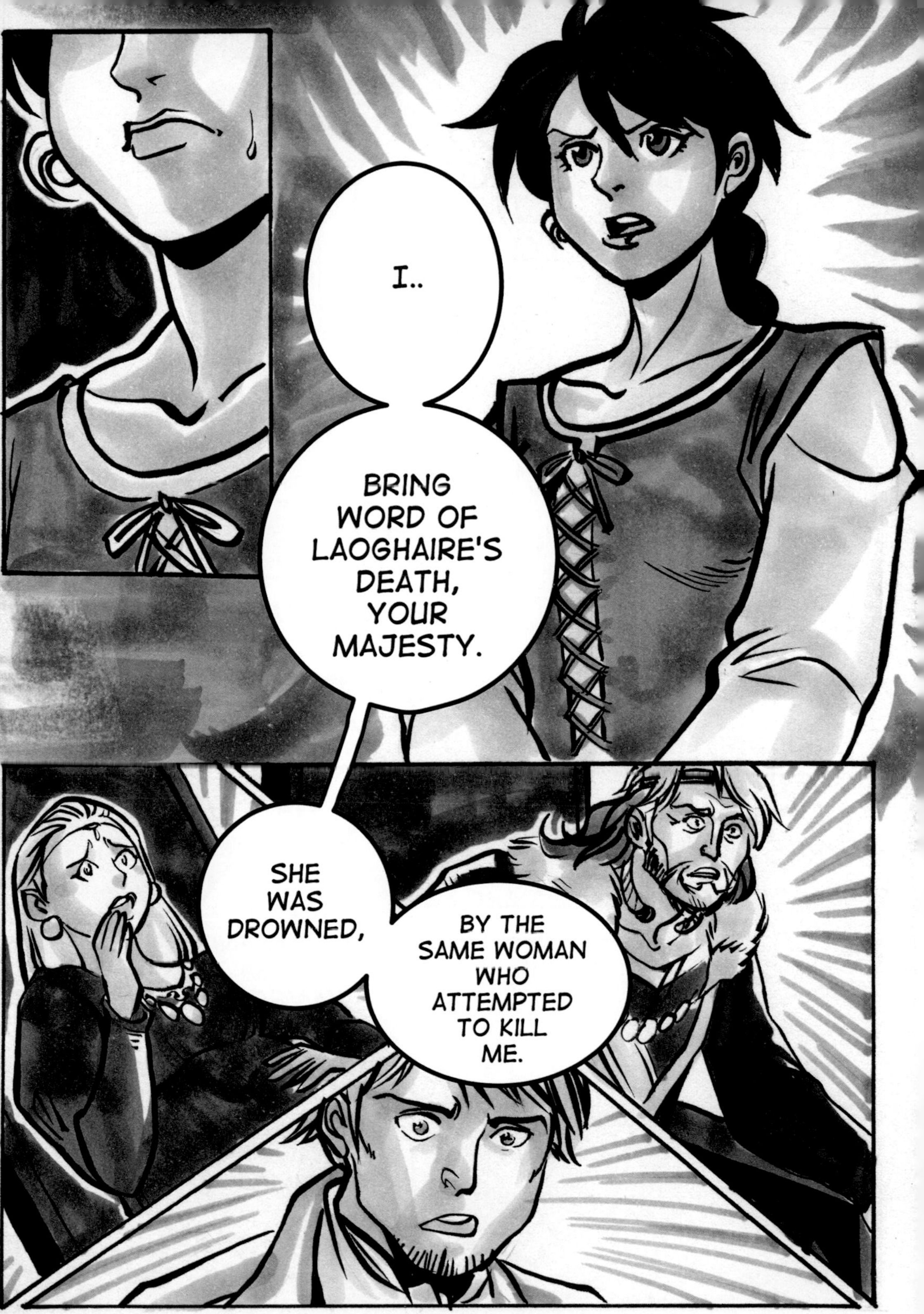
I..
BRING WORD OF LAOGHAIRE'S DEATH, YOUR MAJESTY.
SHE WAS DROWNED,
BY THE SAME WOMAN WHO ATTEMPTED TO KILL ME.

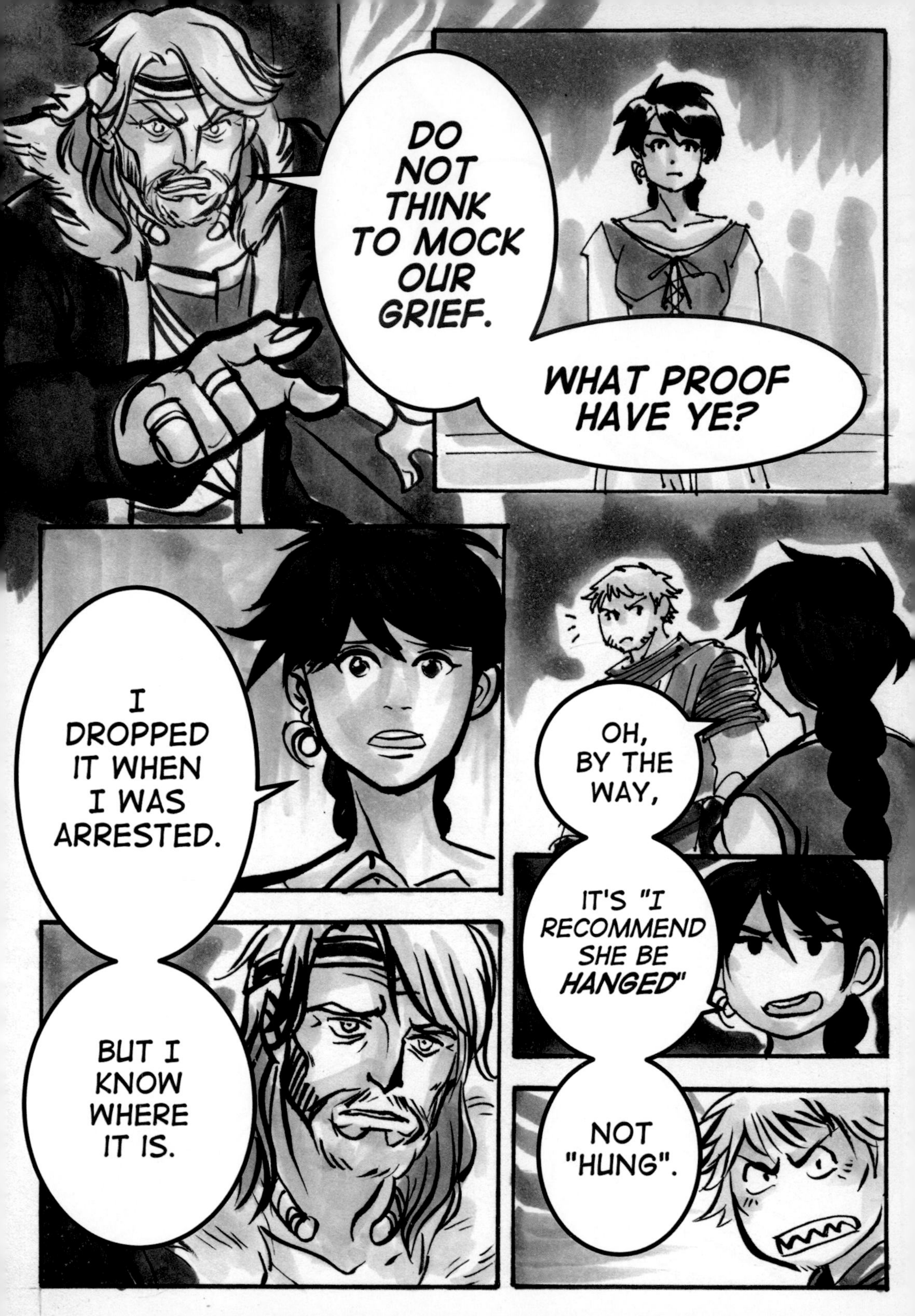
DO NOT THINK TO MOCK OUR GRIEF.
WHAT PROOF HAVE YE?
I DROPPED IT WHEN I WAS ARRESTED.
BUT I KNOW WHERE IT IS.
OH, BY THE WAY,
IT'S "I RECOMMEND SHE BE *HANGED*"
NOT "HUNG".

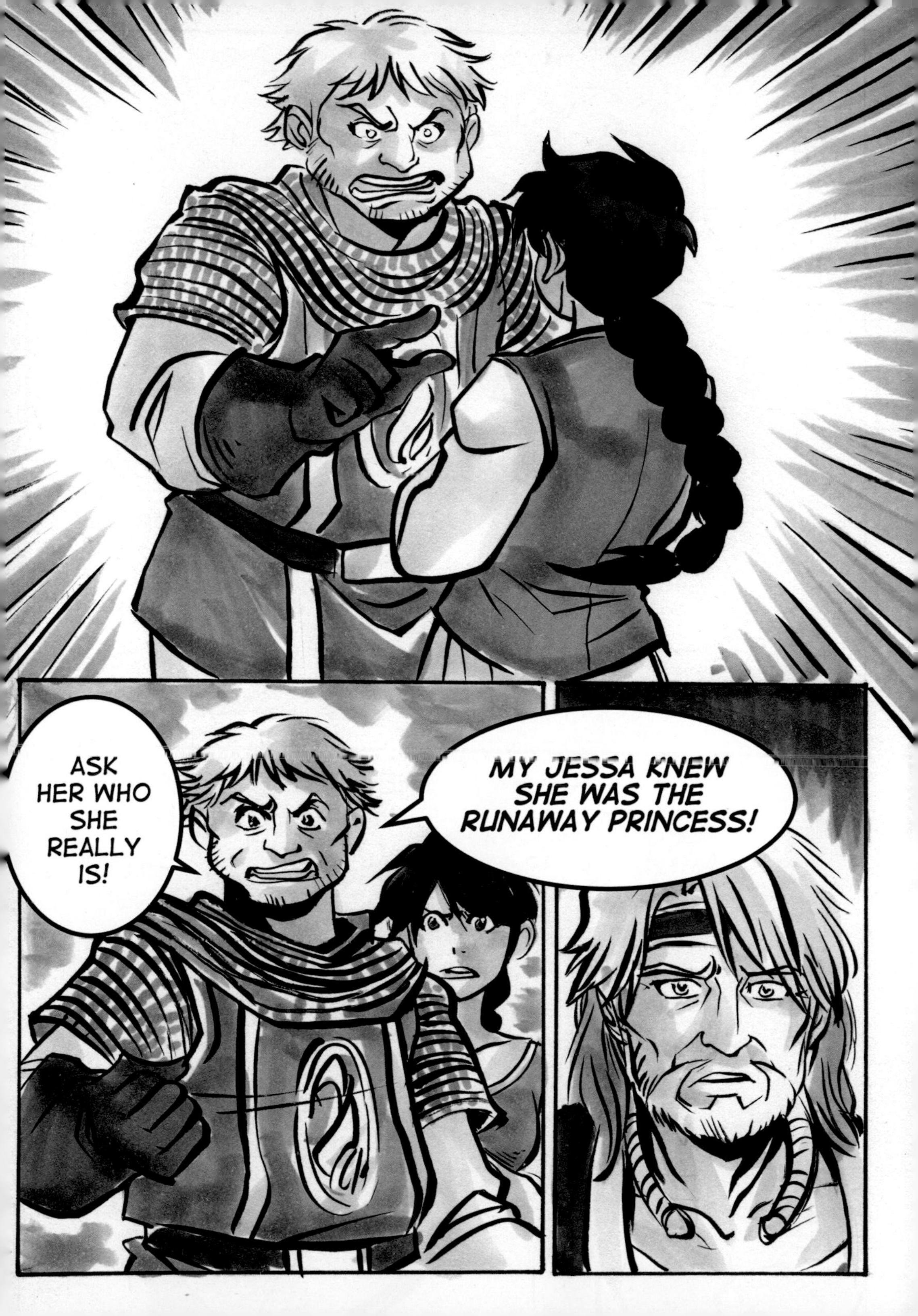
ASK HER WHO SHE REALLY IS!
MY JESSA KNEW SHE WAS THE RUNAWAY PRINCESS!

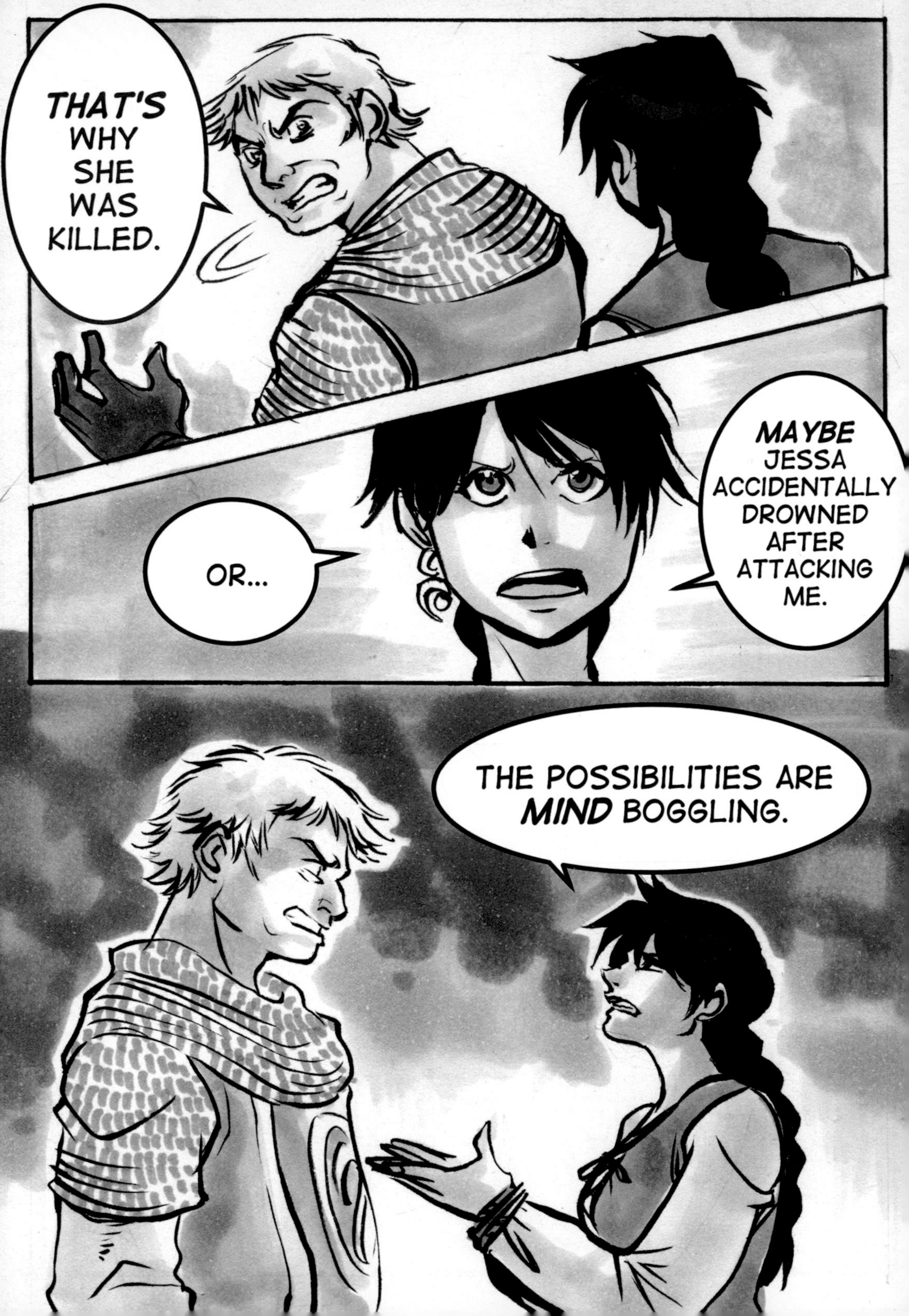
THAT'S WHY SHE WAS KILLED.
OR...
MAYBE JESSA ACCIDENTALLY DROWNED AFTER ATTACKING ME.
THE POSSIBILITIES ARE ***MIND*** BOGGLING.

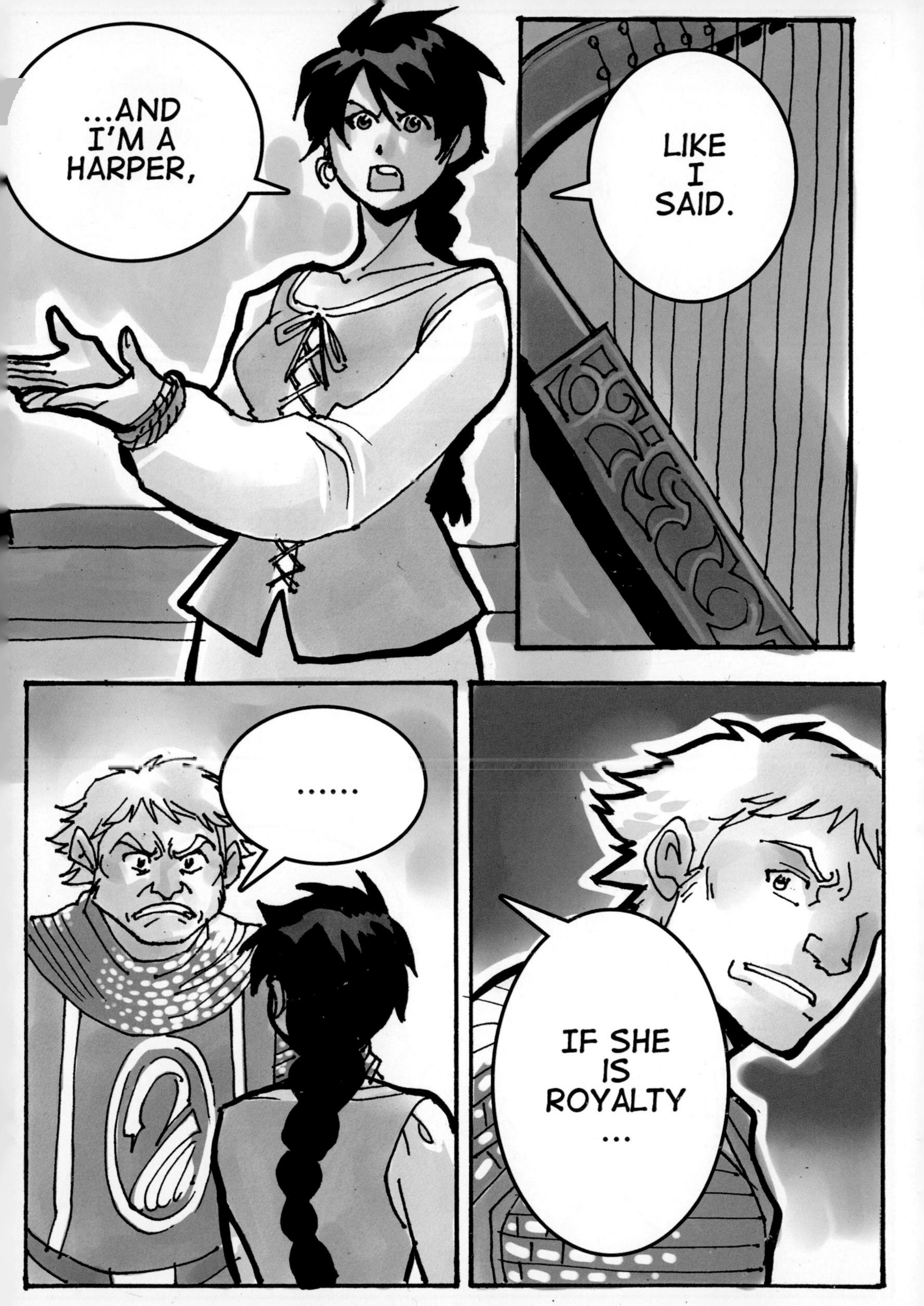
...AND I'M A HARPER,
LIKE I SAID.
......
IF SHE IS ROYALTY ...

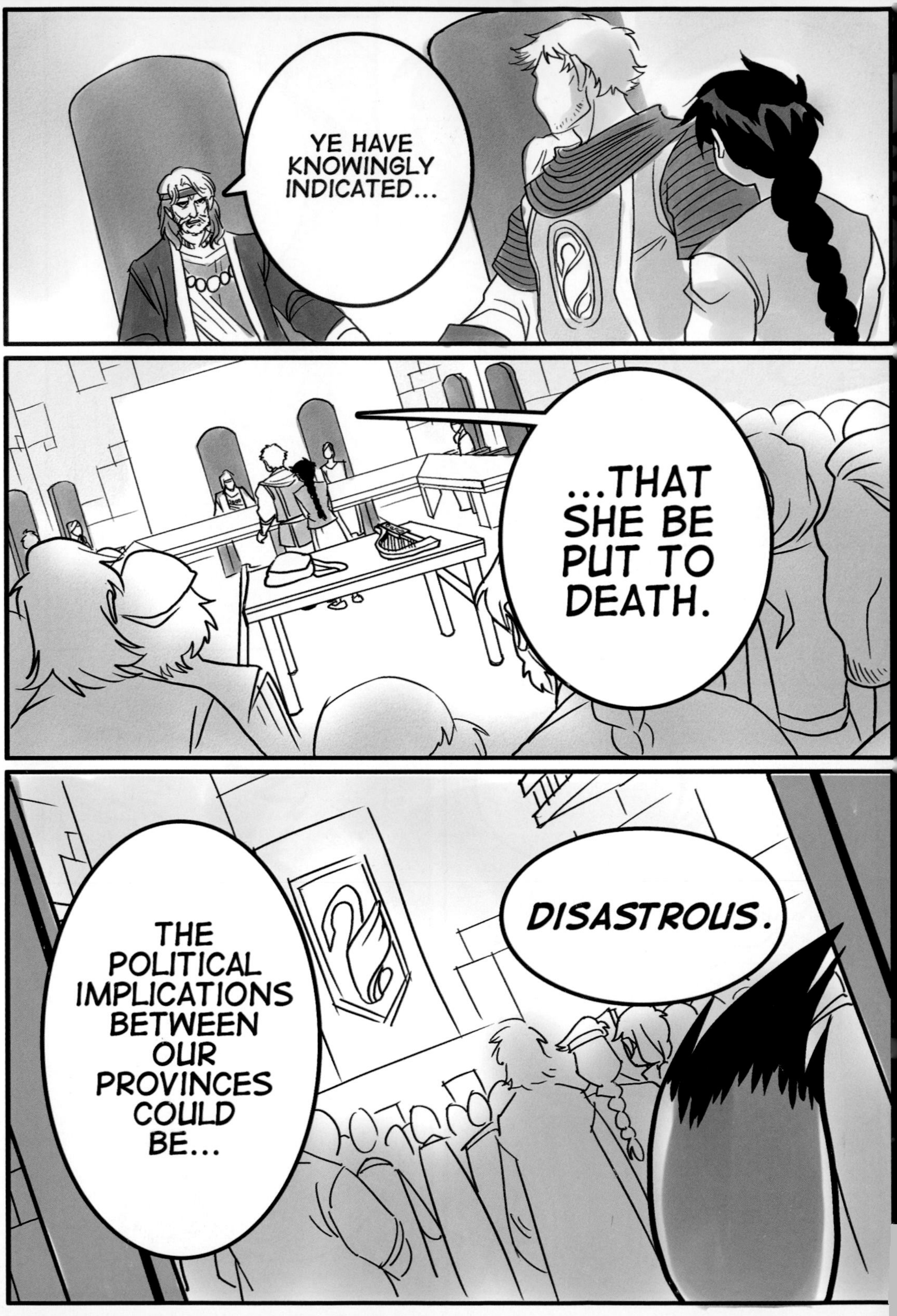
YE HAVE KNOWINGLY INDICATED...
...THAT SHE BE PUT TO DEATH.
THE POLITICAL IMPLICATIONS BETWEEN OUR PROVINCES COULD BE...
DISASTROUS.

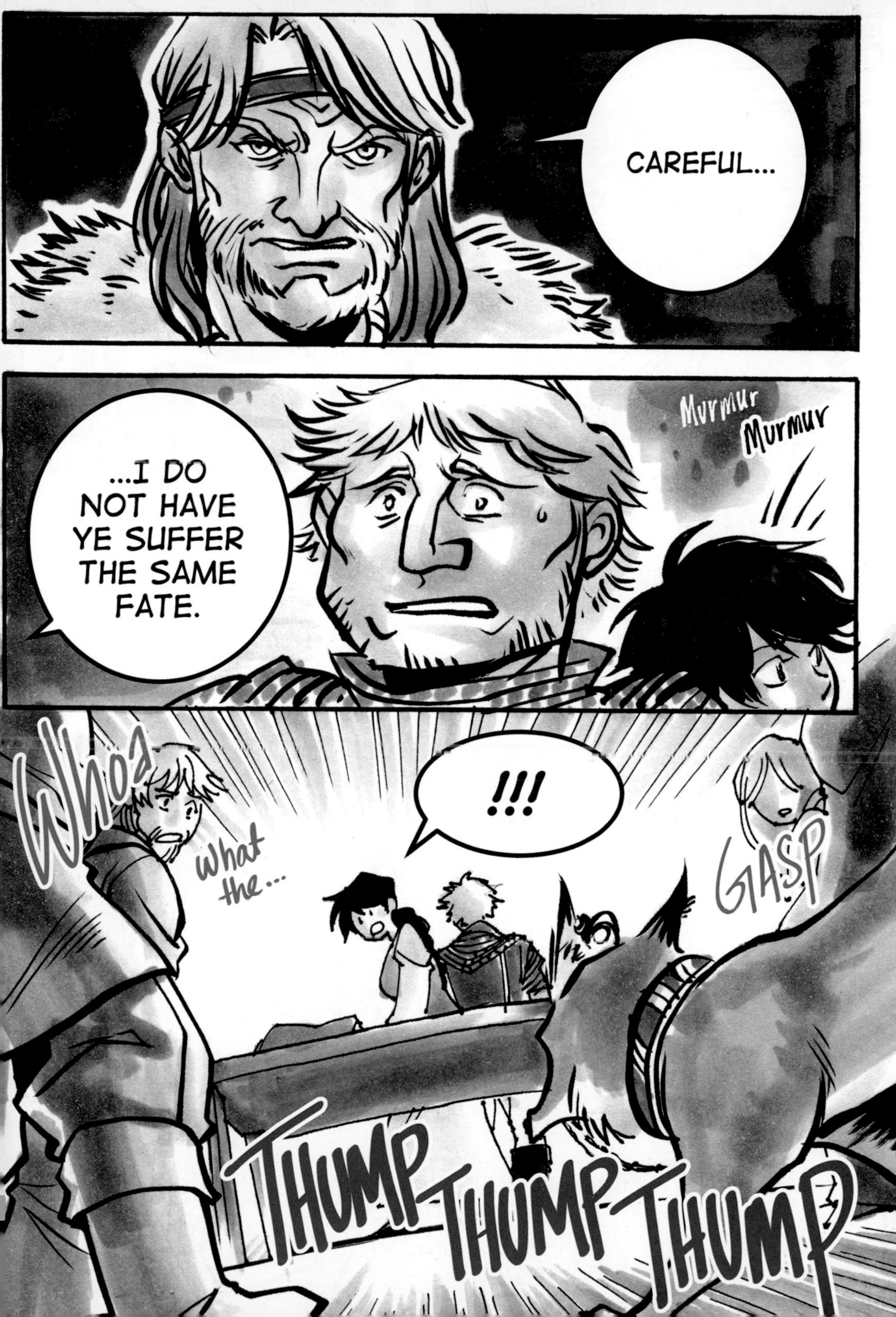
CAREFUL...
...I DO NOT HAVE YE SUFFER THE SAME FATE.
Murmur Murmur
Whoa
what the...
!!!
GASP
THUMP THUMP THUMP

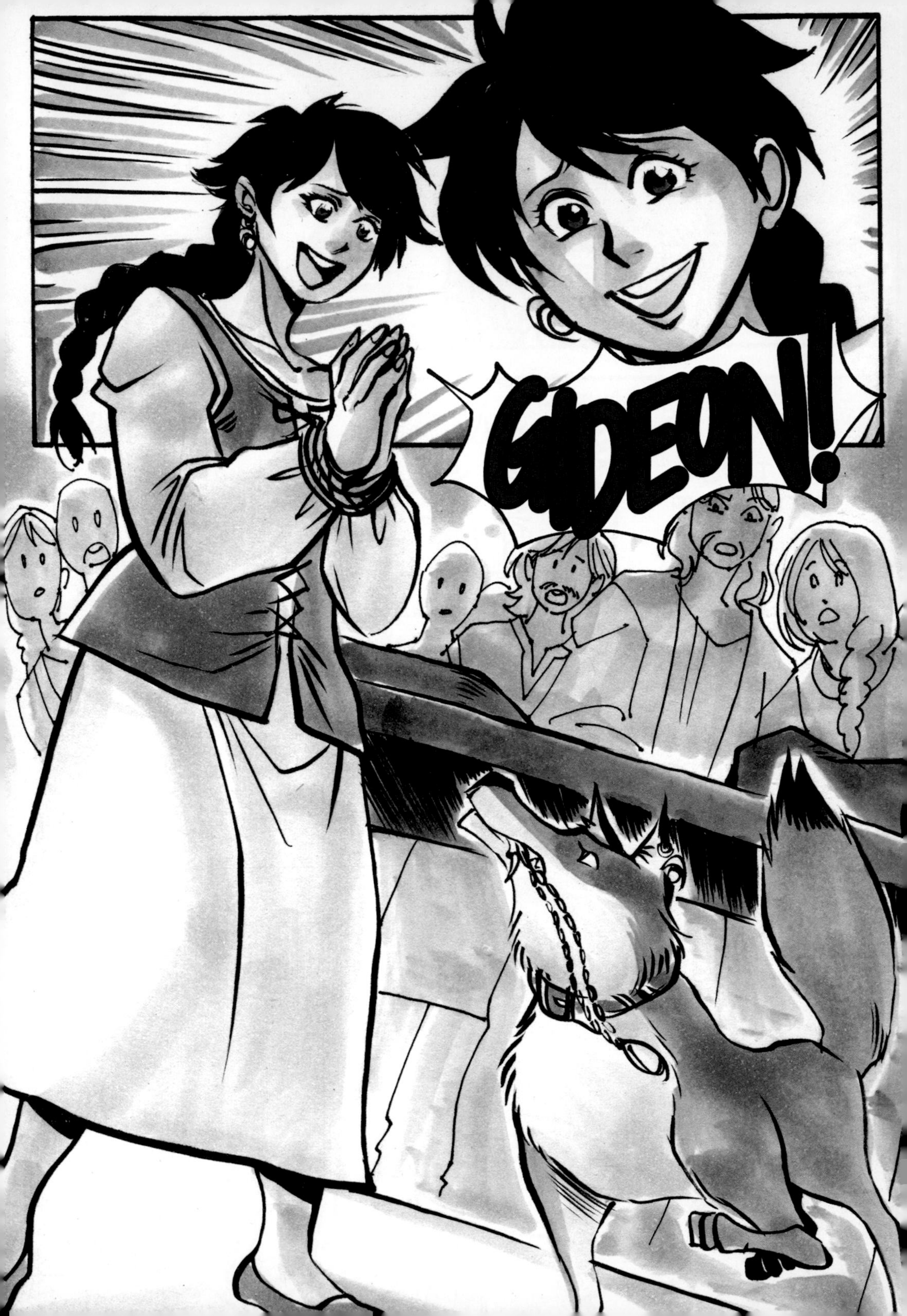
GIDEON!

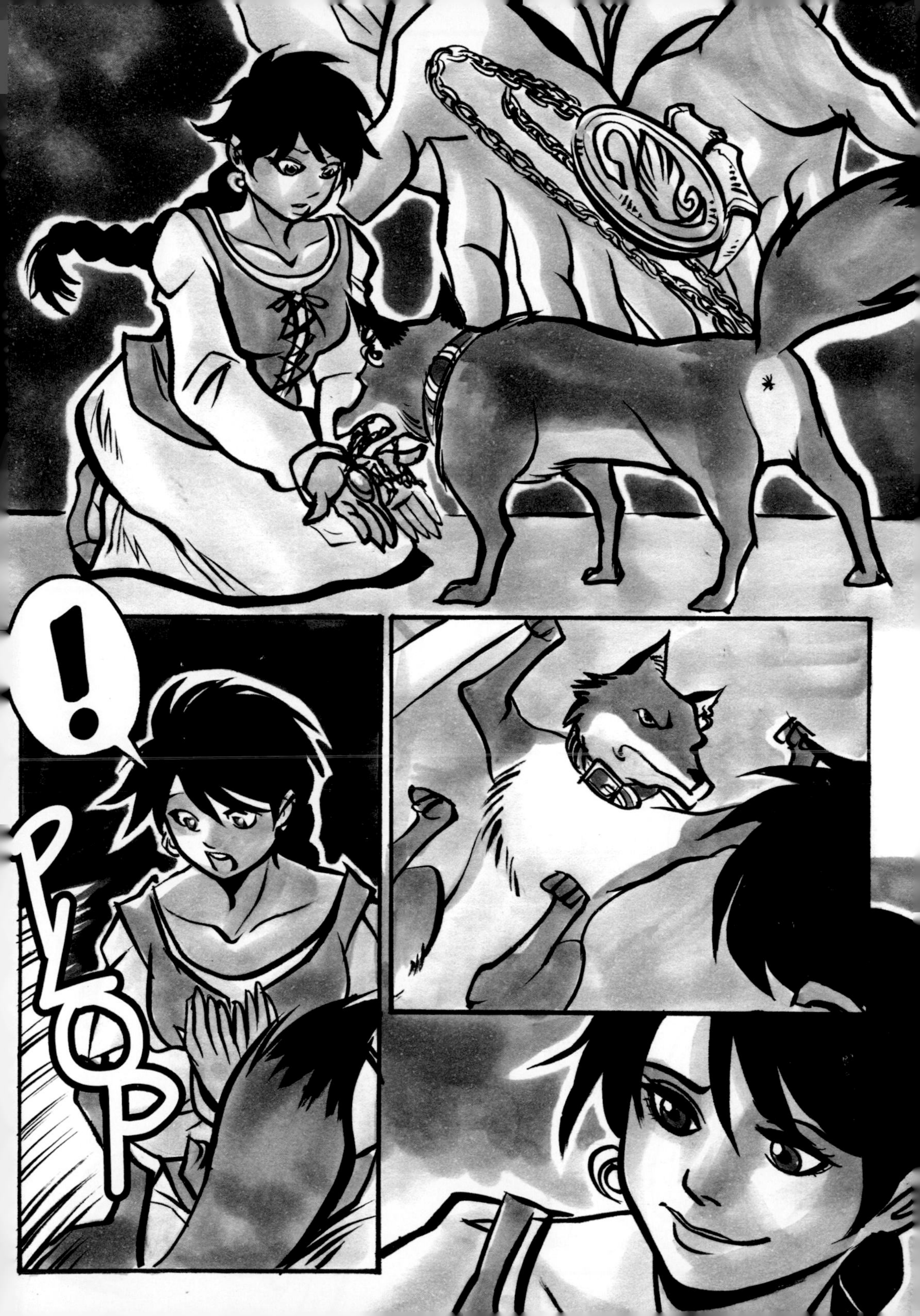
!
PLOP

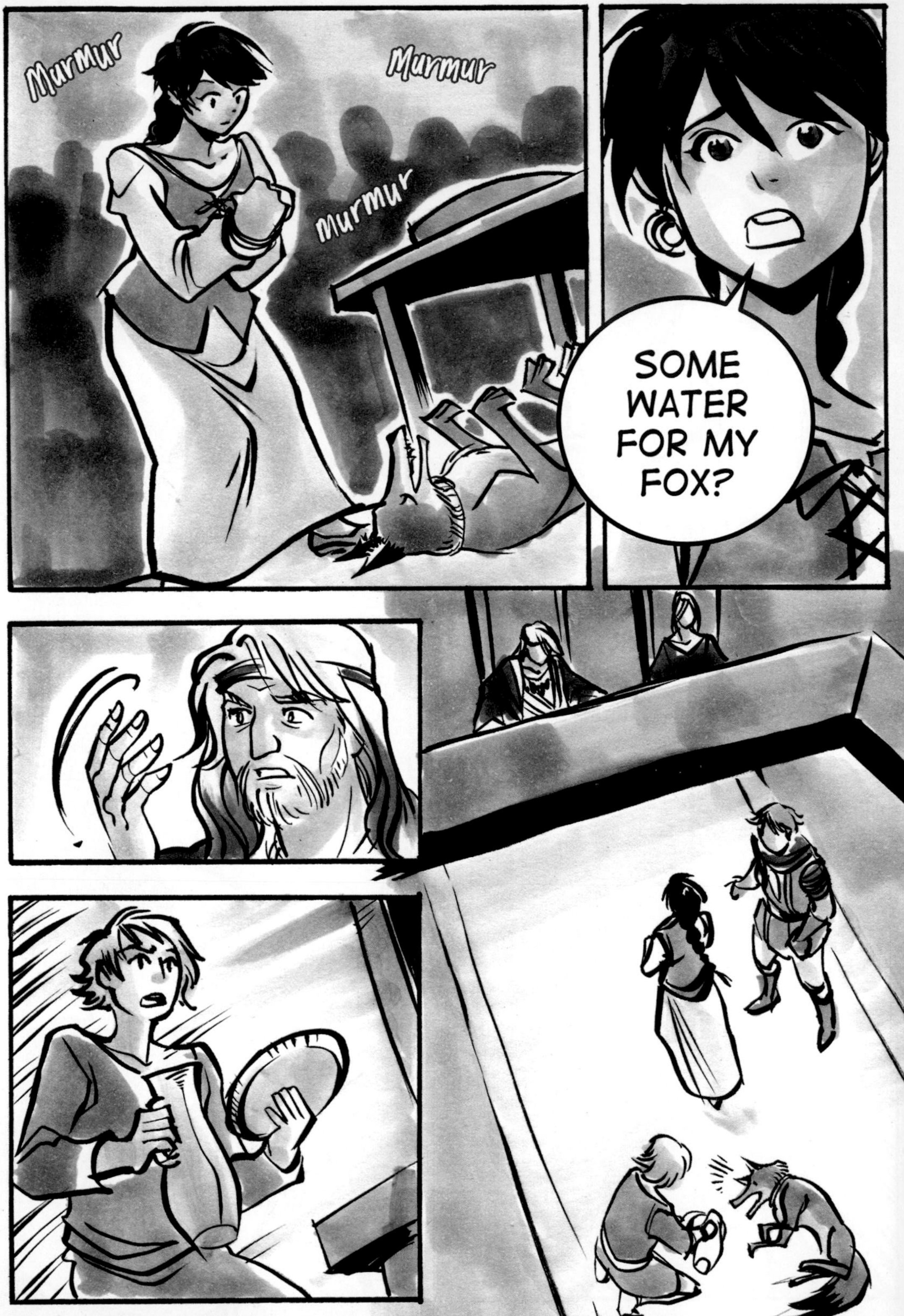
Murmur
Murmur
Murmur
SOME WATER FOR MY FOX?

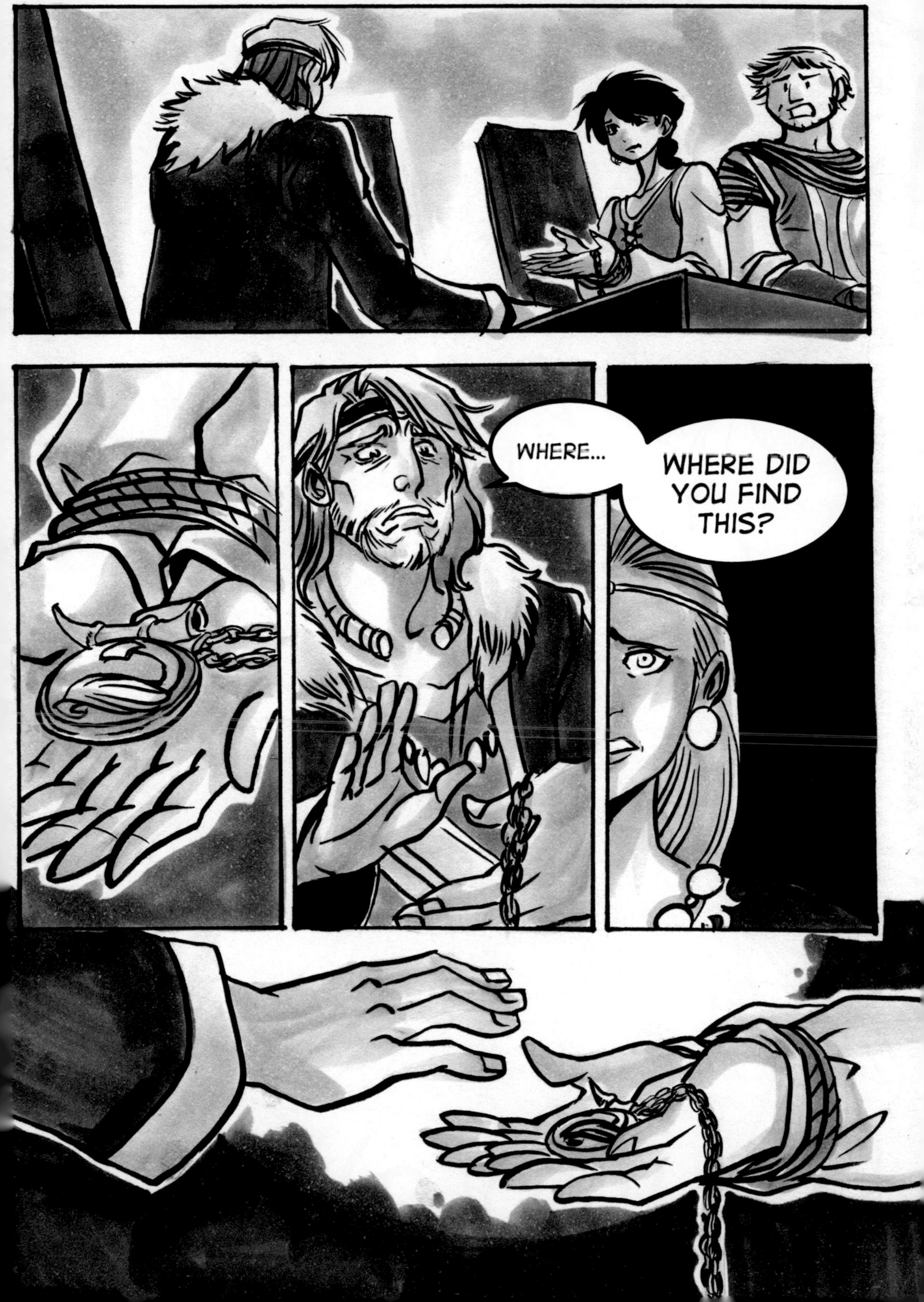
WHERE...
WHERE DID YOU FIND THIS?

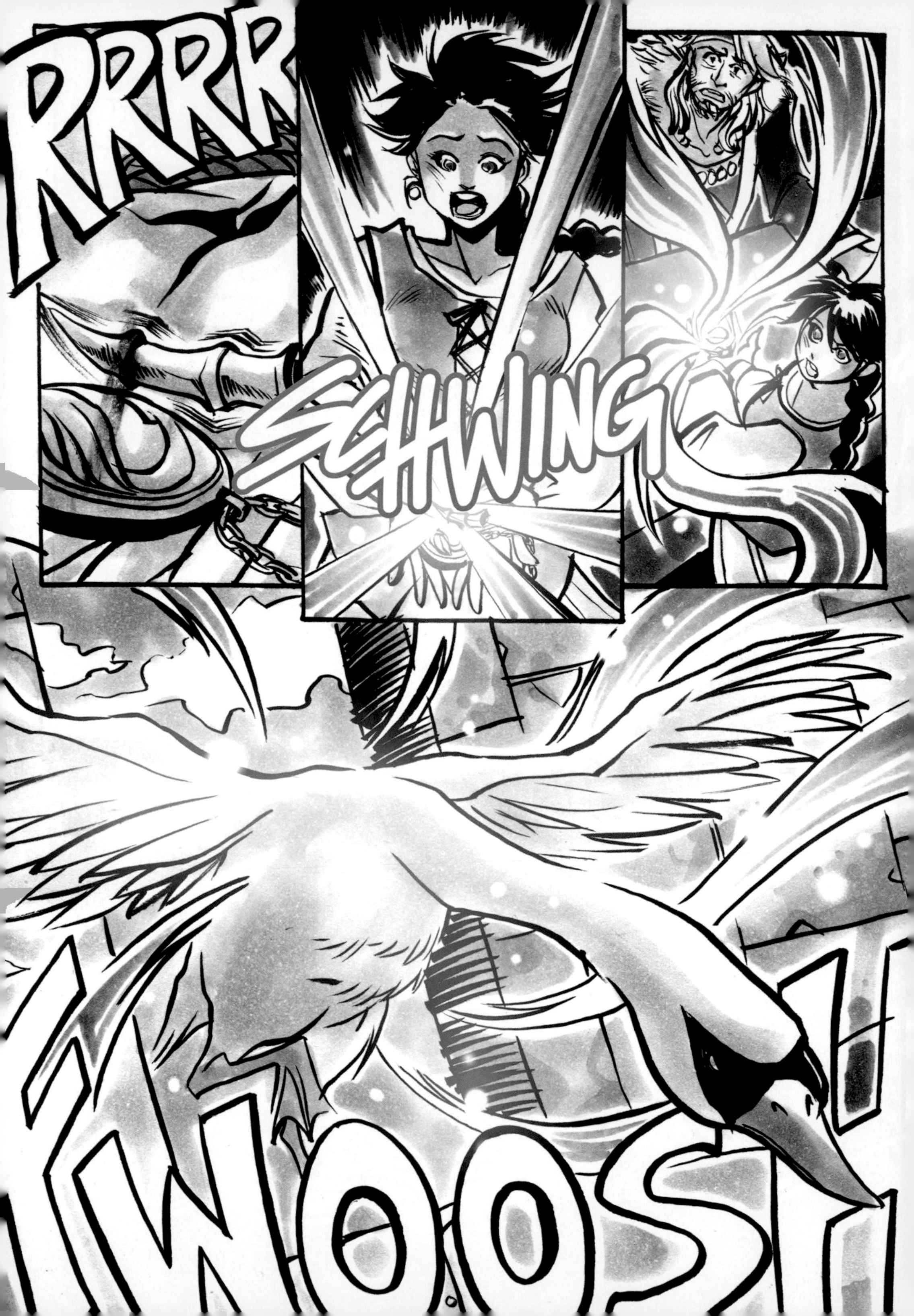
RRRR
SCHWING
WOOSH

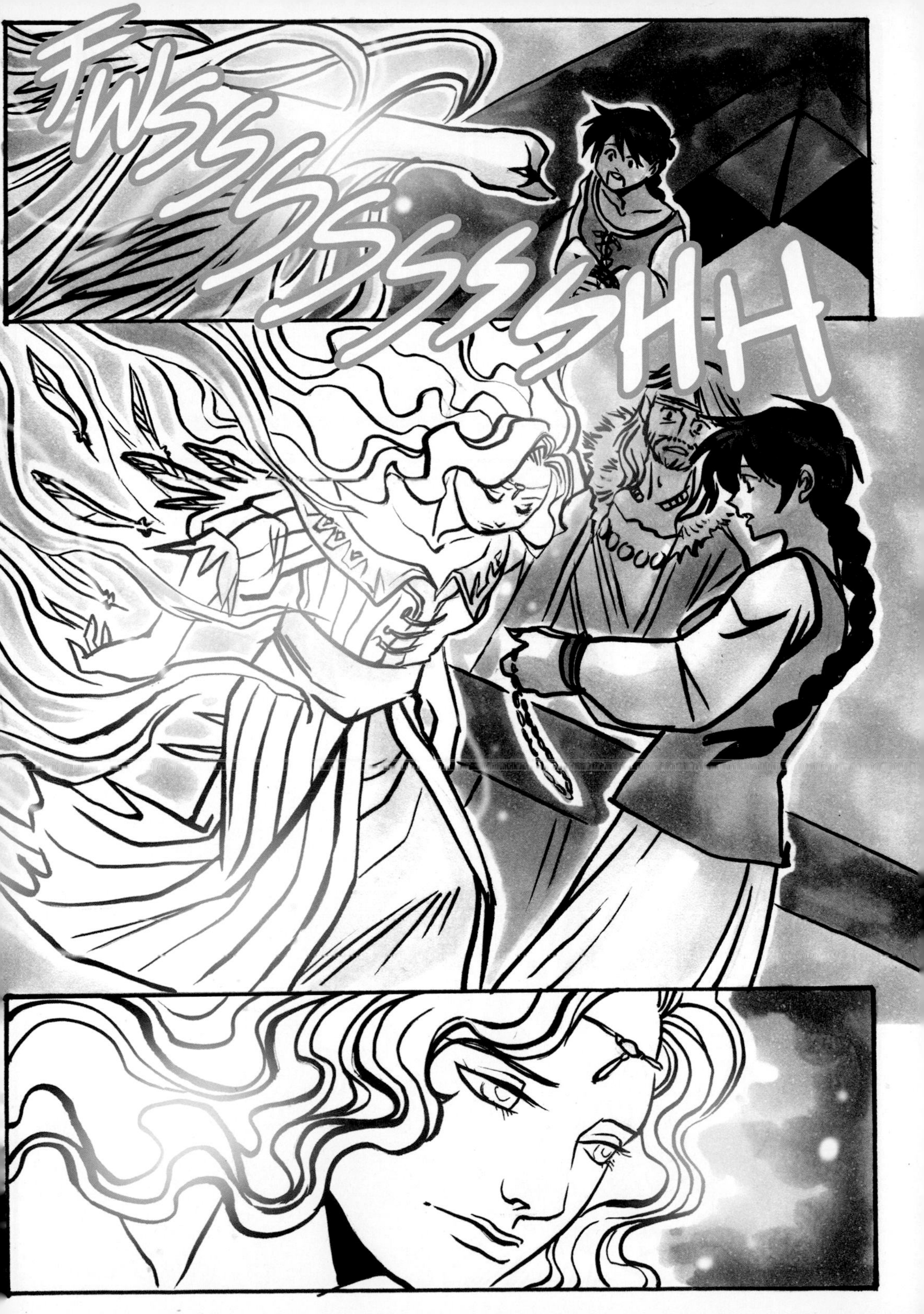
FWSSSSSSSHH

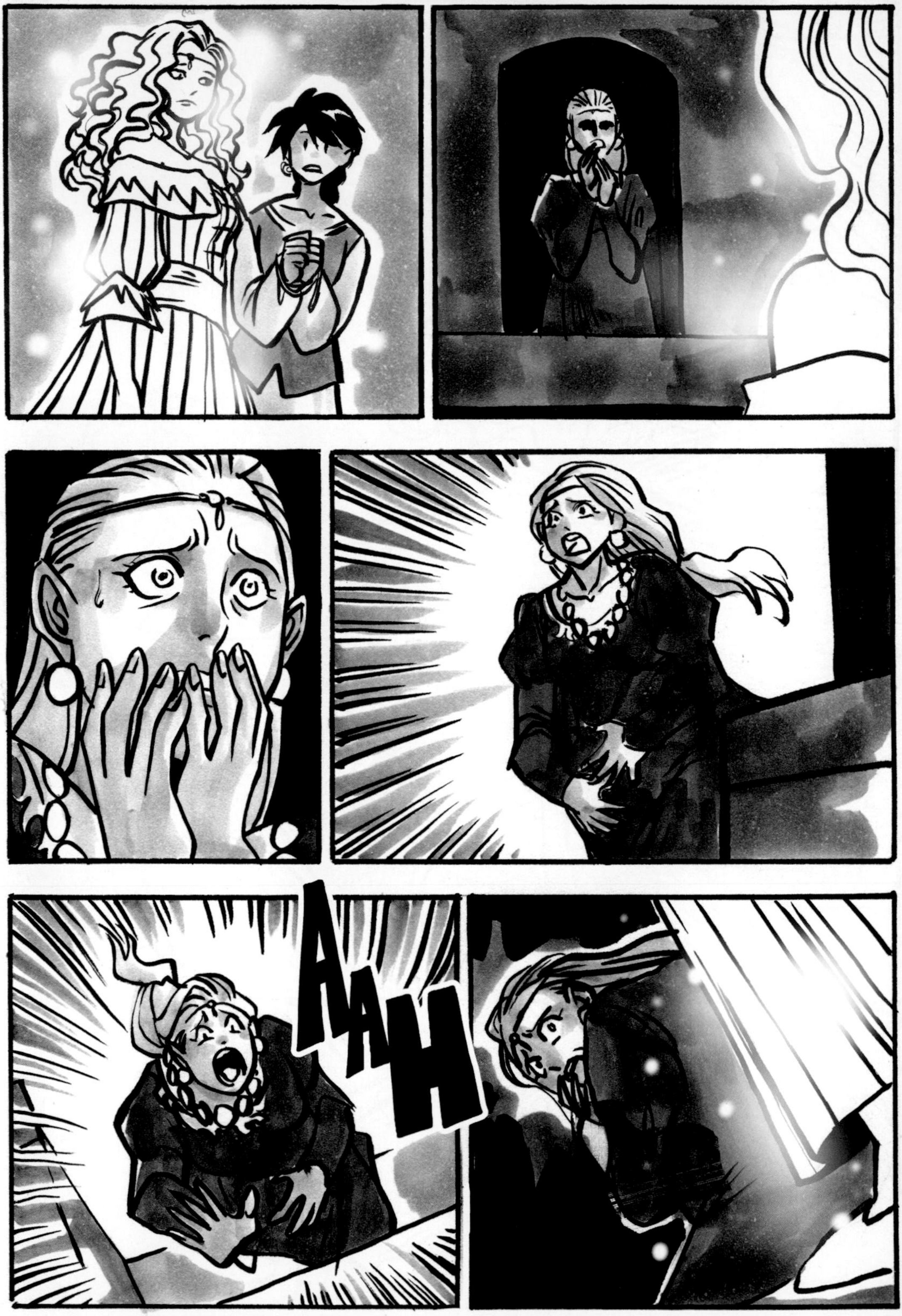
AAAH

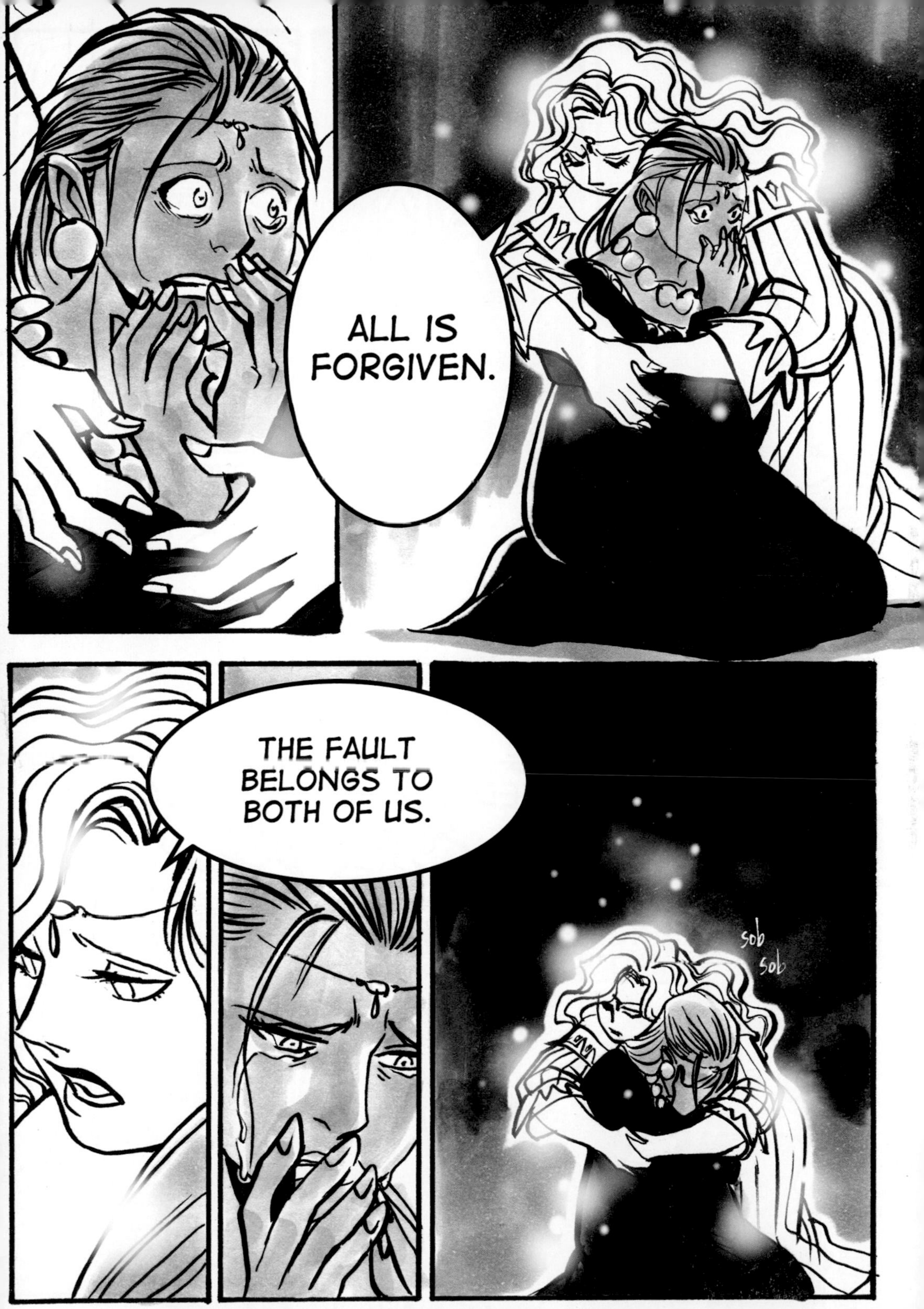
ALL IS FORGIVEN.
THE FAULT BELONGS TO BOTH OF US.
sob sob

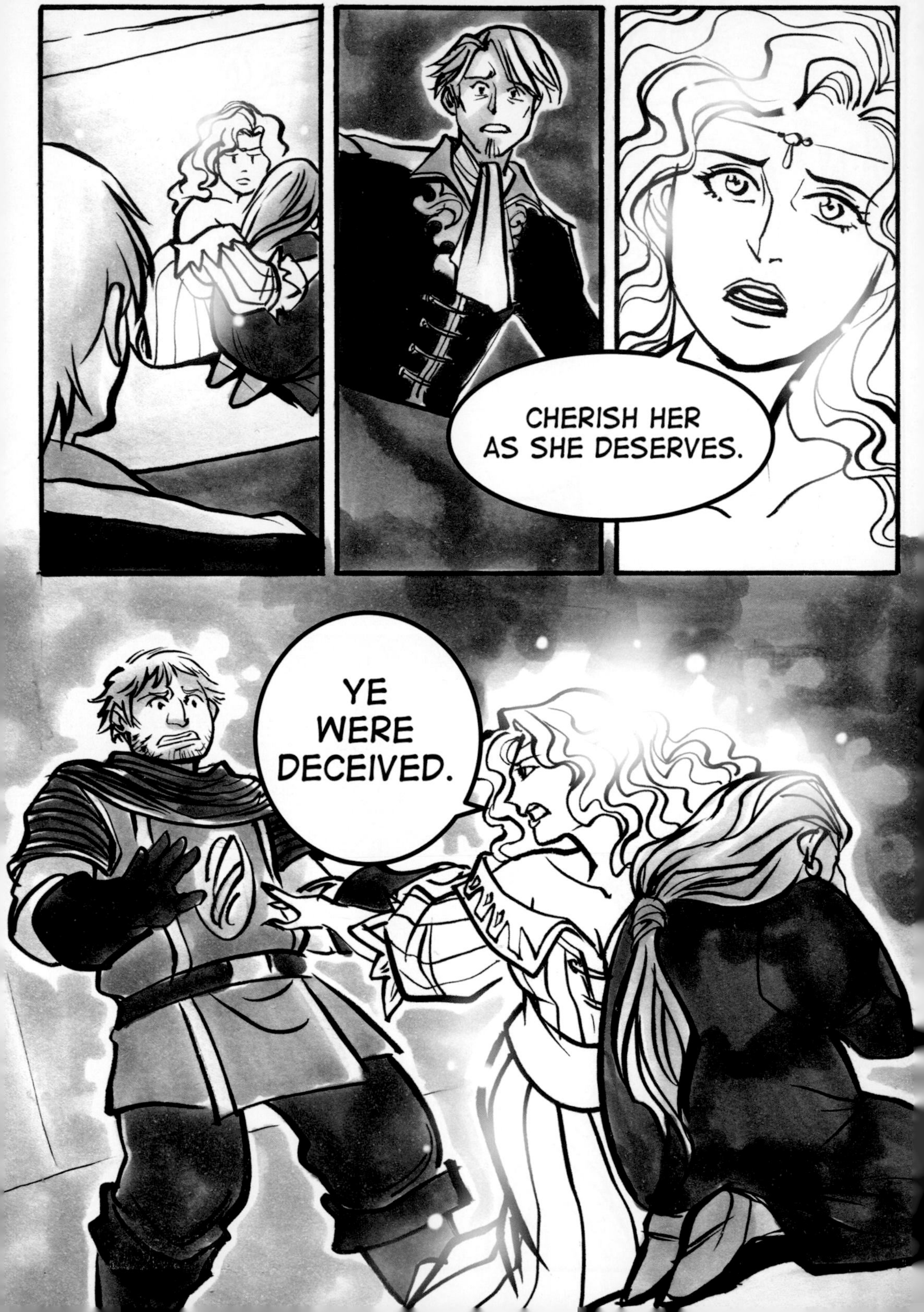
CHERISH HER AS SHE DESERVES.
YE WERE DECEIVED.

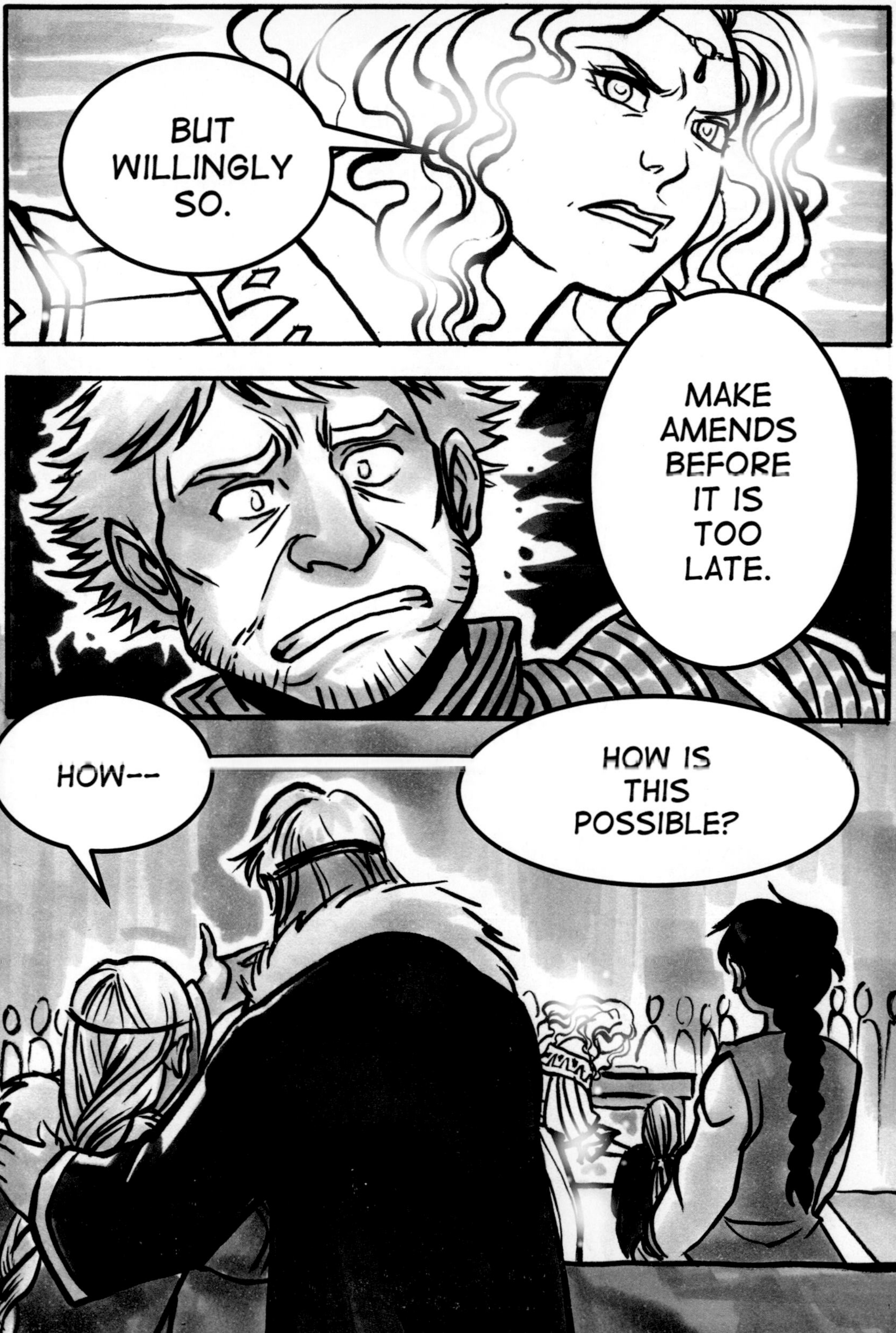
BUT WILLINGLY SO.
MAKE AMENDS BEFORE IT IS TOO LATE.
HOW--
HOW IS THIS POSSIBLE?

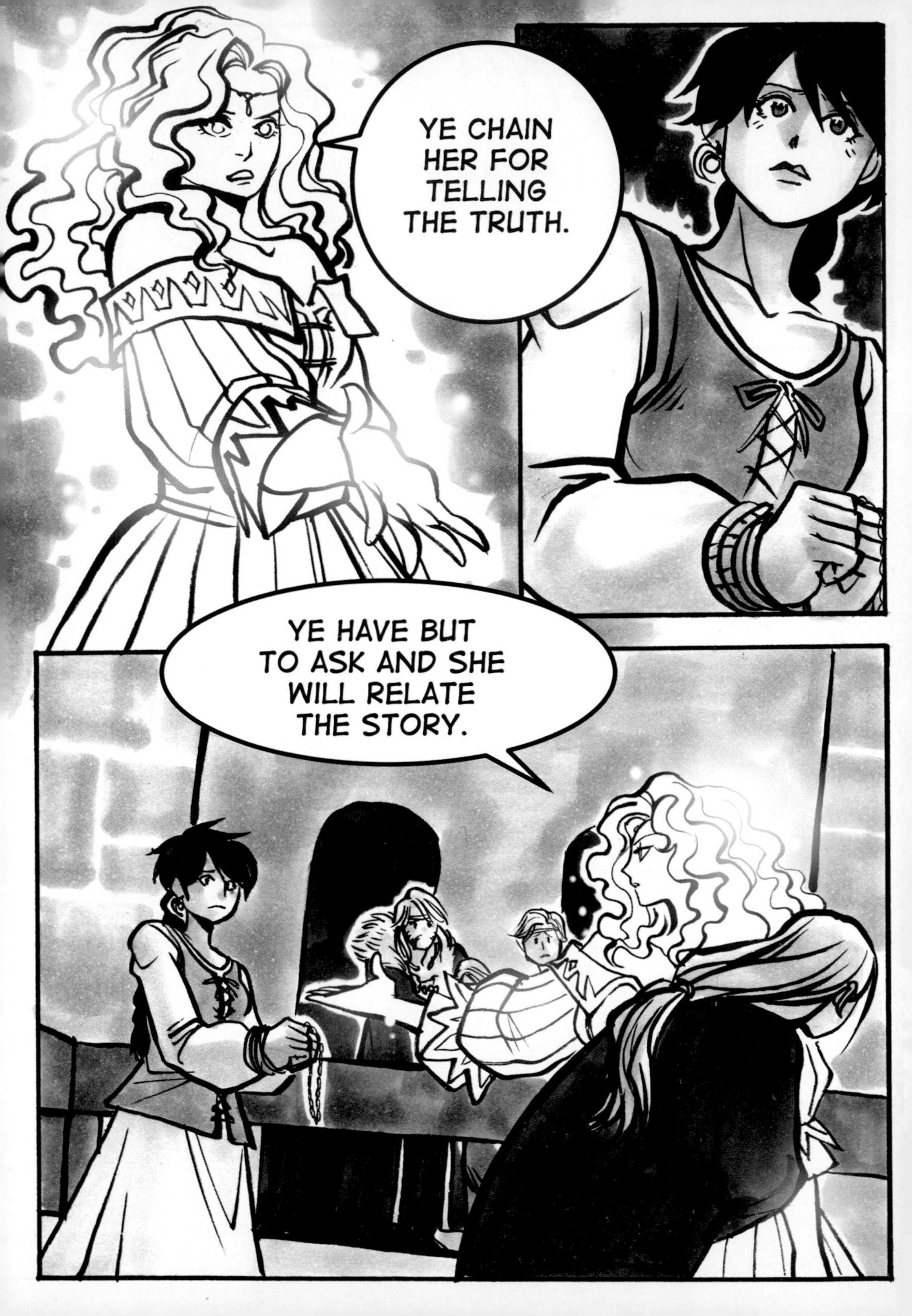
YE CHAIN HER FOR TELLING THE TRUTH.
YE HAVE BUT TO ASK AND SHE WILL RELATE THE STORY.

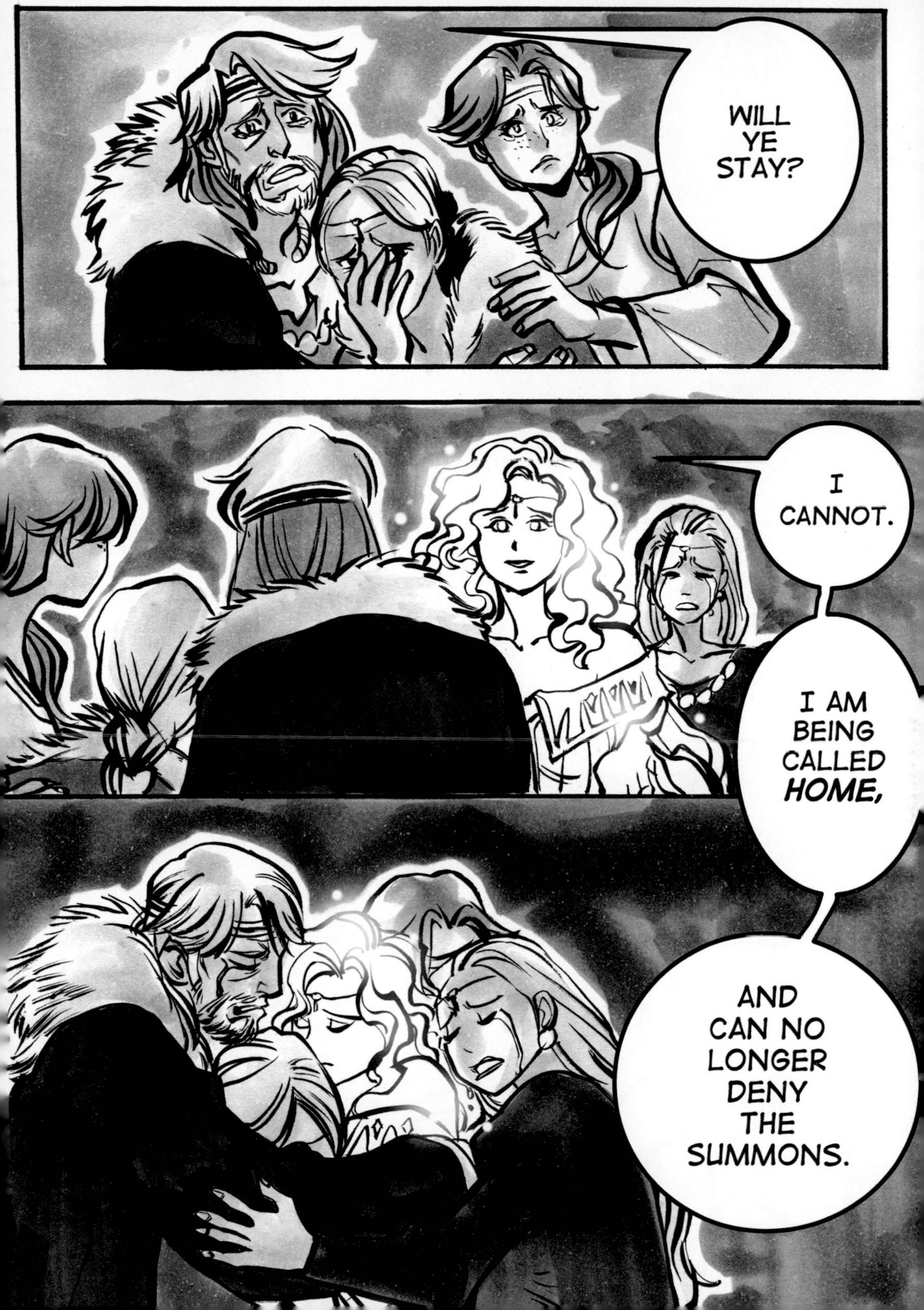
WILL YE STAY?
I CANNOT.
I AM BEING CALLED *HOME,*
AND CAN NO LONGER DENY THE SUMMONS.

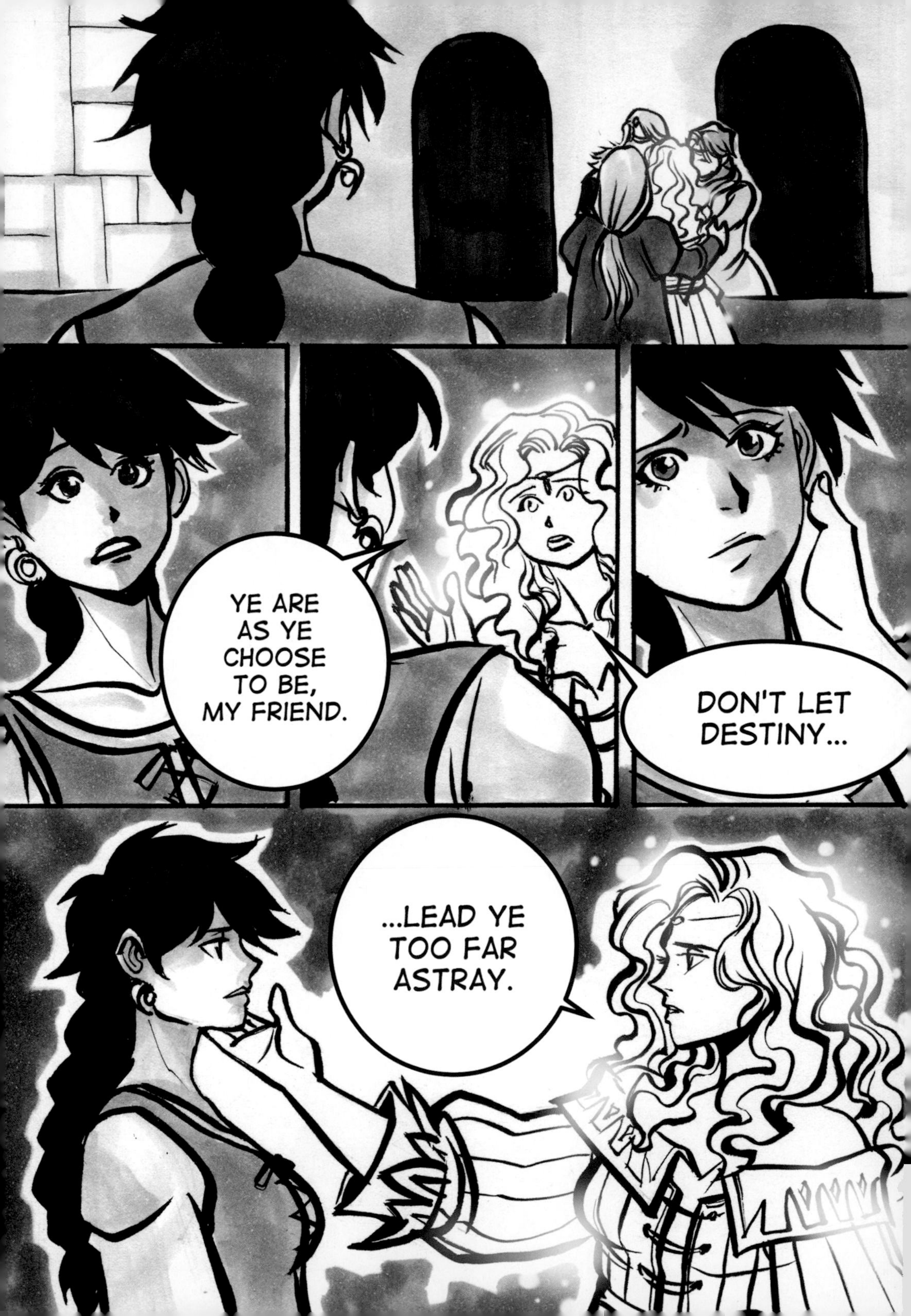
YE ARE AS YE CHOOSE TO BE, MY FRIEND.
DON'T LET DESTINY...
...LEAD YE TOO FAR ASTRAY.

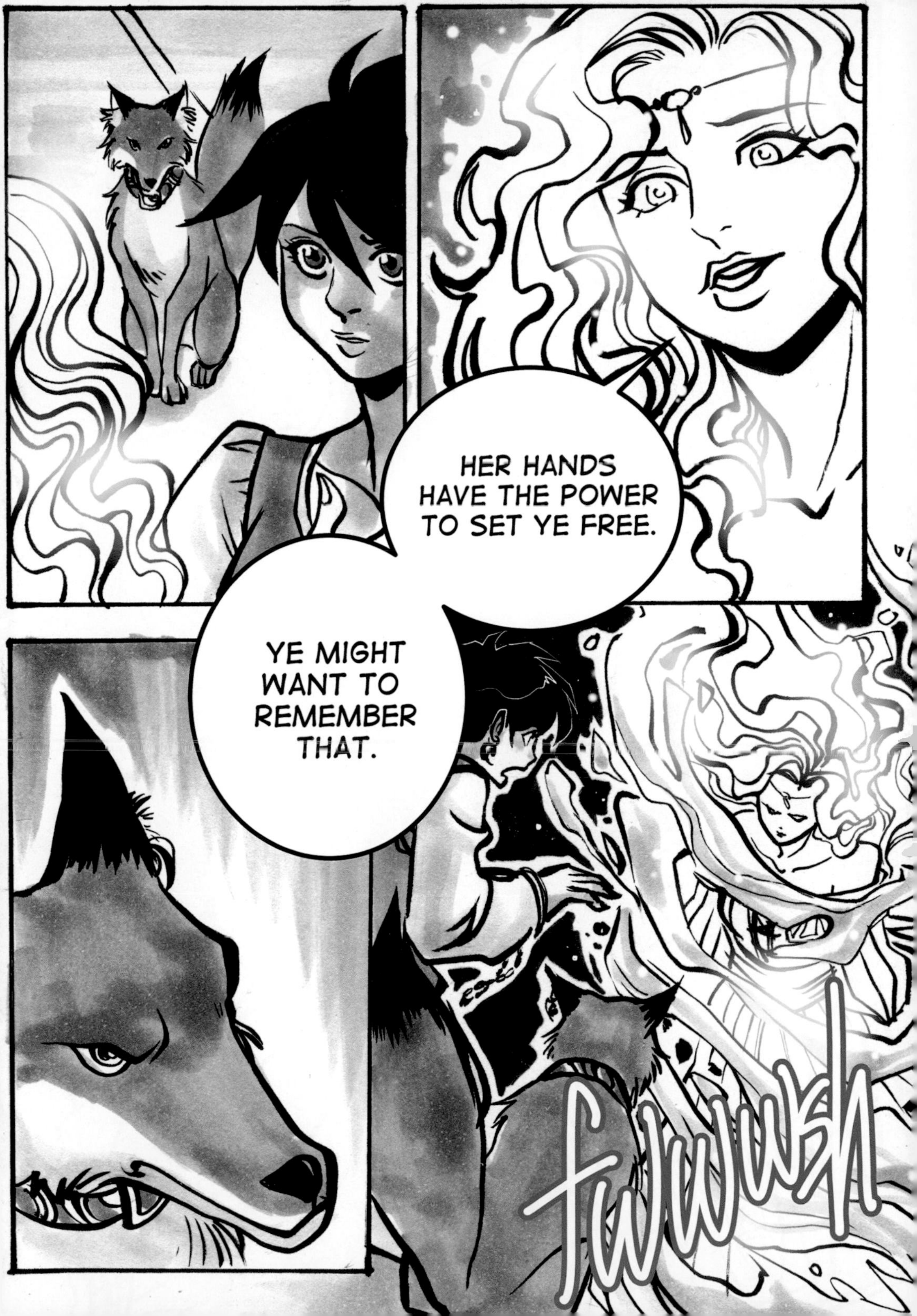
HER HANDS HAVE THE POWER TO SET YE FREE.
YE MIGHT WANT TO REMEMBER THAT.
fwuush

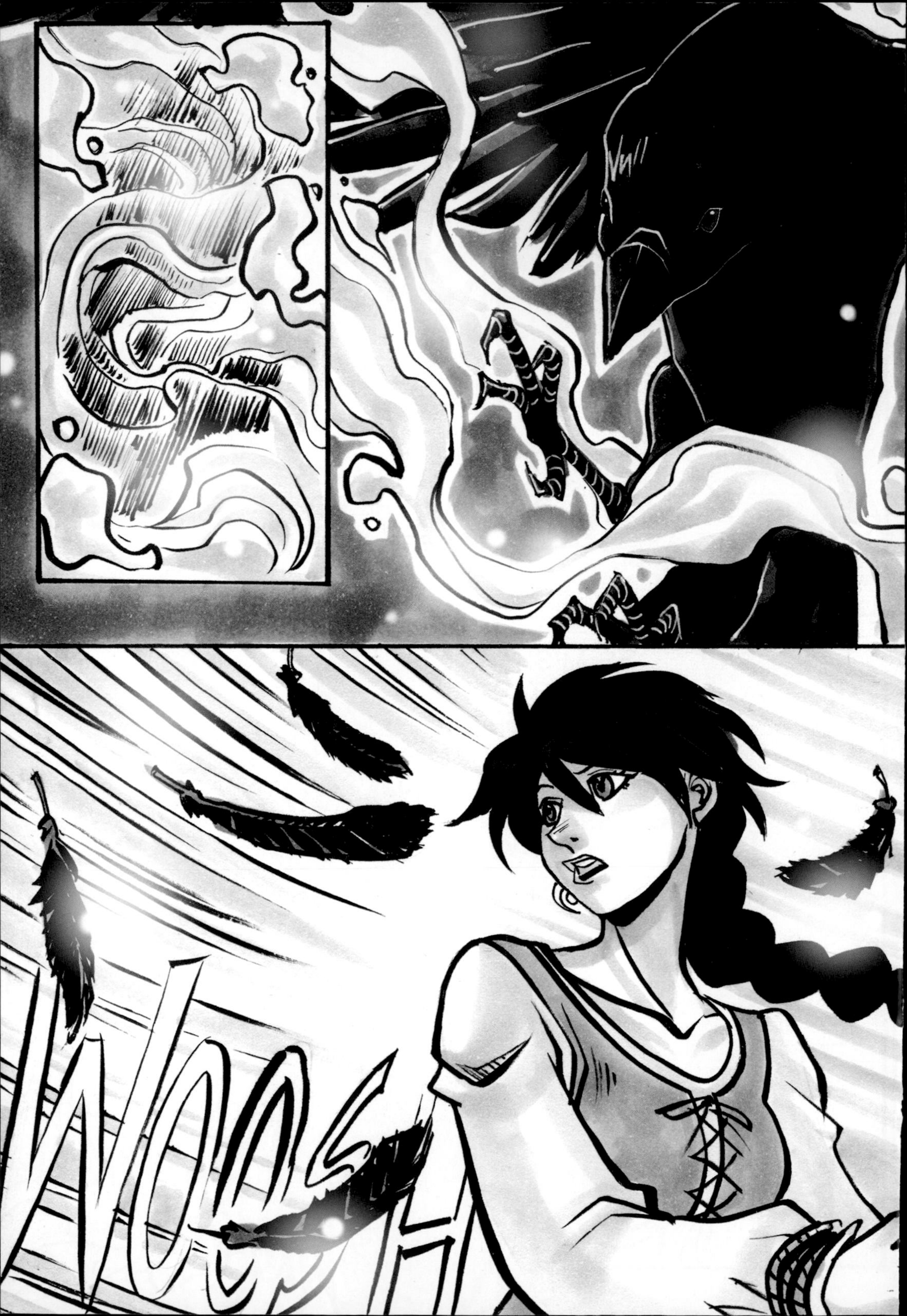
Woosh

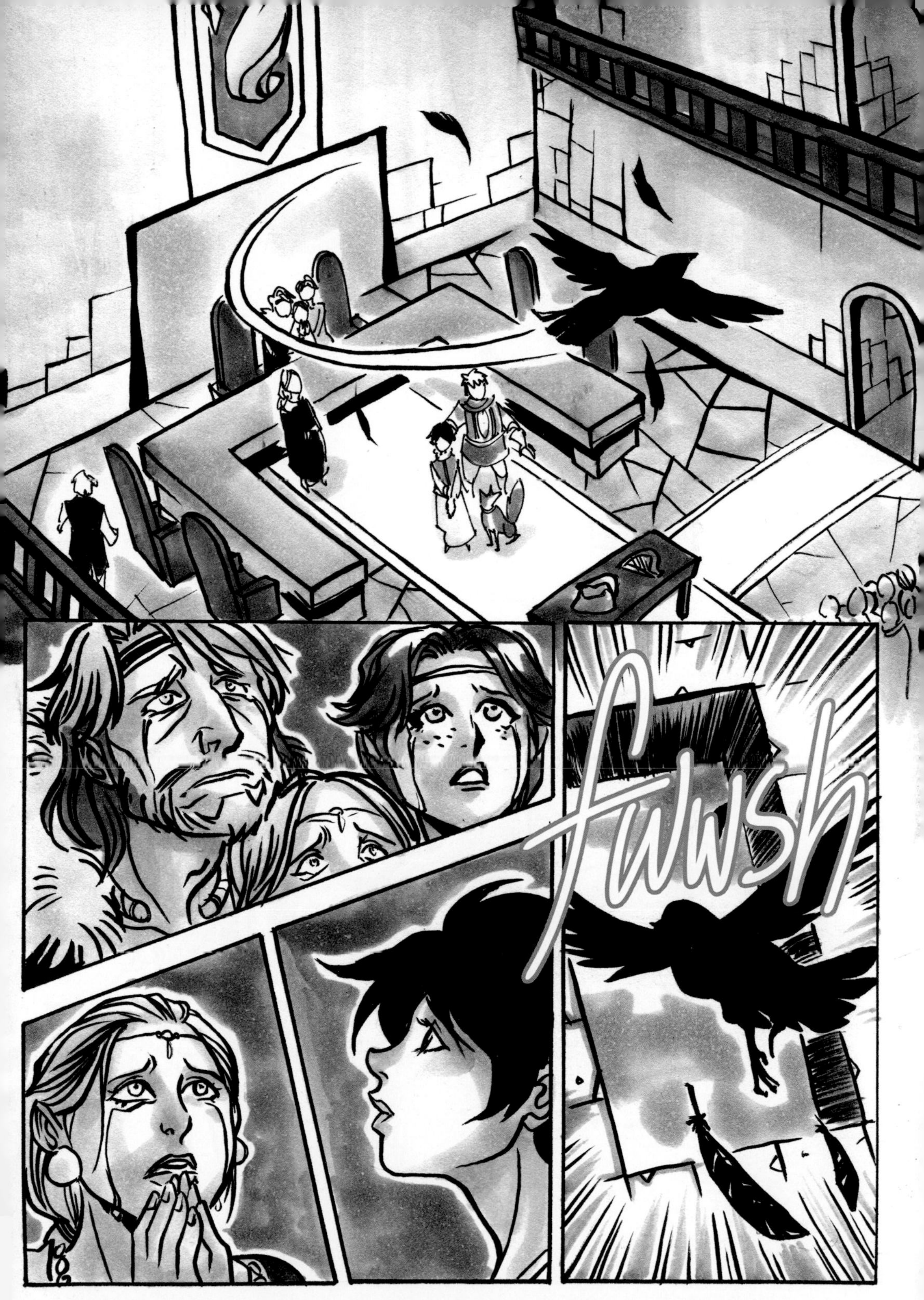
fwwsh

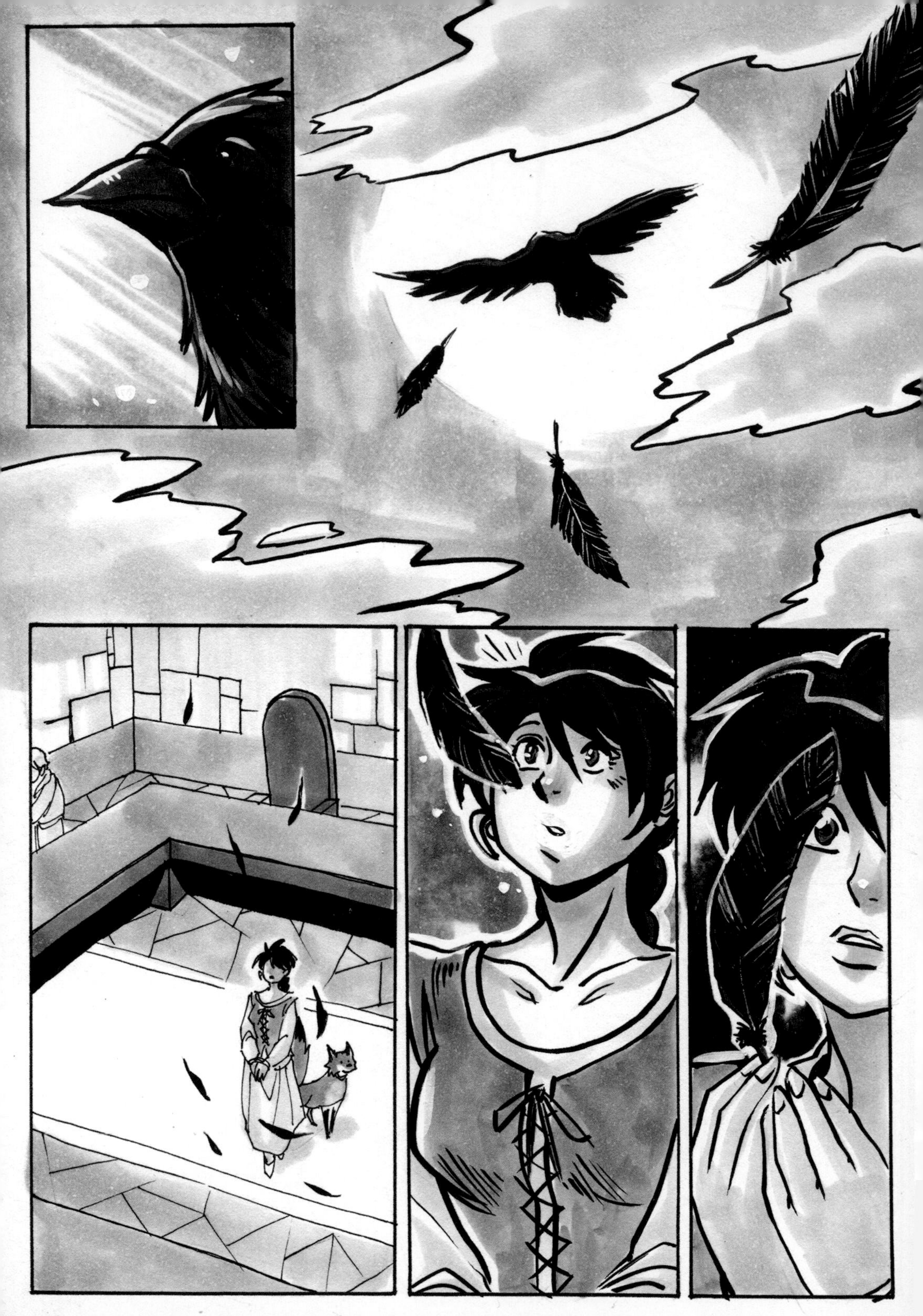

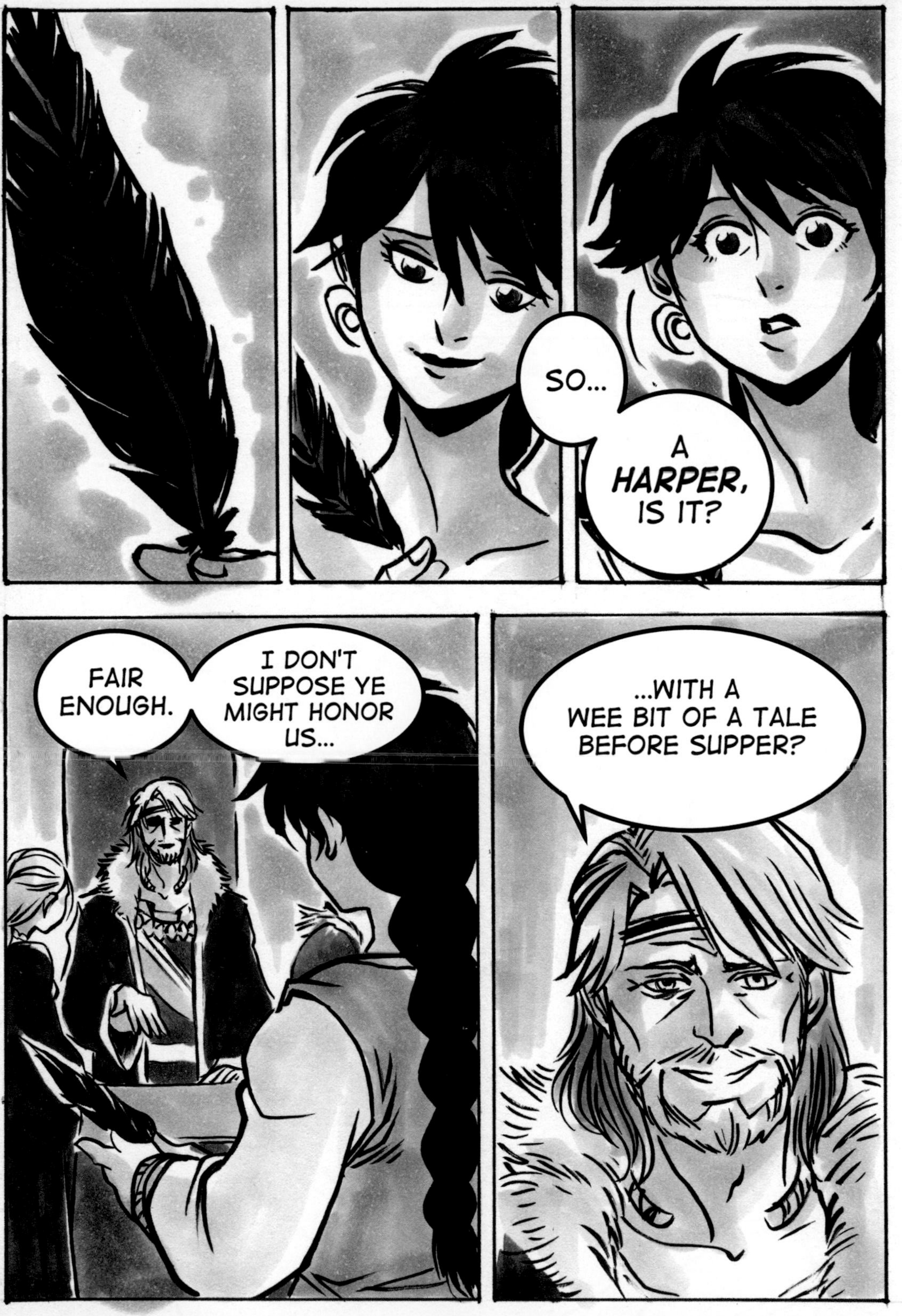
SO...
A *HARPER,* IS IT?
FAIR ENOUGH.
I DON'T SUPPOSE YE MIGHT HONOR US...
...WITH A WEE BIT OF A TALE BEFORE SUPPER?

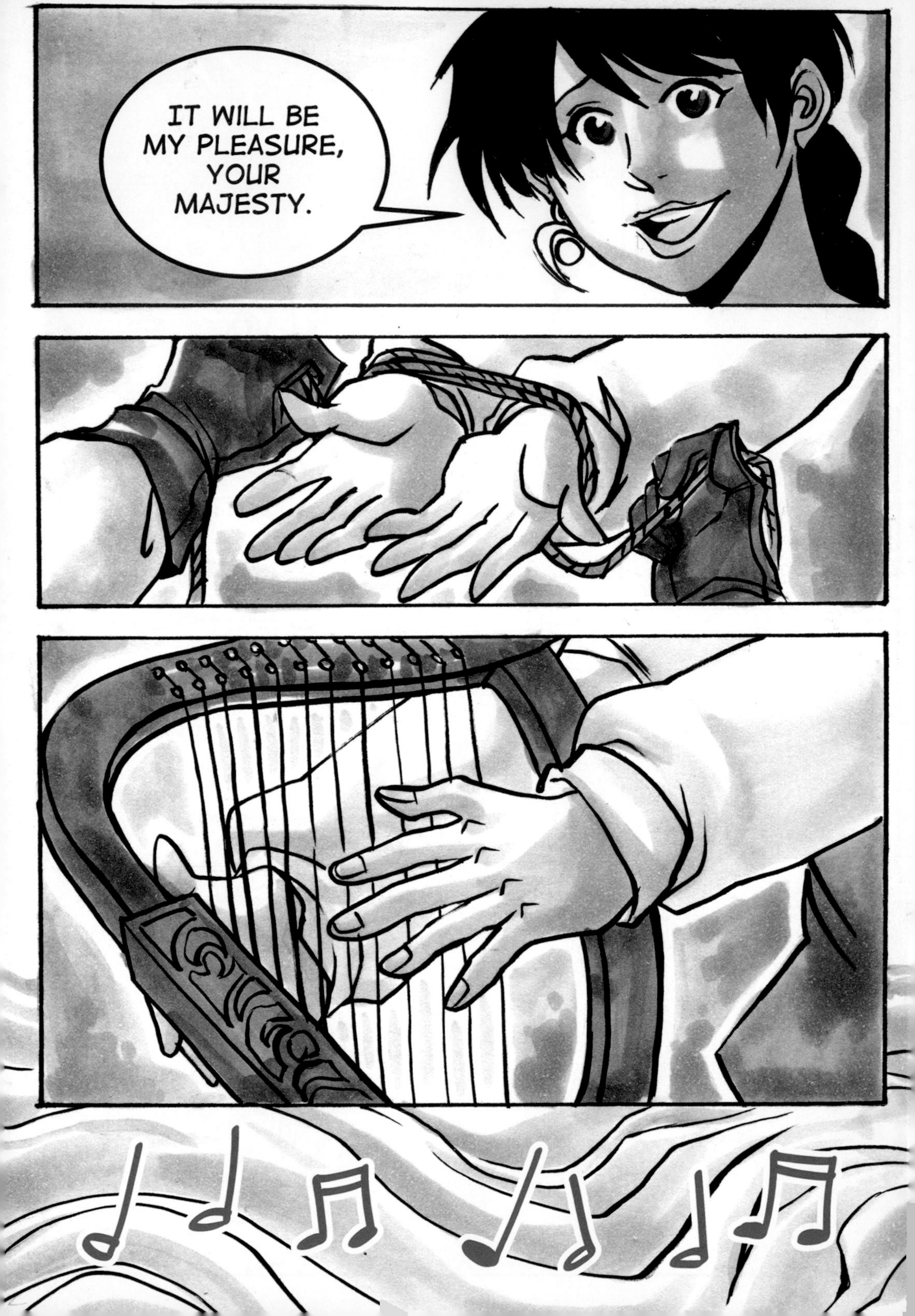
IT WILL BE MY PLEASURE, YOUR MAJESTY.

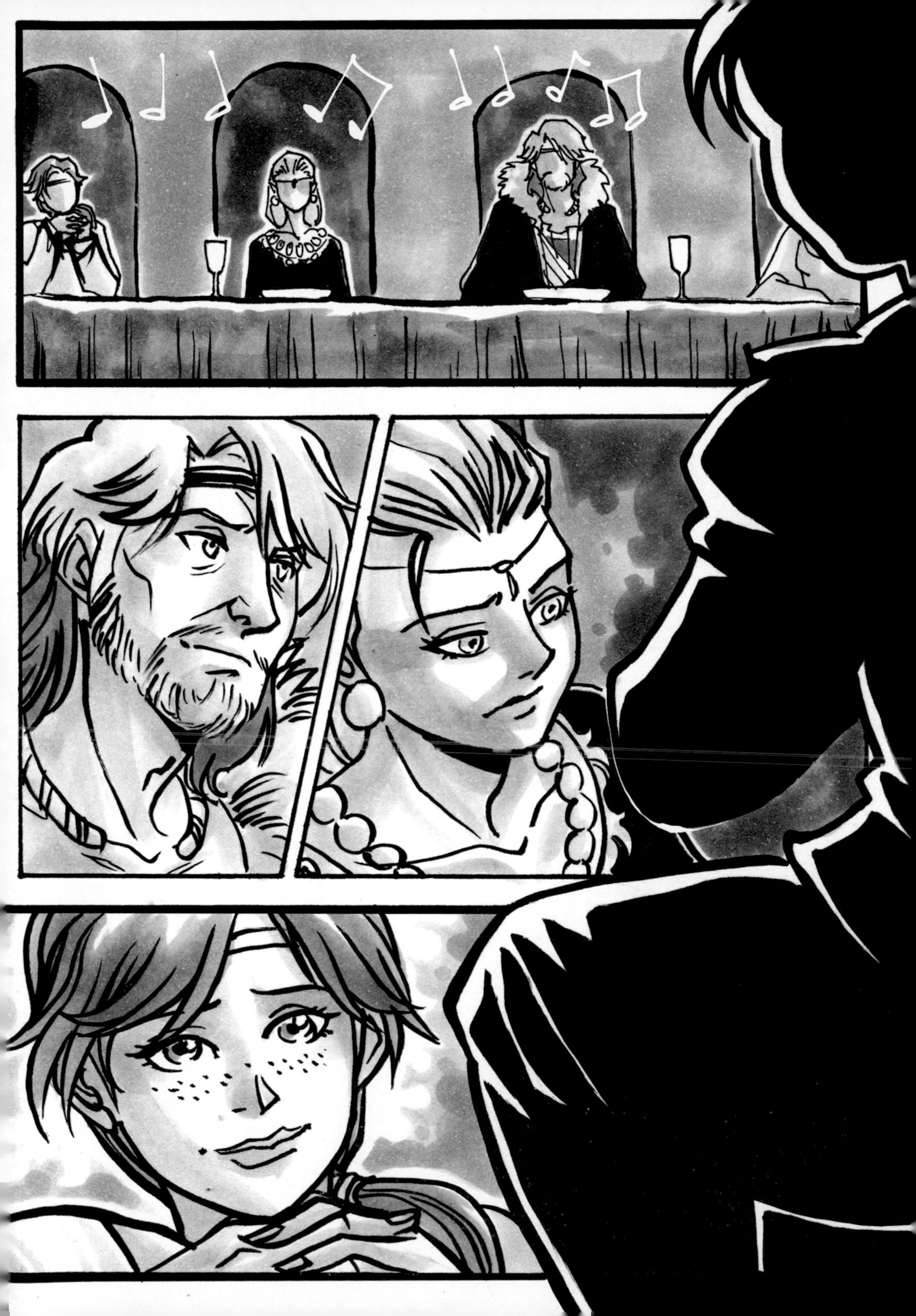

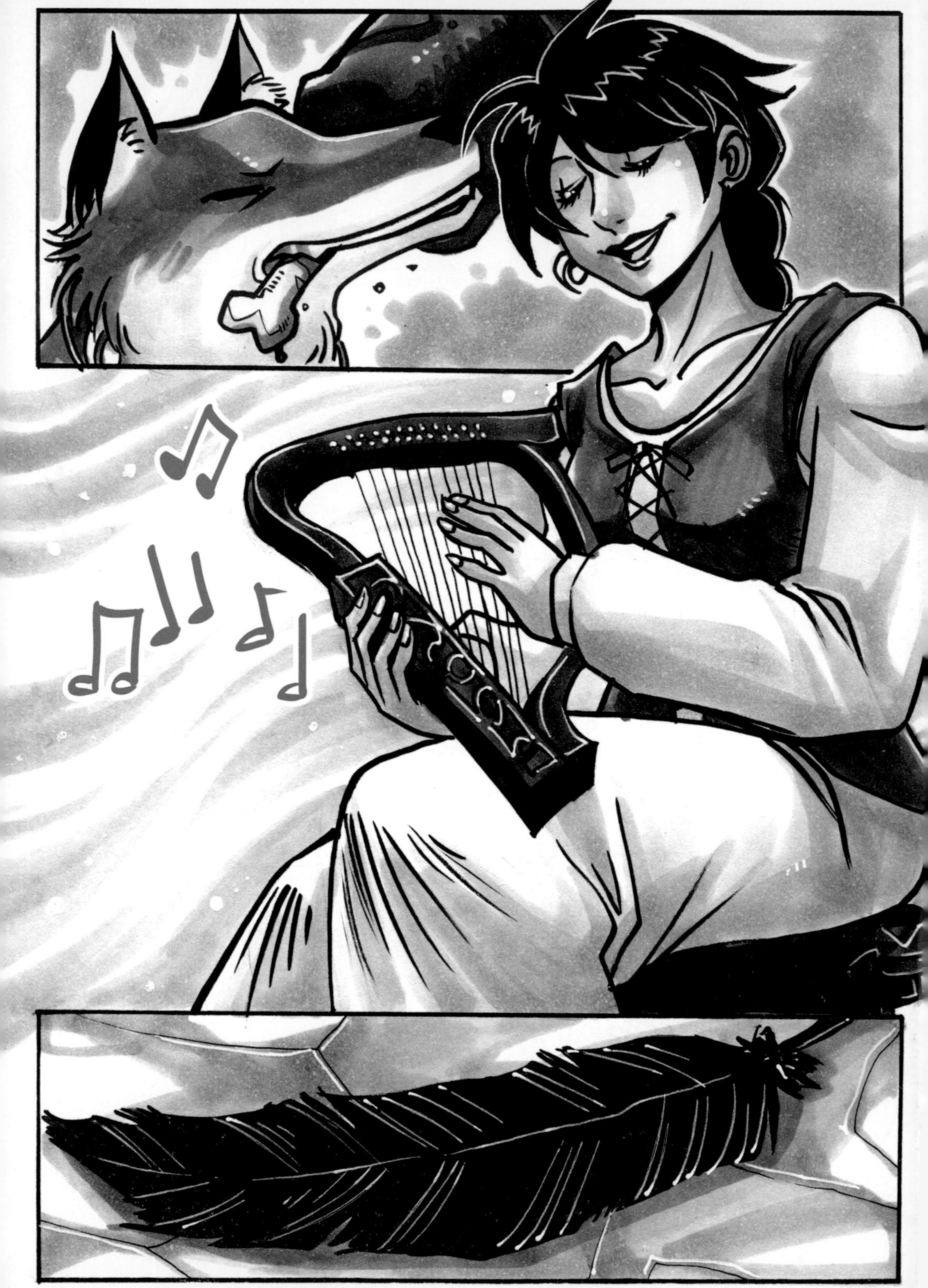

EPILOGUE

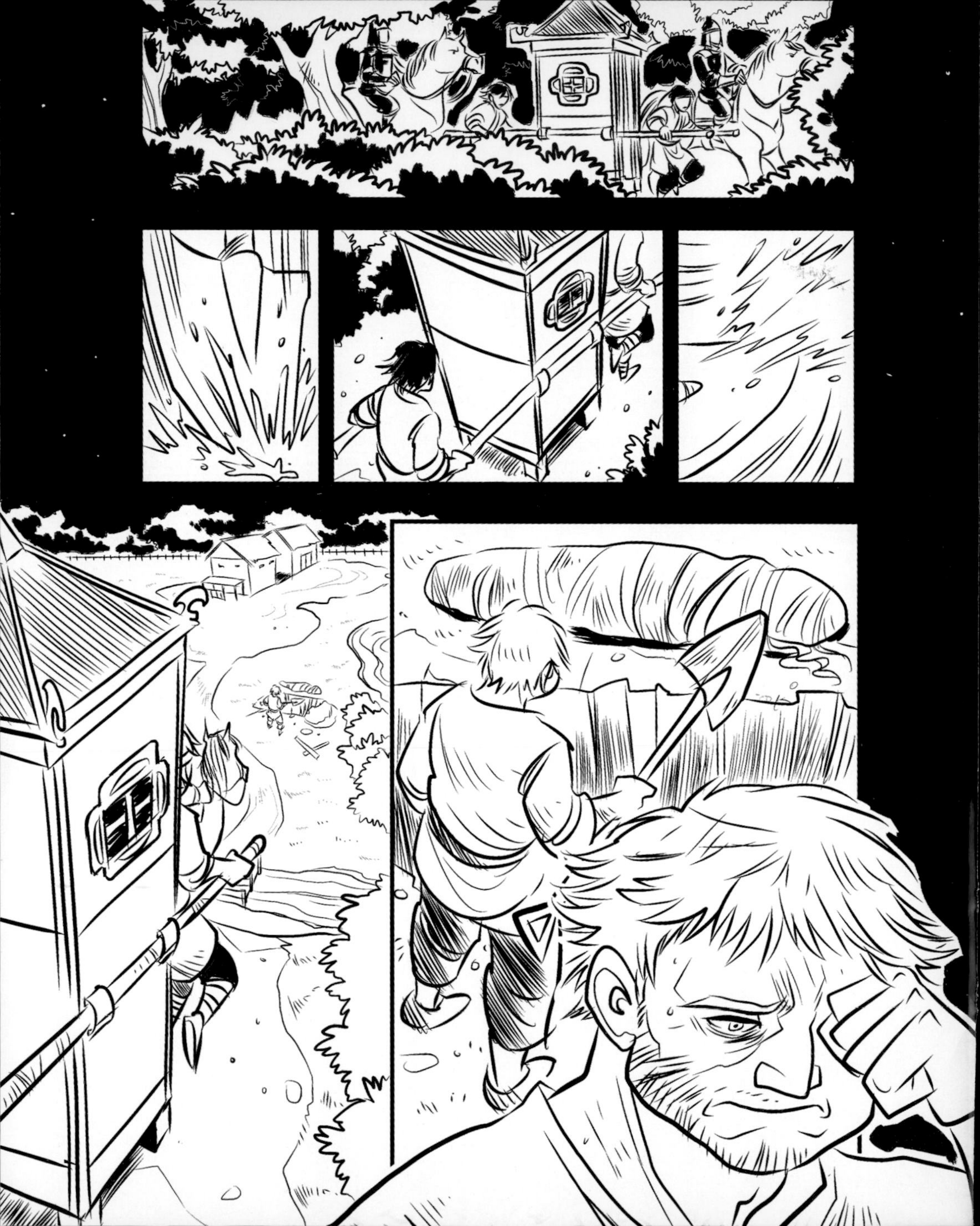

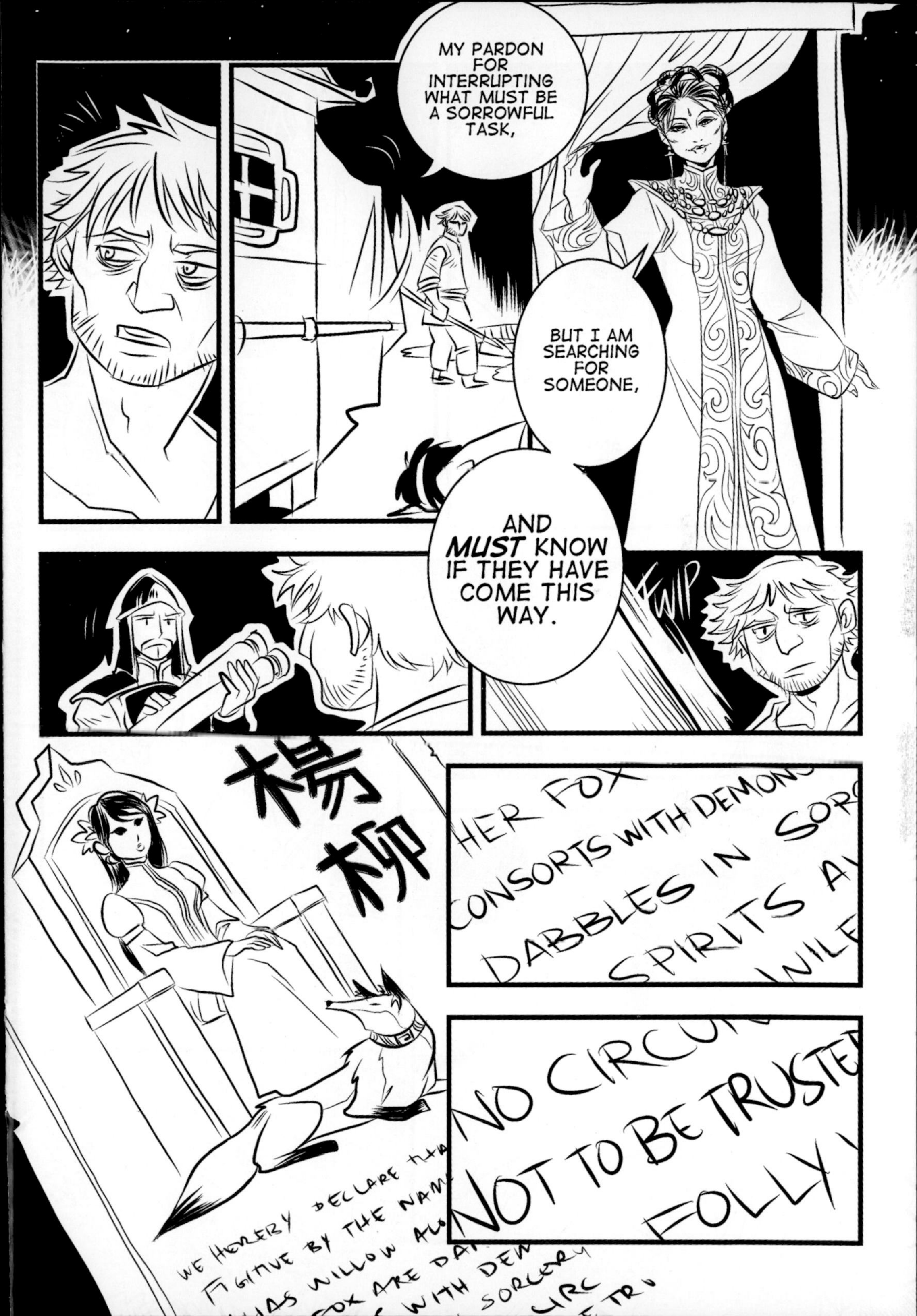
MY PARDON FOR INTERRUPTING WHAT MUST BE A SORROWFUL TASK,
BUT I AM SEARCHING FOR SOMEONE,
AND *MUST* KNOW IF THEY HAVE COME THIS WAY.
FWIP
楊柳
HER FOX
CONSORTS WITH DEMONS
DABBLES IN
SPIRITS
NO CIRC
NOT TO BE TRUSTE
FOLLY
WE HEREBY DECLARE
FUGITIVE BY THE NAM
WILLOW
FOX ARE
WITH DEM
SORCERY

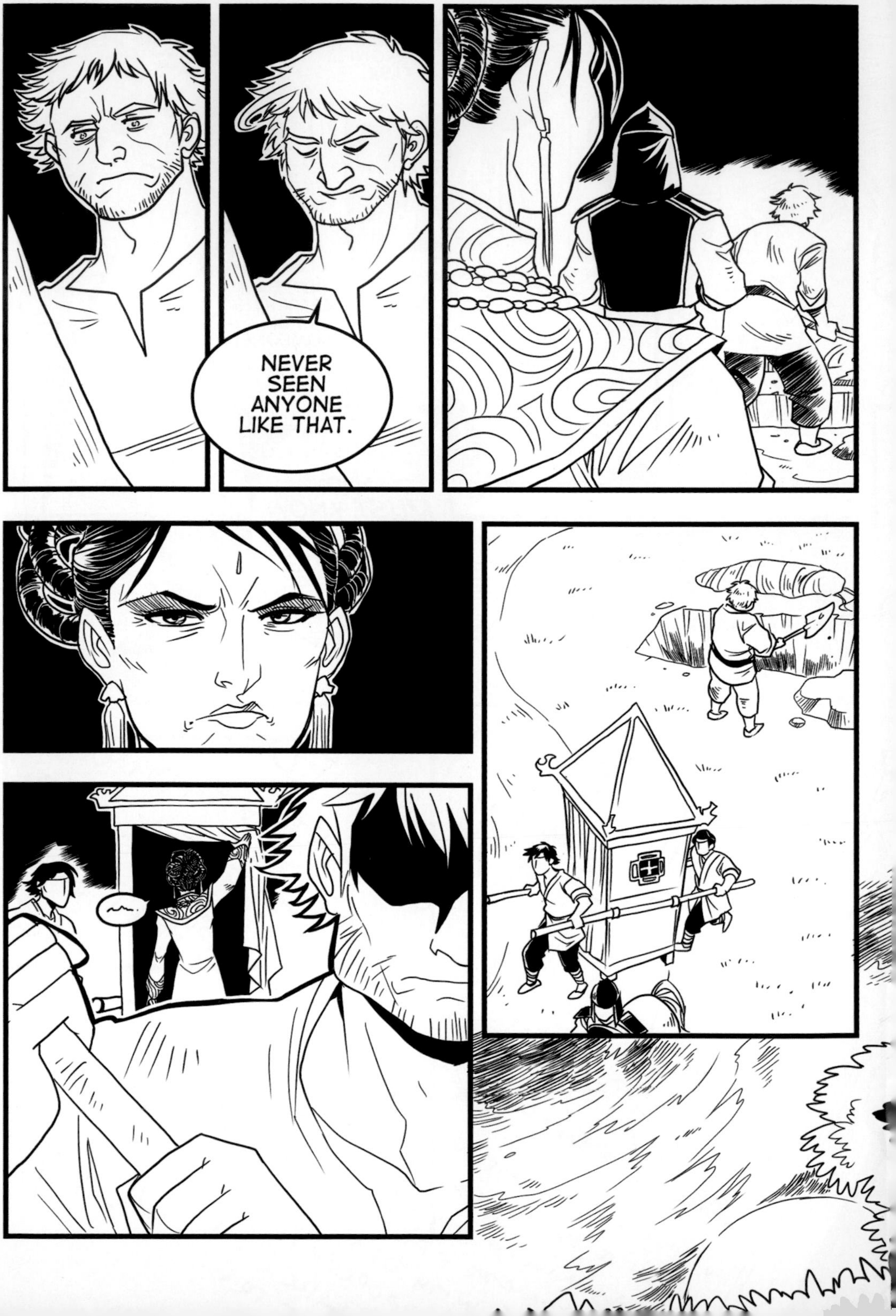
NEVER SEEN ANYONE LIKE THAT.

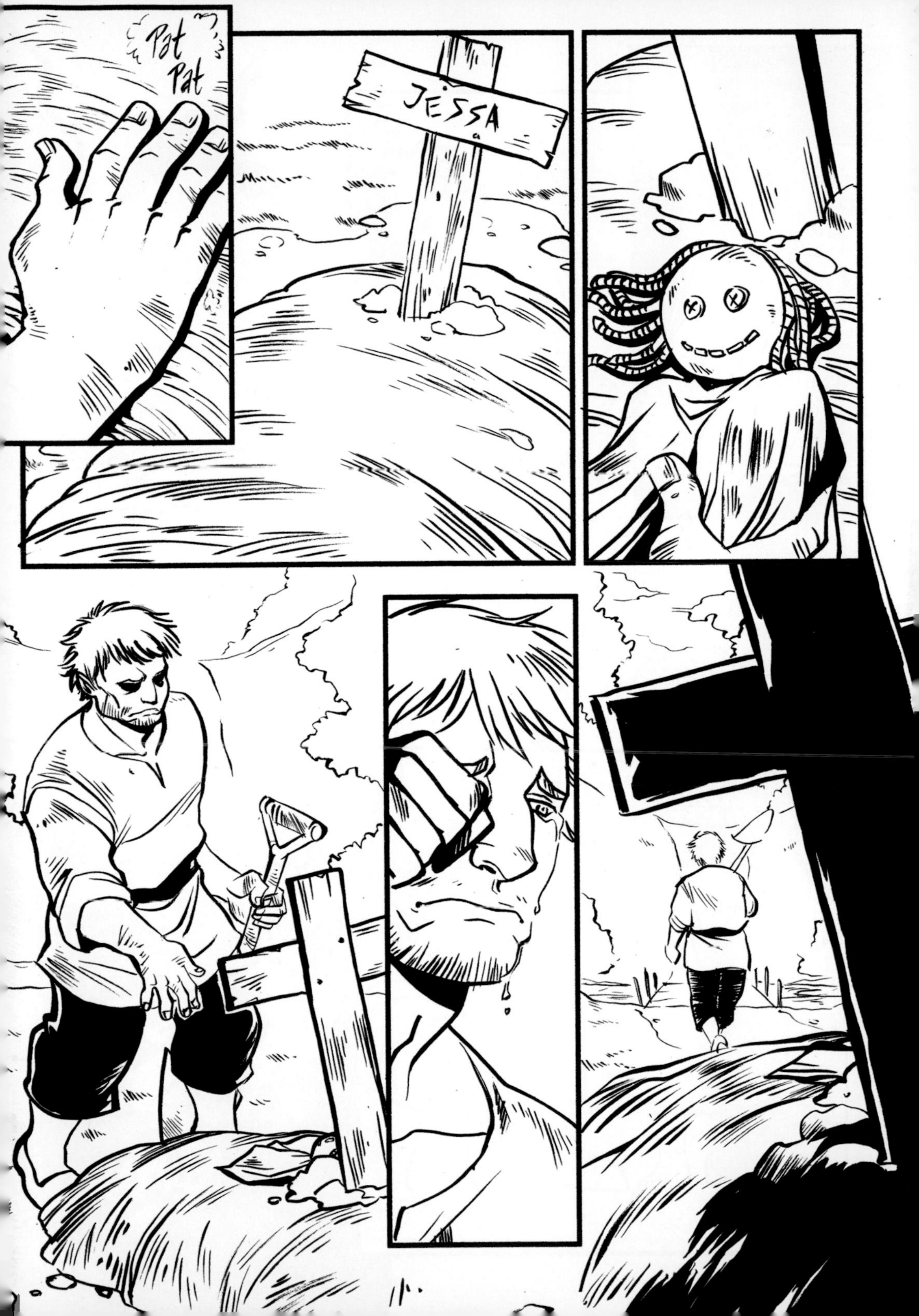
Pat
Pat
JESSA

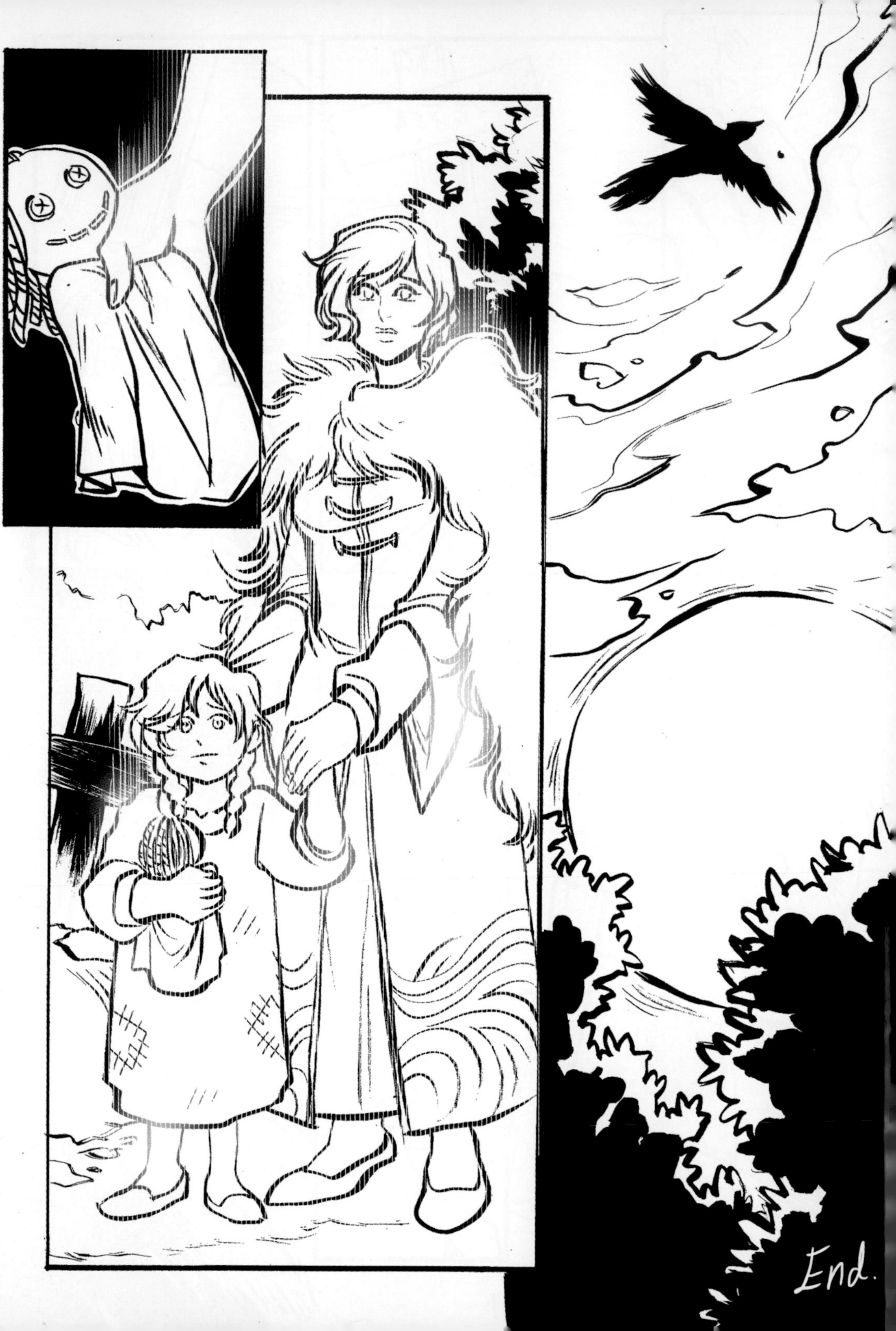
End.

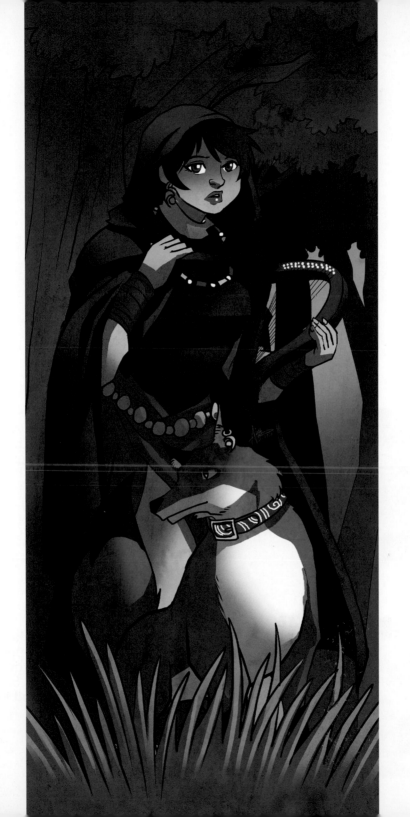

READ MORE *FOX & WILLOW* AT
www.sadsausagedogs.com

ABOUT ALLISON PANG
Allison is the author of the Urban Fantasy Abby Sinclair series, the steampunk IronHeart Chronicles series and has also written several short stories and comics for various anthologies. She likes LEGOS, elves, LEGO elves…and bacon.

Find more at her website -
www.heartofthedreaming.com

ABOUT IRMA 'AIMO' AHMED
Aimo is a professional sketch card artist who has done work for card companies such as Topps, Upper Deck, and Rittenhouse Archives on properties of Lucasfilm, New Line Cinema, and Marvel. She has a big love for comics and pretty pictures. And kitties. FAT AND FLUFFY KITTIES.

Find more at her Patreon -
www.patreon.com/aimostudio

FOX and WILLOW